VIKING
Mystery
Suspense

Jesse
Sublett

Boiled

in

Concrete

Viking

VIKING
Published by the Penguin Group
Viking Penguin, a division of Penguin Books USA Inc.,
375 Hudson Street, New York, New York 10014, U.S.A.
Penguin Books Ltd, 27 Wrights Lane,
London W8 5TZ, England
Penguin Books Australia Ltd, Ringwood,
Victoria, Australia
Penguin Books Canada Ltd, 10 Alcorn Avenue, Suite 300,
Toronto, Ontario, Canada M4V 3B2
Penguin Books (N.Z.) Ltd, 182–190 Wairau Road,
Auckland 10, New Zealand

Penguin Books Ltd, Registered Offices:
Harmondsworth, Middlesex, England

First published in 1992 by Viking Penguin,
a division of Penguin Books USA Inc.

1 3 5 7 9 10 8 6 4 2

PUBLISHER'S NOTE
This is a work of fiction. Names, characters, places, and incidents
either are the product of the author's imagination or are used
fictitiously, and any resemblance to actual persons, living or
dead, events, or locales is entirely coincidental.

LIBRARY OF CONGRESS CATALOGING IN PUBLICATION DATA
Sublett, Jesse.
Boiled in concrete / Jesse Sublett.
p.   cm.
ISBN 0-670-83888-8
I. Title.
PS3569.U218B65   1992
813'.54—dc20   91-22041

Printed in the United States of America
Set in Times Roman
Designed by Brian Mulligan

For Lois

Author's Note

This book is the story of a legendary Texas blues musician killed in a plane crash. The first draft was completed in 1988, then set aside until the summer of 1990. On August 27, 1990, while the manuscript was being revised, Stevie Ray Vaughan was taken from us in a tragic helicopter accident. The similarity between Stevie's story and the plot of this book goes no further than the fact that both musicians were from Texas, and both played the blues.

In my gallery of heroes, Stevie, the Fabulous Thunderbirds, Lou Ann Barton, Howlin' Wolf, Muddy Waters, Elmore James, Willie Dixon, Raymond Chandler, Dashiell Hammett, Richard Stark, Chester Himes, and many, many others stand side by side, trading riffs, giving inspiration, being cool.

I'd like to thank my editor, Roger Devine, for helping me tune this one up.

L.A. Exile

1

Looking something like a cross between an Elvis impersonator and a tow truck driver, he swaggered over to my booth in the back of the bar, his bulky body a tight fit in gray mechanic's coveralls with the name "Chuck" stitched above the pocket. His black hair was lacquered into a rockabilly pompadour as stiff and tall as a shark's fin, and a strange gleam glittered in his puffy, bleary, bloodshot eyes.

His voice was a twangy baritone drawl: "You Martin Fender, the bass player from Austin?"

I nodded and said, "You must be Cyclone Davis."

"Yep," he said, "that's me all right." His face lit up and broke into a grin, as if the sound of his own name gave him immense pleasure. He slid into the booth and pulled out a pack of Kools, shook one out, set fire to it with a Zippo lighter, and inhaled deeply. As he blew out the cloud of smoke and sprawled out in the booth, he looked me up and down, nodding his head approvingly, his grin stretching into a wide, openmouthed smile that brimmed over with confidence, despite the presence of several chipped teeth. He also reeked of whiskey, cigarettes, and stale pomade.

"You said you got some session work for me?"

"Yep," he drawled, still nodding, still grinning. "Simple, raw

R&B. I seen you play bass before, you won't have no problem with it."

A waitress came over. He ordered a Seagram's and 7-Up and I ordered a scotch rocks. It was a little after ten P.M. on my eightieth day in Los Angeles. Back in Austin, it would be a little after midnight. I didn't care what time it was anywhere else.

"When's the session?" I said.

The grin had faded by this time, and a speculative expression had taken its place, but he still exuded the type of iron-willed conviction observed in the newly converted and the permanently deranged. "I told you on the phone it might be real soon, didn't I?"

"You also said something about five hundred bucks."

He tossed me a wink as he dug into a zippered pocket in the jumpsuit. "You 'vailable tonight, 'round midnight?"

I pretended to think it over for a few seconds. "For five hundred I might be."

The waitress brought our drinks. Cyclone paid for them with a worn-looking ten dollar bill, tipped the waitress a buck, then grinned lustily at her backside as she walked back to the bar. Still grinning, he turned back to face me and slapped a fat number-ten envelope down on the table by my drink. I peeled back the flap on the envelope and thumbed through its contents: bills of various denominations—fives, tens, twenties, and lots of singles.

"That's your down payment—a hundred bucks," he said. "You get the other four after we finish the session." He threw some of his drink down his throat, then glanced suspiciously over each shoulder and shuddered as the booze hit home. "Might take all night. That OK with you, Martin?"

"I got nowhere else to go," I said. Except for back home to Austin, I thought to myself. The five hundred was going to take me there. I stuffed the envelope in my jacket and took a drink.

"All right, then," he said, "let's make us some noise. You got a car, don't you?"

"Actually, I don't. Not in this town, anyway. My apartment's only a few blocks from here, though, and my bass is there. If you could give me a ride—"

The big man was glaring at me with bemused disbelief. "Man," he bellowed, "I can't believe a guy like you got no wheels in a town like this. You call that living?"

"Call it whatever you want. I call it temporary."

He stopped laughing, stopped grinning—as if something I'd said or the way I'd said it had blown out his candle. But the expression lingered no more than a second before he belched and tilted his head back to dump the rest of his drink in his mouth, laughing as he chomped on the ice. "Guess we better get started, then. I'll give you a ride, drop you off, then come back for you 'fore the session. Got me an important errand to run."

We were heading down Ventura Boulevard at about thirty miles over the speed limit in a late-model Cadillac with Texas plates. Though I hadn't been able to pinpoint the origin of his drawl, the Texas plates hadn't surprised me. At that point, I wasn't all that curious about it, either. All that really concerned me —as he narrowly avoided sideswiping a beer truck by zipping through a gas station driveway—were his five hundred dollars and his ability to navigate that Cadillac in the condition he was in. In that order.

As the sushi bars, Thai restaurants, goat-cheese pizzerias, and neon-lit boutiques of Studio City blurred by, he sank back into his seat, steering with the heel of his right hand. "Tell me something, Martin," he said, his voice suddenly throaty, his tone pensive. "How you feel about the Rockin' Dog?"

I thought about the question as the traffic light in the intersection ahead of us went red and he made no move to slow down. I slid down in the seat and braced myself for a collision or the wail of a siren, but we sailed through without incident, as if guided by the hand of a whimsical angel.

Richard "the Rockin' Dog" James was a Texas-based R&B

singer/guitarist who'd had a string of hits back in the late seventies. But like Roky Erikson and Bobby Fuller, he was one of those rock 'n' roll legends whose influence looms way out of proportion to their own success. By the beginning of the last decade, James didn't even have a record deal, and he'd been reduced to playing nostalgia shows by the time his plane crashed on a Colorado mountainside on February 3, 1984, exactly twenty-five years after Buddy Holly's own fatal plane crash. But Dovie de Carlo, James's lover and backup singer, survived the crash and became a legend herself, embarking on a solo career that quickly eclipsed her late mentor and lover's own success. Her last three albums, each one a compilation of her own versions of his songs, had gone gold.

Though James had been based in my hometown of Austin for the last few years of his career, I'd only seen him play twice, just after the release of his first album back in 1977, and I'd never seen Dovie de Carlo at all, except on MTV.

I told Cyclone Davis I liked the Rockin' Dog just fine.

"Good," he drawled lustily as he made a hard right onto Laurel Canyon, the Cadillac lurching as the right wheels bumped a curb. "We gonna have fun, then."

"You've got the other musicians lined up already?" I said.

He nodded. "Drummer's booked, and the engineer'll be waitin'. That's all we need. I'll drop you off and then I gotta go run that errand. I gots to meet a man about a song."

"A song?"

He pulled a cassette tape out of his pocket and held it so I could see the label. In bold block letters, someone had written "THE WHOLE DAMN TRUTH." He popped the tape into the cassette deck in the dash and turned up the volume. The sound quality was that of a demo recording, with drums, bass, and a reverb-tinged guitar plucking out a melancholy minor key melody, and a suitably reverb-drenched male voice singing in a gritty, bluesy twang.

An ambulance siren drowned out the first few lines of the vocal. After the ambulance passed us, I caught these words:

Hearing those angels singing
A sweet, sweet song, but it's not for you,
Cold as a coffin nail, boiled in concrete
Buried alive in the blues
and you'll never know, baby you'll never know,
the whole damn truth.

I said, "The singer sounds a lot like Richard James."

"He sure does, don't he?" drawled Cyclone, grinning and giving me a conspiratorial wink as he popped the cassette out of the deck and stuck it back in his pocket. "Yes sir, this song'll pay for our little session and a whole lot more."

"Someone's going to give you some cash for this song?"

"Oh yeah. This here ain't no ordinary song. This tape proves that Richard James, the Rockin' Dog, is still alive and kickin'."

I didn't say anything. I wanted that five hundred dollars, and I would've played a session with anyone short of a mass murderer to get it. I was that ready to get out of L.A.

"They say you're some sorta detective back in Austin," said Cyclone.

"Part-time skiptracer for a collection agency," I said. "I look up people after they move."

We swerved into the left turn lane to pass a slow-moving Mercedes, then swung back. He shot a look in the rearview mirror and cackled sarcastically. "I heard there was more to it than that. I hear you pack a pistol as well as a P-bass."

"Sometimes. Some bandmates of mine have been robbed leaving gigs back in Texas. But the measly amounts I've gotten for playing in this town aren't worth risking a concealed weapon charge. I didn't even bring the gun out here with me."

"Don't worry." He slapped his thigh pocket and let out a brief, husky laugh. "I'm packing."

"Great." I couldn't tell if the bulge in his jumpsuit was really a small-caliber gun or a pack of 100-millimeter cigarettes. "For your little meeting, or in case the drummer misses the backbeat?"

At first, I thought he either hadn't heard me or was pretending not to. Finally, he said, "You just never know what'll happen, Martin. You just never know."

I shook my head as he turned on the radio and the rowdy primal sounds of Howlin' Wolf blasted from the speakers. Cyclone immediately stomped the accelerator to the floor, snarling, "That there's the real goddamn thang, man."

"Well, how about pumping up the volume and easing back on the accelerator?"

He hadn't heard me any more than the people in Siberia could hear me. He gripped the steering wheel hard with one hand and pounded it with the heel of the other and shouted over the music:

"The Wolf, Muddy Waters, O.V. Wright, Buddy Holly, Otis, Janis, Jimi, and, God rest his soul, Stevie Ray Vaughan. Goddamn!"

"Amen," I shouted back, "but slow this boat *down* a few knots, for chrissakes."

Instead, he punched the accelerator again, pumping more enthusiasm into his litany: "Patsy Cline, Roy Buchanan, Little Willie John, Johnny Ace, Percy Mayfield, Robert Johnson, Sam Cooke. Good *God,* man!" He whipped a half pint of Seagram's out of the glove box, took a drink, gritting his teeth a few seconds after he swallowed. "You ever think about it?"

"About what?"

He took another drink, gritted his teeth again, then offered me the bottle. I didn't want any. "How all the good ones are dead, man. How screwed up it is they get snatched away 'fore their prime, deprivin' us of all that powerful shit they had in 'em, leavin' us stuck with all this mediocre crap?"

"I agree with you, Cyclone," I said, "but I've got no desire to board the train to glory tonight."

"Huh?"

"Slow *down,* for chrissakes. I don't wanna die, get maimed and scarred or even hauled off to jail with you. I thought you wanted to play music tonight, not try out for the demolition derby."

For the first time since I'd laid eyes on him, an expression that could pass for mellowness came over his face and stayed in place for several seconds. His jaw muscles went slack, his lips drooped like a scolded child's, and, most importantly, he eased up on the accelerator. "OK, Martin," he said. "How's that?"

"Fine," I said, watching as the speedometer needle dropped down between forty and forty-five.

"Martin . . ." His voice was throaty and quiet again.

"What?"

"Used to have a cat named Martin. Cute little rascal, just a little kitten. It died, though. Got that feline leukemia."

"I'm sorry."

He just nodded. Then the muscles in his face hardened again, and his foot jammed back down on the accelerator. The transformation was as sudden as it was complete, and from the gleam in his eye and the sneer on his lips, I could tell it was caused by the sounds emanating from the radio: the Howlin' Wolf song had faded out, followed with "Precious Heart," by Dovie de Carlo.

"Aw hell," he growled. "Just listen to *that.*"

"Precious Heart" was the first Richard James song Dovie de Carlo had recorded. Released as a twelve-inch commemorative single in February '85, the tune had a pensive minor key melody identical to hundreds of other blues songs. But this track was dressed up with synthesized drums and electronic keyboards, primping it up for the slick rock and pop market. While such production values had propelled Dovie de Carlo up the charts, they caused blues purists and diehard fans of the Rockin' Dog to feel the earth rumble to a backbeat as the late musician spun in his grave.

The apartment complex where I lived was just ahead. I pointed it out and Cyclone jerked the wheel and hit the brakes, fishtailing us into a parking spot.

Cyclone slammed the volume control on the radio with the heel of his hand with such violence that the knob flew off, ricocheting against his window. "Shit, man," he snarled.

"It's just pop music," I said.

"Bullshit. Dovie de Carlo? I know a thang or two about her that'd curl your hair, pal. Make you eat those words in a New York minute."

I just looked at him, my hand resting on the door handle and my mind mulling over the doubts I had about tonight's recording session. I kept them to myself, though. It would either work out or it wouldn't, and I would either get the other four hundred bucks or I wouldn't. At least I'd already gotten a hundred bucks, one free drink, and a ride out of the deal.

"You think I'm crazy, don'cha?" A strange half-moon smile lit up his features. "Lemme tell you something, Martin," he drawled. "Sometimes crazy people don't act that way 'cause they're crazy, they act that way 'cause there's no other way to act."

"See you 'round midnight," I said, and got out of the car. As I turned and went up the walk, the screeching of his tires on the pavement sounded like a wild animal who was either horny, hungry, or mad as hell.

Maybe all three.

2

I let myself in the apartment and warmed up my fingers on my bass while I waited for midnight to roll around. The bass wasn't the candy-apple red Precision I'd used longer than the Reagan and Bush crowd had been in the White House, but another vintage '63 model I'd recently picked up. My red bass had been used literally as a blunt instrument in an Austin gangster's maniacal attack on a girl who'd probed too deeply into his affairs, and I hadn't been able to bring myself to use it to make music again just yet.

The L.A. trip had seemed like a good idea at the time. My fellow bandmates needed some time to recover from a bit of post-road-trip madness, so I'd lit out for the West Coast to play bass on some sessions and give some music publishers the chance to hear our tape. A royalty check for a song I'd cowritten for an Austin singer's major-label debut gave me enough cash to pay the rent on my Austin apartment and a month-to-month lease on a tiny space in North Hollywood.

I played a few sessions, spread the tape around. Though the producers liked my bass playing and the publishers liked the band's songs, neither field of endeavor yielded much beyond a few extra business cards stuffed in my Filofax and a little cash stuffed in the pocket of my vintage suit. In fact, my standard

Austin R&B uniform of vintage suits and my '63 model Fender Precision bass seemed to garner more enthusiasm than the music.

I was broke and homesick. I had trouble relating to the L.A. music scene, and I was tired of being around musicians whose idea of music history went only as far back as Guns N' Roses early days on the Strip. And the ratio of clubs to bands was so lopsided that bands often had to pay club owners for the privilege of playing, a practice known locally as "pay to play." My friends back in Austin called it something else.

There were things about L.A. that I liked, but Antone's ("the home of the blues") and dozens of other great clubs were back in Austin. The best flour tacos and the hottest salsa were in Austin. Town Lake was in Austin. The capital of Texas was in Austin.

So was Ladonna DiMascio, a sexy, broad-shouldered Italian with mounds of platinum blond hair, cayenne pepper in her bloodstream, and a picture of yours truly on her nightstand. She'd been supportive when I explained why my L.A. excursion was a good idea. Eighty days and half that many phone calls later, neither of us could remember why, and her precocious eight-year-old son, Michael, had stopped asking if I'd met anyone famous lately.

At a quarter to midnight I put my bass back in its case and started pacing the room. At a quarter to one, I turned on the portable radio and fell back on the sofa bed. After a series of announcements, the deejay spun a set of songs by Elvis Presley, Muddy Waters, Buddy Holly, Stevie Ray Vaughan, and Richard James. I spent the following hour listening to the radio, keeping track of how many of the songs the deejay played were by dead musicians. As it turned out, most were, and I wondered if that was due to the state of mind of the deejay or the fact that that was where the good music was.

Cyclone Davis never showed up.

3

Sgt. Roman was a sturdily built man in his early sixties, with deep squint lines around his eyes and wavy brown hair. He conducted himself with the cool, unhurried manner of a cop who knows his job inside and out, and has known it that way for a long time. The two LAPD detectives who had knocked on my door around noon had introduced us.

A man had been found shot through the heart with a high-powered rifle, a .30-06, on a hiking trail in a wilderness park up in the Santa Monica Mountains just fifty yards off Mulholland Drive above Studio City. There had been no identification on the body, but a matchbook inscribed with the name and hotel room number of a female had been found under a car seat. The female was summoned to the county morgue to identify the body. She said the man's name was Cyclone Davis, and that he had lived in a garage apartment in Van Nuys. But when the detectives went to the garage apartment, they found it had been gutted by an early morning fire. Arson was suspected.

The Cadillac, left at the park entrance, had been wiped clean of prints. The car was registered to an Otis Taylor of Austin, Texas. When contacted, Taylor stated that he had given the car to Cyclone Davis.

Sgt. Roman wanted to know if I knew Otis Taylor.

I told him that I did not.

Roman leaned on one elbow at his desk in the homicide room and said, "Seems like you'd know him. This homicide sergeant down there that you give bass lessons to, Sgt. Lasko, claims you're kind of a fixture on the Austin music scene."

Roman read from his notes. "Otis Taylor owns a music publishing company called Lux de Lux. Lux de Lux publishes Richard James songs. You said the victim started ranting about Richard James being alive just before he dropped you off at your apartment to go *meet a man about a song*."

"Austin is a music town," I said. "You can't throw a rock without hitting a hot guitar player, song plugger, or band manager. I wouldn't know every single music person there any more than you know every cop in L.A. Davis had a tape he said proved that Richard James is still alive. But he didn't mention any Otis Taylor."

The squint lines around Roman's eyes deepened when I mentioned the tape. "We didn't find a tape, but the folks in Sacramento tell us the victim's prints belong to a Kyle Anthony Lynch of Oakland. Ever hear that name?"

"No."

"Lynch served county time for armed robbery up there last February. How about Dovie de Carlo? Tell me what you know about her."

"She's got an OK voice," I said. "She went down in a plane with Richard James in 1984. Now she does pretty well doing his songs."

"But do you know her?"

I shook my head. "I know she's from Austin, too, but the way I understand it, she spends most of her time here. She was in a Top Forty band before she hooked up with Richard James, and that's out of my circle. Now she's in the big time, and that's still out of my circle. I play rhythm and blues in nightclubs, Sergeant. It's a different scene."

"Uh-huh," he said. "My eleven-year-old daughter keeps MTV blasting twenty-four hours a day. Seems like Ms. de Carlo is on there quite a bit. Apparently this Lynch character was part of her, uhm, *entourage,* for awhile."

Something about the way he used the word "entourage" implied that the sex lives of the rich and famous wasn't something that held a great deal of fascination for him. I liked that.

"Was Dovie de Carlo the name on the matchbook cover?" I asked.

"Uh-huh. She was paying his rent, too."

"Interesting."

Roman nodded. "So this Lynch character phoned you yesterday about playing bass on a recording session. You met at a bar, he dropped you off at your apartment, then went to 'meet a man about a song' and never came back. Your downstairs neighbor saw you come in, heard your radio playing, heard you pacing. You say you don't know where the studio was or whom the victim was supposed to meet."

"That's correct, Sergeant."

"You don't suppose this 'meet a man about a song' could've meant meet a man about buying or selling some drugs, do you?"

I shrugged. "I have no idea. I don't use them myself. I don't sell them and I try to avoid people who do."

He nodded. "That's what your friend Sgt. Lasko says. But we've been seeing an increase in drug transactions and drug-related body dumpings up in the hills lately. Lynch was also arrested for narcotics possession in Oakland back in '86. I believe we're going to pursue that angle for awhile."

He pushed his notes around with his pencil like a kid avoiding vegetables on his dinner plate. Then, peering at me from underneath a cynically raised eyebrow, he said, "Richard James is alive, huh?"

I just shrugged.

He grinned slightly, then glanced back at his notes. What he saw there made both eyebrows go up this time. "So you don't have a car out here?"

"That's right, Sergeant."

He shook his head in wonderment. "I can't imagine living in

L.A. without a car. How long you say you've been out here, almost three months?"

"Today makes eighty-one days. Cyclone Davis, or whatever his name was, thought it was pretty incredible, too."

He nodded slowly as he stuck his notes into a folder, closed it, tossed it onto another stack of folders, then reached out and grabbed another from a pile at his elbow. He opened the new file, glanced at the contents, frowned, and shook his head. "I'll get somebody to give you a ride back," he said. "You're free to go."

4

"I'm glad you were able to drop by, Martin," said Carson Block behind his desk in the artists and repertoire department of IMF Records in the heart of Burbank's media district. "Did my assistant take care of your cab fare and everything?"

I nodded and sat down as he straightened one of the stacks of scores of cassettes that competed for his attention and elbow room on the desk. His blond hair was tied in a ponytail in back, and his casual, unconstructed suit was oversized and boxy on his lightweight frame.

"Are you still sore about that other thing?" he said.

"That other thing" was the fact that he was the person who had secretly hired Retha Thomas to investigate the Austin gangster's past music business dealings. Retha looked at the assignment as a way of bolstering her chances of landing a job at the record company; Carson had looked at it as a way to put out some fires on a shady record deal. I'd met Retha on my first night back in town after eighteen weeks on the road. She gave me a ride to a party and asked me a few odd questions, and I ended up drinking a spiked drink that had been intended for her. I left my bass in her car, and later that night, the gangster tried to kill her with it.

I told Carson that since he had paid her doctor's bill and

promised her a job at IMF as soon as she wanted one, I was no longer as sore as I had been.

"Good," he said as he bit the side of his lip and made a plosive sound, which I had come to learn meant that something troubled him. "Now I've got something else to apologize to you for: I'm the one who gave Cyclone Davis your phone number."

The news didn't floor me. Carson was the guy who'd signed Dovie de Carlo to IMF. "I'm just glad the cops found one body up off Mulholland instead of two," I said. "Otherwise I wouldn't be here to accept your apology. Did you send the police to talk to me, too?"

He nodded. "I had to, Martin. You're the only person I know besides Dovie who might have known him."

"What about Otis Taylor?"

"Dovie's publisher, yeah. What about him?"

"The cops say Otis Taylor gave Cyclone Davis the Cadillac he was driving."

"Yeah, I know him. But I didn't know about his connection with Cyclone Davis. You OK with the cops?"

"I guess so. They seem to think it might've been drug related."

"And you?"

I shrugged. "He didn't say anything about drugs, but he was real excited about a tape of a song he had called 'The Whole Damn Truth.' He said it proved Richard James is still alive."

"Yeah right," he said as he rolled his eyes, "and he's jamming down at the China Club every Tuesday with Jim Morrison and Robert Johnson. Look, I don't know much about this guy— Davis or Lynch or whatever his name was—and I never heard about that song or any of that garbage. But he was a kook, so what you're saying he said doesn't exactly surprise me. All I know is, Dovie picked him up after a gig one night. He wasn't the kind of person I'd hang around with, but she seemed to like him. He claimed to be a songwriter, too, and Dovie needs some help in that department. And, actually . . . "

"Actually, what?"

"Actually, that's the main thing I wanted to talk to you about—writing songs."

"You want me to write songs with her?"

"Look, Martin, let's be blunt. Dovie de Carlo is cool. She goes down with Richard in a plane crash, survives a grueling two weeks on that mountainside, gets rescued, then sings his songs. Christ, our publicity hacks couldn't make up a better story than that. She's sexy and she makes great videos. She's from Texas, more or less, and her records go gold."

He made a fist and cleared his throat into it. "Now on the other hand, her voice is no great shakes. Appearance-wise, she's no Madonna, and she can't dance. She's spoiled rotten and she's had her whole career just dropped in her lap. She doesn't have a band, and she isn't the kind of artist who attracts top name musicians to back her up. She has a drinking problem and I think she still does drugs sometimes, even though I don't need to tell you that doesn't leave this office. Actually, none of this does."

"Goes without saying," I said.

"Right." He nodded. "But the biggest problem with Dovie is her material. I'm not speaking just for myself when I say that, although Richard James put her where she is today, it's wearing a little thin. I mean, an artist needs to grow, you know? I don't know how many more of Richard's unrecorded songs are left, but the bottom line is I don't think we can afford to keep putting out her records unless she comes up with something fresh."

"Gold records aren't enough?"

He slumped inside the flimsy suit. "Frankly, no. We didn't make diddly from her last two albums. And Dovie doesn't just operate in the red, she bathes in a sea of it."

"I seem to remember hearing about a hefty advance when you renewed her contract last year."

"It all went to Otis Taylor, since he owns all the songs, and that's his deal with her. Otis is the guy who came to Dovie when she was still recovering from the plane crash and asked her if she'd record one of Richard's songs for a single, a tribute sort of thing. She did it, and Otis brought it to us to distribute. We did a one-off type deal with Otis. Well, as you know, the record took off, so I looked into getting my hands on the rest of Richard's unpublished material, but I was too late. With the money we'd given him for the single, Otis had gone to Richard's mother and bought up all his publishing. Turns out Richard left quite a few unrecorded songs behind, and now Otis owns them all. So we're sort of married to the guy.

"Otis pays Dovie out of his own company, Lux de Lux, like she's just an employee or something. We don't get a split of the publishing at all, which is unusual. You know that. We want to hold on to Dovie because we love her and believe in her, and because she's a prestige act. But we need more incentive, like a breakthrough hit, one that this company has a piece of. I know it sounds cold, but hey, you've been around long enough to understand that."

"Does she have a manager?"

He shook his head. "Just Otis. He tells her what to do. But if she didn't have to rely on him so much for her material, it would be easier for us to work things out for her. If you could help her write some songs, it'd be good for all of us. I could book some studio time for you—"

"I'm no pop songwriter, Carson."

"So? You're a craftsman, a journeyman musician. You'd be nothing but good for her. Believe me, I trust my instincts on this thing."

"I don't. I don't like the sound or smell of this thing."

"Hey," he protested. "At your age, aren't you ready to go for it? If you wanna get somewhere—"

"Yeah. I wanna get somewhere, and it's the hell out of this town. It's fine for some people, but I'd rather be a fence post in Austin, Texas, than have a star on Hollywood Boulevard. I just wanna play the blues. I'm not cut out for baby-sitting, either."

He was chewing his lip again.

"Don't you get mouth ulcers from that?" I said.

He let the lip go and snorted indignantly. He took one of the cassettes off a stack at his elbow and placed it in front of him, standing it on end. Then he took another and set it down the same way, a couple of inches from the other. "Would you consider doing this thing, just for a little while? For money?"

"Maybe."

"Maybe? What kind of maybe?" He cocked his head attentively as he took several more cassettes and lined them up in a semicircular arrangement with their brothers.

"The kind they have in Austin."

His eyebrows shot up. "Austin?"

"Yeah, you know, capital of Texas, home of the blues. My band could back her up. We'd work up the new songs and she would get more royalties, which you'd get a split of, and she could start getting independent from this Otis character."

"I don't know, Martin." He was leaning on his elbows, staring at the tapes in front of him, thinking. "See, there's the fact that Otis is in Austin, and so are those weirdos who come to her gigs and hang around. I wanna get her away from all that."

"What kind of weirdos?"

A couple more cassettes closed the circle. "Just creeps," he said as he placed a cassette in a horizontal position atop one of the standing ones. "I guess they're old Richard James fans. Backwoods weirdos, I guess you could call them. They're not nice people, Martin."

"Austin has its share. I'd imagine there are plenty out here, too."

"I guess you're right. Well, Martin, what's it gonna take, man?"

"I'll think about it."

"You will?"

"Yeah. I'd need to talk to her, see if we might be able to get along."

"She's staying at the Mondrian Hotel on Sunset. I already

talked to her about you, so she'll be expecting you. I'll have my assistant give you some cash for cab fare. I can't believe you've been living in L.A. almost three months without a car."

"I can't either."

He nodded and focused his attention on the circle of cassettes, made a minor adjustment in the placement of a couple, and smiled. "Look, Stonehenge."

"Nice," I said. "And all those bands who send you their demo tapes probably think you actually listen to them."

His expression turned serious. "I hope you'll do it, Martin. I can only lose so much money on Dovie before the guys upstairs pull the plug."

I nodded and stood up. He stood up then, and stuck out his hand. "I'm not guaranteeing it'll be easy," he said. "I love Dovie, but she's got problems. If she didn't, we wouldn't have this trouble with people like Otis Taylor and Cyclone Davis. But she's special, Martin. She's been through a lot. Neither you or I can imagine what she must've gone through up on that mountainside."

"I know," I said.

There was an oddly emotive look on his face, and it stayed in place even as he summoned his assistant into the office, and instructed him to give me two hundred dollars cash. I followed the assistant to his desk, took the cash, and signed a receipt.

There was a cab waiting when I got downstairs.

On the way to Dovie's hotel, I thought about Carson Block. I didn't trust him as far as I could throw him. First he gives my phone number to a lunatic who got himself blown away shortly after we'd met. Then in one breath, he tells me that Dovie de Carlo isn't the kind of artist who can attract top-drawer players, but she needs a breakthrough hit. In the next breath he asks *me* to try working with her, to help her write songs, to help him drive a wedge between Dovie and her tightfisted publisher.

Why would I even consider playing with a spoiled, troubled

pop star whose style was more Madonna than Muddy Waters? One reason was that I'd never done it before. Another was that I wanted to know a little more about the man who'd said that the Rockin' Dog was still alive.

But mainly, it sounded like there was plane fare in it.

5

Her door wasn't shut all the way. I knocked several times, then went in, cleared my throat, and looked around. The seventh-floor suite was about three times the size of my efficiency crib in North Hollywood, but instead of a view of the Hollywood freeway, this one offered the sweeping panorama of West Hollywood and the smog-enveloped basin far to the south. The phone was ringing and the suite was littered with clothes, magazines, CDs, guitars, and assorted music paraphernalia. Dovie de Carlo was sitting on a couch, bent over an acoustic guitar.

"Hello," I said. "I'm Martin Fender."

She quit playing long enough to shoot me a look of mild reproach for interrupting her. "Just a minute. Come on in."

The phone stopped ringing. I walked around the sofa and sat in a comfortable chair. Wearing an oversize black T-shirt and black jeans, she looked nothing like she did on MTV. Her black hair sprawled about the top of her head, with thick, swirling bangs falling down into blue eyes with dark circles under them. Her cheekbones were high and rounded, and her small mouth bore a sort of pinched expression as she concentrated on playing the guitar.

She ran through a three-chord grouping a couple of times, switched to an awkward transitional section of minor chords, then returned to the same three chords of the first section, played with an added emphasis that suggested that, this time around, they constituted the chorus.

"OK, I think I've got it now," she said as she stopped playing. "I didn't want to forget what I was doing."

"Why don't you run through it one more time," I said.

She gave me a look with a bit of challenge in it, but started playing again, singing along, sometimes with words, sometimes just with a throaty hum. When she came to the chorus the second time, I made a motion for her to stop playing.

"The chorus and the verse have the same chords," I said. "C-minor, B-flat, and F, right?"

She nodded, unsmiling. "The chords between the verse and chorus sort of make a little bridge for it, but I'm still working on that part."

"If it was my song, I'd get rid of the transition section and cut straight to the chorus."

"Why? I think it needs something."

I shook my head. "Keep it simple. Your chorus shifts gears once you get to it anyway, because the vocal goes higher and the melody turns melismatic. That's all you need to distinguish it from the verse."

"Well I know what you're saying," she said, nodding her head as she bent over the guitar again. "But I still think it needs this part, you know . . ." She started to stab out the awkward chord grouping again, trying to leave the verse and come back to it again from a different direction.

I made her stop. "Why? You've got a cool groove going. Why mess it up by pasting something in that just distracts?"

I had the feeling she liked my suggestion, but hated to admit it. "Simple is always best, isn't it?" she said.

I nodded.

"What would you do for a middle eight?"

"Start in D-minor," I said.

She strummed the chord and gave me an inquiring look.

"Go to, say, G-minor," I suggested.

She tried it. The look came back, we didn't like the G-minor.
"Try B-flat." The B-flat sounded good. "Back again," I said.
I kept time with my foot as she ran through the D-minor to B-flat change several times, then said, "Next time, get off the D-minor by driving on the G-minor, since that's your fifth."

She did a little flourish on the E string before hitting the G-minor and hammering it, muting the strings back by the bridge with the heel of her right hand, then slashed out the chords to the verse again. Her face lit up a bit as she strummed a final chord.

"Think you're pretty smart, don't you?" she said.

"Nah. That kind of stuff is in the air, in your blood. You just have to let it come out. Then trust your instincts and keep it simple."

"Keep it simple, huh." Her eyes narrowed. The challenging look was still there, but it was softening. Finally she smiled. There was something reassuring about that smile, and she held on to it even after she nonchalantly answered the phone, which was ringing again. She put the guitar down and walked to the bar, phone cradled on her shoulder, glancing back at me and wiggling her fingers over the various bottles on the counter in case I wanted something.

"Yeah, I'm OK . . . ," she said into the phone. "Really . . . No, he hasn't been here . . ."

I didn't want a drink. She nodded and poured some wine in a long-stemmed glass. It was more or less well known that Dovie had spent a couple of months recovering from "alcohol and substance problems" in a private hospital in Austin after the plane crash experience in 1984. Then, after signing with IMF Records, she'd taped a number of antidrug and alcohol public service spots. It seemed that I'd just seen one a couple of days ago. She swished the wine around in the glass, taking medium-sized sips.

She hung up the phone and frowned. "Record companies," she said as she topped off her glass and came back over to the couch. She drew up her legs and held the wineglass in both hands, tracing the rim of it with a fingertip, making a squeaking sound. "I heard you were in on some wild deal in Austin last May," she said. "You shot somebody and everything."

"I was being shot at. I was under a table and two guys were trying to kill me because I knew some things I wasn't supposed to know. I fired a shotgun at them and they stopped shooting at me. Why?"

"Do you know Otis Taylor?"

"No. I know he owns all of the Richard James songs you record. The police tell me he gave Cyclone Davis his Cadillac, and Carson Block tells me Otis tells you what to do. Is he your lover, too?"

"No. Cyclone was. Otis is just Otis. Otis killed Cyclone," she said with a matter-of-fact but brittle tone.

"You should tell the police," I said. "Or have you already?"

"*No*. No way."

"Look, I just came here to see about writing songs—"

"Stick around awhile and help me, Martin. I'm all fucked up." Her nose was red, her eyes were swelling up, but there were no tears. "You say you like things simple, huh? OK, how's this: I want you to kill Otis."

I looked away from her. Outside, the horizon was an astonishing smear of grayish gold, dotted with the fringe tops of palm trees that looked like stick figures with fright wigs.

"Did you hear me?" Her voice was harsh and pathetic. "I said I want you to kill Otis Taylor."

"Yeah," I answered. "I heard you."

Then she started crying and throwing things. I sat there and watched her, ducking whenever I had to.

6

The room had taken a beating. A bedside lamp and a clock radio were total losses, an abstract painting now looked surrealist with a wine bottle sticking through it, and an unopened bottle of Macallan was hurled at the wall with enough force to send it back to Scotland. Luckily, it didn't break. At that point I'd decided enough was enough and pinned her arms to her sides till she promised to calm down and talk to me.

I was back in my chair, sipping on some of the salvaged Macallan, watching her fortify herself with wine and a cigarette as she told her story. It started out like a lot of other stories.

She hadn't been popular in high school. Her dad was in the air force, so her family moved around a lot, so there were a lot of schools she was not popular in. During her senior year the de Carlo family moved to Austin and she met a guitar player named Nate Waco.

"He was a real cool rockabilly-looking dude," she said, "short hair, tall and thin with no ass at all. His jeans, no matter how tight they were everywhere else, just hung down empty in back, because there wasn't anything there. Nothing at all.

"Nate wanted to be a songwriter, but he dropped out of school to go on the road with a Top Forty band, the Number Sevens. We got married and I took my GED so I could go out on the road with him. They let me sing backup, and even let me sing lead on one song.

"One night in Dallas we opened for Richard James, and after our set, he came in our dressing room in his gold lamé suit, his hair dangling down in front of his face like it always did, and he said he really enjoyed our set and his guitar player had fallen off the back of a pickup truck that afternoon and did Nate think he could fill in for him?"

She sighed heavily, smiling nervously at the memory, then drank some more wine, lit another cigarette, and went on.

"Well, Nate filled in so well that he quit the Sevens and went on the road with Richard for three months. Nate and I didn't have a place of our own yet, so I had to stay with my parents, and it was no picnic. Mom was one of those people who still thought rock and blues was evil, you know, the devil's music, that whole trip. To make matters worse, Nate started fooling around with groupies on the road and taking a lot of speed.

"Meanwhile, the Sevens got another guitar player. The bass player, Preston Drake, called and said he'd been writing songs and he'd like me to sing on them. They had a tour booked and did I want to do it? I said hell, yes. Mama shit bricks, but I didn't care.

"After Richard's tour was over, it was Nate's turn to come back and be alone while I was on the road. The next thing that happened turned the tables around even more: The Sevens were playing a club in Lubbock the night Richard flew in to see his mama and he dropped in on us. He was wearing that gold lamé suit again." She paused again to blush at the memory. "Richard had a thing about Lubbock, you know. He'd bought his mama a house there, and he always was a big Buddy Holly fan. Well, Preston knew all these Buddy Holly songs, so Richard couldn't resist getting up and singing on them. Then we played some of Richard's songs—'Tornado Man,' 'Six Foot Rattlesnake in Tight Blue Jeans,' 'S.O.L.,' and 'Do the Dog.' It was great. During a break, Richard bought me a drink and we talked and hit it off pretty well. Then after our last set, he took me back in the dressing room, locked the door, and showed me what 'Six Foot Rattlesnake in Tight Blue Jeans' was really all about."

She blushed and let out a lusty laugh, then her expression turned serious again. "Well, Richard liked the Sevens well enough to ask us if we'd be his new backup band, and he liked me well enough that I forgot all about Nate and how he'd treated me."

"What happened to him?"

"Well, like I said, he wanted to be a songwriter, but it always seemed to bring him more grief than success. I mean, like his ass, it just wasn't there. He had a bad attitude. He'd always fought with Preston in the Number Sevens, and I think he fought with everybody else he ever played with, too. He gradually slid into crummier and crummier gigs. Plus, there was the speed thing. I guess he started with Richard. Everybody who played or hung around with Richard was into it back then. People weren't so worked up about drugs back then like they are now, you know. I did a line occasionally, but I passed it up more often than not. And it was *always* around, so it was hard to turn down. I guess Nate just kept on doing it."

"And you stayed with Richard?"

She nodded. "Until the end, along with the drummer, Cokey, and Preston. Richard didn't have a record deal, and by 1984 he was sort of a novelty act. Sometimes it's worse being a legend than being unknown, you know. We'd done a revival show in Grand Junction with Chubby Checker where five people showed up and we were flying on to do a gig in Denver the next night. I remember we were really looking forward to that gig because Richard's original guitar player, L-Tone Rogers, was gonna sit in with us. But not long after we took off the plane started having engine trouble and the pilot decided to turn back. Then we hit the storm."

She went on talking as though a tape were playing inside her head, her cigarette left smoldering in the ashtray, fouling the room with the fumes that untended cigarettes give off.

"Lightning hit the plane. It was almost like in the cartoons when you see people's skeletons and stuff. Preston really got zapped, it actually knocked him out of his seat. Then we hit a snowbank on the side of a mountain, but the plane didn't break up. We just kept sliding down it, forever, it seemed like. I remember just waiting for us to explode or something. We kept going down, and then we hit a big drift or something and slowed down. The rest of it is just a jumble—guys screaming, parts of the plane and luggage and guitars flying all over the place, and then all of a sudden we stopped.

"We were all alive, except for the pilot. His seat was jammed up against the instrument panel, and something was sticking through his back. Preston had a head injury, bleeding a lot, which made it look a lot worse than it was. Cokey, the drummer, didn't *look* like he was hurt too badly, but he didn't seem to understand what had happened. Richard had some bad cuts on his face and his nose was broken in a couple of places, teeth knocked out, and I just knew that, even if we got out of there alive, nobody'd ever pay to see him sing again, not ever.

"The radio didn't work. The next day we started to ration the food. We had lots of chocolate bars, the deli spread from the gig the night before, two big bags of sunflower seeds, some nuts, and a big bag of tortilla strips from Seis Salsas in Austin. It was bad. We were weak and so freaked out, and the cold was worse than you can imagine. Cokey was like a baby, just useless. On the ninth day we were down to one tortilla chip a day and a bite of chocolate.

"On the eleventh day the snow let up early. Richard went down and checked out the gorge below the ledge the plane was on and said he thought he might be able to make it down the mountain to get help. Preston decided to go with him. I stayed with Cokey. About twenty minutes after they left, there was a rumble. At first I thought it was helicopters, coming to rescue us. The plane started to shake. I looked out the window and saw it was an avalanche. It looked like it was gonna bury us for sure. But the stuff hit this ridge just on the other side of us, and it all passed right by.

"Preston and Richard never came back. On the fourteenth day there was another rumble and I thought this time we'd get buried for sure. But then I heard someone knocking on the outside of the fuselage. I looked up and saw this big beard and sunglasses in the window and he was the most beautiful thing I'd ever seen. This time it *was* a helicopter.

"They loaded us up and took off. I remember looking down and thinking how beautiful that mountain looked. But when we passed over the gorge and I saw how those mountains had dumped a million tons of snow and ice down there, I knew I'd never see Richard or Preston again."

She absentmindedly reached over and brushed her fingers against the strings of the guitar, took a deep breath, and let it out quickly. "I need another drink."

I took her glass over to the bar and emptied the rest of the bottle into it. I gave her the wine and asked if I could bum a cigarette and she nodded.

I dropped two out of the pack, gave her one, then lit both. She inhaled hers deeply, then watched me as I did the same. I hadn't smoked a cigarette in three months. These were Gitanes, and the dark aromatic tobacco sent a jolt into my bloodstream that insisted on another sip of scotch.

"I don't remember much else after they put me in the helicopter," she said. "I know there was a hassle with the FAA and some kind of aeronautics safety board, because the guys who rescued us, who were from Austin, just loaded us up in their plane at St. Ascot and flew us back to Austin without stopping to talk to the officials in Colorado, though they did radio the air strip and tell them where the plane was. They just left the pilot there. They could see Cokey and I were in bad shape, and that was all they cared about. A doctor treated me for exposure and everything, but I ended up spending a couple of months in Oak Tree sanitarium anyway, bouncing off walls and stuff. When I got out, well, you know the rest of it."

"It's a hell of a story," I said. "I've read or heard about parts of it, but not the way you just told it."

She made the sound of a laugh but it was joyless. "Cokey never came out of it. He's still at Oak Tree, and hell, I try not to complain, but on the other hand, it's hard not to dwell on it sometimes. I mean, it's part of my life." She gave another dead laugh. "But I *am* alive, aren't I?"

"You're lucky."

"I'm lucky, all right. I'm lucky six crazy guys from Austin who were big Richard James fans jumped in a plane and flew up there and combed those mountains for us. Rock 'n' roll, it saved my life, but it killed Richard. He gave his life trying to save mine."

"They never found their bodies, did they?"

She shook her head. "Except for the pilot. Half those mountains fell on Richard and Preston. Every couple of years some nut calls the press and claims he's found Richard's skeleton, but it always turns out to be an animal or somebody who got lost years ago."

"Speaking of nuts," I said, "what about Cyclone, or did you know him as Kyle Anthony Lynch?"

"I don't know anything about this Kyle Lynch stuff," she said. "But Cyclone was a full-tilt nut all right. All he ever said about his past was that a woman in a trailer camp found a baby on her doorstep one morning and kicked it out the back door thirteen years later after she got tired of beating on it. He was another Richard James fanatic. I can always tell, the way they come to the gig and get real close to the stage, taking in every word, every bent guitar string. They stare at you with their arms crossed or their hands in their pockets and they subtract points for every chord that isn't just like those kooky chords Richard used, divided by every melody that doesn't go just the way they think Richard would've sung it.

"But Cyclone was different. He did the usual thing, standing up close, not smiling, not dancing, but he really drank it all in and took it to heart. And after one of the shows he came backstage and asked me to marry him. Not because I was Dovie de Carlo but because he was Cyclone Davis and he was going to turn the world upside down and show everybody what color panties it had on. I thought he was funny. We had some good times.

"Anyway, I tried to talk Otis into signing him up to a publishing deal because I thought he had talent. But they met and Otis didn't like him. Not at all. I made him give Cyclone his old Cadillac anyway. Otis gets a new car every couple of years and so it was no big deal. I thought it would make Cyclone happy, but instead he got kind of morose and disappeared for awhile. Then one night a few weeks ago he calls me from Lubbock. He was real weird, mumbling and not making any sense. That was the last I heard from him."

"Do you remember what he said when he called?"

She shook her head, a faraway look glazing her eyes.

"Why do you think Otis killed Cyclone?"

"Just before Cyclone disappeared, someone broke into my room here. I know it was him. Some cash and some jewelry and a Telecaster were missing, too, but I think it was just to cover up for the tapes. When I told Otis, he went crazy."

"What kind of tapes were stolen?"

She shrugged. "I don't know exactly which ones, but at least a couple were some of Richard's songs that Otis had sent me."

"Was 'The Whole Damn Truth' one of them?"

She shrugged. "I don't know. That title doesn't ring a bell. What you have to realize is, Richard wrote tons of songs. I don't even know if Otis knows how many. He sends me tapes of the ones he thinks I should do, and I work them up in the studio with the musicians."

"Cyclone seemed to be pretty convinced that 'The Whole Damn Truth' proved Richard is still alive. He said he was going to meet a man about a song. Do you think he was trying to blackmail Otis with the tape, or maybe just trying to sell it back to him?"

She shook her head. "Forget the tape. I mean, I can imagine Cyclone doing what you said. He was crazy enough. But the tape isn't why, it's just a clue. Otis is very possessive, and stealing the tape and trying to sell it back would've been real stupid. Otis is also very jealous, and that's more like the real reason."

"I thought you said he wasn't your lover."

"And I said Otis is Otis. Love isn't quite the right word for what we have. Love's not enough to keep us together. It's beyond that, way beyond. He told me if Cyclone ever came near me again, he'd kill him, and maybe me too. So when Cyclone came back, that's what he did. Otis killed him."

"But doesn't Otis live in Austin?"

"He's here now. He called this morning, when I came back from the morgue." She shuddered as she drew on her cigarette. "The police talked to Otis, too, you know."

"I know. I just assumed they called him in Austin."

She shook her head. "Look, Otis runs my life and my life sucks. Cyclone was just about the only bright spot and that's why I want you to—"

"Don't say that—"

"—kill him. Blow him away, like he did Cyclone."

Her breathing was heavy and labored as she drained the rest of the wine from her glass. I went over to the bar, got another bottle and a corkscrew, and brought it back to the table. I stripped the seal off and went to work on the cork. I didn't want her to start throwing things again.

"Will you promise to quit asking me to do that for a minute?"

"Why?"

"What if I said it's because I'm starting to like you and every time you say that it puts me off?"

Her lips pressed together in a kind of smirk. "You're starting to like me, huh?"

"I'm not sure. I don't know many other pop stars and I hate to offend the ones I do, even when they ask me to kill someone for them."

She looked at me like I'd hurt her feelings. "I'm not a pop star, I'm just a broad who got a break. You know, a helluva break. Promise to help me?"

I got the screw started in the cork and started twisting. "Tell me why we can't just call the police."

I kept working on the wine bottle. There was a strange haunted look in her eyes that had nothing to do with needing another drink. The cork was giving me trouble. It was starting to split down the side. I gave the screw a couple more turns, trying to spear part of the cork that wasn't split.

"Because," said Dovie, "I'm not the only one who's lucky. Otis is, too. If he gets arrested he'll get that old fart lawyer of his to get him out on bail so quick it'll make your head spin. And then he'll kill me."

I yanked on the cork. It came free, but a big chunk of it fell back into the bottle and bobbed there, looking ugly.

"Well, I don't know him," I said, "but—"

"Let me finish. I *do* know him. Otis is a monster, an evil, mean person, the meanest evilest man I've ever known. And besides not wanting to get murdered, I don't want the attention. I've had magnifying glasses and spotlights and video cameras out the ass ever since I crashed on that mountain and didn't die. Maybe that sounds trite, huh? *I don't want the publicity.* Well, I don't just not want it, I don't think I can take it. I think I'd rather Otis go ahead and kill me first."

"This is going to be hard to make simple, Dovie."

"Well, you can start by giving me some more wine. In fact, if you don't gimme that fucking bottle I'm gonna knock you in the head and take it from you."

I filled up her glass quickly. As she drank it down, I poured some in my own glass, drank some, and lit a couple more cigarettes. Her hand shook a little when she took the cigarette from her mouth and exhaled. She'd been tearing at her cuticles with the stubby nails of her fingers, and at least two of the fingertips were bleeding.

I said, "Is Richard James still alive?"

"Christ, what do you think? I loved him, Martin. I'd trade everything I have, everything I am, just to have him back. I don't give a fuck about being famous. The only reason I do what I do is because it's the only thing I know. I mean, now that you know more about it, what do you think of my glamorous life?"

I didn't know how to answer that. I said, "Cyclone sure seemed worked up about that song."

"I don't remember any song like that," she said. "Maybe I heard it but I forgot. I don't know."

She drank some more wine. I drank some wine, but it tasted like cheap candy after the scotch. I bummed another Gitanes from Dovie, chunking three months of abstinence out the window. I got the cigarette going with a Zippo lighter not unlike the one Cyclone had used the night before, stood up, and checked out the view again. The grayish gold band that had first appeared to be part of the horizon was now rolling over West Hollywood, and, as it came nearer, it took on the more ordinary brownish gray hue of everyday smog. The afternoon was starting to fade into evening and, like many things in L.A., was not aging gracefully. I was starting to feel drunk and I wanted that plane ticket more than ever.

7

"Where's Otis now?"

She was biting a nail. With her teeth still firmly clamped down on it, she said, "I don't know. He didn't say."

"Where does he usually stay when he's out here?"

She jerked the finger in a tearing motion. "I don't know. Not here, he doesn't like big hotels."

"Do you remember where he stayed the last time?"

She shook her head so that more of her hair fell into her face. "He doesn't come out very often. He doesn't like big cities, either, especially L.A."

"But you're sure he's here."

"I *told* you. He called this morning. The last time before that I talked to him was, oh, three days ago. Today's Friday, right? Then it was Tuesday. He was in Austin then."

I tried to put myself in the suspect's position. If I were flying out to L.A., ostensibly to meet a grifter and/or kill him, I probably wouldn't want to be seen hanging around town too long. Maybe he'd flown in early yesterday.

"Does he fly Continental?" I asked.

"Yeah. How'd you guess?"

"He doesn't like big hotels and I have a feeling he doesn't like flying. And if he likes to save money—"

"He does."

"Continental has the cheapest Austin-to-L.A. fares right now, and, last I heard, they were the only nonstop service."

"So what?"

"Before you try and fry this guy, we should make sure he was even here to do the deed. Knowing that he usually flies Continental makes it easier to check up on him. I could make some calls . . ."

She was tearing at her fingers again, looking distracted.

"Look," I said, "I came here to see if we might write songs together. I didn't come here to kill anybody."

"I guess it's a lot to ask. I don't even know you. You probably think I'm a balls-out nutso case."

"No. But there's got to be a better way to deal with this situation than drinking wine until you're mindless and picking your fingers down to the bone. Maybe you could ask him about it. Do you think you could get him to show you his plane ticket?"

She crossed her arms over her chest and gave me a disgusted look. "You don't know Otis."

I started to say something, but the phone rang. She continued glaring at me for several rings, then answered it. She listened for a moment, said, "Yeah, sure," and hung up.

"That was Otis," she said, still staring down at the phone. "He said he'd be here in two minutes."

She stood up suddenly, as if the full import of her words had just sunk in. "Martin, you gotta get out of here."

"Why? Maybe I should meet this monster."

She shook her head and grabbed my arm. "No. Don't try to mess with him."

She yanked on my arm and hurriedly walked me to the door, pausing at the mirror to fuss with her hair and straighten out her T-shirt.

"What if I said I didn't want to go?" I said as she opened the door and peeked down the hallway.

The coast was clear. She ducked back in and put a hand on

my chest. Her hand was shaking. "Just go, OK? I can handle Otis."

"Are you sure?"

She nodded and pushed on my chest. Her eyes looked glazed, her chin unsteady. I stepped backward, over the threshold, out into the hall, and she shut the door.

I waited in the stairwell with the door open a crack so I could keep an eye on the hall. In about three minutes the elevator doors opened and three men got out.

All three wore black cowboy hats and boots. One was a real Marlboro Man, big boned and tan and well over six feet, towering over the other two, who looked about average in height. One had a shock of snow white hair sticking out from under his hat. The other one's hair was either slicked back or pulled into a ponytail. Both shorter men wore sunglasses and the brims of their hats pulled down low, making it hard to distinguish any facial features.

The white-haired man was bundled up in a knee-length duster, the collar turned up in back and his hands jammed in the side pockets. It seemed odd, since it was a warm day. The other two carried jean jackets under their arms.

The Marlboro Man led the way to Dovie's door, knocked, and smiled lustily as she opened it and said, "Hi, Otis." The Marlboro Man put one of his big hands on the door and pushed it the rest of the way open. The short men walked in first, ducking their heads only slightly to slip under his outstretched arm. I eased the exit door shut and started down the stairs to the lobby.

I guessed that the Marlboro Man would be Otis, and he looked like one bad hombre. Apparently, guilty or not, he did have amigos. I was a stranger in town with no amigos. I tipped one of the valets a couple of bucks to call a cab to take me back to the valley.

8

Dovie came over to my apartment just after midnight huddled inside a long black leather coat, wearing gloves, a beret, and oversized Jackie Kennedy shades. I couldn't help being reminded of the white-haired man's getup. She sat down on the sofa bed and took out her cigarettes and offered me one. I lit them both and said, "I've got a couple of beers in the fridge if you want one."

"No thanks, I can only stay a minute," she said in a small, hoarse voice. Her face was puffy and pale, her lips waxy. "I just wanted to bring you this."

She reached inside the coat and brought out a Continental Airlines receipt. I took it and read it, though I already knew what it would say. I'd called the airline reservation department myself and gotten the same information: Otis Taylor had arrived on the 7:30 flight Friday morning, seven and a half hours *after* Cyclone Davis had been shot through the heart.

"Do you think he might've had someone else do it for him?"

She shook her head. "Not Otis. He's the kind of guy who'd do it himself. Believe me."

"What about Cyclone's apartment getting burned down?"

"I can imagine Otis doing that," she said. "Even if he didn't kill him, he'd still want to get even with Cyclone for stealing the tape." She took a drag on the cigarette and said, "Do you think Richard is alive?"

"No, I guess not. Why?"

"Because I'm sick of reliving nightmares, sick of being stuck in the past. But I still love Richard, you know, he's still in my heart, and I think he'd want me to go on, to quit being fucked up. That's why I want to break with Otis and get out of this sick town, too. Carson said you wanted to try to work with me in Austin."

"I'd like to give it a try. I called my band this afternoon and ran the idea past them, and they liked it, too."

Her mouth curled up in the corners, but the result was not a smile. "I'm glad. I just kept thinking about it today, when I told Otis that was what I wanted to do. It also gave me the courage to get that plane ticket."

"Was that all it took?"

"What do you mean?"

I reached for her sunglasses. She tried to bat my hands away but I persisted. When I got the shades off, I saw what getting that airline receipt had cost her.

Two black eyes.

9

It took several minutes to get through to Sgt. Roman. When he came on the phone, he said he wasn't sure he remembered me.

"Martin Fender, Sergeant," I said, "the bass player you questioned about Cyclone Davis yesterday morning."

"Excuse me?"

"Kyle Anthony Lynch."

"Oh yes," he said. "Now I remember, Martin."

"I'm glad."

"Listen, Martin, there've been five murders in my division's jurisdiction since I last spoke with you. Try to bear that in mind. You said you were thinking of leaving town?"

"That's right, Sgt. Roman," I said. "I need to go back to Austin. Dovie de Carlo is going with me. As a matter of fact, our flight is boarding right now."

"You shave it pretty close, don't you, Martin?"

"Did you want me to stick around? In another couple of days, you'll have forgotten me and Cyclone Davis completely."

"Go on back to Texas, Martin. I think we'll be able to find you if we need you. Thanks for calling and have a nice flight."

■

Dovie insisted I take the window seat. No one seemed to recognize her at the airport or on the plane. She was still wearing the sunglasses, but sitting next to her gave me a constant reminder of Otis's handiwork. She'd already had a couple of glasses of wine by the time I arrived at the hotel, and she polished off the bottle while I helped her pack. She had two more glasses at the bar in the terminal, and now she was looking over her shoulder anxiously.

"Why can't they just start serving drinks as soon as you get on the plane, even in the Greyhound section?" she said. "It'd make things a helluva lot easier on everybody."

"You didn't drink a drop last night when you came over."

"That's because we didn't talk much. I don't drink when I play, either. I don't need to."

I didn't say anything. The flight attendants were going up and down the aisles, making sure things were secure for takeoff, and Dovie didn't bother them. Finally she stopped fidgeting for awhile and sighed heavily.

"I'm glad we're going to Austin, Martin."

I nodded. "I didn't think it would be so easy to get you to leave L.A."

"Why? You're the one who says to keep things simple. Like the song, remember?"

I nodded. "It's still a big transition. And then there's Otis."

"Well, the truth is, I'm actually more dependent on him when I'm in L.A. The cost of operating out here, staying in a hotel, finding musicians to work with—it's outrageous, you know. But in Austin, I have a house to live in, for one thing. I'll have to kick Nate out first, though. I guess I'll check into a hotel when we get there. Nate's probably hocked all the furniture and appliances, anyway."

"He still lives off you?"

"We never actually got divorced. And he doesn't live off me, he just exists, by dumb luck and whatever he can scrounge off me and anybody else. He's sort of a human tumbleweed, rolling over the landscape, picking up dirt, just a blur across the road in the middle of the night."

"Something'll have to be done about Otis, too," I said.

She adjusted her sunglasses and turned her head toward the window as the flight attendant made one last pass and the captain came on the p.a. and explained that we were waiting for clearance.

After the announcement, Dovie started gnawing on one of her fingers. "Don't worry about Otis."

"We can't allow him to get near you again. You could file a peace bond or something."

"I don't want to get involved with stuff like that. Remember? Otis won't be around when we get back for awhile, anyway."

"What do you mean?"

"He just won't be, that's all. Damn, I wish I had a drink. If only they'd . . ."

I stared at her as her last sentence dissolved into a soft, low moan. Her complexion was as pale and waxy as a wilted magnolia blossom.

"You know, this is so cool, this new beginning thing," she said, the words floating on top of a dreamy sigh. The abrupt transition was startling. Her voice had the timbre of a young girl reciting her Christmas wish list before drifting off to sleep. "New songs, new town, new freedom. I'll go shopping and get some new clothes, too. It reminds me of back in 1982, when Richard couldn't get a record deal so he decided to put out an album himself. Richard thought that if he could just get a record out, he'd get back on top."

She paused and closed her eyes, and for a moment I thought she'd passed out. "*Ninety Minute Man* was the name of the record," she said, slurring the words. "That one came out in '83. Do you have it?"

I shook my head.

She shrugged and went on. "Richard was really excited, and it was fun being with him and playing with him. No matter how small the club or the crowd, Richard was really revved up. When he was hot, he was *really* hot and wild, you know. Did you ever see him play?"

"Just a couple of times, a long time ago," I said.

"Well, anyway, when the record came out it sank like a stone. It lost a lot of money, and that was bad. Real bad. Those people who put up the money to do the record just couldn't understand that their investment was just gone, you know? It was gone and it wasn't coming back. Are we *ever* gonna take off?"

The plane started to vibrate and move down the approach to the runway. The captain came on and said that we'd been cleared for takeoff. Dovie shuddered and sank down in her seat, folding her arms across her chest, her eyes squeezed tightly shut.

"Who's they?" I asked.

She mumbled something unintelligible.

"Who'd Richard borrow the money from?"

She grimaced at the sound of another jet taking off. "Just some guys. You know, big fans with loose cash."

A tear was rolling down her cheek, and her knees were knocking together. She looked very small and afraid.

"Are you OK?" I asked.

Her lips were pursed together so tightly that they were gray. Finally she slurred, "You think . . . You think I *like* to fly??"

I put an arm around her and pulled her close. She reached over and grabbed my other hand with both of hers and squeezed it. "Take it easy," I said. "Don't think about it."

"Don't think 'bout it? Don't you realize that thing's gonna haunt me till the day I die? Till the day I fuckin' die."

"Nothing's going to happen."

She sighed and the grip on my hand fell loose. "I won't know 'bout it, anyway," she mumbled. "I took some pills. The doc takes care of Dovie."

The plane lurched slightly, started to roll, and quickly picked up speed. By the time the rear landing gear left the pavement, Dovie was snoring softly, making a damp spot on my shoulder.

I thought about Carson Block and how he'd said neither of us would ever know what it had been like up on that mountain.

A few minutes later, as the plane swung out over the ocean and headed back east, she stirred and mumbled something, the words tumbling out half-sung and barely audible. I strained to make out the words: "cold as a coffin nail . . . boiled in concrete . . ."

They were words from "The Whole Damn Truth," the song that Cyclone Davis had said proved the Rockin' Dog was still alive. The song that Cyclone Davis had gone to meet a man about.

I nudged Dovie, but she was out.

When the flight attendants rolled their cart past us, I asked for a pillow and blanket for Dovie and a double scotch for myself.

That got us all the way to Austin.

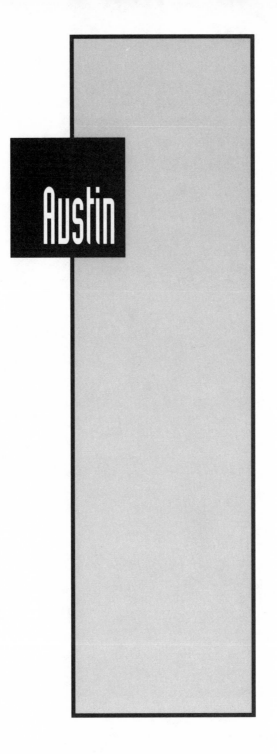

Austin

1

When I opened my eyes, Ladonna was still sitting on top of me, her exquisite mane of platinum blond hair falling down around her bare breasts. Humphrey Bogart was sneaking a look at us out of the corner of his eye as he took a drag on his cigarette, standing in the six-foot poster tacked to my bedroom door. Something soft and furry rubbed against the bare sole of my foot as it dangled off the bed. When I used the toes of my other foot to pinch a tuft of fur, the thirty-pound striped cat meowed and galloped out of the room. He'd be back.

I closed my eyes and pinched myself, and when I opened them again, Ladonna was still there, Bogart was still there, and the cat was back, digging his claws into the bedspread and stretching. I reached down, scooped him up and held him down on my chest.

"You let him get fatter while I was gone," I said.

"He missed you," she said. "It was his way of coping."

I moved my hand from the cat's rounded chassis to Ladonna's smooth, taut frame. "Looks like it wasn't so hard on you. Or did you find some other way of coping?"

The cat suddenly sprang off my chest and landed with a thud on the floor. "There's only one way," she said, cupping my chin with her soft hand with perfect, long nails, bending down and brushing my chest with her hair, then mashing her breasts against me and saying, "All I could do is think about how we were going to make up for it when you got back."

"I guess I've got work to do," I said.

After we took a shower together, I made some ice tea and filled Ladonna in on the rest of my L.A. saga, concluding with Dovie's drugged mumblings on the plane.

"And did you ask her about it when she woke up?"

I shrugged. "She was pretty groggy, and the plane was about to land, and that put her out of sorts, too. She said maybe she *had* heard the song and those lines just stuck in her head. But she didn't remember anything else about it."

"Do you think she's hiding something?"

"Everybody has something to hide. But she seems to keep some bad company. I don't know if it's by choice or just bad luck. She *is* a person that things happen to. Some of the things are good, and some of them are bad."

Ladonna pressed her hands against the cold tea glass and shook her head. "She sounds like trouble with a capital *T* to me. You don't think it's possible that Richard James is alive, do you? You're not the type to go in for things like that, Martin. You don't even laugh when people say they saw Elvis at K-Mart."

"No. Maybe it's because somebody shot Cyclone through the heart, stole the tape that he said proved Richard James is alive, and then set fire to his apartment."

Ladonna's eyebrows came together at that. "And then there's Dovie and Otis. This isn't just a gig for you, is it?"

"Well, it got me home, anyway. Have you seen anything about L-Tone Rogers playing around town lately?"

"I think he was doing a happy-hour set at some place on the East Side last week, but I can't remember where. Why?"

"L-Tone was supposed to meet up and play with Richard in Denver the night after his plane crashed. I seem to remember reading that L-Tone drove up to St. Ascot, where they were coordinating the search parties, and he waited up there until it was all over. Maybe he could tell me something."

Ladonna finished her tea without saying anything. Finally she said she had to go pick up Michael from her mom and dad's. I walked her out to her car and kissed her good-bye, then went back inside and pored over the club listings in the newspaper, looking for L-Tone, fighting the urge to go and buy a pack of Gitanes.

I had no luck.

Later that evening I was relaxing over at Ladonna's condominium after a welcome-home feast of grilled eggplant with bufalo mozzarella, fried calamari, and linguine and clam sauce. Ladonna's mother had sent half a homemade cheesecake back with Michael, and I was washing down the last bite of a wedge of it with a cup of steaming espresso served in a bright orange Bakelite cup, brewed in a stainless-steel Italian espresso maker of '50s atomic design. I was sitting on her new rattan couch, part of a matching set she'd picked up for a song at a flea market. Ladonna's petite black-and-white cat, Betty, was lounging at the other end of the couch, bathing contentedly after having been cut in on the cheesecake.

Michael was seated on the floor playing a Nintendo game and Ladonna was in the kitchen. Dovie was at the Driskill Hotel downtown. She'd decided to stay there until she figured out what to do about her lake house and its unwanted tenant.

"Martin, are you glad to be back?" said Michael.

"Yes, Michael," I said. "I'm real glad. How's school?"

"Pretty cool, I guess." He shrugged his bony shoulders, hunching over the video controls, wearing the yellow fedora from his Dick Tracy costume. Halloween was less than two weeks away. "For school, you know," he added.

I finished the last bit of espresso and sighed, lying back and studying the tropical jungle design on the couch cushions, the sweep of the pink formica boomerang coffee table, and the cyclops eye of the antique Philco TV set in the corner. The whole place was a cozy art deco and '50s modern nest, reflecting what seemed to be a perfect blend of comfort, practicality, and kitsch.

Hell, yes, I was glad to be back. Tomorrow, sometime after Ladonna was at work at the real estate office and Michael was in school, I'd walk back to my apartment, feed the cat, put my bass in the back of my convertible Karmann Ghia, and meet the boys for our first get-together with Dovie. Later on in the week, after we had a few rehearsals under our belts and possibly a tentative gig or two booked, I'd decide whether I needed to call the collection agency and volunteer my part-time services to make some of my own bills go away.

Ladonna looked irresistible in her tight jean cutoffs and bare-midriff tank top, the usual gold hoop earrings dangling, carrying two brandy snifters on a tray. The doorbell rang just as she put the tray down on the boomerang table. She went to the door, peered out the peephole, then opened it a crack.

"Excuse me, ma'am," came a deep, somewhat gruff voice.

"Yes sir?" Her voice sounded a little shaky.

"I'm real sorry to disturb you, but I was patrolling the neighborhood when a report came over the radio about a dangerous felon being spotted near here."

"What is he charged with, Officer?"

"Well, he's suspected of smuggling hot Rolexes, Mercedes hood ornaments, cellular phones, a couple of screenplays, and some stale sushi in from Lotus Land, or, as you civilians may know it, L.A."

"Oh dear," she said. "You'd better come in and have a look around."

She swung the door open and a broad, bearded man wearing cowboy boots, jeans, a brightly colored Hawaiian shirt, and a gimme cap walked in. The tip of a leather holster protruded just below the hem of his shirt as he leaned over to give Ladonna a peck on the cheek, and a gold stud earring glistened in the lobe of his left ear.

"You'll never take me alive, Sgt. Lasko," I said.

"I *heard* that," he said as he pushed the cap back on his head and walked over, looking me up and down for traces of a tan or the glint of a gold chain on my chest. We shook hands and he took a seat across from me.

"Will you have a cognac," asked Ladonna, "or are you on duty?"

"No thanks, darlin'," he answered. "I'm always on duty, seems like." His jocularity faded a bit as he looked at me and said, "Like when I got that call from L.A. Thursday night."

"Did you give Sgt. Roman a good reference for me?" I said.

"Shit. I told him you're a helluva good bass player, but you hang around the wrong people now and then. How's that?"

"I think he figured at least half of that out on his own, but thanks anyway. Have you talked to him since?"

"Uh-huh," he drawled. Lasko had the kind of laconic drawl that sounded the same when he woke up in the morning as when he'd been up forty-eight hours straight, working a grue-some homicide case, or weighing the merits of one Mississippi Delta blues musician over another. "What's your side of the story on this Cyclone Davis–Kyle Lynch character?"

"We were supposed to be doing a session, but I think he was more of a loony tune than a player. Not much more to it than that. I'll tell you about it later. Sure you don't want a drink?"

He nodded. "I can't stay anyway. Just thought I'd drop by, say howdy and way to go on this gig with Dovie de Carlo. Guess you did OK in L.A. after all."

"It's good to be back."

"How'd you hook up with her, anyway?"

I brushed my fingernails on my lapel and said, "I guess my reputation preceded me."

"Yeah," he drawled, stretching the word into long syllables, wringing several possible meanings out of it. "Well, whatever. I was kinda fond of the way Richard James used to do his own songs, myself. I don't go for the MTV versions. Her last record sounded like it had Macintosh computer keyboards on it when it called for Hammond B3, and Eddie Van Halen licks where it could have used Ry Cooder bottleneck. You ain't gonna be a party to that kinda thing, are you?"

"Don't worry, Lasko. I brought her back here to get her away from all that."

He slapped his thigh and smiled, then stood up. "Good. Glad to hear it. Ladonna—" He touched the bill of his cap and said, "You're looking better than ever, and damn it sure smells like there's been some good eating going on here." He wrinkled his nose, grinning. "What's that other smell? Don't tell me Ladonna's lettin' you smoke cigars in the house."

"Gitanes, Lasko."

"Gitanes?"

"French cigarettes. The unfiltered kind."

"Hell, I know, the kind in the cute blue box. Next thing we know, you'll be wearing a beret and reading poetry in a coffeehouse."

"I don't think so."

"Yeah, well, that'll be the day I shave my beard and move to Tarrytown. Anyway, Martin, it's good to have you back."

"Thanks, Lasko. Bring your bass over sometime this week and I'll show you a couple of new riffs or something."

"You got a deal there, bro. Sure you won't be too busy with Dovie?"

"Never too busy for Austin's finest," I said. I shook his hand again and showed him to the door. Soon the quiet Austin night was interrupted by the sound of his pickup engine revving, and it was just the three of us again.

Ladonna went over and checked Michael's status on the video game. "One more, Michael, then it's off to bed."

"Aw, Mom," he protested.

"It's late," she said firmly, "and tomorrow's Monday. A big Monday for everybody." She hoisted her brandy snifter and clicked it against mine. "Cheers, you dangerous felon."

"Cheers." After making sure that Michael was more interested in saving the universe than in the silly things that grown-ups say to each other, I said, "Can I interest you in some only slightly stale sushi?"

She wrinkled her nose and laughed. "You big ape," she said.

We drank our cognac and it seemed to send a warming sensation from the top of my head to the tips of my toes. We kissed, and other warming sensations came into play. I made some more bad jokes, we kissed some more, and finally Michael decided it was time to go to bed.

2

Leo Daly, who played guitar like a man who'd had more cheap whiskey and bad women than a road scholar twice his age, had one of my cigarettes screwed into the side of his mouth, sending snaky blue-gray ribbons up past his youthful scowl as he rested one of his size-twelve sneakers up on the monitor wedge and peeled out riff after stinging riff. Billy Ludwig pounded out a steady shuffle, sweating buckets, a packet of nicotine gum showing through the pocket of his yellow nylon shirt and a mileage logbook sticking out his back pocket. Ray Whitfield stood on his corner of the stage, fedora at a jaunty angle atop a head of black, slicked-back hair, sharp and icicle cool in an avocado green gabardine suit. His pencil-thin mustache appeared to levitate just slightly in one corner whenever Leo hit an especially hot lick. When the guitar solo was over, he would raise his saxophone reed to his lips and blow like a West Texas tornado.

I pumped out the bottom end on my Precision and watched Dovie smile and nod her head in appreciation of the instrumental workout as she stood back from the microphone, tapping her foot to the beat. The ugly little South Austin warehouse we rehearsed in was a long way from a soundstage in Hollywood, but Dovie looked like she felt right at home.

A long-brimmed black velvet cap sat backwards atop her riot

of black hair. She wore an oversize black sweatshirt with the Chanel logo on the front, black bicycle shorts, white athletic shoes, and the sunglasses that hid as much of the black eyes as they could.

Leo finished off his solo with a flurry of whammy bar action and Ray started to blow, approaching the tonic note from a place that seemed far removed from the melody, then racing to close the distance with raw, urgent figures. Leo ducked his chin down and snickered; it sounded like he'd inspired Ray to try to go him one better.

The song was actually an instrumental of ours that Dovie had ad-libbed some verses to, but it sounded like something that might turn into a pretty good song with a little inspiration and polish.

We were a couple of hours into our first rehearsal and everyone seemed to be having a good time. Even Ray, the most mercenary member of the combo, who often had two or three side gigs a night when he wasn't playing with us, had thrown himself into the proceedings without bringing up the subject of how much he'd be earning for his time. I wondered if the two men outside in the beat-up Monte Carlo were enjoying it, too. I didn't know whose friends they were; it had been too dark when I'd arrived to get a good look at them, but one of them had looked slightly familiar.

When Ray's solo was over, Dovie sang the chorus a couple more times and we ended the song. Leo took another drag on his cigarette, stomped it out, and put his guitar down.

"'Scuse me," he said. "Call of nature."

"Why don't we take five?" I said. No one objected.

The four of us toweled off and sat down on amp cases and listened to the equipment hum for awhile. Ray and Billy and I opened fresh beers. Dovie sipped from a large bottle of Evian.

"It sounds good, you guys," she said. "Especially that last one."

"Thanks," said Billy. "Sounds pretty cool to me, too."

"It's sounding quite nice indeed," said Ray. "Quite nice."

Dovie took another sip of Evian and said, "I've got a little ballad kind of thing we might try. It's a sort of a minor key deal that does a slow build after a kooky bridge."

"Good," I said. "We'll try it next."

Leo came back in, got a beer, bummed a cigarette. "They're still out there."

"Who?" asked Dovie.

"A couple of guys wearing cowboy hats and boots," said Billy. "They helped me unload the van. I figured you guys knew them."

I shook my head and waited for Dovie to say something. Finally she opened her purse, rifled around in it, withdrew a pack of cigarettes. Ray quickly offered her a light.

"One of them has red hair pulled back in a tail," said Billy. "The other one is black, with a scar on his forehead. He's got a finger missing, too. His right index finger, I think."

Dovie took another drag on her cigarette. "Red Fred and Nubby Maxwell," she said finally.

Ray shook his head, his lips puckered with disgust. "Hillbilly trash."

"You know them?" I said.

"*Acquainted*," said Ray, an astringent snarl in his voice. "And only by accident, I assure you."

"And you know them, Dovie?" I said.

She shrugged. "I guess you could say that. Red Fred is the red-haired one, and the black one is Marcus Maxwell, but they call him Nubby, because of his missing finger. They were big fans of Richard, used to party with him a lot."

"And this is their idea of a party, too?" said Billy. "Helping with the gear, then sitting in the car, drinking beer while we rehearse? Hey, these guys might make ideal roadies. Maybe we should talk to them about it."

Dovie shook her head and said, "Just ignore them. Maybe they'll go away."

"The police don't like people hanging around in parking lots in this neighborhood," I said. "And we've got roadies we can call when we need them, anyway."

"But if they're big fans of Dovie's, maybe they'll work for free, you know? Just for the privilege. Let 'em get their jollies, I say."

Ray took off his hat and inspected it slowly, then smoothed out the brim before putting it back on his head. "I don't like the idea of those hillbillies hanging around."

Leo was back at his amplifier, tuning his guitar, making the awkward conversation more so.

"Why don't we try that ballad?" I suggested.

No one said anything one way or the other, but a few minutes later, we were back in our usual places, working on the ballad. The song got off to a rough start. Dovie stopped us midway through it several times and said something about the guitar chords not being right. Leo would shrug and try something else, and we'd start over again, but we never made it all the way through to the end. No matter what inversions of the chords Leo tried, the music never quite matched up to the melody Dovie was singing.

Finally we gave up on it. We spent the rest of the evening jamming on some Ann Peebles, Wanda Jackson, and Barbara Lynn songs, then called it quits.

When I ducked outside to answer nature's call just before leaving, the Monte Carlo was backing out of the parking lot. As it passed under the streetlight, I got my first decent look at the two men in cowboy hats. The one behind the wheel was black, so the one in the passenger seat had to be Red Fred. He seemed vaguely familiar.

They were gone when Dovie came out a minute later. I helped her put her acoustic guitar in the backseat of the Lincoln Town Car she'd rented. She had a black '65 Mustang, she said, but Nate had it. She'd get it back when she got him out of her house.

"Richard's fans left," I said.

"Maybe they're not into load out," she said, and smiled weakly. Her voice was hoarse.

"One of them, the red-haired one," I said, "looked like a guy I saw going to your room with Otis the other day."

She didn't say anything. She was digging through her purse.

"The other guy was about the same size," I said. "He had white hair, but he didn't look old and didn't look like the type who would have it bleached."

She stopped digging and gave me a puzzled look. You'd think she'd never heard of a guy having white hair.

"Is something wrong?" I said.

"Have you seen my car keys?"

"Yeah." I took them out of the door lock and handed them to her.

"Thanks, Martin. I guess I'm tired."

"Me, too. We'll try the ballad again tomorrow. Leo's a quick study, he'll figure it out."

The puzzled look was back. She seemed to have forgotten all about the ballad. I kissed her on the cheek, then watched her get in the car and drive away.

A couple of minutes later, I went back inside and packed up my bass. The other guys were talking about Dovie, wondering how she got two black eyes. I wouldn't tell them.

3

I pulled up in my parking lot just after midnight. Situated on the hilly west side of South 1st Street as it slopes down toward Town Lake, the apartment complex consisted of a series of buildings built on the banks of a small, winding creek and two buildings on a high rise, situated around a pool and sunbathing decks—which I rarely used. I lived in one of the buildings on high ground, with a balcony that looked down on the creek-side units.

There was a black '65 Mustang parked in front of one of them.

I parked the Ghia, took out my bass, and put the rag top up. I walked down the hall to my door, unlocked it, went in. The cat didn't come up and demand to be fed, which was somewhat unusual. The place still smelled stale from being unoccupied for almost three months, which would have been normal, but as I put my bass down and looked around the living room/ kitchen area and went over to open the drapes and sliding glass door, I detected another odor: sweat, not my sweat, but the odor of perspiration mixed with ether.

Cassettes were scattered on the floor by the stereo. The cushions had been pulled off the couch. I walked back to the small room where I kept a desk and spare amplifiers and other music hardware. Someone had been there. In the bathroom, the faucet was still dripping, and back in the bedroom, the bed was still unmade. I looked under it; the cat was there in the dark, staring out at me with big green eyes.

That only left the walk-in closet. A tall, wiry long-haired man was coming out of it, pointing a small-caliber automatic at my head.

"I didn't hurt him," he said. "I wouldn't hurt an animal."

"Glad to hear it," I said. "He's a good cat. Spends ninety percent of his time either eating or sleeping, which I suppose you'd find hard to relate to."

The automatic was gripped in both hands. They shook a little. His upper lip was shiny with sweat, and his face had the bony, shrunken look of a man who has taken too much methamphetamine for too long. The mane of hair that pouffed up on top of his head and cascaded down past his bony shoulders added to the shrunken-head effect. His leather jacket hung limply since he had no chest, and though his jeans were tight in the legs, I had the feeling they would sag in back.

"Let's go back in the living room," he said.

"Mind if I change shirts first?" I said. "I've been jamming in a hot warehouse and this one's starting to get rank. All right with you, Nate?"

Something in his neck twitched at the sound of his name, but he didn't try to stop me as I moved toward the dresser.

"Sure, unless you're looking for this—" He reached back to his hip pocket and pulled out my 9-mm Beretta sixteen-shot automatic pistol.

"Oh well. You're sweating enough for both of us. I'll just stop."

"I might as well tell you right now I don't have a sense of humor."

"You mean you didn't come over here to watch David Letterman with me?"

"Uh-uh. Let's go."

He used the gun to point the way. When we got to the living

room I sat on the couch and he braced himself on the kitchen counter.

"All right," he said. "Free it up."

"Free what up?"

"Don't try to con me, man. You probably knew I'd come looking for it so you hid it somewhere special. It doesn't matter. Either I'll turn this place upside down and you with it or you'll get smart and free it up, so why don't you get smart and quit wasting my time?"

"Look, Nate, why don't you put that gun down before you put a bullet through the ceiling and kill the guy upstairs? He's a lead-footed republican and he wakes me up every morning by running his garbage disposal, but I think if anyone's going to murder him it oughta be me. You're shaking so bad I doubt you could hit your own shadow if you tried. And I honestly don't know what you want."

"Bull. Quit wasting time." He gritted his teeth and tried steadying his hand. It didn't work.

"Come on, Nate," I said. "If you were going to shoot me, you'd have done it back there in the bedroom. Besides, the damn drapes are open and somebody might see you."

"Close 'em."

"Come on, Nate."

"Close 'em," he demanded.

I closed the drapes.

"The tape," he said. "I want the damn tape Cyclone Davis had."

"Oh, that one."

"Yeah, that one. Free it up."

"Why? What makes it so special?"

"It's mine is why I want it."

"How'd you hear about it? Did Dovie tell you, or Cyclone? Or did you know him as Kyle Lynch?"

"I just heard, is all. Who's Kyle Lynch?"

"A guy with a toe tag in L.A. and a criminal record in Oakland. You heard of Oakland?"

"I told you I've got no sense of humor, so stop wasting time. Cyclone told me about it, and I heard you were with him that night he got killed, so I figured you and him were going to try to make a deal with it. Cyclone was stupid, just a stupid rockabilly redneck, and I'm sorry he had to get killed like that, but he had no right to the tape."

"Did you kill him?"

"Hell, no. You think I got money to go flying out to L.A. like some jet-set rocker?"

"I didn't think so. What kind of scam do *you* want to pull with the tape? Maybe we could work something out. Did you have some sort of 'Richard-James-is-alive' type thing in mind, or did you just want to sell it back to Otis Taylor?"

"Bullshit. Richard James *is* alive and I'm gonna find him and I'm gonna kill him. He deserves to die. He was a thieving bastard."

"Because he stole your wife?"

"Because he stole my *songs,* dammit. Every one of those songs on his last record were things he ripped off from me, and I never got a penny off it. He'd listen to me fooling around on the guitar in the dressing room or at sound check, then he'd write some lyrics a couple of days later and say, 'Hey, I got a new song, goes like this.' He's a thief. He always was a thieving bastard, still is one, and always will be."

"But his last record was a flop. The way I heard it, everybody lost money on it."

"Doesn't matter. All those songs Dovie's doing right now, they're all stuff Richard stole from me. The albums before *Ninety Minute Man,* too. The guy has made a career out of things that came out of my head, out of my soul."

"You mean even songs like 'Nowhere Train' and 'Six Foot Snake in Tight Blue Jeans'?"

He nodded. His eyes bugged out and shone with a fierce gleam. "You're getting the picture, man."

"But those songs came out a long time ago, back when you were a teenager playing in your daddy's garage. Are you going to tell me you wrote 'Louie Louie' and 'Johnny B. Goode,' too?"

He laughed hoarsely, shaking his head from side to side, with a look that said I was a slow-learning moron who was trying his patience. "Don't you get it? The guy was evil. I should've known the first time I heard him on the radio and felt the electricity going through my bones. He was tuned in to me just like that radio was tuned in to the station. He could drill a hole right into a person's brain from a thousand miles away and suck the thoughts and ideas right out of it. Don't you get it, man?"

"You're saying Richard James had some sort of telepathic connection to your brain, even five, ten years before you even met him, and that's where a lot of his songs came from?"

"Oh yeah. He still does. And that's how I know for sure he's alive, because he's still ripping me off. Don't tell me you can't see it, the way she keeps coming up with all those songs they say Richard wrote, after he supposedly died in that plane crash. There's no use in me picking up a guitar anymore, because as soon as I do, he's out there with his tape recorder running, ready to rip me off again."

I had a Stratocaster plugged into an amp in the office in case I wanted to test his theory, but I doubted he could make a barre chord without getting his fingers knotted up in the strings. Nate Waco was out there where the buses don't run, in a land where cows jump over the moon, where Richard James, Elvis, and Jim Morrison faked their own deaths, and the president is always right. Suddenly I was a lot more worried about him having a gun in his hands.

"They never found a body, you know," he said. "And anytime somebody learns too much, they get rubbed out. If you heard the song, you know he's still alive."

"All right, Nate," I said. "I guess you deserve it more than anybody. Give me a minute to find the tape. I dubbed the song onto another cassette and left the original in L.A. That's why you didn't find it."

"Ah-ha," he said, nodding in a self-assured manner that was

as scary as it was ludicrous. "Go ahead. Quit wasting time."

I went over to the stereo and started rifling through the stereo cabinet, looking for a potential weapon. Headphones, a Walkman, speaker connectors, fuses, CDs, a cassette of a Judas Priest concert that someone had given me as a gag gift last Christmas.

"I think this is it," I said.

"Lemme have it."

"Hold on, I need to make sure." I loaded the cassette into the deck and made some adjustments on the amplifier. "I blew a fuse in the amp last night so I'll have to use the headphones, OK?"

"Give 'em to me," he demanded.

I shrugged and turned them over to him. He adjusted them on his head, still holding onto the gun.

"Nothing coming through yet," he said.

"That's funny. Let me see." I stepped over to the amp, turned the volume up full blast, and *then* I hit play.

Even muffled against his head, the sound blasting out of the headphones was painful to my own ears. He screamed, his hands flailing to knock the headphones off his head like a man who's just stuck his head in a hat full of bees. I swung around and smashed him in the throat with my fist. The throat is a damn good place to hit people when they need hitting, and it's easy on the knuckles, too.

The automatic flew out of his hands. I yanked him off the bar stool and threw him face first onto the carpet, got my Beretta out of his hip pocket, and planted my foot in the small of his back, then reached over to the tape deck and put an end to the Banshee wails of Judas Priest.

Nate was sobbing. "Goddamn, man. You didn't have to hit me. Goddamn."

"You need help, Nate. Your brain is fried. If you don't stop doing speed you'll die soon. And I don't have the tape. I never had it."

"Bullshit."

"No, truth."

"Bullshit."

"Why would I lie? I'm the one with the guns and you're the one getting rug burn on your face. Why should I lie?"

He didn't say anything for a moment, and his sobs began to subside. "Let me up, man. I'm sorry."

"Do you believe me?"

"Uh-huh. I do."

"Are you going to try something stupid if I let you up?"

"No, man. I believe you."

I took my foot off his back. He rolled over and sat upright, rubbing his throat. He looked passive, but just as stupid as ever.

"Hey, I'm sorry," he said as he got to his feet. "But what do you expect? The guy ripped me off. He ruined me. Everybody knows that. Now I can't get a gig because his guys are still after me, watching every damn move I make. I just can't do right, I know too much and there's not enough time. Now Dovie's back in town and his guys will be all over her, and you, too. You're all against me."

"That's the speed demons talking," I said, "not you. Why do you think other people like to sleep and eat instead of running on crystal and nerves? Other people have nightmares, but if you don't sleep, you have to manufacture your own."

"Just say no, huh? Man, you just don't get it. Time's running out and you just don't get it, but you will."

I didn't know what to do with him. One voice said call the police, another said let him go and make Dovie do something about him. She could get him checked into a place with nice padded rooms and purer drugs that would make him see butterflies and froggies instead of dead blues musicians with an eternal supply of multitrack tape.

Nate made a rasping sound. "I need to get some air, man. I think you broke my windpipe."

I let him walk over to the sliding glass door and go out onto the patio. There was a twenty-foot drop off the patio and then a steep slope down to the parking lot, so I wasn't worried about losing him.

I got his gun off the floor and stuck it in a kitchen drawer. The phone was on the counter, and I knew the Austin police department's number by heart. As I closed the drawer, the knives and forks inside rattled, reminding me that there was a barbecue pit on the balcony, with the usual assortment of long-handled implements hanging from one of the side handles. One of them was a large meat fork.

I went over and jerked the drapes back. The fork was still there, but the speed freak wasn't. I went out and leaned over the railing just in time to see Nate brush himself off after rolling down the slope. I watched him as he limped over to the Mustang, got in, and peeled out.

Dovie was right. The guy had no ass.

I called Dovie and told her what happened.

"He's a kook, Martin," she said. "He takes too much speed."

"I *know* that," I said. "Unfortunately, people who take too much speed often have too many guns. I've got his gun, but we've got to do something about him."

"It's my problem, Martin. I'll take care of him. Don't worry about it."

"I guess that means you don't want me to call the police."

"Well, Martin . . . ," she said in a voice that sounded tired and full of resignation. "I guess I couldn't blame you. But I don't think he has another gun. That automatic is one I used to keep around the house in case of burglars."

"Swell."

"I said I was sorry."

"You did. You can stop now. At least he didn't break a window or let the cat out. He's a real pro. There's hardly even a scratch on my door lock."

"So should I get dressed and go to the police station, or should I come over there?"

I didn't answer right away. I was wondering how Nate Waco knew Cyclone Davis. I asked her.

"Cyclone was a Richard James fanatic. I guess when he took off last month he looked up Nate because Nate used to play with Richard. I guess that's where Cyclone got some of his crazy ideas. Or vice versa. Are you gonna call the police?"

"No. Go to bed. I'll see you at rehearsal."

"OK. Thanks, Martin. I don't know what I'd do without you. You're really quite a guy."

"Yeah. Good night."

After I hung up, her last words still rang in my ears. Dovie de Carlo, the pop star, thought I was quite a guy. Going by what I knew of her taste in men, it was hard to get much of a boost from it.

Out of three men I knew she'd been involved with in the past, one was the late blues rocker who had stolen her from her husband. Another had been killed shortly after he intimated that he had a tape that proved the wild blues rocker wasn't really dead. The third—her husband—also claimed that the wild blues rocker wasn't dead, but he wanted to change all that. And he wanted that tape.

Nate Waco, a textbook case of methamphetamine-induced paranoid schizophrenia. Cyclone Davis, a guy with a criminal past and no future. Richard "the Rockin' Dog" James, another dead legend. Legends are always dying in plane crashes, by murder, by OD. Rarely of old age. And when they crash and burn, they always seem to leave a riot of weirdos in their wake. The Rockin' Dog had been no exception.

What did I have in common with these gentlemen? We were all musicians, for one thing. The only other guy that I knew she'd been involved with was Otis Taylor. He knew about the tape, but as far as I knew, he wasn't a musician. That made him special. He only liked to run her life, tell her what songs she could sing, and beat her up.

I took Nate's gun apart, walked down to the creek, and

scattered the parts in the shallow water. When I came back in, I got out of my suit and stuck it on a hanger. It was too late to call Ladonna, so I opened the last Molson in the fridge, lit a cigarette, and sat down on the couch. Soon the cat came out of the bedroom and lay down next to me. In less than a minute he was asleep. When the cigarette and the Molson were gone, I moved the cat into a position that made it possible for both of us to sleep.

I dreamed that men with guns and men with guitars were chasing each other. I couldn't figure out who was chasing whom exactly, because they were all running in a circle. There was a girl in the middle of the circle, with hair as black as night and skin as white as snow. Her fingers were bleeding. So were her feet.

Suddenly a bolt of lightning arced down from the sky and struck the circle of running men and they all fell down dead. After a few minutes, some of the men got up again and left with the girl.

4

Tuesday afternoon I found L-Tone Rogers finishing off a plate of barbecue ribs and beans in a joint on East 7th. There was a small stage in the back, with a stool, a mike stand, and a battered tweed Pro-Reverb amp like Leo's. L-Tone had to be almost sixty, but he could've passed for thirty-five or forty. He pushed his plate away and worked at the barbecue grease on his fingers with a damp napkin, a gold crown flashing in his grin.

"Yes sir, Martin," he said. "I been doin' just fine. Time's right for my sound. People from all over just now rediscovering that extra-special L-Tone sound. Nobody else got it, 'cause nobody else L-Tone."

"You do play a mean guitar, L-Tone," I said.

"Yes sir, Martin. And I may not be rich, but I ain't desperate. That's why, when that moron who called himself Tornado Smith, or what was it?"

"Cyclone Davis," I said.

"Yeah, whatever," he said, nodding. "Cyclone Dave, then. Well, I'm here at my headquarters last week and they says, L-Tone, you got a phone call. I picks it up and some fool says, Howdy, L-Tone, this here's the Rockin' Dog. How you doin'?

I say, the hell you say? And he says, this here's Richard James, the Rockin' Dog. How you like to play with me? Shit."

"Then what?"

"Shit, I hanged up on him. What you think? Then the fool calls back and says, this here's Cyclone David, and I got a gig for you. Got me a hot song, I want you to come out and play on it. I thought about it for a minute, then I hanged up on him again. I'm too old for that kinda shit."

"You didn't take him seriously at all, then?"

He shook his head. "Too old and too good-looking for that stuff."

"Do you know this guy Otis Taylor?"

He shook his head again. "Who's he?"

"The guy who bought up all of Richard James's publishing after he died. He's been sort of managing Dovie de Carlo."

"Don't really know her, neither. She was with the Dog last couple of times I jammed with him, an' I saw her that day they brought her an' Cokey down off the mountain. But no Dog. They didn't find no Dog."

L-Tone looked down at his hands, then looked away, blinking.

"Richard was a dummy," he said. "Just a big, overfed white boy jacked up on R&B and white powder. Couldn't play guitar worth a shit, couldn't sing that well, neither, to my way of thinking. Never could get along with the same people for too long, either, 'cause they get fed up with him, but he was a good fella, and I think that's what folks liked about him. Fella tried hard, played hard, loved hard. Just couldn't get enough of playing the blues, drinking whiskey, driving Cadillacs, and chasin' pussy. And the pussy chasin' stopped once he met Dovie. Way I heard it, he never went with no other woman after he met her."

"I guess it hit you pretty hard when he got killed," I said.

The smile went out of him. "Like I said, he wasn't much of a fella, couldn't sing right, didn't play right with that gimpy hand of his. You know he broke his index finger on his fretting hand when he was a kid, and it never healed up right, so he never could make a chord worth a shit. That boy would steal your last cigarette, your song, your gal, even your band. He was a damn tightwad, too, and I wouldn't hardly fool with him when them hillbillies started following him everywhere, neither. But hell, the Dog was just one of those fellas you couldn't help but like. I sure do miss that old mutt."

"So you hung around at the airstrip when they were searching for them," I said.

"Oh yeah, up at St. Ascot. Not much of a town, really, jest an airstrip an' a coffee shop. I reckon they did some skiing up there, too. Anyway, that was the last place they had radio contact, so everybody figured they must of gone down somewheres around there. I's supposed to play with them in Denver, and when I heard maybe they crashed, I drove on up there. I got a bad lung, so I didn't go up in no plane or no egg beater, just hung around, waitin'."

"Who were the guys who rescued Dovie and Cokey, anyway?"

"Like I said, a bunch of no good go-fast hillbillies used to follow the Dog around. They were all from Kilton, over in East Texas. They flew up there and rented that beater in St. Ascot. I was hangin' round, talking to all the folks who were going up. At first, there were folks from the county, reporters, and what all, shuffling 'round there, but by the end of the second week, the weather was real disagreeable and nobody was hangin' round but me, and only those boys from Kilton were going up, on account of the weather.

"Finally that last day they come back and they had Dovie and Cokey with 'em. I went over and give Dovie and Cokey a hug, but they were sick and all freaked out, you know, 'specially old Cokey. He wasn't worth a damn. They tell me the Dog and Preston got killed in an avalanche. Next thing I know, they up in that plane and gone. Didn't even stop at the office to look for the gentleman who rented them that beater. They was some folks plenty riled up at 'em, law included. They try hasslin' me, but I just said 'L-Tone's goin' home now. No use hangin' 'round here no more.' And here's L-Tone. What you pokin' 'round in this pile for, Martin?"

"Cyclone Davis got in touch with me, too," I said. "He wanted me to play on that session. He had a tape of a song called 'The Whole Damn Truth.' I think he thought it proved that Richard James is still alive."

"Well, shit. Got to you too, huh?"

I nodded. "He was going to meet somebody about the song after midnight last Thursday."

"Then what?"

"Somebody shot him through the heart."

"The devil you say."

"Yeah."

L-Tone scratched his chin. "You think maybe the Dog didn't really die, he just been playing dead?"

"Cyclone seemed to think so."

He shook his head. "Shit, Martin," he said, "why you think the Dog would wanna go and play dead? Not even give old L-Tone a phone call."

"I don't know, L-Tone. Do you know anybody else in this Kilton gang?"

He shook his head. "No, but you be better off you avoid that bunch, Martin. Why you wanna give any credit to this Typhoon Charlie don't make sense, neither. If the Dog was alive, he be tearin' it up again, don't you reckon?"

"Seems like it," I said. "Did you ever hear a song called 'The Whole Damn Truth'?"

"Nah. I never paid no attention to what he was singin' anyway. The Dog wrote some pretty goofy songs, but I sure miss that scruffy bastard."

"I guess other people do, too," I said, "the way they keep buying Dovie's albums. Too bad Richard didn't live a little longer, he could've sung those songs himself."

"Shit," said L-Tone, his lips curled in a snarl. "The Dog

wasn't much of a songwriter. I don't know where they keep digging up these songs of his anyhow."

The remark struck me as being a little strange, but I didn't say anything. It seemed that L-Tone was still feeling hurt that his old friend had abandoned him.

"It just don't go right when they don't find a body," he said after awhile. "Like somebody got up and left without sayin' good-bye."

I met Dovie and the band at the rehearsal hall at nine o'clock. Red Fred and Nubby showed up a couple of hours later. Around midnight they were still slouched in their Monte Carlo like crows on a fence. A white Ford Taurus was parked across the street, too. The next time I came out, the Monte Carlo was still there but the Taurus was gone. Around two A.M., I came out again in time to see the Taurus cruising slowly by. The windows were tinted and I couldn't make out anything about the two men inside except that their hair wasn't long and they weren't wearing cowboy hats.

I stood there for a few minutes. Finally the Monte Carlo's lights came on and it pulled out and drove away.

5

Writers and painters used to go to Paris. Moslems go to Mecca. Every day in Austin, a lot of musicians trek down South 1st Street to Seis Salsas for lunch. Wednesday I was one of them.

"Dangerous," said Ladonna.

"What the hell?" I said. "No guts, no glory."

I was drenching my enchilada plate with generous swaths of my two favorite salsas, the fiercely hot orange *chile de árbol* and the dark reddish brown *chipotle,* which is made from smoked jalapeño peppers. I topped it all off with fresh jalapeño slices and a couple of pinches of cilantro, just for the hell of it.

"Your gut must be made of iron," she said.

I took a bite and savored the heat. The rehearsal with Dovie had gone on long into the night and I was just starting to wake up. Ladonna took a bite of her own enchilada, over which she'd cautiously dribbled *pico de gallo* and *chipotle* salsa. She was only conservative with her spices and peppers when compared to an extremist like me. Also, she had to go back to work after lunch and have a bunch of real estate clients and agents breathing in her face.

She was wearing a conservative but classic suit consisting of a tobacco brown bolero jacket with padded shoulders and a single ornate button the size of a silver dollar, a matching skirt, and a white cotton blouse. On her feet were a pair of Donna Karan pumps I'd sent her from L.A.

"I've got a dozen people who want to sell their houses," she said, "and they want to know why they can't get a third of what they paid for them five years ago. I've got a retired salesman who paid eighty thousand dollars for a three-bedroom tract house near Cherry Creek after the oil crash, a real bargain. The house next door to him is identical. It went on the market this morning for forty-five, and they'll take less."

"And I thought I had it rough. I just have to talk Wayne over at the Continental Club into paying us fifteen hundred dollars to play on Saturday night."

"You're playing Saturday night?"

"Uh-huh. That's the plan. Just to try out the new songs and get some more adrenalin into the project."

"And he's getting Dovie de Carlo plus you guys for only fifteen hundred?"

"Yeah, but he can't use Dovie's name. We don't want a mob scene, and like I said, it's just for practice and inspiration. He'll have a full house just by word of mouth, easy."

She dabbed at her lips with a napkin and smiled. "Just watch the adrenalin. I think you've had enough of that. So how *are* things going with Dovie?"

"We've got half a dozen new songs worked up," I said. "She has notebooks full of song ideas and we're working on some hip cover versions, too. It's definitely a new direction for her. She's got a cool, emotive style of singing, and with the band doing our usual R&B thing, it's a good combination. We've tried a couple of new things that were more in the Richard James groove, but those haven't worked out and I don't know why."

"What about Nate?"

"He seems to have dropped out of sight since our little encounter. Dovie's having the locks changed on her lake house today so she can reclaim it."

"What does Dovie say about the guys in the Monte Carlo?"

"She seems to think putting up with this kind of weirdness is her lot in life. I think she feels guilty about surviving that plane crash and being famous for it. Anyway, it sure seems to bring all the snakes out from under their rocks."

"Martin—"

"I know," I said. "I'll be careful."

We finished our lunch in silence.

I paid the check and walked her out to her car. Our good-bye kiss went beyond the *hasta luego, mi amor* stage and progressed on to something much more heated. After she broke away and started the ignition, I reached in and stuck my hand down her blouse.

"Adrenalin," I said. "Can't ever get enough."

"That's all you get for now, sweetie," she said.

But after watching her drive away, I walked over to the Ghia and got another jolt of the stuff. The Marlboro Man was getting out of a blue-and-tan pickup with a rifle rack in the back window. He wanted to talk to me. We didn't bother with introductions. I don't shake hands with men who beat up women, anyway.

"You don't wanna fuck with me, Fender," he said as he placed a viselike grip on my upper arm. "Believe you me, you don't."

"I don't want to call the cops or sue you for assault, either, so take your hand off my arm."

He didn't say anything, and he didn't take his hand off my arm. The tall crown of the black cowboy hat topped off at about seven feet, which made him only about half a foot taller than me. He was deeply tanned except for a blanched area on his upper forehead, which showed that he rarely went outdoors without his hat, and though his nostrils seemed naturally flared, he seemed to do most of his breathing through the gap between his two front teeth.

Other than all that, he was your average redneck in a shirt

with imitation pearl inlaid snaps and piping on the yoke, faded blue jeans with a snuff can in the back pocket, diamondback rattlesnake skin belt, and diamondback rattlesnake skin cowboy boots. The pearl-handled nickel-plated .38 revolver in his belt seemed redundant.

"Come over here," he said. He walked back to the bed of the pickup. His hand was still attached to my arm, so I followed. He reached over the sidewall of the pickup bed, picked up a gunny sack, and shook it till a dead seven-foot rattlesnake spilled out.

"This morning when I was driving in, I seen this fella crossin' the road. I pull over, walk up, grab him by the tail, and pop the sonuvabitch like a god-dang bullwhip. See?"

He reached over with his left hand and lifted the snake's body so that its head dangled limply, like a hanged man's.

"Whaddya say, Fender?"

"Where does the neck end and the tail begin? The tall tale, I mean."

"Don't fuck with me, dang it."

His grip tightened around my arm. I wiggled my fingers, just to make sure gangrene hadn't already set in. I could barely feel them.

"OK," I said. "I guess this is the part where I ask you what you want. You tell me to stay away from Dovie and I say, OK, you win. Then we both walk away and we all live happily ever after unless I die in a car wreck or you grab the wrong end of a rattlesnake some morning."

"You got a smart mouth, Fender, but the right idea. I was afraid I might have to beat some sense into you."

"I'm no snake. But this is a free country. Even a redneck republican like you must still believe that."

"Yeah, but your dang freedom ends where my fists begin."

One set of knuckles caught me just below the sternum, and as I collapsed, the other set plowed into the hard bone just behind my left ear. Before I hit the pavement, I was hoisted up by the back of the collar and slammed face first into the side of his pickup. He let go of me, and I slid down the side of the truck like a raindrop on a windshield.

I was lying on my back, staring up at the endless blue sky as he got in the pickup and drove away. I knew I shouldn't have brought politics into it.

Dang.

I was the last one to arrive at the warehouse. Dovie's rented Lincoln was there. So was the band's Dodge van. Billy had the most equipment to haul around, so he usually drove the van, and Leo, who didn't have a car and whose girlfriend rarely trusted him with hers, had probably ridden with him. Ray's immaculate '53 Buick Special with the leopard-print seat covers was there, parked in the shade of an oak tree.

The warehouse was set back from the street, off an alley behind an auto parts store. Next door was a pool hall that a group of perpetually unemployed construction workers kept in business. The Monte Carlo was parked there. Across the street was the white Taurus.

Mixed in with the noise of the cars going down South Congress, I could hear the muffled sounds of the band playing. They'd started without me.

I got my bass out of the Ghia and walked over to the driver's side of the Monte Carlo. Nubby was behind the wheel, Red Fred was on the other side, the crowns of their cowboy hats brushing the car's headliner.

"If you guys are looking for curb service," I said, "you should try Dirty's Cum-Bak Burgers on the drag."

"Huh?" said Nubby. His forehead was shiny, even where the scar creased it. Attached to his belt was a leather holder for a big knife with a grip carved out of deer antler.

Nubby sat bumping the steering wheel with the nub where an index finger used to be on his right hand, and Red Fred glared at me with a sort of unfocused rage. From where I stood I could see the interior of the car was littered with empty beer cans, cigarette butts, and junk-food packaging. The smell was enough to draw flies and kill them on contact.

"There's no curb service here, gentlemen," I said, "and no loitering. If you're planning on sitting here all day again, I'll have to go into the pool hall there and tell George, the owner, that you're out here exposing yourself to teenage girls and listening to rap music."

Red Fred came to life, hacking a ball of phlegm from some deep cavity, then flinging it out the window. "What's yer problem?"

"You're the ones with the problem," I said. "Especially after I tell George that, in addition to your prurient behavior and musical preferences, you made a disparaging remark about Willie Nelson, insinuating something about Austin's poet laureate engaging in an unnatural act with a blackface sheep wearing a Madonna getup."

"You're fucked up, man," said Nubby. Red Fred squinted at me, nodding his head enthusiastically. Their jaw muscles marbled as they ground their gray teeth in the same dead-giveaway manner as Nate Waco had the night before, and the Monte Carlo reeked of the same ether-sweat bouquet he'd brought along with him. They were speed freaks, too, sure as hell.

"Not as fucked up as you'll be," I said. "George in there is an old-time hippie from way back. That means Lone Star beer and 'Whiskey River.' That means remember the Alamo and don't forget that Texas women are good as gold. That means there's a poster of Willie in his Texas-flag jogging shorts over the Wurlitzer and a twelve-gauge under the bar. And it means that ever since I turned George on to Stevie Vaughan back in 1974—back before he added the 'Ray' in the middle—he thinks I'm a cool guy even though I don't wear a ponytail and a beard and you'd better get the hell out of here."

Nubby went for his knife, but Red Fred put his hand out and shook his head.

I stepped away from the car just in time to miss a big blob

of spit shooting out of Nubby's mouth. They each gave me their most dangerous scowls before Nubby fired up the Monte Carlo and they backed out onto South Congress and drove away.

I committed their license plate to memory and went inside.

I stood there for a couple of minutes and listened to the band playing without me. It didn't look like they were going to stop any time soon, so I turned on the Bassman amp, plugged in my bass, and started playing along. The tune was a Richard James song.

"Lay Down and Cry," which had been a minor hit for the Dog back in '77 or '78, wasn't a morose slow ballad as the title implied but actually an uptempo rocker. Dovie's singing sounded strong, even though it recalled the kind of numbed out, semiflat style I'd heard on her records. Leo was playing a sort of choppy rhythm using strange, somewhat dissonant chords, leaving several open droning strings. Though the chords didn't do much to suggest a melody, the vocals did, and I soon figured out that the song was basically in a sort of mutated key of G, and there was a lot of room for loping major and minor melodic runs on the bass. I had fun with it.

After the bridge, Ray played a short sax solo, then laid out for the rest of the song. When the song ended, everyone looked pleased with it.

"An old Rockin' Dog tune," said Leo.

"I noticed," I said.

Dovie's eyebrows shot up as she got a good look at my face. "What happened to you? There's a big lump on your forehead."

"Otis happened to me."

"Otis? *Otis* put that lump on your head?"

"Yeah. I know it's hard to believe, since he's such a teddy bear of a guy, but he did. I think it was his way of telling me he wants you back."

"Oh hell, I'm sorry, Martin." She looked away. Her fingers, quickly knotted together, began to tear at one another. "I'd better go call him, I guess."

"No. And quit trying to rip your nails out."

She untangled her fingers and stuck one hand behind her back. I could tell she was working at the nails on it, though, by the expression on her face. It was too calm. "Well, if he beat you up—"

"Don't call him. Don't go see him. You've got to ignore him or you'll never get away from him. And I'm calling the police on him."

"No, you can't."

"Yes I can."

We stood there, trying to stare each other down, as the rest of the band stared at us. Finally Dovie said, "Just let me handle this, OK, Martin? I'm sure he won't do it again."

"I'm not agreeing to anything yet," I said. "That guy's dangerous."

"Oh, Martin, I really think you're overreacting. Why don't we take a break? I need to run to the store and get some cigarettes and then we need to get to work. We've got a lot of ground to cover if we're going to be ready by Saturday. Anybody else want anything?"

"Some beer would be nice," said Leo.

"You got it," she said.

"I need to check my answering machine," said Billy. "Why don't I drive?"

"Let's go," she said. She grabbed her purse and they left.

Ray and Leo wanted to know what I'd gotten them into. I told them the whole story, ending with my mugging in the Seis Salsas parking lot.

"Think he might be out to hammer the rest of us," said Leo, "or is it just you he's pissed off at?"

"I don't know. He's not exactly brimming over with good-will, that's for sure."

"She seemed pretty surprised that he'd take you on," said Ray.

"I noticed. I don't know why, the guy is big as a house. Ray, the other night you said something about knowing Nubby and Red Fred by accident."

"Hanging around with those hillbilly trash cans wasn't my idea, my friend," he said.

"How'd it come about?"

"It was quite a while back, in 1978, I believe. Richard James had a three-night stand in Dallas at a new, rather large club. The club hired me, apparently at Richard's request. The money was quite good. Richard was red hot then, too, driving audiences crazy. It was his birthday—he was twenty-four or twenty-five, I believe—and he had a couple of hits under his belt.

"Unfortunately, he also had a rather large entourage consisting of these hillbilly types. Probably about a dozen or so at various times, with a core of possibly six or seven individuals, including Nubby, Red Fred, and by the way you've described this Otis character, him also. Although I don't remember him answering to that name, the Marlboro Man description is quite apt. Anyway, they were all in all most disgusting group of people I've had the misfortune of sharing facilities with in my entire career. And you fellows know I've been around."

"What was so disgusting?" asked Leo. "Let's hear some dirt."

Ray twisted one of the ends of his pencil-thin mustache into a snarl but kept his voice low and his manner calm. "Well, for starters, they snorted speed constantly. Not just a little toots, mind you, but literally ounces of the stuff. There seemed to be a never-ending supply. They also chewed tobacco and spit on the floor. They not only drank all of our comp beer and liquor but brought in some sort of moonshine and drank that, too. I think that may have been even more toxic than the speed.

"They procured girls for Richard. Richard seemed to have some pathological need to have sex at least once an hour, except when he was onstage, which was a sort of sex surrogate in itself. One night, Nubby and Red Fred brought an obese woman backstage. She had an infant almost certainly less than a year old, with another one on the way. While she was nursing the baby on one breast, Richard gave her five dollars to let him nurse on the other.

"I left the room rather than witness much of this activity, but some of it was unavoidable and I'm sure there was quite a bit of depravity that went on without my knowledge. Some of them carried guns openly, and I suspect that actually all of them were carrying them. I overheard a couple of them boast of having killed people. In addition to all that, they stank horribly. And that's why I referred to them as hillbilly trash."

"Anyone ever tell you you're a snob, Ray?" said Leo.

"Frequently. It grieves me terribly."

"That was before Dovie and the Number Sevens were his band," I said. "But now Otis hangs out with these cretins," I said, "and he's the guy who has the Richard James catalog."

"Strange indeed," said Ray.

"I don't think I've ever seen him around," said Leo. "For such a big local music broker, he sure seems to keep a low profile."

"Not low enough," I said. "What about that song you guys were playing when I came in?"

Leo shrugged. "I didn't think you'd mind, you know. I wish I'd known the guy who owns the rights to it was beating you up, but hey . . ."

"That's all right. It sounded good. But it's kind of a strange song, the chords and everything."

"Yeah, that's what I thought when I first heard it," he said. "After rehearsal the other night, when we were having trouble with Dovie's ballad, it reminded me of the Dog's songs, so I went over to a friend's house and borrowed all his Richard James albums. Then after rehearsal last night I stayed up till noon and pretty much figured out all his songs. Once you learn three or four, the rest are easy."

"Do all of them use the same sort of exotic chords?"

He shrugged. "Kinda like that, yeah. They're not exotic, really, they're primitive. See—I read about this somewhere, or maybe one of the roadies told me about it, I don't remember

—Richard James had a gimpy index finger. Got it broke when he was a kid or something, playing baseball."

Leo paused and massaged his own right hand, which had been broken just a few months back under some strange circumstances. He grinned uncomfortably as he realized what he was doing, and went on. "So he played these odd chords, you know, and his index finger attack was kinda crippled sounding, but he worked it into his style. I can figure out any Richard James song I hear now, I betcha."

"Maybe someday that'll come in handy."

He just shrugged.

"How many records did you say you got, Leo?"

"All four. I already had the first one."

"How many songs does that make?"

He scratched his head and said, "Oh, a little over three dozen, I guess. The last album had live versions of a couple of old songs on it. Why?"

"Never mind," I said. I was thinking that Dovie had released three albums of previously unrecorded Richard James songs, an amount roughly equal to Richard's total output while he was alive. Supposedly there was yet more where those songs came from, which meant that Otis Taylor could keep getting royalty checks for a long, long time. But L-Tone had said that Richard wasn't much of a songwriter.

"What are we gonna do, guys?" I asked.

"I don't know about y'all," said Leo, "but I'm gonna smoke a cigarette."

It was my last one. Leo halfheartedly offered it to me, then lit up after I declined. I could wait until Dovie came back from the store with a fresh supply. One thing about playing with Dovie, she kept us in cigarettes, beer, and Doritos. A lot of bands would kill for that kind of patronage.

Ray took off his fedora, combed his hair back, then replaced the hat. We heard the sound of bottles clinking as the door swung open and Billy and Dovie walked in. Dovie had a big smile on her face, Billy had his usual basset hound expression as he carried in two grocery bags. There were six-packs for the guys in one, three bottles of wine for Dovie in the other.

Dovie had already opened one. We fired back up again, and she belted out credible performances on an Otis Clay song called "You Don't Miss Your Water," James Carr's arrangement of "At the Dark End of the Street," and a song by Cloud 19 called "Rained All Night" before finishing the first bottle of wine. During the second bottle, she almost managed to do a convincing version of Ann Peebles's "99 Pounds."

The band already knew the song, and she tried hard to do a good job on the vocal, but it didn't seem to be in her range. I voted for moving on, but she had it set in her mind that the song was perfect for her and that we should keep playing it until she got it right. "I know I can do it," she kept saying. "My throat is a little tight, that's all."

We tried it a couple more times before she opened the third bottle, and once after. All it did was prove her wrong.

6

Dovie was in no condition to talk her way out of a DWI, so I volunteered to drive her out to her lake house in the Lincoln. New locks had been installed, and she was determined to sleep there that night. She'd packed an overnight bag, but she wanted to stop by the Driskill to pick up her portable 4-track cassette recorder. Once upon a time, she said, she'd had a 16-track reel-to-reel recorder at the lake house, but that had found its way up Nate's nose—along with a lot of other things.

The air was cool and crisp. Some of the store windows on Congress Avenue were decorated with jack-o'-lanterns, cardboard skeletons, witches, and black cats, but many of the displays—more and more every year, it seemed—showcased *Día de los Muertos* (Day of the Dead) art—clay skeleton figurines lying in coffins, playing guitars, and dancing the lambada, their grinning skull faces laughing at death and laughing at you for being afraid of it.

It was after two A.M. and 6th Street looked almost deserted as I crossed it, a few bands still loading out of the clubs, drunk fraternity boys trying to remember where they had parked their cars, and moussed-up packs of androgynes heading for after-hours dance clubs.

I parked the Lincoln at the curb in front of the Driskill lobby.

"Give me the key," I said. "I'll run up and get it. Anything else up there you need?"

Dovie, slumped down in the seat, hiccuped. "Nope."

"OK. I'll be right back."

She put a hand on my arm and dug her fingers in. "Martin—"

"What?"

Her head lolling against my shoulder, she said, "You're so good to me."

"I know," I said.

I got out of the car, gave the valet a buck just for the hell of it, and took the elevator up to her room.

As I put the key in the door, I thought I heard the jangle of an acoustic guitar. At first it seemed like a faraway sound, then muted and intimate—and it seemed to be coming from inside the room.

I opened the door and walked in. A thin man sat on the foot of Dovie's bed, playing one of her acoustic guitars. He was facing away from the door and the mirror on the dresser, but in his reflection on the window I could see he had a shock of snow white hair raked back from his lined forehead. His complexion was pale and waxy, and his cheekbones stood out from his face, high and angular and unsymmetrical, an effect that was almost as jarring as finding him there in the first place.

The last time I'd seen him was in the hallway of the Mondrian Hotel, on his way to Dovie's room with guys I now knew as Red Fred and Otis Taylor, the Marlboro Man. But I didn't know this one's name.

I said, "Who the hell are you and what are you doing here?"

He didn't answer me. I guessed he was about fifty, but his eyes looked younger and his slinky poise reminded me of a teenager slumped in front of a TV set with a soda in his lap. I repeated my question.

The black raincoat slung over his shoulders moved in a shrugging motion, and the toes of his cowboy boots curled up like leaves in a fire. "Friend of Dovie's," he said.

"How'd you get in here?"

"She gimme a key."

"Where is it?"

He put the guitar down gently and felt around in the pockets of his raincoat. He put them inside the pockets of his jeans, his shirt, and several other places, but they always came out empty.

"Your hat," I said.

He grabbed the black Stetson off the pillow and felt around inside the crown.

"I didn't mean look for the keys in it," I said. "I meant insert your head in it and get your ass out of here."

The raincoat moved in a shrugging motion again. "Cool."

"Not the way it strikes me, stranger."

"Whatever you say, Jack." He stood, pulled the raincoat together in front, and shuffled toward the door. "No problem, I'm outta here."

I grabbed the tape recorder and the cords that went with it and hurried downstairs. I scanned the lobby and the bar and the street in front of the hotel, but there was no sign of the white-haired ghoul. He was gone like a turkey in a storm.

Dovie was passed out when I got to the car, but she woke up again on the drive out Ranch Road 2222, which is one of those curving Hill Country roads that makes you drive a little faster than you should, even though a spooked white-tail deer or an uninsured drunk driver could appear in your headlights just around the next bend.

To get to her place meant taking a switchback turn off 2222, then winding through the dense woods over half a mile of axle-scraping and tree-limb-ducking endurance-test driveway. When we pulled up in front of the house, Dovie got out and stretched, taking in big gulps of air. She seemed to have sobered up a little.

"There was a little white-haired guy in your room," I said.

"Oh, shit," she said. She stuck a finger in her mouth and started gnawing on it. "What happened?"

"He said you gave him a key, but I threw him out anyway."

She squeezed her still-purple eyelids together and stretched her arms again. "Well, at least he didn't beat you up."

I grabbed her guitar and the 4-track and followed her into the house, not saying a word.

The house was the type of low, rambling country getaways built of native rock and big timber beams that doesn't look like much from the front, but once you're inside, remind you that you always wanted a fireplace, vaulted ceilings, and maybe even a wagon wheel chandelier. Dovie put her bag down on the floor and started walking around, turning on lamps, and frowning at the state of unkemptness. Everything was dusty, the ranch-style furniture, the red tile floor, the air. When she pulled back the drapes, the view of the hills at night was fine. I stood there and looked at it.

Dovie walked back down a hallway and came back quickly, cursing.

"What's wrong?" I asked.

"It's just gross, you know," she said, shaking her head with disgust.

I walked back to the room she'd come out of, finding what had been, at one time, a nice bedroom, with a four-poster bed, blond maple dresser and matching vanity table, and adjoining bathroom. The window looked down the hill toward the lake, looking like polished silver under the moonlight, providing a jarring contrast with what was on this side of the window: the bed was stripped down to the mattress, which was a battlefield of cigarette burns, the better part of one corner charred down to the springs. The ceiling was splattered with old blood, squirted there from syringes. The walls were covered with Richard James posters, defaced with felt-tip pens and more blood. The floor was piled ankle to shin deep with clothes, paper, bottles, and food wrappers. In one corner, rising up out of the sea of garbage like an iceberg, was a Marshall fifty-watt amp with a battered Les Paul leaning against it. I didn't bother to inspect the bathroom.

Suddenly Dovie screamed as a mouse darted out from a hole in the mattress, shot down the bedpost, and disappeared under the bed.

The next thing I knew, she was down on her knees, banging the floorboards with one of her shoes. "Come on out, you fucking rodent," she snarled.

She rummaged around under there for awhile, cursing and hammering the floor with the shoe, then got back to her feet and shook her head disgustedly. "I need a goddamn drink."

We went back to the living room. She was shaking, but she lit a cigarette instead of reopening the wine she'd brought along.

"Martin," she said, "I know it's silly, but I hate mice."

"Maybe you should get a cat."

She wasn't amused. "What if there's a whole nest of them under that bed?"

"I'll go check it out."

That seemed to calm her down a bit. I left her and went back to the bedroom. I crouched down by the bed and looked under it. The floor was covered with newspapers and magazines. I moved some of them around, trying to flush the little mammal out. Nothing came of it. Finally I cleared all the debris out from under the bed and threw it in a pile in the corner by the Marshall amp. I looked under the bed again. No mouse.

I struck a match so I could see better, and spotted a crack in the floor boarding about a foot from the bedpost against the wall. The gap didn't look big enough for a mouse to crawl out of, but when I rapped on the area with my knuckles, a foot-long section of floor boarding gave way and fell through.

Now I'd done it, I figured. No telling what was down there —scorpions, centipedes, even snakes. More mice would be preferable. I got up and reluctantly pushed the bed over a couple of feet, then got back down on my knees and pulled the board out of the hole.

No animal life at all. Just a Sony microcassette-corder.

I pulled it out of the hole. The thing was a little smaller than a pack of cigarettes. The buttons had been left in the recording position, and there was a cassette in the chamber. I gave the device a closeup exam and determined that it was a voice-activated model. I spoke into the microphone, but the little red recording light stayed dim. I pressed the play button, but nothing happened. Apparently the batteries were dead.

Dovie was standing by the window when I came back into the living room. "Did you get the little bastard?"

"No, but I found this," I said. "It was hidden down a hole in the floor under the bed."

"What?"

She took the machine from me and rolled her eyes distastefully. "That makes sense. Nate is so paranoid. He's one of these people who used to put his initials on all his albums. He even used to hide his toothbrush so I wouldn't use it."

She shook her head and put the recorder down on the windowsill and dusted off her hands.

"Want to go back to the hotel?" I said.

"No. I'm staying here. Goddammit, this is my house and he's not keeping me out of it another goddamn minute."

"Is there another bedroom back there?"

She nodded. "A couple, actually, but I got rid of the beds back when I was trying to set up a studio here. I do have a queen-size futon in the hall closet. It's still there, I checked already. I'll fix that up in here by the window. I like to look at the stars before I go to sleep. That's why I wanted to come out here."

"Sure that's what you wanna do?"

She nodded. "Yeah. Now go home. I know you're tired and you were supposed to see your girlfriend tonight."

"She probably gave up on me a long time ago."

"That'd be her loss. Good night, Martin."

I bent down to kiss her and she put her arms around me and mashed her breasts against my chest. Her body was hot and damp, her lips soft and wet and hungry. We broke apart slowly.

For a moment our eyes locked on each other. I could still taste the wine on her lips and I knew what the sweat on her breasts would taste like. I knew the sounds she would make when we made love there by the window, the stars reflecting in her eyes. I knew how her hair would tangle up on her head and how her legs would lock around my back. These were warm thoughts.

She knew she was having that effect on me, and she wasn't backing away from it. But whether the attraction was the real thing or just the wine and the trials we'd been through together stirring something up, I didn't know. There were a lot of things I didn't know about her, and they made my skin prickle. They were cold thoughts.

The cold thoughts and the warm thoughts fought each other all the way back to town.

When I got to Ladonna's place, I let myself in with my key, slipped off my shoes, and tiptoed into her room to watch her sleep. Michael would be in his room, sleeping peacefully next to a Fernando Valenzuela poster. Once in awhile, as Ladonna stirred in her sleep, her hand would reach out to where I would have been lying had I been in bed with her.

I went over to the window and looked at the night-softened profile of the sleepy city on the Colorado River, the little town with the big sound. It seemed odd that it would rest so quietly. There was the occasional whoosh of a car going down Riverside Drive, the low snore of a truck going down the interstate, and the crickets conducting their all-night jam session. Maybe I still had a case of nerves from living in L.A., but it struck me that everything was too motionless, too still.

Finally I decided that the city could rest however it wanted, that the only thing to do was crawl into bed, close my eyes, and lie skin to skin with the woman I loved. To hell with the rest of it.

7

I woke up alone, a little after ten A.M. Ladonna had left the coffee on, but no note. I poured a cup of coffee, picked up the newspaper, and went into the living room to turn on the radio.

At the window I saw a black Ford LTD pulling up next to Dovie's Lincoln in the parking lot. There were no other cars in the lot. I put down the coffee and newspaper and went downstairs.

The passenger window on the LTD rolled down as I walked up. Dovie was the passenger, the white-haired man was the driver. He was still wearing the raincoat, and his hair jutted out stiffly from underneath his Stetson like a scarecrow's straw stuffing. Sunglasses hid his eyes and some of the rest of his face.

"Martin, I came for the car," said Dovie. She looked at the white-haired man, then at me, but only briefly. Her hands were in her lap, the fingertips once again under siege.

"The keys are under the mat," I said.

She looked at her companion again. "You've met Otis."

"Otis? *This* is Otis?"

"Yes." The purple around her eyes had faded considerably, but she looked very tired. She glanced again at the white-haired man who was the real Otis Taylor. "I think there's been a misunderstanding."

"Hello, Otis," I said. I couldn't think of anything I wanted to say to him. Apparently Otis couldn't think of anything to say to me, either. As he moved his head, I noticed a Band-Aid on the upper part of his ear, mashing it against his head. It made the ear look like it had been taped on.

Dovie took in a deep breath and said, "I've decided the band thing isn't working out."

"I thought it was working out fine. Especially compared to—"

"It ain't right for Dovie, man," said Otis.

She looked over at him as he spoke, as if he'd said exactly what she'd been thinking. "It isn't right for me, Martin."

I stepped back from the car and took a breath of fresh air. The city was awake again. Birds were singing, traffic was flowing down Riverside Drive, and overhead, a jet left a fine white vapor trail through the clear blue sky. Inside the LTD, Dovie and the man with the taped-on ear were looking at each other, linked together by the strange impermeable bond that couples sometimes develop, the kind that makes two people talk and think as one, the kind that makes everyone else an outsider at best, an enemy at worst. I kicked some gravel, just for the hell of it. Dovie gave me a frown, then unlocked her door and got out.

"Listen, Martin," she said, "I appreciate what you've done, but, you know—" She looked back at Otis. Otis looked at her, drumming his fingertips on the steering wheel like a driver patiently waiting for a red light to change to green. Like a pimp waiting for his girl to pick up a trick.

"I know," I said, "it isn't right for you. But he said 'it *ain't* right' and you say 'it *isn't* right.' Do you guys want me to leave so you can hash this out? Maybe after you get the wording worked out you could sing it together, do a little harmony thing."

"Look, Martin." Some of the edge came back into her voice. "Don't be a pain in the ass."

Otis stopped drumming his fingertips on the wheel and casually glanced at the two of us. I thought about kicking some more gravel. "Fine," I said. "Whatever you want."

"That's better," she said, and gave me a light peck on the cheek. She still smelled like wine, but the sexual challenge from the night before was gone. "I think we'll all be better off this way."

I turned around and walked back upstairs. I heard the ignition on the Lincoln, then the sound of two cars leaving the parking lot.

Together.

I walked back home to feed the cat before heading over to the warehouse to pick up my car. While the cat ate, I checked the answering machine. The only message was from Leo.

"Hey man, where are you? You'd better get down to the warehouse soon as you get this. The police will wanna talk to you. It's, uh, about ten-thirty."

I threw on a clean shirt, locked up, hit the pavement.

A blue-and-white police car was parked in front of the pool hall, a black officer behind the wheel talking on the radio. Leo's girlfriend, Nadine, was sitting on the hood of her station wagon, which was parked behind the Ghia. Billy and Leo were talking to a blond policewoman by the roll-up load-in door of the warehouse. No beat-up Monte Carlos or white Ford Tauruses today.

Our van wasn't there, either.

"Hi, Martin," said Nadine. Her hair was cut in a bob, dyed an eggplant shade of black. Her eyes were full of worry.

"What's going on?" I said.

"Somebody broke in, and the van is missing," she said.

"Damn it," I said.

"Uh-huh. Leo's fit to be tied, because his favorite amp is gone." She glanced at her watch, biting her lip. "And I have to get to work pretty soon."

"I'll give them a ride, if they need it. You working today?"

"Yep," she said. "I hate to miss the lunch rush."

"I know," I said. Waitresses generally feel the same way all over the world, especially when they have guitar players for roommates.

She glanced at her watch again. "I'll stick around a minute."

When I walked over to Billy, Leo, and the female cop, they stopped talking and stepped aside so I could peek inside the warehouse. One look was all it took. Except for empty drum cases, a couple of loose guitar cords, and the empty beer and wine bottles from the past few days, the place was empty. The heavy padlock that had been used to secure the door was sitting atop a three-legged stool inside, its shackle sheared off.

I didn't feel much worse than I had when Dovie had told me she was dropping the band. The sinking feeling in my stomach just went a few fathoms lower.

"Officer Petit, this is Martin Fender, the bass player," said Billy.

She underlined my name on her clipboard and said, "Do you have any idea who might have done this, Mr. Fender?"

I thought about the customized Bassman 135 that had served me so well over the years, and I thought about the screwy chain of events that had started with Cyclone's meet-a-man-about-a-song routine and ended here, with a missing van and a cleaned-out warehouse. Otis Taylor, Nate Waco, and the hillbilly thugs were the links in between, and it looked like Dovie was in the middle somewhere.

I told her that I had no idea at all who the culprits might be.

Officer Petit adjusted her sunglasses as she made a low sound in her throat. "You sure about that?"

"Yes," I said. I was lying because I wanted to follow that chain back to its beginning and snap its head off, like one of the Marlboro Man's rattlesnakes. The snake analogy was no accident: Down at the edge of the door frame, a half-inch piece of scaly reptile skin dangled from the jagged edge of the tin siding. There was little doubt in my mind that it had come from one of the Marlboro Man's boots.

"I told her about the hillbillies in the Monte Carlo," said

Leo. His face was taut, his eyes glassy. He'd had his old tweed and black face Pro Reverb almost as long as I'd had the Bassman.

Officer Petit read from her clipboard. "A Marcus Maxwell and Scotty Fredericks?"

"They're fans," I said. "Why would they rip us off?"

Billy and Leo gave me blank looks that made the lie threaten to lodge in my throat. Billy spoke up. "What about Otis Taylor?" he said.

"That was a case of mistaken identity." I looked at Officer Petit and explained. "I got into a scrape with a redneck about a parking space. Later on I found out he wasn't the person I thought he was."

Officer Petit gave me one of those dead looks that cops are so good at. "So you have no idea who would steal your band's van *and* your equipment the same night?"

"Not right now," I said. "But I'll give it some thought."

Leo fixed me with a glassy stare. Billy's expression was harder.

"I got home around two-thirty after taking Leo home," said Billy. "I got up at nine-thirty to take a leak and saw the van was gone."

"What about Ray?" I asked.

"What about him?" said Billy. "What'd he have to lose? An ashtray? A box of reeds or a martini glass?"

Billy was right. It was our tragedy, not the saxophonist's. Ray carried all his gear—a tenor sax and a couple of spare reeds—with him, with one hand. Only hookers traveled lighter. Though we compensated him for its use, the van was in Billy's name, and the p.a. system was something that Billy, Leo, and I owned jointly.

Officer Petit was scratching something on her clipboard as her partner came walking up. "Hey," he said. "I got news for y'all."

"Martin, this is Officer Hayes," said Billy.

"Nice to meet you," I said.

Hayes hooked a thumb on his Sam Browne belt and stood there kind of loose limbed, sizing me up. His mustache and sideburns looked a little past regulation length, and his uniform looked strangely out of kilter, as if it had been thrown on in the dark. I half expected him to say that it had all turned out to be a joke of some sort.

"They found it," he said finally.

"Where?" said Leo.

"City workers over at the street-and-bridge-maintenance department found it," he said. "Over by Red River Street."

"Can we get it?" said Billy. "Or is it being towed in to the police station?"

Hayes plucked at his mustache with his thick fingers and cocked his head to one side. "Might be awhile," he said. "It's in the lake."

"In the *lake?*" I said.

"Uh-huh. Not all the way under. That's what drew attention to it."

"What about our gear?" said Billy. "Is it in there?"

"Hard to tell, son."

"Why?" demanded Leo. "I thought you said it wasn't all the way in."

"Well it ain't, but—" The cop glanced over at his partner, pressing his lips together like he was trying to suppress a laugh. Finally the words tumbled out:

"Boys, your van is full of concrete."

The cops burst out laughing. The musicians did not.

It was a tough ride over to Red River.

"I don't care if you know what you're doing, Martin," said Billy, "just as long as somebody makes this up to us."

"Yeah, Martin," said Leo. "If this is some kinda frammus Dovie's messed up in, she could just write us a check, right? Buy us a new van, new equipment, and all?"

"One thing about her," said Billy, "she sure is generous. I haven't had to spring for a six-pack or a pack of gum since we've been working with her. I'm sure she'll want to do the right thing."

"Yeah, right," I said. I couldn't blame them for looking at the short view of the situation. "Maybe we can save some of the gear, anyway. The cement couldn't have been poured more than six or seven hours ago. Maybe it isn't dry yet. Maybe it can be hosed out or something . . ."

I caught myself before I said anything else stupidly optimistic. Now I was trying to look on the bright side. I didn't know why, either. Maybe because I didn't think things could get any worse.

"Can't go no further," said Officer Hayes.

The van had come to a stop about thirty feet from the shore, in about three feet of water. One of the detectives who'd waded out to it said it had rolled to a stop atop a rocky ledge. The road we'd been halted on was blocked off by police cars, and the strip of land between it and the lake was roped off with crime-scene tape. The road ran alongside a tin maintenance building and a fenced-in lot where various dump trucks, pick-ups, and street-repair vehicles were garaged and/or serviced. Policemen milled around inside the building, looking at things, taking notes.

Across the road from the maintenance outfit was a paved lot bordered by the hike-and-bike trail, now blocked by a cement truck that was being dusted for fingerprints. On the other side of the trail, where the riverbank dropped off sharply down to the water's edge, twin trails of mashed-down grass and weeds marked the path of the van into the lake.

"They stole the cement truck from a construction site over on the East Side," said Hayes. "They broke in this building and stowed the truck here, went and got your van and equipment, brought it over here, busted out the windshield, and filled the thing up with cement down there by the trail, then used the cement truck to push it down the bank. You guys insured?"

"Yeah," said Billy. "I don't know if it covers something like this, though."

Leo raked his hair back with his fingers, grimacing as if the motion would help sort things out. "I just wonder if that Pro Reverb is in there. God I hope not. You think they'll manage to tow the thing out any time soon?"

Hayes just shrugged. The first tow truck hadn't been able to budge the van, so they'd sent for a bigger one. None of the city vehicles there were suited to the job. Between the muck and rocks it was sitting in, the extra tons that had been injected into it, and the steep slope of the soft sandy banks, recovering the van was going to be some trick. And we weren't allowed to go down there and get in the way because the detectives were still combing the area all the way down to the water's edge for clues. So far, no prints had been found in or on the cement truck, in the tin building, or around the busted gate.

A half dozen city workers sat in the shade of a tree, eating their lunches, waiting for the foreman to tell them that they could have the rest of the day off.

Billy looked at them and shook his head. "I guess we oughta put off rehearsal for tonight," he said sarcastically. "I mean, we all got spare equipment, but I just don't feel like it. You gonna talk to Dovie, Martin?"

"I'll talk to her," I said. I didn't feel like telling them the gig was off yet. Leo was distracted almost to the point of being in a stupor, but Billy kept staring at me.

"Goddammit," said Leo. "I gotta know if that amp is in there. That baby sure has a sweet tone. You think they might've saved it so they could pawn it or something?"

"I don't know, Leo," I said.

"I gotta know, man," he said in a high-strung whine. He walked over to Hayes. "Why can't we go down there, anyway?"

Hayes stuck his jaw out and said, "'Cause Watson said so."

That got my attention. "Detective Tom Watson?"

"Yep," said Hayes. "He's in charge here. You know him?"

I shook my head and walked away from the group rather than acknowledge the peculiar bond that Watson and I shared: I didn't care for born-again hardass cops from Abilene even if their fathers had been Texas Rangers, and he didn't like musician scum.

I wondered why Watson, who, last I'd heard, worked with the robbery and assault division, would be giving the orders on the scene of a case of grand theft auto. Maybe he knew something about this case that I didn't, and maybe he'd known it ever since a couple of his boys sat inside a white Ford Taurus, keeping an eye on a beat-up Monte Carlo outside of our warehouse every night we had rehearsed with Dovie.

The more I considered the likelihood that Watson knew more about our situation than we did, the angrier I became. The sensation was something akin to belatedly feeling the full intensity of a bee sting as you notice the insect sinking its stinger into your skin.

Leo came running after me when he noticed that I was getting into my car. I told him I had to treat a bee sting and got out of there.

8

Inside a piss yellow brick building on the north shore of Town Lake just off Congress Avenue was a vast inventory of vintage clothes, used appliances, musical instruments, and many items that defied classification. Some of the merchandise was junk, some of it was priceless. Sometimes it just depended on who you asked.

The place was called Vick's Vintage, after its grossly obese proprietor, Vick Travis, who'd spent a good many years doing what he felt was his part for the local music scene, providing cool vintage clothes and fine used musical instruments at a reasonable price, donating same when the whim struck him, running a small record label that featured hot but undiscovered local acts, and giving certain desperate and cash-short local scenesters a small stipend in exchange for entertaining certain sadomasochistic fetishes of his.

Vick and I had last crossed paths back in May, when I was trying to find out who had beaten Retha Thomas with my bass. I found out that although Vick hadn't committed that particular crime, he was far from innocent. He'd vowed to change. No more sadistic hobbies, no more lots of things.

I still thought that he'd gotten off far too easily and I still felt like taking a walk through a car wash after each conversation

I had with him, but I had a hunch he could give me the lowdown on local hillbilly trash quicker and easier than I could get it anywhere else.

When I went in, ringing the cowbell on the door, I heard grunting, wheezing, and a few curses, then finally the dry scraping sound of shoes on the concrete floor behind a packed-solid rack of used suits. I knew he'd be there.

He was getting too fat to make it out the door.

"I don't know why in hell you'd wanna ask me about this crap," he said, leaning back in the chair by his desk in the back of the store. He was sweating heavily, using a red bandana to blot his greasy forehead and push back a lock of curly hair that would fall forward no matter how many times he coaxed it back. "Buncha methamphetamine-crazed backwoods sisterfuckers."

"Your class of people, Vick," I said.

"Aw, get off that soapbox, Martin. I never sold crank to nobody and never had no sisters, neither. Hey, I look like a guy who pushes appetite suppressants?"

He laughed and patted his stomach. He looked just this side of four hundred pounds, on his way to a quarter ton. I said, "You get off your own soapbox before you crush it, Vick. You sell plenty of things here you can't use, including size-thirty trousers and sequined G-strings, and you wouldn't be so quick to feel insulted unless you knew a little bit about these hillbillies, so spill."

"Well, I'll tell you one goddamn thing, you better stay away from this Marlboro Man you thought was Otis Taylor. Name is Graves, Neville Tyrone Graves. They say he's killed a couple of people, but could be that figure's a mite low. Him and Nubby Maxwell and Red Fred are members of a no-'count group of go-fast gangsters from the backwoods near Kilton, East Texas. Real thick piney woods, nothing but trees and trailer houses, once in awhile a satellite dish. Used to be moonshine country."

"And now they brew methamphetamine out there?"

Two chins became four as he nodded. "I hear they still cook

'shine for the hell of it, but crystal's the thing these days. Same situation. See, your crystal meth is easy to make. You have to worry about blowing yourself up or inhaling too much solvent, but the chemicals are easy as hell to buy—they're legal. The smell is the problem, that ether stinks to hell for miles and miles. That's why you don't find that many speed labs in the city. But when you're back in those woods up around Kilton, you're in the middle of nowhere, Jack. I bet they made enough shit up there this summer to keep the whole state buzzing through double shifts till next Easter. People out there are either making it themselves or they like living too much to criticize. It's always been that way, moonshine or meth."

"So what brought these backwoods creeps to Austin?"

"Well, Graves is an ex–bull rider. 'Bout ten, twelve years ago he give it up and got on as foreman for Dolph Moreland, the rancher with a million cows and twice as many bucks."

"I heard he lost most of his money in the oil crash," I said.

"Martin, you know well as I do these kinda folks don't let go of all of it once they got it. He may have sold off some land and a couple of Cadillacs, but he ain't hurtin', believe me."

"What does Moreland have to do with these hillbillies?"

"Well, like I was saying. Graves went to work for Dolph out at his ranch, and later on brought in a bunch of his old pals from Kilton, supposedly to help work the ranch. Dolph has him a bigger spread down in South Texas, but these days he pretty much stays up here on the one just west of here, a couple miles from Sweet Bay City."

"Maybe Dolph just sped his way through the oil crash," I said. "Is that what you're saying?"

"I don't know, Martin. I told you I don't truck with no meth-abilly crowd, and Dolph Moreland is way outta my league, too. What I do know, these boys and a couple others they traveled with were big Richard James fans. They hung around all his gigs, especially the last couple of years before he got killed."

"What about Otis Taylor? Is he part of the gang?"

"I wouldn't know. I only know the others by reputation and

what I've seen from upwind. Otis—all I got is a couple of rumors. They say he came down from Lubbock, but I never heard of him in connection with any music business out there."

"I saw him in L.A. with Graves and Red Fred."

Vick turned his palms up. "They were Richard's fan club and Otis has Richard's songs and Richard's old girlfriend. Maybe it's the best they can do, hanging out with the people he left behind."

"No, there's more to it than hanging out. Otis wanted me to stay away from Dovie. This morning he got his wish and I got a van full of concrete."

"Well, maybe they're all one big happy family—Otis, Dovie, the Kilton methabillies. The Saint Richard James Club."

"That's not funny," I said. "I still don't see any reasonable explanation as to why Dovie would still be slumming around with these creeps. She doesn't do speed."

"Got me hangin', Martin."

"L-Tone Rogers said some of the same type of crowd were on the team that rescued Dovie and Cokey after the crash. You know anything about that?"

Vick shook his head. "I seem to recall there was some kinda hassle 'cause they hurt the Civil Air Patrol's feelings by not stopping in on 'em before they headed back here, but the way I recall, nobody ever said who those fellas were."

"Have you heard of a Cyclone Davis or Kyle Lynch?"

"Nope."

"How about a song called 'The Whole Damn Truth'?"

He shook his head and yawned.

"What about Richard James's last record?" I said. "*Ninety Minute Man* was released on Richard's own private record label. Maybe these hillbilly mobsters bankrolled it. It wouldn't be the first record financed with drug money."

Vick smiled sheepishly. "I wouldn't know, Martin. Ask me something else. Ask me about one-shot record labels out of Houston and San Antone, ask me to name all twenty-nine songs Robert Johnson recorded, ask me to name the top ten songs of 1956, and I can tell you. But this is starting to remind me of a goddamn courtroom drama. You know I'm allergic to those and besides, I don't see what it has to do with anything."

"Dovie took some pills for the flight back from L.A.," I said. "Just before she passed out she said something about how Richard's investors hadn't been very cool about losing their money on his last record."

"Hey, I've lost money on ninety percent of my music ventures, but you see me putting a bomb on somebody's plane because their record stiffed? Hey, at least the asshole was still flying to gigs even after no one was buying his records. You dig?"

"You've got a point there. But wasn't Richard still getting royalties from his other hits?"

Vick shrugged. "Not off the kinda deals Richard made. The guy was dumb, a throwback to the days of the early sixties when half the artists didn't know any better than to trade all their publishing for a new Cadillac. Later on, after he got dropped, nobody'd touch his publishing, which is how this fella Otis cleaned up. But back when he was hot, Richard was wild and stupid, a goddamn rock 'n' roll rhino in heat. He'd sign anything, just so he could rush back over to the hotel and plow vulva. That's why he didn't have no royalties to be flying in no plane."

"Then how'd he die in one?"

Vick shook himself so that his copious rolls of fat jiggled in a wavelike motion, from his chins down to a paunch the size of a medicine ball. "Hey, I don't know everything."

"Tell me more."

"Fuck you, man. I gotta take a nap." He pulled out the bandana and wheezed into it, then mopped his head again. When the bandana came away from his face, it was hard to say which was redder. "I thought you were the felony melody expert around here. Why don't you know any of this shit about Richard?"

"Maybe because he used to be on speaking terms with the

pop charts, and, this five-minute gig with Dovie aside, I only play with the legends on the fringe. I never hung around with the speed crowd, either."

"Well, whatever," he drawled. "But Martin, you oughta be staying away from Graves and Moreland. You ever hear that story about Dolph's son getting run over on his motorcycle?"

"They figured one of his neighbors accidentally did it, right?"

He nodded somberly. "Then the poor bastard goes out to feed his hogs one night a couple weeks later and never comes back. They never found him."

"Sounds sort of like a certain east coast mafia don," I said. "Not high on forgiveness."

"Well, we all got our shortcomings." He snorted into the bandana again and struggled to his feet. "Tell you what, I'm gonna lay down for a couple hours. Go over there to the bookshelf by the coatracks and borrow yourself *Sweet Soul Music* by Guralnick, *That Texas Thang* by B.B. Berry, and *Rock of Ages* by Ed Ward et al., plus whatever else looks like it might have something on the Dog in it. Take 'em home and read 'em but make damn sure you bring 'em back. And on your way out, flip the sign on the door around so it says 'closed, owner asleep with loaded gun under pillow.' "

"Thanks, Vick," I said. I would have shook his hand but the greasy, sweaty bandana was still in it. I got the books he'd recommended and reversed the sign on the door for him on my way out. Instead of being a warning about a grumpy owner with an itchy trigger finger, the sign said:

sorry we're
CLOSED
but have a nice day
anyway!

I was shocked. It seemed so inappropriate, so unlike the lumbering blob inside the building. It seemed so . . . Californian.

Maybe that was the joke.

I got back in the Ghia and headed down South Congress. I was anxious to look over the books I'd borrowed, but they would have to wait. Right then I was hungry for a different species of information. I had doubts, questions, suspicions, and innuendo, all scattered like random dots on a canvas. I hoped that the collection agency's resources would give up a few things that could connect those dots.

9

Jack Green, the office manager, ducked into the cubbyhole office I'd appropriated during his lunch break and stuck out his hand. "Hey, Martin, how the heck was L.A.?"

"Wild and crazy," I said. "When I wasn't dodging bullets on the freeway I was avoiding them during midnight rendezvous in Laurel Canyon. I got offered a hit record contract and a contract to hit somebody all on the same day."

"Wow," he said as he brushed his blond hair out of his eyes. Jack wore turtleneck shirts and prefaded jeans with poorly fitting blazers he'd bought on sale at The Gap. He looked like a guy who wanted to be a yuppie but just didn't subscribe to the right magazines. Somewhere in his heart, though, was a secret desire to be a rock 'n' roller, and ever since he'd rediscovered his roots at a Stones concert, he treated me like a buddy. "You're kidding, right?"

I laughed. "Right, Jack. But it is wild and crazy out there."

"Good. I mean, don't let me down, Martin." He smiled, then his expression turned serious. "How long you think you're gonna stick around this time? I mean, last time, you were only here what, two, three hours before the cops came and got you. That's gotta be some sort of record, even for you."

"Well, actually, Jack," I said, "I wanted to see if I could break that record. I've only been here thirty minutes, but I was hoping I'd get arrested after no more than an hour or ninety minutes. If I'm gonna get any work done, I'd better get started."

He snickered good-naturedly and left, and I went back to the computer. I pecked at it for over an hour, feeding it information, coaxing it to return the favor. When I was done, the printer had vomited about four feet of continuous form paper through the teeth of its tractor feed, and with it, a comparative amount of information from the local credit bureau.

Dolph Moreland, age 68, still lived with his wife, Vera, on his ranch west of Austin. The address was a rural route number in Sweet Bay City, a town so named not for its proximity to a large body of water but for a certain species of native trees whose leaves provide the sweet bay seasoning sometimes used in Creole cooking. Moreland had several outstanding loans, but they were well secured.

Neville Graves, Marcus Maxwell, and Scotty Fredericks apparently lived in a house on Moreland's property. They shared a common address, with the same rural route number as Moreland but a different box number. Graves was 43 years old and had a fair credit record. Beside the occupation blank, it said "ranch foreman." Maxwell and Fredericks, 32 and 34, respectively, had several repossessions back in Kilton, but none since they'd moved to Central Texas and gone to work for Graves and Moreland. Their occupational histories said nothing about a talent for the manufacture and distribution of methamphetamines, or for B&E, auto theft, vandalism, or fun with concrete.

Otis Taylor had excellent credit. He owned a house in one of the newer developments on the western edge of town. His credit report gave his date of birth as January 7, 1954. Pretty young to have such white hair and ghostly white skin. I got a red felt-tip pen and circled all the addresses on the various reports and skipped out of there, less than two and a half hours after I'd punched in. It was shorter than the last time, but I hadn't been arrested.

I left a note for Jack anyway.

Vick's dark insinuations about Dolph Moreland aside, I couldn't help feeling that a man who ostensibly raises cows for a living would approve of his hired hands stealing a blues band's van and equipment and trying to sink it in the lake just in case that blues band's bass player didn't take Dovie de Carlo seriously when she said Later, gator.

On the other hand, Dolph Moreland's credit record had turned up an interesting fact that made me want to distrust that feeling: Up until 1984, Moreland was still making monthly payments on two small planes, both Cessna 414s. In May of that year, an insurance company paid off the note on one of those planes. Even without calling the bank or insurance company, that sounded an awful lot like a settlement for a Cessna 414 that would have crashed in February of that year on a Colorado mountain pass carrying a pilot and a four-piece band.

This information made me wonder if it was Moreland's patronage that had kept the Rockin' Dog airborne long after he'd ceased making enough money to pay for such extravagance. Or was the rancher just a front for a drug gang who had carted the Dog from gig to gig in their private plane while he was alive and was now trying to run the career and life of his surviving backup singer?

The facts I'd gathered and the semisordid possibilities they suggested were really starting to rev my engine. I still didn't know how Cyclone Davis's murder fit into the picture, but when you have a hillbilly speed gang and a pop singer and a dead blues singer and a millionaire cattle rancher involved, things can happen.

All sorts of things.

Maybe I'd even find out why the Kilton gang had gone to all the trouble with the van caper the night before, even as Otis was working on Dovie to woo her back to his fold. If it was their way of sending us a message to stay away from Dovie, it seemed like overkill if she was just going to drop us the next day anyway. But maybe they didn't know about that. I knew I'd pissed them off when I'd run them off from the warehouse, so maybe they'd done it out of spite.

Maybe they *were* disorganized and spiteful instead of organized and sinister. Either way, they'd gone too far, and that was their mistake.

10

Heading west out of Austin, the suburbs and developments gradually run out of steam along Highway 290, giving up to a scenic drive past open fields and rolling, rock-strewn pastures full of cactus and mesquite and grazing livestock. It's white-tail-deer country, where armadillos and rattlesnakes blend in and yellow Karmann Ghia convertibles exceeding the speed limit don't.

I was topping the hill just before the Sweet Bay City limits when I saw the big cruiser sitting on the shoulder of the highway. As I passed by, I saw the shield on the door and the words "Sweet Bay City Sheriff's Dept." I took my foot off the accelerator and let the engine do the braking, holding my breath as the speedometer needle fell just under sixty. The cruiser didn't come after me. I breathed a sigh of relief and headed on into Sweet Bay City.

It's a little hangover of a town, the kind you could wake up in one morning and get the hell out of without bothering to find out how or why you'd ended up there. The Pedernales River winds haphazardly through the northeast side, as if looking for the quickest route out of town, and the highway splits up the rest with a Y intersection at the junction of another state road heading to the north. They have two rest homes and two gun shops but no hospital, and the kids who grow up there have two things to do: drink and drive. Most of the billboards along the roadside are advertisements for better places you could be. All the small-town mainstays—gas station, feed store, burger joint, drive-in grocery, bank, courthouse, and more gas stations—were either on the highway itself or had signs pointing out their proximity. I stopped at the feed store to get directions to the Moreland ranch.

They were as polite and helpful as you'd want them to be, but they didn't mistake me for a local.

I drove slowly past the main gate, finally pulling over at the top of a hill about a half mile down the road. From there you could see the main ranch house, which was a good hundred yards from the gate. A herd of rust red herefords grazed over the gently rolling grasslands between the house and the county road.

The house was a big, stodgy-looking thing made out of rough-cut native limestone, possibly old enough to have been built back when homes like it were considered attractive as well as practical. A good bit of the yard was drenched in the shade of a couple of oak trees that were almost as wide as my car at the base of their trunks. Back of the house was a concrete slab patio with tables, chairs, and a steel barrel barbecue smoker. The fence around the yard was buttressed with limestone and mortar corner posts that looked ready to give out in the next fifty years or so. The private road leading off the main gate wasn't quite twice as wide as the county one, but it was better paved.

A three-car garage had been added on in the last decade or so. One of the bays was open, showing the rear end of a late-model Cadillac. But as I sat and watched the place, I decided that Dolph Moreland wasn't home.

I figured he'd drive a pickup truck. He'd park it just outside the fence under the shade of the overhanging limbs of one of the oak trees, right where the bermuda grass was thinned out from its heavy tires. He'd roll up in a cloud of dust after running a chore out in the back forty, go through the gate and wash his hands with the garden hose by the garage, then enter the house from the garage or go on through it to the back patio, where his wife would bring him a beer and his dog would lap up some water from the battered tin bowl at the slab's edge.

On a rise about a hundred feet beyond the house was a large red barn. In separate pens next to it were several horses and some very large bulls. A short distance from the barn compound stood a large turkey pen, and about thirty yards from that a paved runway with a twin-engine plane parked at one end. The plane was one of the things I'd come to see, and seeing it made my heart beat a little faster.

But it still didn't look like the kind of place a hillbilly speed gang would operate out of. I rolled farther down the road, looking for the place where Graves, Nubby, and Red Fred hung their hats. Just a quarter mile down the county road was a hairpin turn that headed off to the left and a small dirt road veering right. At the mouth of the dirt road was a mailbox. There were no names on it, but the number on the lid was the same as the one on the credit reports. The box was empty. I took the small dirt road.

After heading up a steep incline and winding around several switchback turns, the road entered a deep thicket. The road was hard on the Ghia, even rockier and narrower than Dovie's lake-house driveway. Thorn shrubs and short, squat cedars were thick as thieves, and in the few gaps that existed in the junglelike growth, the ground was strewn with flinty rocks of all sizes, as if Mother Nature had bought them at a fire sale and dumped them there. After five minutes of road and scenery that refused to improve, I turned around and headed back to the county road.

Once the Ghia was back on smooth pavement, I hit the gas, determined to go ring Moreland's doorbell. But the next sound I heard was the whoop of a siren.

It looked like the same cruiser I'd passed coming into Sweet Bay City. I pulled over, he pulled over. He got out of the car and walked up to mine. He was tall and thin and the hair that wasn't covered by his straw hat was no more than a quarter inch long. I watched myself looking up at him in the mirror lenses of his sunglasses as he said, "Lemme see your license, son."

I gave him my license. A nickel-plated .44 revolver hung from his Sam Browne belt, and a deputy sheriff's badge gleamed from his khaki shirt pocket.

He took my license, looked at it. "What's your hurry, son?"

"I'm kind of anxious to talk to Mr. Moreland."

His lower lip pushed up underneath the upper one as he thought that one over. He said, "Where you come down from, Austin?"

"That's right."

"Uh-huh. Then how's it you come from that direction up yonder? Miss the gate the first time?"

"That's right."

"You *know* Dolph Moreland? He expecting you?"

I made a sort of cool Indian hand signal, like something James Dean might have done in *Giant*. "We have some what you might call mutual acquaintances."

He did the thing with his lower lip again, then went back to his car. A few minutes later he came back and handed me a clipboard. Under the clamp was a speeding ticket that was going to run me about eighty-nine dollars. I signed it and gave it back to the deputy. He tore off my copy and handed it to me along with my license.

"You wanna find the highway," he said, "you foller this road here aways 'bout a half a mile. You wanna veer to the left after the cattle guard, then you foller it on all the way out till you see the state highway. You don't wanna take that jog right less you wanna head south back toward San Antone. That'd be the long way."

"Thanks a lot, Deputy," I said.

"Just slow it down now, son." He nodded and stepped back from the car. I fired it up again and headed down the road toward Moreland's gate. When I got to it I whipped the wheel over and drove through, bumping over the bars of the cattle guard. I was a little surprised when the deputy didn't follow me up Moreland's driveway. He did, however, stop the cruiser just short of the gate.

When I pulled up in front of Moreland's house, a gray-and-blue Chevy pickup was parked just where I thought it would be.

A big man with silver hair and a white straw hat was climbing out of the cab, wearing White Mule gloves and toting a .30-30 rifle under his arm. A lanky dog with floppy ears and short burgundy colored hair leaped from the driver's seat and loped over to me. His eyes were curiously pale, his gaping jaws full of teeth.

"Ho, boy," hollered the silver-haired man. "Come on back here, Duke. Come on, boy."

"Howdy," I yelled. We were about twenty yards apart, and the dog was barking. "I wanted to ask you about your plane."

The dog circled back to his owner as I walked up, but refused to completely back down, barking, lunging at me, snarling. "Don't worry 'bout him," said the silver-haired man, taking off his gloves and slapping them against the legs of his blue coveralls. "He'll sure enough nip ya, but he won't bite. Not 'less there's a need."

"My name's Martin Fender," I said as I extended my hand.

He gave me a firm grip in his hard, calloused hand as he studied my face, not saying anything. As his mouth gaped open a little and his eyes shone wide and glassy, I at first assumed he was trying to decide if he knew me, then began to wonder if he'd forgotten his own name.

"Dolph Moreland," he suddenly announced in a gritty baritone. "How 'bout some ice tea?"

I drank some tea and tried to get comfortable in a chair fashioned from an old tractor seat. Dolph sat back in a rawhide-backed chair on the other side of the concrete table on the patio while Duke barked and romped after birds outside the yard. The millionaire rancher watched the dog's shenanigans with the same wizened squint I'd seen him wearing in photographs shaking hands with Lyndon Johnson, two former governors, and countless other legendary Texans. Though his deeply tanned face was deep set with lines, he looked a lot younger than sixty-eight.

Even though we were sitting in the sun, it was cooler out there, and there seemed to be less dust in the air. Through the slats of the pens on the other side of the barn, you could just see the tail of the plane.

"Said you wanted to buy a plane, son?" he said.

"I'm thinking about it," I said.

"Well, it ain't exactly in shape right now, but it could be fixed up. Sure you're interested?"

"What about the one you used to have?"

"Come again?"

"The one the insurance company paid off. I was wondering, would that be the one Richard James crashed in, back in 1984?"

His squint could have been lines engraved in hardwood. "Just who the hell are you anyway, son?"

"I'm a musician," I said. "I just got back from L.A., but Austin is my home. Lately I've been playing with Dovie de Carlo."

His squint softened noticeably, but I could tell he still hadn't made up his mind about me. "She back in Austin, is she?"

I nodded. "She seems to still be a bit haunted by her past."

He shifted his legs and took a sip of his ice tea. "Well, I reckon that's understandable, considering."

"What about that other plane?"

"Yup, that was mine, all right," he said. "What about it?"

"I was just curious. How did Richard James end up using one of your planes?"

"Well, first off, the reason I had two planes, you see, is 'cause sometimes I used to need to fly down to my spread in South Texas an' I'd end up drivin' a truckload of livestock back up here. Sometimes I had a pilot workin' for me, sometimes I flew myself. So if I's to drive back up here, I didn't much like bein' stuck with no plane. That's how I come to own two of them. Didn't always need both of 'em, but it come in handy sometimes."

"So did Richard James rent one from you, or what?"

"Well-sir, my foreman used to run with James. You see, sometimes I run into a need to spend some money on myself or people who work for me rather'n let Uncle Sam have it. So I let Neville—that's my foreman—arrange for James to use the plane once in awhile. He did use it, and it did crash."

"You say Graves used to 'run' with Richard James. You mean they were real close, or what?"

"Well, hell, bein' a musician, you must know what I mean. These rock 'n' roll sumbitches get together an' do what they do, chase women, play guitars an' holler all night. You know, that kinda thang."

"And borrow planes from their bosses," I said. "I wish I had some fans like that. I understand Graves and your other hired hands are still big rock 'n' rollers. Do you know who their favorite is now, by any chance?"

He cleared his throat loudly, making a sound like an old tractor engine starting up, and spit something into the grass. "You ask some funny questions, son."

"Oh yeah? Well I think you're giving me some mighty funny answers."

His face started to flush with anger and a deep growl came out of his throat. "Son—"

"Listen, Mr. Moreland, don't get too riled up just yet. I know I ask funny questions, but I've got not-so-funny problems and it looks like you're involved in them whether you know it or not. So I thought I might come out here and test your patience just a bit instead of going straight to the police."

"I think you better explain yourself, son."

I laid the whole thing out for him, beginning with Dovie's decision to break away from Otis by moving to Austin, only to go back to him and leave me with a van full of concrete. I told him about the threats from Graves and the surveillance from Nubby Maxwell and Red Fred, but left out Cyclone Davis because I wasn't sure how to work him into the story.

When I was finished, Moreland sat there with a troubled, contemplative expression on his face. The dog came into the yard and put his head in the old rancher's lap, and for a moment, it was hard to say who looked sadder. But then the dog's eyes lit up again as his ears were stroked by big hands, and Moreland's voice boomed:

"You come out here onto my land sayin' you wanna buy my plane, then try an' hand me a bunch a shit 'bout a boy who's worked for me for over ten years. I don't like rock 'n' roll, son. I can't tell one goddamn song from another. But old Neville, he seems to like it.

"Neville liked this Richard James fella. Said that boy played rock 'n' roll like a bull rider doggin' a mean old Bremmer who had his balls set afire, an' Neville Graves oughta know 'cause he used to be the best goddamn bull rider there ever was. One day he got throwed off one bull too many so I told him to come an' work for me. He does damn good work an' I let him do as he pleases around here. If he wants to plant corn, I let him plant corn. If he wants to use my plane, he uses my plane. So that's how come Richard James was in my plane when it crashed. Come on inside. Wanna show you somethin'."

We got up and went into the house. I followed him through

a screened-in back porch into a kitchen, down a hall, past a bedroom where a woman about Moreland's age was sitting in a rocking chair, watching a soap opera and drinking a diet soda. She glanced up, gave Moreland a funny look, then slowly turned back to the TV, the look frozen on her face. A large framed photo in the room caught my eye, a photo of a smiling adolescent boy with blond hair. I figured the boy was Moreland's dead son.

We followed the hall to a small den. Moreland bent down to turn on a lamp and closed the door. At first glance, it was a friendly, manly room, with a fireplace and a bar in the corner. Thick carpet, dark wood paneling, a low couch and recliner of well-worn dark leather, brass spittoons in front of a bar in the corner. Just above the stone mantel of the fireplace, a shotgun rested on a pair of deer legs jutting out from the wall. On the opposite wall a buffalo head stared down at us.

On the wall behind the bar was a framed Japanese Rising Sun flag. In the lower right-hand corner of the frame was a snapshot of a young fighter pilot sitting in a cockpit—Dolph Moreland minus half a century. Framed photos on either side of the flag for the most part appeared to feature men with guns posing with dead animals. The most striking of these was one of Moreland, a former Texas governor, and two freshly killed deer. Next to that photo was a five-by-seven with a group of people standing next to a plane. Moreland took it down and handed it to me.

Six men and one woman, most of them hunkered in parkas or down vests and wool caps, stood by the tail section of the small plane. One of the men was black. The background was all white. Snow.

The black face in the photo belonged to Nubby Maxwell. Next to him was a wide-eyed, bearded man I didn't recognize. Red Fred was huddled inside a hooded down jacket, and Graves stood tall and menacing, with one arm around a drawn and pale Dovie de Carlo.

Cokey Kossmeyer, the drummer, stood close at Dovie's side,

staring openmouthed, a blanket slung over his shoulders. To his left stood a smiling man with light-colored hair and small, pale eyes. He was the only one in the photo who looked happy to be there; everyone else looked dazed and out of sorts. Maybe the fur-lined hood on his leather coat was tickling him, or maybe something in the large leather bag slung over his shoulder was keeping that artificial smile pasted on his face. The wide-eyed, bearded man seemed to be glaring at him.

"Who's the beard?" I asked.

"Hell, I don't recall that boy's name," said Moreland.

"How about the poseur in the nice jacket?" I said.

"Chester White," said Moreland, "the doc. He's the one flew up with 'em an' gave 'em first aid. Once they got back here, he took care of Miz de Carlo when she was bouncin' 'round that rubber room at the Oak Tree, seein' spiders an' what all. Wasn't nothin' he could do about that drummer boy, though. Sumbitch's still in the drool ward. See the number on the tail of that plane, son?"

I looked at the number, then at him. He took the photo out of my hands, put it down on the bar, and motioned for me to follow him back through the house. As I lingered and gave the buffalo a commiserating glance, I noticed Moreland shoot me a look of disapproval. When he reached over to turn off the light, I snatched the photo off the bar and stuck it in my jacket.

We'd already walked past the small landing strip, so I knew the number on the tail of the Cessna there was the same as the one in the photo. Moreland had not only provided Richard James with a plane to fly to his gigs in, but sent one to rescue him, too.

The tires on the plane were flat, and the body was caked with a thick layer of dust. The landing strip was dotted with weeds.

Now we were walking up a gradual incline that was an obstacle course of slippery rocks, cactus, and other things that my shoes weren't made for walking on. The dog ran ahead of us, barking threateningly at anything that moved. Moreland had the .30-30 in the crook of his arm. When I asked him why he was carrying it, he just said, "Snakes."

We were high enough on the incline that I could see all the way back to the county road. The deputy's car was gone.

"Look here, son," he drawled in that deep, gritty voice. "Like my daddy use to say, Where I come from, men are *men*. Ride all day an' fuck all night. Treat all women, whether they're ladies or whores, like *ladies,* except when your own old lady acts or talks like a whore. Then you pop her one upside the head, an' if she got the right stuff she'll take it an' straighten her ass up. So don't come to me whinin' about Miz de Carlo gettin' a black eye or a busted lip. She must like this sumbitch or she wouldn't be with him. I don't know him. I don't have no reason to know him."

"I find that hard to believe," I said. "Especially since your boys seem to be pals with Otis Taylor, and since the same morning Dovie delivers the news that she's back with him I find out my band's van and equipment have been stolen and trashed."

We'd made it to the top of the incline and were now heading down the other side. For fifty yards or so, it was the same rugged, rocky ground. But just on the other side of an excavated area we were headed toward, the low cedars and shrubs took over, like the thicket I'd driven into searching for the methabilly hideout.

"All right," said Moreland, clearing his throat once again. "For one goddamn thang, I don't s'pose it occurred to you that Miz de Carlo feels obliged to these fellas 'cause they saved her damn life? So if she's hangin' around with 'em, hell, if she's *sleepin'* with every goddamn one of 'em, I 'magine that's un-derstandable, too. It might seem distasteful to you an' me but, I 'magine it's a damn sight more pleasant 'n freezin' your butt off on the side of a goddamn mountain."

We stopped by an old dead tree trunk. The bark had been rubbed away at about waist level, by a deer's antlers, I assumed.

Kernels of dry corn were scattered on the ground. As I looked around the area, I began to see a lot of corn scattered on the ground, along goat trails, on top of large rocks, and at the bottom of tree trunks.

"For another goddamn thang, if these boys were to get a mite overprotective of Miz de Carlo, well, I can see where that might happen an' I think it's damn understandable, too. An' from what I seen of your behavior, I can plumb understand why you might have an enemy or two. But my boys were here last night, I can tell you that for damn sure. We were out scatterin' this here corn for the deer. Huntin' season's comin' up in just a few weeks, an' I got a dozen day hunters comin' down the first week an' they like their deer fattened up."

"You trying to tell me you were out spreading corn all night?"

"Not the whole thang," he drawled. "Round 'bout seven, Neville's mean old hound treed a goddamn ringtail. Duke here got all excited, too, so we run over to the boys' place, got us some lamps, an' went varmint huntin'. Them dogs had a time, I tell ya."

"Yeah, I bet." I wanted to say that I thought he was still spreading the corn around, but I kept my mouth shut.

Moreland could tell I was skeptical. "Son, you just don't get it, do ya? Come over 'ere."

We walked on toward the excavated area. As we got nearer, I could see it was about the size of Moreland's three-car garage. Dirt was banked up along the sides, and the contents of the pit itself were covered with white powder. Lime.

Then the smell hit me. It was like sticking lit cigarettes up your nostrils. Moreland grinned. The stench didn't seem to bother him.

"See, it's hard for a rancher to make it these days, even a big old rancher like me. That's why that money a feller gets off leasin' his property to deer hunters is sorely needed. Take this here pit, son. Last year we had a brucillosis outbreak on the west end of the ranch. The county boys come down an' say I gotta kill ever damn one of them cows. I got no choice, so we herd 'em over here put a bullet in every goddamn cow's head. Fifty-three of 'em in all, right here in this goddamn pit. That lime eats 'em up in a hurry. Well, hell, if I shot you right now an' throwed you in there an' dumped some lime on top of your ass, wouldn't be nothin' left come Christmas. Teeth are the last to go."

I got the point. "A guy *could* get shot out here, couldn't he?"

"Now, son, don't get the wrong idea. I mean, hell, somebody starts some shit with me, I don't need to git ugly. I's born an' raised here. I don't just own this goddamn land, I *am* this goddamn land. I call the sheriff down there, he'll ask me, Dolph, what the hell can I do for you? An' that's the way I am, too. You come straight with me an' I can sure enough do thangs for ya, do a favor, or pass on a good word for ya. Ya start some shit with me, well, God help your sorry ass."

"You mean it?"

"Hell yeah, son."

I pulled the speeding ticket out of my pocket and gave it to him. He looked at it and laughed. "Well, shit. You gonna try an' make me prove it, ain't ya?"

"If it's no big deal—"

"Hell no, kid. It's nothin'." He stuffed the ticket in his pocket, but I could tell he wasn't keen on the idea of having it fixed for me.

I pointed toward the big thicket and said, "So Graves and the boys live back in there?"

He nodded. "Yup. They got 'em an old cabin back in them woods."

"I bet it reminds them of home," I said. "Wind whistling through the trees, the smell of ether in the air, crystal meth cooking on an open fire—"

"Now looky here, son," he growled. "You stay outta there. Fact, I don't expect to see you again, 'less you wanna do some deer huntin' come November. But you'd 'specially be wise to stay clear of that cabin. That old hound of Neville's ain't like

Duke. He's mean as Satan, an' he will sure enough goddamn bite ya."

"I get the message."

He cleared his throat and spit again as we turned around and headed back toward the house. I didn't say anything for the rest of the way back.

11

The old rancher's voice drawled and droned on inside my head all the way back to Austin, but I gradually became inured to it, and by the time I was back in the city proper, fighting the five-o'clock traffic, it was hard even to imagine how characters like Moreland and Graves could exist.

They still scared the hell out of me, but I was sure they'd both exaggerated a little about how tough they were and how far they'd go to prove it. I just wasn't sure how much. People who talk as much as Moreland are usually lying at least part of the time, and the relatively reticent Graves came on too strong to not be scared of *something*. So how much of Moreland's act was hot air, and what was Graves scared of?

Certain things Moreland had said *had* to be lies. There had to be more to his relationship with Richard James. His casual contention that he let the wild bluesman use one of his planes for the hell of it, for income tax purposes, or because his foreman was a big fan, just didn't cut it. And even though lots of big Texas ranchers had their own planes, I couldn't see a legitimate reason why even an ex–fighter pilot would need two of them.

Drugs were an easy answer. Maybe Moreland was a front for

the Kilton gang; he let them use his plane, and Richard James had been their mascot or something. Maybe that was how Cyclone Davis had originally come into the picture. I hadn't forgotten how, back in L.A., Sgt. Roman had been awfully anxious to chalk up Cyclone Davis's murder as drug related.

But the drug angle was too easy. I didn't like it, and I couldn't see Dovie fitting into the picture. I swung the frame back to Moreland.

There were things the rancher couldn't lie about: Graves and the Kilton gang had hung around Richard James for the last couple of years before he was killed in Moreland's own private plane; Graves and the Kilton gang flew Moreland's other Cessna up to Colorado to try to rescue James and the band; they failed to save James but they did bring back Dovie and the drummer, and even that was a miracle.

But was even a miracle enough for Dovie to hang around with these cretins the rest of her life? I just couldn't see it, especially when one of them was a woman-beating creep. I thought back to my first meeting with Dovie in L.A., back when she'd thought Otis had killed Cyclone. Cyclone was her lover, she said, but—

Otis is Otis . . .
Love is not enough . . .
It's beyond that, way beyond . . .
way scarier.

Love was not enough.

Either Otis and the Kilton gang had something on Dovie from the old days with Richard, or they were using intimidation and guilt to keep her on the hook, an emotional hostage to a bunch of twisted sleazoids who would be coming to her rescue for the rest of her life whether she screamed for help or not.

Just to thicken the stew, there was a doctor involved. That

just increased the possibilities for treachery. I'd never trusted doctors.

I pulled over at a pay phone and called the collection agency. When they put Jack on, he sounded surprised to hear from me.

"Two and a half hours, Martin," he said.

"Something came up, Jack. I'll work twice as many hours next time."

"Whoa, man. Don't overextend yourself. What's up?"

"A friend of mine sold a car to this guy on credit a few months back. The guy missed the last couple of payments and it turns out he's moved. My friend's worried the car's been wrecked or something, so I was wondering if you could run the guy's name through the computer for me, find an address so I could just drive by and see if the car is there."

"Are you sure this isn't one of your, uh, things you get into, Martin?"

"No, honest. I'm just helping a friend."

"All right. What's the guy's name?"

"Chester White. No middle initial that I know of."

"Chester White? The doctor?"

I lied. "I don't know if he is or not. Why? You know him?"

"Well, my mother does. He did her nose. Don't tell anybody. He's not really a licensed plastician but he did a real good job and cut her a deal, too. Here, I'm punching the name in now, let's see what else comes up . . . Chester White, the doctor, has an office on 38th Street. Got a house, too, on McCullough Street over in Tarrytown. Single, no dependents. Don't tell me *he's* having trouble paying his bills."

"Is he well off?"

"Huh? Is he a doctor? Does he have a house in Tarrytown? Would my mother get her nose done down at the free clinic? Come on, Martin."

"What do I know? I'm just trying to help a friend find his car."

"Well, good luck. Nothing else is showing under that name. You want the doctor or not?"

"Well, he's probably not the right one, but go ahead and give him to me," I said, trying to sound casual.

"All right, Martin. Here you go—"

I scribbled both addresses on a matchbook, read them back once to make sure I had them right, thanked him, hung up, jumped in the Ghia, peeled out into the rush hour traffic.

There were five doctors' offices in the building, but I doubted that any of the others resembled a postmodern furniture showroom as much as Dr. Chester White's did. His waiting room had black carpet speckled pink and blue, deep-set black leather Corbu couches and chairs, glass-topped wrought iron tables, and angular black torchieres—gangly things that looked like they'd make lousy reading lamps, but made the furniture in the empty room look good.

The Latina receptionist with the bright blue contacts in her eyes waited until I was standing two feet in front of her before parting her coral red–daubed lips to say, "Do you have an appointment?"—the five words running together, coming out as one.

"Actually, no. Is Dr. White in?"

"I don't know, I'd have to check. *Wouldyouliketomakean-appointment?*" Besides her tendency to hammer words together, her voice had a certain brassy notch in it that caused a sharp pain in the left front portion of my skull.

"I'd like to see him right now. It's about an accident."

"Oh? Are you injured? *Haveyouseendoctorwhitebefore?*"

"Listen, darlin'. Would you just buzz the good doc and tell him Martin Fender would like to see him about an old injury that keeps acting up, an old injury from a plane crash in Colorado."

She gave me a funny look, then picked up the phone and pressed a button. The blue contacts glistened at me until someone on the other end picked up. "Dr. White? *There'samanhere-whosays . . .*"

I couldn't hear the rest because she turned away from me and spoke in a voice just above a whisper. As she held the phone in both hands, I noticed that her nails were maybe two inches longer than Dovie de Carlo's, filed down to sharp points and painted hospital white.

She'd barely hung up when the door by the counter swung open and a small, trim man came out of it, offering a hand that was awfully tanned for one belonging to a guy who supposedly did all his work indoors. He had a wide smile of perfect teeth and a full head of blond hair hanging loose but not so long in front that it would interfere with his vision during a tennis match. Instead of a stethoscope, a Walkman headset showed just inside the collar of his shirt, the wires trailing down to the pocket of his smock.

"I'm Dr. White," he said as we shook hands. Cool, calm, but just a trifle mystified. "And aren't you sort of a minor local celebrity?"

"Martin Fender is my name," I said. "You might have seen me in a club, but not the kind where you have to be a member."

He grinned. "That's what I mean. I know I've seen you play, somewhere, with somebody, but I can't remember. It escapes me."

"Up until today I was playing with Dovie de Carlo. I think she was a patient of yours."

Something went on behind his eyes as he thought about that. After a moment he glanced over at the receptionist, then put a hand on my arm and said, "Well, I'll probably remember where I saw you play the minute you leave, so why don't you come on back so we can have a look at you? The sooner we get that over with, the sooner I'll remember."

I followed him down a short hall with several adjoining rooms furnished with the usual strange devices and the usual antiseptic smell, back to a small office. He sat on the edge of his desk and nodded at one of the black, cube-shaped chairs behind me in case I wanted to sit, but didn't insist on it.

"Well, Martin, what's the problem?" he said. His tone was kind of snappy, and the way his arms were crossed over his chest didn't suggest any kind of bedside manner.

"Are you still treating Dovie de Carlo?"

"That's none of your business. Surely you know doctors don't discuss things like that."

"I could ask her myself, but I'm here now. And I figure that you're probably still treating her. I also figure that if you were hanging around a bunch of speed-freak backwoods gangsters back in '84, then you're still hanging around with them. And that's why I'm here."

He feigned disgust with a curled lip and a limp-wristed wave. "Aw, come on, Martin, get real. Those guys called me up in the middle of the night and said they were going to fly up to Colorado to see if they could find the Rockin' Dog and did I want to go with them. What do you think I said? I'm a doctor and I'm a music fan. What if you were a physician back in 1977 and someone called you and said come over right away, the King had a heart attack, but I think he might still be breathing?"

"Sort of like Hippocrates sung to the tune of Chuck Berry, huh?"

"Look, Martin. We didn't find the Dog but we saved Dovie and Cokey's life. The way you're acting, you'd think we committed some sort of crime by saving their lives. I don't think Dovie could have held out much longer."

"What about Cokey?"

His mouth twitched a little. "His injuries weren't that serious, but the shock was too much for him. He's still at the Oak Tree, semicatatonic. If Dovie weren't such a resilient person, the same thing could have happened to her. She recovered physically in almost no time, but before and immediately after the plane crash thing she was abusing drugs and alcohol to a serious degree, and she was way out there, Martin. Take my word for it. She checked into Oak Tree on the condition that I act as her personal physician there."

"Is that normal?"

He shrugged. "What's normal? It was what she wanted. I spent another three, six, sometimes ten hours every day with her for two months. When she left, she was as cured as you can get from that sort of thing and she was grateful. I imagine she's also grateful to the guys who flew up there and rented the helicopter that pulled her off that mountain. So, once again, Martin, what's the problem?"

"I got lots of problems," I said. "I got problems with hillbillies who jump me, spy on me, and steal and trash my band's van and equipment when they think I'm becoming too tight with Dovie de Carlo. I got problems with silver-haired, barbed-wire-tongued ranchers who threaten me with lime pits and hick cops when I ask too many questions about the planes they used to have and what certain hired hands are doing deep in the thicket in the back forty. And I got problems with doctors who have too much money and bad taste in furniture and friends. I got problems that you would help me with, if you were smart."

He smiled and shook his head. "You need help all right, Martin, and you definitely need to see a doctor, but I don't treat people with drug problems anymore and paranoid schizophrenics never were my field. Frankly, I can't think of any other explanations for your behavior, coming in here like this and making these bizarre, malicious insinuations."

"Bullshit. You know what I'm talking about. You're either with these assholes or you're against them. And if you keep covering up for them, you must be with them."

He shook his head. "Look, Martin, I'm serious. You're externalizing your own private conflicts here. If you're accusing me of being a fan of Richard James and Dovie de Carlo, then you got me, guilty as charged. If you're accusing me of still caring about her, still seeing her when she's in town, bam, guilty as charged. Have I hung around with people who were on drugs, who might have sold drugs? Hey, I don't know. You play in a band, you hang out in nightclubs and recording studios, are you gonna tell me you haven't associated with some strange people you wouldn't take home to your mother? Come on, what's your problem?"

"Forget it, Doc."

"Are you sure? Have you got it out of your system or do you want to get a search warrant for my house to see what kind of CDs I listen to? Christ, Martin, are you working for Tipper Gore or something?"

"Just forget it."

"I will if you will." He smiled. I didn't.

He took his smile around to the other side of his desk and sat down and turned the page on his desk calendar. Tomorrow was Friday. It didn't look like he had many patients, but he didn't seem worried about it.

I turned around and walked out of there, knowing I'd have to talk to the doc again, but it would have to wait. He was too cool, too accommodating to be as innocent as he said he was.

12

I dropped a quarter in the pay phone and called my answering machine. The tape played back nine messages:

LADONNA—I just called because I just heard about the van, sweetie. I'm sorry. Call me at work. Bye.

LASKO—Hey, bub, they been talking about you up here since your van got in the lake. That fucking tightass holy roller Watson came over and pulled your file, said did I think maybe you'd done it yourself to collect the insurance. Hope you didn't lose another damn bass. Gimme a ring here if you want. If I'm not in, try the beeper. You got the number. See ya.

RAY—I just talked to Billy and Leo at Matt's El Rancho. I think Leo would have traded the whole van and its contents for that ragged little Pro Reverb of his. You can leave a message for me at Antone's after nine if there's anything I can do. And let me know if we're still rehearsing on Friday, otherwise I could pick up a gig on 6th Street. Cheers.

BILLY—It's a total loss, man, unless some modern art museum wants to buy it. By the time the second tow truck got there and pulled it out, all we had was a concrete empanada on wheels. Shit. Can you believe it? I just got the oil changed and a new head on my snare. The police are checking the prints they found on the cement truck against the construction crew and stuff, but there doesn't seem to be much to go on. Nobody in the neighborhood saw anything. I'm gonna call Dovie's house and see if you're over there. Later.

LEO—I just wanted to tell you, man, that the cops knew about those guys in the Monte Carlo already, OK? I know you wanted us to hold off telling them, so I didn't say anything about it. But they knew about those guys already. Turns out they were out in the woods shooting squirrels all night or something. Can you believe it? I sure don't. Weird. I'll try to call you later, or come by Nadine's. *Adios,* pal.

LADONNA—Martin, one of the guys here was out showing houses this afternoon and he drove by the Continental Club. He told me the marquee in the window says, "Saturday night, welcome home Dovie de Carlo, Austin's own." I thought you'd want to know. Call me at the office, OK? I'll be here until six or so. I think I might take Michael out to a movie, so if you want to share my popcorn and Red Hots, let me know. Bye.

A RASPY VOICE—This is Nate Waco, remember? I want that tape, man. It's mine and I know you got it. So quit fucking around and wasting time. I want it. Uhm, don't try to call me back, because I won't be where you think I am, ha ha.

CARSON BLOCK—Martin, this is Carson from IMF calling. Hey, man, how are things going down there? I talked to the queen bee herself on Tuesday and she said it was really groovy, maybe you guys were gonna play on Saturday night. I've tried calling her today, but no luck yet. Hey, maybe I'll fly in and check it out. Later, dude.

DOVIE—Martin, this is Dovie. I heard about the van and I'm sorry. Some, uhm . . . *other* things have happened, too. Can you come out and talk to me? I'm at the lake house. It's a little after five, Martin. Call me or just come. Don't worry, Otis isn't here. Bye.

The sun was smoldering in back of the hills to the west when I turned onto the tortuous little road up to her house. The woods closed in behind me, squeezing out the daylight. The temperature was cooler in the thicket, too, though it felt still and humid, as if the dense flora were too stingy to share it with intruders. I parked behind the Lincoln, got out, and looked back down the drive, feeling a little strange, like I'd forgotten something. I chalked it up to ragged nerves and walked up to the door. Dovie was waiting.

She let me in and double-locked the door behind me, then peered out the peephole. She was wearing jeans and an oversize Dodgers sweatshirt, and she had a wineglass in her hand, a cigarette going, too. Her hair was more of a mess than usual, and she wore no makeup. She looked fragile, like someone who'd just gotten out of the hospital, or received news of a death in the family.

"Did you see anybody else on my road?" she said.

"No."

"Are you sure? I'm pretty sure I heard a car coming up the drive right before you drove up."

"There's no way I'd have missed it. Isn't this the only house back here?"

She gulped some wine, nodding. "And the woods are solid along my road, they couldn't have turned off. There's barely room to turn around, but that must be what they did."

"Someone must've pulled in the wrong drive, realized it, and backed out."

"Yeah, that's it," she said, but she didn't sound convinced, and she took another look through the peephole. "I don't have any scotch. Want some wine?"

"No. Just tell me what's been happening, then I've got some big questions for you that need some simple answers. Are you OK?"

"I guess so. I haven't had any sleep. Otis left not long ago."

She plopped down on the couch, wringing her hands. I sat down a couple of feet away, studying her as she spoke. "Carson called this afternoon while Otis was here. When I told him things weren't working out, he blew up. I mean, he was really mad. I've never heard him like that before. I told him I'd call him back. Otis and I, uh, were having a fight."

"Did he hurt you?"

She shook her head. I couldn't see any bruises, but I didn't believe her, either. I had the same kind of feeling looking at her now as when I'd first seen her black eyes.

"After Otis left," she said, "Billy called here, looking for you, and told me about the van. He kind of got to me, too, because I realized you hadn't told him I said it wasn't working out, and he was telling me not to worry, you guys all had spare equipment we could use Saturday night, and he said he might have a little trouble getting a good p.a. system to rehearse with tomorrow, but he'd come up with something."

"He would, too. That's Billy. Did you tell him not to bother?"

She shook her head, staring down at the wineglass. "I don't know what to do, Martin. I feel stupid. My relationship with Otis is sick, but I can't fight him and I can't say no to him."

"You can't say no to him, or his friends?"

She looked up at me. "Who?"

"You know, the search-party boys, the Kilton all-star speed team. I think there's something sick about your relationship with them, too. What have they got on you?"

"Nothing, Martin. They saved me from dying and I owe them for that. Otis gave me a life and I owe him for that, too."

"Otis doesn't look capable of flicking on a light switch, much less giving someone a life."

"He was in a car wreck years ago and his hair turned white. I know he looks strange and you think he's horrible, but—"

"But what, he's funny? He's got a mean right? He sure knows how to fill a van with concrete? Where'd you find this prince, anyway?"

"I was really down after the plane crash, Martin. I mean, it's like part of me was still up there, with Richard. And I had no other life, nothing, not even a place to stay. All I had was this nightmare I walked around in. So Chester, the doctor—"

"I've met him."

"He was the one who introduced me to Otis. Otis had just moved here from Lubbock and he was a big fan of Richard's. He'd just bought all of Richard's publishing from Richard's mom, and he thought it would be nice if I cut a couple of the songs for a single, you know, as a kind of a tribute. Richard's fans, the Kilton gang, as you call them, were paying the studio costs. They'd paid for Richard's last record and lost a lot of money on it, so it seemed like a nice thing to do, to help them get a chance to do something else. And it gave me something to do, too."

She lit another cigarette and thought about what she was going to say next. Finally she said, "Otis was just what I needed at the time. He got IMF to distribute the single and it took off. You know how the rest of it goes, I guess."

"Yeah, it goes like this: Everybody's so right for each other, the next few years they just go around being nice to one another. Otis was nice to you, except for maybe when he blackened your eyes or said he'd kill you and Cyclone if he caught you together again. You kept on being nice to the Kilton gang and Dolph Moreland and what's wrong with that? Except for when they jump me, steal my van and fill it up with concrete and push it in the lake, or take me out to a lime pit in the middle of the woods to show me how tough they are, they've been real nice to me, too."

"I'm sorry, Martin. But in their minds, I think they think they're just looking after me. I didn't know anything about the van until Billy called, and I don't think Otis did, either. You shouldn't have told them off last night, Martin. I think you really pissed them off."

"Well that's just too bad. Listen, the way it looks to me is they owned a piece of Richard, so they think they own you. And they don't plan on letting go."

"Martin, I know they aren't good people, I'm not that stupid. I wasn't wild about them when they followed Richard around. Now Richard's gone and they follow Otis and me around. But that's all there is to it."

"Are you sure?"

"What do you mean am I sure?" she snapped. "Believe me, there's no crime involved. There's no secret triple-X-rated Dovie de Carlo film, nothing like that, that they have on me. I mean, I know what these guys used to do back in Kilton, and I know they probably still sell drugs and who knows what else. But my ties to them are just, you know, the plane-crash thing. That thing is always with me and it's always gonna be."

"Look, Dovie, it was a catastrophe, something that happened to you and four other people. You made it, they didn't. Maybe you can't stop thinking about it, but you've got to bear in mind that it wasn't your fault."

"But it *was,* to some extent," she said. "I didn't want to do those dates. Part of the reason was I didn't want to be in a van with a bunch of guys all the way up to Colorado and back. Richard didn't want to do the gigs without me, so he got the plane for us. Mr. Moreland's regular pilot wasn't available, so we hired the other guy from Fort Worth. But that's not all.

"After the crash, after the second day, Preston got weird. First he started being really abusive to Cokey, then to me and Richard. Richard, you know, was heavy but not that big, same as Preston, but Preston was mean. And he always resented me anyway. He started taking more food than the rest of us. The third night Preston tied Richard up and raped me. He did it again the next day, and every day after that.

"But Richard didn't give up. We kept hearing this rumbling sound, and Richard said that it must be helicopters, looking for us. I think he really knew the sound was from avalanches, but I don't know for sure. What I do know is he finally convinced Preston that they could make it down the mountain, that there might be a ski lodge or something down there. But I think he knew they wouldn't make it, but he had to do something to lessen my misery. He did it, and he took that other bastard with him. When the search party found us, Cokey and I were both stark raving mad. That's why they rushed me back here so fast and that's why this thing will always be with me."

I took one of her hands and squeezed it. Her eyes bored into me as she squeezed back, then pulled away, folding her arms across her chest. She didn't want to be hugged, didn't want to be pitied. "Forget about it, Martin."

"Did you tell anyone about this, about what happened up there?"

She gave me a funny look. "No."

"Not even Otis?"

"No. Why?"

"Because when I asked you what Otis was to you, you said that love wasn't enough to keep you together. I understand that you feel indebted to him, but enough's enough. I just can't see why you'd let these people drag you down."

"They're not dragging me down, Martin. I admit that my relationship with Otis isn't normal, but how can I expect anything normal? It's a crazy world. Every day I get up and I can't believe I'm here, alive, semifamous. And Richard's dead. I still miss him. It's bullshit when they say time heals. Maybe that's why I go in for this kind of treatment with Otis, so I can take my mind off the other thing. I don't know. But you're the guy who likes things simple, aren't you, so why don't you just accept it the way it is and quit looking for some big evil plot?"

"I'm sorry," I said. "Maybe the plane crash will always be with you, but these cretins don't have to be. Besides, they went up there to rescue Richard, not you."

She didn't like the remark much more than I liked delivering it, but she took it pretty easily. "You're right," she said.

"Do you think they'd stop following you around if Otis were out of the picture?"

She took a deep breath and said, "Probably. Like you said, I'm not Richard, I'm just his sort of widowed chick backup singer, you know? Otis is one of them, one of the boys. They were only coming to our rehearsals because they thought Otis would want them to until he got back to town, and I'm sure they filled your van with concrete because they thought he wanted them to do that, too."

"Wait a minute," I said. "That reminds me of something—"

"I'll pay for your van and equipment, Martin, if that's what you mean. I told Billy that. I don't have the cash right now, but—"

"Wait a minute. Just then when you said 'concrete' I remembered something. In 'The Whole Damn Truth' there's a line about being 'boiled in concrete.' What does that mean?"

"It means just what it sounds like," she said. "It means hard."

"You sound pretty sure. Have you heard it before?"

She gave a nonchalant nod. "Cyclone used to say it all the time. It means tough, you know, hardboiled. He'd say that about a song he liked, and sometimes he'd say it about his own situation, you know, his life being tough. Richard had a lot of little sayings like that."

"Richard?"

Her eyes squinted as she shook her head and corrected herself. "No, Cyclone."

"But you said Richard."

"I *meant* Cyclone. I just got mixed up."

"But the phrase is from Richard's song. Cyclone sang that much of it, and you mumbled it in your sleep on the plane."

She bit into a nail and twisted it. "I don't know. Maybe it's an old saying. Maybe Cyclone started using it after he heard the tape. I don't know, I still don't remember the song, but I guess I must have heard it. Memory is a strange thing, Martin."

I lit a cigarette, took a long drag, and blew it out slowly, watching the patterns of smoke stretch languorously up toward the ceiling beams, like escaped ghosts, and I thought about memory.

I said, "What does Cyclone have to do with all this?"

"How would I know? I didn't even know his real name, remember?"

"Remember when you thought Otis was the one who killed him?"

"Of course. But we figured out he didn't. Why?"

"Because since I've met some of these other *hellbillies* I wonder if Otis might've gotten one of them to do it for him."

She shook her head. "I told you, Otis would've done it himself."

"How can you be so sure?"

"Because that's the way Otis is, for one thing. And I only met Dolph Moreland once and he seemed like a nice old guy, like a character on *Dallas* or something. Nubby Maxwell was here in Austin when Otis was in L.A., and Red Fred has an eye condition or something, he can barely count fingers in front of his face."

"How do you know Nubby was here in Austin?"

"I saw him out at the airport when we got here."

"Maybe he'd just flown in himself."

She shook her head. "He was picking someone up. He was waiting at the curb in the Monte Carlo when I saw him."

I decided to file that one away for later. "What about Graves? He's the one I was thinking of, anyway."

"Well, he's a different case, but I know it wasn't him."

"I've heard he's killed a couple of people."

She nodded. "They say he killed one with his bare hands, in east Austin, and the other, in a San Antonio nightclub, with a gun. Supposedly several people saw the San Antonio one, but they kept quiet because they were scared of Graves and besides, the other guy supposedly pulled a knife and cut Graves before he shot him. The point is they say Graves had a revolver and kept shooting at the guy, kept reloading and shooting up the place, this tiny bar, a place no bigger than this room. They say he reloaded twice and kept shooting until he was out of bullets, which means he shot at him almost twenty times."

"Is this supposed to make me less worried about Graves?"

"He only hit him once," she said. "That's why I know Otis wouldn't send Graves to shoot Cyclone."

I took another long drag on the cigarette. "What part of the body did he finally hit?"

"The head." She sighed heavily and slumped farther down on the couch, so that her chin was resting on her chest. Suddenly the room seemed very quiet, very still.

So Graves, the deadly redneck, was a lousy shot. What the hell.

"All right," I said, "can you think of anyone besides Otis who would have wanted to shoot Cyclone dead and go burn his apartment down?"

She looked up at me with a blank expression on her face, looking like a thing that was all used up. "No, I can't."

"Then Otis must have done it."

"But why?"

"Because he stole the tape, because Otis was jealous of him, and because he was a loose cannon going around talking about how Richard James is really alive and you guys have been covering it up all these years. Don't those sound like good enough reasons to kill somebody?''

"I wish you wouldn't talk like that, Martin. And I told you the tape was just—"

"Just an excuse, just a clue, I know. But I'm really starting to wish I'd gotten to hear the whole thing for myself. None of this other crap makes sense. Everybody has such a reasonable explanation for every little thing, but when you put all the pieces together, it's all wrong. I get the feeling that if I could just hear that song again, maybe it would make sense to me. Hell, maybe it's not called 'The Whole Damn Truth' for nothing."

She didn't say anything and I was glad. I got up and went over to the window and looked out. It was dark outside.

"Do you see anything?" she said.

"No. Did you hear something again?"

"No, but ever since I came out here last night I've felt like someone was out there, watching me. I mean, I'm used to it when I'm in a crowd, when I go to a mall or something, but out here, I don't like it."

"What's the nearest house?"

"About a quarter mile, I guess. Those woods go all around the place. The places on either side of me go all the way down to the lake, and they're fenced off, too. Maybe it's just bums or something. Kids, maybe."

"Maybe it's just nerves," I said. "I've got them, too, but I'm going to try to get them to work for me instead of against me. Will you be OK here, or would you rather go back to the Driskill?"

"Where are you going?"

"That all depends," I said. "If you want, I'll start working on getting Otis Taylor off your back for good. If not, I'm going to a movie with my girlfriend and her kid, and I won't have anything else to do with you again. I understand about your mixed-up feelings about the plane crash, but like I said, enough is enough. If your relationship with the search-party gang is just how you described it, I think there's a good chance they won't give us any more trouble. Dolph Moreland may be above the law over by Sweet Bay City, but I don't think he'd let his hired help get out of hand again like last night."

"You're probably right. Like I said, if I got rid of Otis, I'd probably be rid of them. But no police, please."

"I hate to sound like a broken record, but is it really because you don't want the publicity, or is there something I need to know?"

"No, I just don't want those old wounds opened again. OK?"

"OK. I'll just talk to him and explain the benefits of his staying out of the picture. There are laws against beating up women, you know, and I know at least one cop, one who takes bass lessons from me, who takes a special interest in seeing them enforced. But you've got to decide to take a stand, be strong. If you aren't willing to do what it takes on this, you're wasting my time as well as breaking my heart."

Something flickered in her eyes. "OK. You're right. I can't keep living like this."

"All right. Let's get rid of Otis."

She raised her glass and said, "*Salud*—get rid of Otis," and tilted her head back and drank. The glass was empty when she took it away from her lips, and her hands were shaking.

13

It was a little after eight o'clock when I pulled up in front of Otis's house. His was the last house on a street that ended at the edge of the densely wooded meadow being slowly overtaken by the subdivision. A wildly overgrown hedge bordering Otis's yard looked like something that had either just crept in from the wild, or was trying to return to it. The house across the street had a FOR SALE sign in the yard, and did not look occupied.

Otis's garage door was open, the LTD inside. I walked up to the front door, knocked, waited, knocked, waited. I opened the screen door and pushed on the inner one. It came open. I poked my head inside and called out, got no response.

I walked over to the LTD until I heard sounds from the engine cooling off. That was enough for me. I went back to the front door.

I went in through the living room, into the dining area, then into the kitchen. The kitchen had a connecting door to the garage. I glanced in there, then moved through the rest of the house. Even in the rooms where lamps had been turned on, the place was dark and stuffy. It reminded me of Dolph Moreland's trophy room. Not only was there an abundance of wood paneling and drawn curtains, but there were deer head trophies on the walls and a shotgun over the fireplace in the living room.

But unlike Moreland's place, this house reeked of the same ether sweat that followed the members of the speed gang around, the rank aura that had permeated my apartment when Nate Waco had come to visit.

I went down a hall and found a bedroom that didn't look lived in—no clothes in the closet, no clutter of personal belongings on the nightstand or dresser—but the covers had been pulled off the bed, the mattress left askew. The light was on, but the ceiling fan was off. I moved on.

The next room was an office. The first thing that got my attention was the door jamb. The locking plate had been knocked out of place, the frame splintered. Someone had kicked the door in.

This room had a ceiling fan, too, along with a desk, file cabinets, more deer head trophies, and a stereo setup complete with a dual cassette deck and a quarter-inch reel-to-reel tape recorder. It all looked like near top-of-the-line equipment, and the dozen or so custom-labeled cassettes scattered over the floor were all professional grade. A lamp on the desk had been left on, but the ceiling fan was off. This room reeked strongly of the ether odor, and of something far worse.

Otis was crumpled on the floor in front of the desk, his face shot off. I crept a little closer, careful not to step in the spreading sea of dark red that he lay in. He'd been shot in the face so many times that he was not only unrecognizable as an individual, but as anything human. But it had to be him. The white hair was no wig, and his skin had the same waxy, translucent appearance as when I'd seen him last.

A .44 magnum lay just beyond the reach of his right hand. I crouched down low enough to sniff the barrel and peer into the exposed chambers. It didn't appear to have been fired.

I tiptoed around to the other side of the desk. There were at least two bullet holes in the wall, where more than one shot had passed through the now faceless man's skull while he was still standing. Gray and pinkish matter had been flung against the wall, too, and a reddish spray still ran in rivulets down the seams of the paneling. The way the fluids were still running down the wall and spreading on the floor, I doubted the shooting had occurred more than a few minutes ago. There was nothing of interest on the desk, just the usual stapler, pens, letter opener, ashtray, phone, and a brass armadillo paper weight the size of a large rat.

I went over to the stereo setup. It was a nice enough collection of gear, nothing out of the ordinary, but well suited to a song-plugger's needs. Quarter-inch dubs of songs would be recorded onto cassette, and the master cassette copy used to run off copies for the record company, the artist, and other interested parties. I glanced down at the cassettes. All the J-cards bore the titles of Richard James songs, which was no surprise.

I decided to check out the rest of the house, then call the police.

The bedroom down the hall, unlike the first one I'd seen, looked lived in. The closet doors were open, the dresser drawers were open, and the nightstand drawer had been pulled out completely and left on the floor. The bed was unmade, clothes were scattered, and an acoustic guitar was lying on the floor in the corner. Next to a shotgun. The ceiling fan was still turning.

A pair of cowboy boots lay in front of the closet door, with little scraps of material beside them. Closer inspection revealed the scraps to be chunks of foam rubber. I shrugged it off and resumed my expedition.

The bathroom had been searched.

The hall closet had been rifled.

The last room on the right, just before the door leading out to the backyard, was a utility room. There was a washer and a dryer, a ceiling fan, and some household cleaning utensils in the corner. The washer and dryer were empty.

The door leading out to the backyard was unlocked, too, and it didn't appear to have been jimmied. The hedge was even thicker and wilder in the back, and only the roof of the house on the opposite lot was visible over it. I saw no one lurking by the barbecue pit, behind the two lawn chairs, or under the young peach tree. But a pile of fresh coals was in the barbecue pit, recently doused with charcoal starter.

I went back through the house, looking over each room again. There was a bottle of Seagram's and a liter bottle of 7-Up on the kitchen counter, the makings of the Rockin' Dog's favorite cocktail, and two large T-bone steaks thawing in the sink. Apparently Otis had been expecting someone for dinner. I moved on. I found an old Vox teardrop-shaped bass guitar under the bed in his bedroom, an engraved Winchester rifle lying next to it.

I went back to the office and looked at the dead man. Why was he in front of the desk? I looked around the room, imagined the killer kicking in the door and entering the room, gun drawn. Otis had his own gun, so why didn't he just pop the guy off from behind his desk? Maybe he didn't have the gun in his hand, maybe something else. I looked over the desk again, saw a dusty smudge on one corner. On closer examination, the smudge appeared to be a footprint. The ceiling fan was just overhead. I climbed up on the desk, a position that, to a man of Otis's height, would put the blades of the fan just within reach. But being taller, I could actually see the top side of the blades, and the cassette tape resting atop one of them. I nabbed it with shaky hands. The label on the cassette said "The Whole Damn Truth."

Dang.

I jammed the tape in my back pocket and stepped down from the desk, careful not to slip in the awful goo.

Now I replayed the killing scenario again. Victim hears killer enter house, panics. Locks his door, looks for clever place to hide tape, decides on the ceiling fan. Killer kicks in door and enters room, just after victim steps down from desk. Victim whirls around with gun, too late. Killer blasts away, makes quick search for tape, splits.

But why did the victim bother to hide the tape? He had plenty of firepower. Why not just wait for the killer and say Fuck you, no chrome high bias cassette tape for you, just old-fashioned lead.

The victim knew the killer. He didn't want to sit and wait and kill him, like a hunter waiting in a deer blind. His mistake.

Then I thought about the steaks thawing in the kitchen, and the charcoal waiting to be lit. Maybe he'd come back here to get matches or something, then heard the killer enter the house.

I was ready to call the cops. I knew I had to. I picked up the phone, then put it down again. Just one more quick look around, I decided.

I decided to check out the garage. Maybe there was a phone in the car I could use to call the cops. The car was unlocked. Not much in the glove box, just a pair of Isotoner driving gloves, insurance papers, registration certificates, and a parking receipt for four dollars worth of parking at LAX. The receipt seemed halfway interesting, so I stuck it in my pocket.

Nothing under the seats. I was checking out the ashtray when I noticed the odometer. The car had over thirty-three thousand miles on it, and it was no more than a year old. Apparently Otis Taylor liked to drive.

When I got out of the car I felt a tingling sensation. My hands shook badly. Need to call the cops, I told myself. That's all it is. You just found a dead man and they'll want to know.

I still felt shaky. I glanced around the garage. Other than a couple of gallons of antifreeze and a couple of spare tires, it was barren, no lawn care tools or sets of golf clubs. I stepped out onto the driveway and ran into a brick wall.

The brick wall was about half a foot taller than me, and it was topped off by a big black cowboy hat. Under the brim of the hat, Neville Graves's eyes glowed angrily, like the headlights of a car speeding down a country road. There was a black cylindrical object in his right hand.

"Oh, shit," I said.

"I told you not to fuck with me," said Graves.

My mouth opened but no wisecracks came out. I saw him

start to swing and I ducked, but not quickly enough and not low enough. It was like having a bank vault dropped on your head.

I fell back and ate stars for awhile.

Voices.

Screeching tires.

Car doors opening, slamming shut.

Sirens whooping, big feet tearing across the lawn. Low voices hollering, threatening, *Don't move!* Did someone tell me to freeze? Man, I was an ice cube.

Black-and-blue uniforms towered over me, looking down as if peering into a deep, dark well. I tried waving at them so they'd see me lying at the bottom of that well, but could only manage a twitching, fluttering movement with one hand. The other was miles away, at the end of an arm that was made of wood.

A face came close to mine. The mouth was moving. Red whiskers surrounded the mouth. The bearded face belonged to a large, brightly colored Hawaiian shirt. People were surfing on the shirt, lying underneath palm trees, cavorting with voluptuous native women wearing grass skirts, leis, and nothing else. I wanted to be there.

Men in orange suits came over, their mouths opening and closing, their hands feeling me, clamping something over my mouth and nose. The Hawaiian shirt stepped back. More men in orange suits came over and put me on a stretcher and carted me away. I was glad. Voluptuous bare-chested women were waiting.

14

It was four in the morning. I knew because it said so on the generic office clock that hung on the blank white wall instead of a full moon in a cloudy tropical sky. I was drinking bad coffee out of a styrofoam cup instead of a piña colada out of a coconut shell.

I wasn't in Hawaii. I told Ladonna that when I called her hours back and promised to call her again when I got a chance, but Lasko had already called her once, so she wasn't surprised that I was in a small room upstairs at the Austin police department. A bandage was taped to my forehead, courtesy of Brackenridge emergency room. After a couple of hours in their care, I'd come to my senses enough to be discharged and given a ride to that small room, and that small room was where I stayed, talking to the same two men off and on for the better part of three and a half hours. The two men stayed a discreet distance apart, rarely interrupting each other as they asked their questions, giving each other the kind of wide berth that a porcupine and a skunk might give each other, not out of fear but professional courtesy.

Sgt. Jim Lasko was the bearded homicide detective in the Hawaiian shirt, and Detective Tom Watson was the grim-faced man with iron-gray hair and straight-line mustache in the plain

brown suit who absorbed every word I spoke and every gesture
I made like a doctor tracking the progress of a killing virus.
They were not bare-chested, voluptuous native women.

I was in a foul mood for many reasons. Some, like the late
hour, the bump on my head, and the presence of Watson, were
obvious. Some, like the fact that I'd lost the damn tape before
I got a chance to listen to it, were not so obvious. The subject
of the tape had not been brought up.

"I'm getting tired of doing all the talking," I said. "You guys
haven't even said if you were gonna charge me yet."

"We'll let you know when we feel like it," Watson said
calmly, his eyes locked onto mine, searching for a reaction as
he tapped a pencil point against the note pad in his hands.

Lasko cleared his throat, bristling at Watson's statement. He
said, "A lady down the street put in the 911 call about five to
ten minutes after she heard the shots. At first she thought they
were firecrackers. Then she looked out her window and saw
you drive up and enter the house. That's when she decided to
call 911."

"What about Graves and his pals?" I said.

Lasko shook his head. "Apparently he took off in the LTD
after he heard the sirens. A guy at the other end of the block
gave us a very good description of him. Seems he jumped the
curb and ran over the guy's mailbox. About an hour ago the
LTD was spotted ditched behind a bar on East Seventh Street.
Witnesses in the area recall seeing Graves's pickup in the lot
earlier this evening. Every cop rolling out there now—city,
county, and state—has a description of him and the pickup. If
he's on the move, we'll like as not spot him."

"Yeah, I bet," I said.

"How's that?" snarled Watson.

"I mean I bet you guys'll find him. Graves'll be out on Dolph
Moreland's place, where he and the old man have been all night,
feeding corn to the deer and bullshit to the cops, same as last
night. And you'll eat it up again, same as you did this
afternoon."

Lasko just shook his head and looked away, but Watson smiled and said, "Fender, for one thing, Maxwell and Fredericks were eating enchiladas in a cafe in Sweet Bay City when this thing happened. For another thing, you seem awfully anxious to peg Graves, Maxwell, and Fredericks for last night's little crime rampage with your van, a cement truck, and the B&E of a municipal facility, and I'm real curious as to why this didn't occur to you yesterday when Officer Petit asked you about it."

"I'm slow, OK?" I said. "How about that?"

"I could possibly buy that," he said, nodding to himself, "since you're such a decadent heathen scumbag, but if you know something that could clear any of this up, you'd best come straight with us pronto. Let's take for example the telephone. Your prints were on it. Who'd you call?"

"A special toll-free number," I said. "You probably already know it."

"What is it?" he asked in a dry voice, his pencil poised over his note pad.

"1-800-FUCK OFF," I said.

I heard Lasko groan. Watson just nodded ever so slightly, a cagey grin putting extra creases in that stoical frontier countenance of his. He was every inch the born-again son of a Texas Ranger from Abilene, the sum total of a childhood of ball-shriveling winter freezes and a story to go with every notch on his father's long-barrel .38.

Lasko spoke up. "Detective Watson, I think we should let Martin finish writing out his statement. The Lieutenant will be coming in a couple hours or so from now and if he finds out we've had a witness in custody since around nine last night and we haven't pressed charges *or* gotten a statement, he'll wanna chew the first ass that walks by, whether it's yours, mine, or one of those dope-sniffing canines of yours."

Watson's eyes flicked over to Lasko's, then back at me. The sworn enemy of all things funky gave me a little wink, then walked out. Lasko gave me a shake of his head, then he left, too.

We'd had a lot to talk about. The van caper appeared to be as unsolved as it had been the previous afternoon. According to Watson, nobody saw anything, and the neighbors off Red River had just assumed the early morning noise was caused by city workers working late or getting an early start. But I didn't like taking Watson's word for anything.

Watson also said Dovie had stated that Otis had been with her, and that pretty much jibed with what I knew. Graves, Nubby Maxwell, and Red Fred had been sufficiently alibied by Moreland's varmint hunting story, and my imagination had already been severely taxed trying to sort out Moreland's other possible tall tales.

It turned out that the white Taurus I'd seen across from the rehearsal studio did indeed belong to the Austin police department. Watson was currently heading up a special narcotics-and-street-gang task force, and as soon as his least favorite degenerate musician returned to Austin (closely shadowed by two suspected narcotics traffickers from the county next door, Nubby Maxwell and Red Fred), two men were pulled off their surveillance of some recently relocated L.A. crack gang members and reassigned band rehearsal detail. After two boring, uneventful evenings, Watson put his men back on the L.A. gangsters, just in time to miss the van-and-equipment heist. Just like his people had been out of pocket long enough to miss a man sneaking out of his house last May when he slithered over to a South Austin motel and tried to bash out Retha Thomas's brains with my bass guitar. Watson and I would never be friends.

I put the tip of my pen down to paper and resumed writing. I had nothing to hide except the suspicions I'd held that Otis and the Kilton drug gang–search party boys had been somehow extorting or harassing Dovie ever since they rescued her and Cokey from that mountain pass in Colorado. But Dovie had cleared that up for me, more or less. Otis was the problem, she said, Otis and their sicko relationship. We just had to get rid of Otis. I went over there to see about that, but someone had already gotten rid of him for me.

If I hadn't bumped into Graves, Nate Waco would have been my prime suspect. The house had reeked with speed sweat, but undoubtedly from Otis's tenancy there. It did occur to me that, being a fellow speed demon, Nate could almost have been a member of the gang, but no one had ever mentioned him in connection with them, and he was in a different class of wacko anyway, a class with only one member. It was obvious, though, that whoever killed Otis had a throbbing hard-on for that tape, and that would tend to implicate Nate. But that implication faded when I ran into Graves—who had apparently been hiding on the premises the whole time—and got bonked in the head with a weighted flashlight. Now he had the tape. Or did he have time to get it? If the sirens had spooked him before he got a chance to search me, that meant that they had it. But they hadn't mentioned it yet. Why?

Maybe they didn't know it had come from that ceiling fan blade where Otis had hidden it in the last panic-stricken moments of his miserable life. I decided I wasn't going to be the first one to bring it up.

I'd just signed my name to the statement when Lasko walked in, closed the door, and sat down. I handed him the statement. He glanced at it and put it inside the folder he'd brought with him. He said, "I gave Ladonna a follow-up call for you."

"Thanks."

He tugged on the bill of the gimme cap on his head and sighed. "Why you wanna go getting excited with Watson? You're just playing his game when you do that. Just encourages the cold-hearted tight-ass son of a bitch."

"Sorry," I said. "I just can't help myself."

He stifled a yawn and glanced up at the clock. He looked as

tired as I felt, but he knew tired as well or better than I did. Lasko had seen sunrise from the wrong side of midnight as often as I had, but he rarely had the luxury of sleeping till noon to recover from it. "What the hell were you looking for, Martin?"

I shrugged. "I don't know. Just a reason for the man's existence, maybe."

"Did you think you found it there in his car?" He unclipped something from the folder and held it up. It was the parking receipt from LAX. "I figured it was Otis's, since there was one like it in his wallet, and you don't seem the type to save a receipt for less than five bucks. What do you get out of it?"

"Well," I said, "for a while I suspected that Otis had killed Cyclone Davis. I checked up on him, found out he didn't fly in until the next morning, and it looked like that cleared him. I suppose the L.A. cops don't suspect him, or you'd have heard about it by now. But maybe I'm starting to again."

"You're not a cop, Martin. Why not let the people who get paid for solving crimes do the work? If you've got information that can help them do their job, pick up the damn phone and call 'em. How was it you and this small-time crook from Oakland got to be such good buddies, anyway?"

"We didn't. He called me and hired me for a session, gave me a strange, scary ride that didn't prove anything more to me than the fact that he was an R&B maniac with a morbid fixation on Richard James. He said that Richard James was still alive, and he had a tape of a song that proved it. Then a bullet from a .30-06 got in the way, which just got him chalked up as another crazy kill in a city boiling over with crazy kills."

"And you think he deserved more 'cause he liked the same music you like."

"*Anybody* deserves more, no matter what kind of music he likes," I said. "But maybe it's also because he hired me to do a gig and I didn't get to play it, or maybe just because he had a crazy dream and I've got my doubts that Otis Taylor wasn't the guy who snuffed them out."

He nodded, tugging on his beard again. "Well, I've got some doubts of my own. Let me tell you about doubts, Martin."

For the next half hour, he did just that.

Lasko knew next to nothing about Otis Taylor, but he did know a thing or two about the people who hung around with him. Graves, Nubby, and Red Fred had been the subject of over a half dozen narcotics investigations over the last ten years. The investigations rarely came to anything. The fact that the trio had come from crystal meth country was common knowledge, and Lasko doubted that the gang members were still free because they were walking the straight and narrow.

Nubby Maxwell and Red Fred had each been busted twice on minor narcotics possession beefs. Both of Nubby's cases and one of Red Fred's had been dismissed, and Red Fred had paid a small fine on the one that hadn't. Lasko seriously doubted those outcomes had resulted from the duo's innocence; it was probably because they'd employed one of the best drug-case attorneys in town.

Graves had been the subject of several criminal investigations, but no charges had been filed except for two assault cases resulting in fines and a few weeks in jail. Lasko doubted that those were the only two times Graves had sent people to the emergency room. The East Side murder case was still unsolved, though all the investigating officers reported finding almost a dozen informants who "knew" that Graves had killed the man, but none of them would say how or why. Once again, Lasko doubted that the informants' reasons for their reticence was due to Graves's winning personality traits.

The narcotics squad maintained an intermittent surveillance on the Kilton gang when they were in Austin jurisdiction, but hadn't been able to connect them with anything big. State police had been out to Moreland's ranch twice, and each time found the boys sitting around fishing, skinning animals, or watching the VCR instead of cooking narcotics. Lasko doubted like hell that the men spent all their free time on the ranch involved in these pastimes.

"You know how it is, Martin," drawled Lasko. "You can see the dust of a car coming down the road for miles out there, and you can sure enough hear a helicopter. They got friends out there, too, and damn few enemies. They know what they're doing. Their grandads taught 'em everything they know, back in those woods around Kilton."

"Now they've got Moreland looking out for them," I said.

He nodded. "He's helped more than one governor into office, and him and the mayor eat ribs once a month out at County Line. He's a decorated World War II fighter pilot, and a good old boy from way back."

"He's a scary good old boy, Lasko," I said. "What about the neighbor who ran over his kid and then disappeared a couple of weeks later?"

Lasko shrugged. "That's Sweet Bay City jurisdiction, Martin. They didn't see fit to do anything about it. Just like the nosy writer killed in a hunting accident a couple of years ago."

"What writer?"

"Bob Jaworski was the kid's name," said Lasko. "I was brought into it because the boy's father kept calling me, kept asking me to look into it. The way it goes, the boy drove out on Moreland's ranch early one morning and got himself mistaken for a white-tail buck. Though they never figured out who fired the shot, the boy was just getting out of his car to walk over to a hunting blind, and he had a rifle on him he'd apparently borrowed from old man Moreland." He sighed and glanced up at a spot on the ceiling. "Case closed."

"What else? I don't like the way you said 'case closed.' "

"Uh huh. The reason his dad kept calling me. Said the kid was a vegetarian. No way he'd kill a deer, he claimed, no way he'd even pretend to be a hunter just so he could spy on someone for a story."

"What'd you do about it?"

"I asked around. That was what everybody said, the kid was a veggie. I talked to a clerk down at Whole Foods Supermarket. They said he'd been by there three times that week to buy this organic, veggie-style deodorant, but they were out. Three times in one week, Martin. OK, so he was a dedicated vegetarian, but that doesn't prove he wasn't accidentally shot by a hunter's stray bullet. Not to the Sweet Bay City district attorney it didn't, anyway."

"Anything else?"

Lasko nodded. "One other thing. On the kid's answering machine, he had a message from Sherm Caswell, saying he wanted to talk to the kid. Caswell was Moreland's pilot at the time. Moreland hardly flies anymore. They say his eyesight's getting bad. Anyway, I looked for Caswell, but seems he disappeared off the face of the earth."

"Was he from Kilton originally?"

"Uh huh," said Lasko. "Another émigré from crystal meth country."

"Disappeared, huh?"

Lasko tugged at his beard. "I'm as tired of saying it as you are hearing it, but it ain't my jurisdiction. And, far as I know, nobody ever came looking for him. Maybe the folks in Kilton are used to things like that."

"Otis have a record?"

"Not here. Kept a low profile, Martin. Neighbors said they hardly ever saw him, except when he'd pull up in that LTD, or the Caddy he had before that—the one he gave your friend from Oakland. Otis did a lot of driving, though. I can tell you that much."

"I noticed the odometer, too. What if he *drove* out to L.A. to kill Cyclone Davis? Maybe he got someone to take his place on that Friday-morning flight, then picked him up at LAX. Maybe that's what that parking receipt is trying to tell us."

Lasko tugged on his beard again, fingering the receipt. "It's possible, I reckon. But the receipt doesn't prove a damn thing. There's nothing on it, no license number, nothing, just last Friday's date, which does jibe with your scenario. If you got real lucky, maybe you could find the attendant who gave it to him, but I imagine the chances he'd remember who was in the car, or anything like that, is slim to none. And still, it's nothing. Wouldn't prove a thing, except that somebody in this crowd was out at LAX last Friday morning."

"I still think it means something," I said. "I remember Dovie telling me not to worry about Otis for awhile, that he wouldn't be here in Austin when we got back. That could've meant he was driving back."

"Yeah, could at that. Why don't you ask her? But once again, this Cyclone Davis–Kyle Lynch case isn't mine, either. It's L.A.'s. Too bad we didn't get a chance to ask old Otis about it before he got his head blown off at close range."

"Close enough even for Graves to hit him?"

"Apparently. You heard that San Antone story too, huh. Well, somebody, Graves it looks like, had a big mad going for this poor bastard, and he knew it. Guess it's why he had so many guns around the house. That, and the speed angle. Though we didn't find much more than a couple of grams in the house, this looks like it'll probably shape up as some sort of drug-related deal, a disagreement between these maniacs of some sort. I know that's the angle that Watson is figuring."

"Is that your angle, too?"

He thumbed the edges of the file folder and made a sour face, as if he'd been chewing on something that disagreed with him and he was trying to decide whether to spit or swallow. "We checked with the phone company, and found that Dovie was talking to her record company guy, Carson Block, just after you left her place. We've talked to Block, and that puts her in the clear, and the woman who heard the shots, saw you drive up, and called 911 puts you in the clear, too. I was just wondering about something. Other than Otis being her sort-of boyfriend and manager as well as Richard James's publisher, plus your suspicions about Taylor and this Cyclone Davis character, could this have anything to do with the Rockin' Dog, far as you know?"

"I don't know," I said, trying to make it sound like the truth.

"Goddamn, I hope not," he said, letting out a big sigh.

"Seems like a musician can't die anymore without everybody trying to make a big scandal out of it, digging up the poor guy's dirty underwear for the next ten years . . ."

I just sat there, nodding my head as my mind wandered. Suddenly Lasko caught the look on my face, interrupted himself, and snarled, "Goddamn it, Martin, you're a lying son of a bitch."

"All right, I think it might have something to do with him."

"Well, you better tell me, Martin. Right now."

I told him everything I knew, starting with my first contact with Cyclone Davis. I told him everything that I'd experienced and most of the things I suspected. I watched as the skin around his eyes tightened when I told him about Otis beating Dovie. It took some doing, but I got it all out, and I felt better afterward.

But I left out the part about finding the tape.

Lasko leaned back in his chair and stared up at the ceiling when I was done. Finally he sighed and said, "But where does all that get us? What does it have to do with here and now, Martin?"

"Those cretins have been sucking around Dovie ever since they pulled her and Cokey off that mountain," I said. "Otis had Richard James's songs and he had Dovie. Graves and his buddies were all over Otis like stink on a skunk, and they're the ones who stole our van and gear and pushed it in the lake. Why they killed Otis, I don't know. Maybe it was just a drug business disagreement and maybe I hope it was. What I do know is that Dovie is skating on thin ice and she deserves better. I'm sorry I messed up your crime scene, but I promised that girl I'd help her, and that's all I've been trying to do."

He took a cigar out of his desk, rolled it around between his fingers, and thought about smoking it. Finally he put it down and took his hands away from it and said: "Look, Martin, I'm damn glad to know you, but on the other hand, you don't make my job any easier. The thing is, I'm damn mad that those boys would do that to you, and if they've been messing with Dovie, I'm damn mad about that, too. But Watson is different than me, in case you haven't noticed. He doesn't give a damn about your van, rock 'n' roll legends, or any of that. What really gets his goat is that some contractor's cement truck was stolen and a city building was broken into. Laws were broken, and criminals are running free, thumbing their noses at God and the chief of police and the ghost of his Texas Ranger daddy. You and those drug-dealing hillbillies are members of the same damn club in his book, and it would sure as shit make his day if he could bring you all in together."

"But I haven't done anything wrong."

"Maybe just not yet," he said. "Maybe you're just working up to a big ole doozy of a wrong. I got me a case of homicide here with a very good suspect I need to track down, and here you are trying to turn this thing into *Eddie and the Cruisers*. I don't want you fouling this thing up any more than you already have."

"Look, Lasko, I just wanna play my bass guitar, drive with my convertible top down, keep searching for the perfect taco, and mind my own business. Dovie's going to need help more than ever now, so maybe I can concentrate on doing what I can for her and you'll find Graves and he'll tell you why he wasted all that lead on Otis Taylor. Maybe Watson will bust the Kilton gang and we'll all live happily ever after."

He looked at me cockeyed and said, "Yeah, right. That'll be the goddamn day. Listen, let's go get your belongings back and then I'm gonna give you a ride back to your car. You're starting to get goofy on me."

I didn't argue with him. I was running on fumes and besides, I had something I wanted to show him.

The neighborhood was quiet once again when Lasko's pickup truck pulled up next to my car. The grass in the yards looked damp and the papers had been delivered. One was on Otis Taylor's doorstep, just the other side of the yellow crime-scene tape. I got out of the pickup, went over to my car, and got the search-party photo I'd lifted from Moreland's den. I took it over to Lasko's window and handed it over.

He held the photo under a map light, pushed his gimme cap back on his head and squinted, then handed the photo back. "So?" he said.

"Have you seen this photo before?"

He nodded. "The vegetarian writer? His mother gave me a copy."

"What do you make of it?"

He shrugged. "About what I did when I first saw it," he said. "A bunch of crazy rock 'n' rollers who got lucky and rescued some people who played with a guy they were big fans of. Far as the doctor goes, maybe he was a big fan like he told you, maybe he just liked hanging around drug dealers. Either way, it's no big deal. The only difference I see is now you say these Kilton guys paid for the Rockin' Dog's last album. I will tell you one thing, though, about the guy with the beard."

"I wish you would," I said. "He's the only one I can't ID. Moreland couldn't remember his name."

Lasko gave me a weird look. "The hell you say. That's what he told you, huh?"

"Yeah."

"Seems unlikely. That's his pilot, Sherm Caswell. The one who disappeared."

"Dang." The news made me a little dizzy. Or maybe there were other reasons. "Speaking of disappearing," I said.

"Yep, I know it. I'm starting to fade, too. But I still have a report to write before I head home to walk the dog. I'll make a few calls for you, Martin. I sure hate to see a lady get beat up and have a bunch of scuzzballs hounding her. Speaking of music, and I imagine you might have other things on your mind, but I don't suppose you reckon you and Dovie'll be playing Saturday night after all?"

"I don't know, Lasko," I said. "But if we are, I'll put you on the guest list."

"All right. Sure appreciate it." He smiled and shook my hand, then put the truck in gear and drove away. I got in my own car, fired it up, slipped it in gear, and headed for a place I could get some doughnuts and coffee to keep me going a little longer. Lasko was wrong about one thing, I did have music on my mind.

Back at the police station, they'd returned my personal belongings to me inside a large manila envelope. The envelope contained my car keys, pocket knife, wallet, some change, and "The Whole Damn Truth."

A light was on in Leo and Nadine's living room when I pulled up. The house was on Guadalupe, within walking distance of Antone's. Nadine was out, working the night shift at the diner, and Leo was listening to old Hi and Goldwax records, playing along with them on a beat-up Silvertone. Sometimes, if no one was around to remind him what time it was, Leo would stay up for days. Sometimes he did it even when people were around, much to their annoyance. Frankenstein, the sad-eyed Doberman curled up before Leo's bare feet, looked like a weary but uncomplaining member of that club.

Leo only had to hear the first verse of the song before he had the music figured out, playing along, slinging chords, and throwing in little lead fills. The critic in me thought the song sounded a bit weak, actually, but Leo only had one comment: "Yeah, yeah, no doubt about it. That's him. That's the Rockin' Dog, all right."

"Are you sure?" I said.

"Look at this," he said, fingering the chords with his middle finger and ring finger, using his little finger sparingly to alter the melody and his index finger to stab short, slightly spastic notes. The effect was unique—the awkward, eccentric fingering created a very spooky melody.

"You're only pecking at the thirds with your index finger," I said. "Otherwise, you're leaving them all out."

He nodded. "See, the Dog's index finger was gimpy from

the accident he had when he was a kid. But he'd already learned how to play chords, and he never really learned them any other way. He did make up a few of his own, but the important thing is, he taught himself to write songs without hardly any thirds in the chords. When he did throw one in, he mostly just stabbed at it with that gimpy finger. That's his style. But the vocal melodies most of the time have the usual flatted blues third in them, and sometimes the regular major third. So do the bass lines. You figured that out yourself, probably without knowing it, when we were jamming. That's why that ballad of Dovie's wasn't working out—I was playing normal chords, and they kind of clashed with the melodic thing she's developed after singing against Richard's funky chords for so long."

As the song faded out on the tape player, Leo said, "Mind if I make a copy?"

"Go ahead, but do me a favor."

"Like what?"

"Stash it away somewhere and don't tell anyone about it."

Leo just shrugged. "Cool."

I felt a strange sort of relief as we listened to the song again while Leo duped it to another cassette. The barefoot guitarist knew what he was talking about, and I was finally dealing with Dovie's mysteries on a playing field that I'd paid dues on. But, just for the record, I asked Leo to tell me one more time why he was so positive about his identification of the song's origins.

Leo smiled and picked up his guitar again and started riffing. "Because that's no way to play guitar, man. It's spastic. Sure, for one song or two, but nobody would intentionally copy that style. I mean, what for? Unless you're Richard James and you got that horny-dog howl to go with it, what's the use?"

I couldn't answer that question. I stuck around for another cup of coffee and half a doughnut with Leo, talking vaguely about the van and the slim chances that we'd be playing on Saturday night, and then went home.

■

I fed the cat and rewound the answering machine. There was a message from Ladonna, left a little after midnight, saying she was going to bed. Dovie had called shortly after that, after one of Lasko's detectives had been by to talk to her. She said not to worry about her, she was taking a pill and going to bed.

I put the tape in my cassette player and played it again. It still wasn't much of a song, but as a clue, it sounded spookier than ever.

Well I just can't shake the hand of fate
Spinning 'round a world of pain
You don't know what it's like
To be struck by lightning, and fall from the sky
They say rest in peace but you didn't die
Hearing those angels singing
A sweet, sweet song, but it's not for you . . .

Cold as a coffin nail, boiled in concrete
Buried alive in the blues
and you'll never know, baby you'll never know . . .
the whole damn truth.

Well I just can't shake the hand of fate . . .

It was just a demo tape, with one guitar track, bass, drums, and vocal, probably recorded at a low-end studio or a small multitrack home setup, probably an 8-track. The vocals and guitar both were drenched with reverb, giving an extra edge of loneliness to the song. I listened to the song over again, and tried to make out the words to the second verse. The first line was the same as the first line of the first verse. The second line was definitely different, but unintelligible. It sounded like the singer had tried to find a different rhyme for the word "fate" and had faltered at the last second. The rest of the lines were only slight variations from the first verse, sometimes with scatted nonsense syllables in the place of words. More than likely the composer had ad-libbed the whole song, probably intending to go back at a later date and put down a final version of the lyrics.

I didn't hear anything on the tape to indicate the song had been written or recorded after Richard James had been supposedly killed in that plane crash. If the song really was performed by Richard James, that meant that I was either listening to the voice of a dead man who'd predicted his fate ("struck by lightning, and fall from the sky") or someone who couldn't help writing a song about it after pretending to be dead.

Either way, I could see why Cyclone Davis had been worked up about it. But was it worth killing for?

Suddenly I realized I was too tired to care, too tired to think. I went to sleep.

The giant woman towered over me so that her head was in the clouds, and it was hard to tell if the great pouf of silvery white that framed her face was really her hair or a swollen bank of cumulus clouds bleached by the sun.

I knew we weren't in L.A., because the sky was too clean and the giant woman too pure, too uncorrupted-looking. She was beautiful, looking down at me with twin sparkles shooting out from both eyes like sun rays on polished chrome. Her lips were moving but they were too far up for me to hear what they were saying. I didn't mind. She was naked. Her breasts were as large as mountains, her navel could have held a lake full of morning dew, and between her legs was a lush, fragrant forest.

But then the cloud around her face turned a bluish gray, and I realized that a cloud far above her had blocked out the sun, making the air turn cold.

Cold and hard. I was in a small room made of concrete. The concrete had been freshly poured, and it was still damp and a weird sort of green. I tried to move but couldn't. It was like struggling in a pool of quicksand, only it wasn't quicksand, it was cement. It weighed a million tons and it was getting harder by the second.

That was when I noticed Cyclone Davis. He was a few feet away from me, using a guitar pick to scratch a message in the damp cement. He turned around and said, "You know what it's like to be hit by lightning and fall from the sky? You hear people say rest in peace but you didn't die. Hearing those angels singing a sweet, sweet song, but not for you. It's like being boiled, man, boiled in concrete."

I tried to ask him to help me but my lips wouldn't move.

He cocked a thumb up at the sky and said, "I know a thing or two about her that'd curl your hair."

I struggled with the sea of cement, trying to get closer to him so I wouldn't miss a word of the secret. His lips moved, but the cement was getting harder and heavier and sucking me down, making the sound travel slower and slower, and I knew that by the time the words reached me, the cement would have turned to stone and so would I.

I woke up with a gnawing sensation in my stomach. I was thirsty. I got up, shaky, and got a glass of water. I drank it down, drew another, and drank that one down, too. I still felt raw and disjointed. There was nothing to eat in the fridge, and I didn't think food would do any good, anyway.

I put the tape on to play again and lay down on the couch. The song didn't seem to mean anything to me then. I felt numb all over and began to wonder if I was actually still asleep. When I pinched myself, I hardly felt anything. I closed my eyes.

The giant woman was more beautiful than ever as she towered over me, but I was just a speck at her feet. I shouted up to her, but she couldn't hear me. She was singing.

Finally I realized that if I honked my horn, maybe I could get a message up to her. It turned out that I was behind the wheel of the van. But the horn wouldn't work. There was someone in the passenger seat. I reached out to get his attention, and that was when I noticed the passenger was Cyclone Davis, sweating up a storm, sucking down seven 'n seven like it was going out of style, reciting another litany of dead musical legends.

"Al Jackson, shot by a woman! Sam Cooke, shot down again! That guy from Tower of Power, drug deal gone bad! Good God! The Big Bopper, plane crash! Patsy Cline, same damn thing! Stevie Ray Vaughan, helicopter crash in the fog! Darby Crash, heroin got him! George Scott, courtesy of Khomeini, Iranian skag glut! Robert Johnson, king of the Delta blues singers, poisoned by a jealous man! Richard James, deader than all of 'em, and madder than Malcolm X!!!!"

I couldn't get his attention, and I couldn't move my arms anymore, anyway. I couldn't move my legs, I couldn't even breathe. The van was filling up with concrete, pouring in through the windshield, instantly hard, instantly cold.

Instant legend.

Instant tombstone.

From the roof of the van came the percussive sound of rain-drops, fat and heavy. I looked out the window and peered up into the face of the giant woman. She wasn't singing anymore.

She was crying.

15

I was still asleep when Ladonna came over during her lunch break. She let herself in with her key, tiptoed back to my bedroom, and woke me up with the sweetest kind of wake-up call there is. Afterward, I lit a cigarette and watched her put her clothes back on.

"Sure you wanna do that?" I said.

She smiled. "I guess the guys at work wouldn't mind, but there's a new girl on the reception desk, and I don't think she'd understand."

"Uh huh. Have to make a good impression. You sure laid one on me."

She came over and gave me a big wet kiss, gently caressing the new bumps Graves had put on my head. "You look like hell, Martin. Do you realize that?"

"I'd be surprised if I didn't. Yesterday was a big day."

She nodded and resumed dressing. Panties, garter belt, stockings, skirt. She usually wore a bra, but not today. "I used to think you got in a lot of trouble when it was just you and the boys. Now it seems like those were the calm old days."

"Things will settle down," I said. "I just need to get some new answers to some old questions."

She pulled her blouse over her head and straightened out her skirt, buckled a wide brown suede belt and stepped into her shoes. She checked her hair in the mirror, shook her head a bit, fluffed it up with her fingertips, then shook her head again. Her breasts jiggled when she did that. I wanted her to do it again, but her hair was now perfect and the show was over. After touching up her lipstick, she noticed the books on the dresser, the ones I'd borrowed from Vick Travis on legendary R&B artists.

"Is our favorite chanteuse mentioned in these?" she said.

"There's not much mention of her in those," I said. "*That Texas Thang* is the only one written recently enough to include both Richard and Dovie."

After fanning through Peter Guralnick's excellent *Sweet Soul Music,* she picked up B.B. Berry's *That Texas Thang* and opened it to the chapter I had marked, the one on Richard James. When I saw her frown, I knew she was looking at the page with the photo of the plane wreckage. "What a nightmare that must have been," she said.

"Yeah, she's been through a lot." I hadn't told her about Dovie's latest revelations about being raped by Richard's bass player.

"And the guys that have been causing you trouble," she said as she put the book back on the dresser, "are they the same six guys it mentions in there, the ones who rescued her?"

"Uh huh. That's them in the photo on the dresser. It was taken at St. Ascot, right after they rescued Dovie and Cokey. After the picture was taken, they got in Moreland's plane and whisked Dovie and Cokey back here for treatment. They were in pretty miserable shape."

She picked up the photo, frowned at it, and put it back on the dresser, then came over and sat on the edge of the bed.

"Speaking of miserable," she said, putting her index finger on my mouth, then slowly tracing a line down my chin, my throat, and chest, "You know, Martin, I've got an eight-year-old boy who has no father, but he looks up to you. It would make me kind of miserable if you weren't around anymore for him to look up to. He might start to wonder about his mother. You know, like if something was wrong with me since the men I love tend to disappear on him. He was too young to understand when his father died, but he's older and smarter now. Maybe not enough to understand the reason you weren't around anymore, but old enough and smart enough to start wondering about me. And I don't want that."

Her fingernail was now digging into my navel. The sensation was a strange mixture of pleasure and pain. "I get the message," I said. "I don't wanna be miserable, either."

"Good. Write songs about it, play other people's songs about it, but don't go looking for it so you have to live it."

"Every day I have the blues."

"Every day you're full of *chorizo*," she said leaning down to kiss me again. "But I love you anyway."

"Me, too." I gave her one for the road and she left.

I was in the shower, thinking about Ladonna, when something struck me. I finished up quickly, toweled off, and went back to the bedroom, doing a little quick addition as I threw on a pair of pants and a shirt. She'd asked about the six guys in the search party. I only knew about five: The pilot, Sherm Caswell, currently among the disappeared, and Chester White made two. Nubby Maxwell, Red Fred, and Graves made five. I picked up the photo I'd glommed from Moreland, did a quick head count, leaving out Dovie and Cokey.

Five people, not six.

I picked up the book Ladonna had been looking at and flipped to the account of the plane crash. It said:

The Rockin' Dog howled for the last time on February 3, 1984, when his private plane went down between White Cap Mountain and St. Ascot. Richard James and his three-piece backing band, the Number Sevens, had just played a gig in Grand Junction, Colorado, with Chubby Checker and they were reportedly anxious to arrive in Denver. An hour after takeoff, however, after passing over the small ski community of St. Ascot, the pilot reported having engine trouble. He attempted to turn back, inadvertently steering the plane into a sudden fierce storm, and shortly thereafter crash-landed high up on a snowy mountain pass.

The pilot was killed instantly, but Richard, Dovie de Carlo, bassist Preston Drake, and drummer Cokey Kossmeyer survived the initial impact. For twelve days, while the Civil Air Patrol and several volunteer groups fought intermittent storms to search for the plane (usually in the wrong area, as it turned out, since the pilot had been lost when he'd last made radio contact), the group huddled inside the wrecked fuselage, subsisting on the backstage deli tray from the Chubby Checker gig and various road snacks. Finally Richard and Preston decided to try climbing down the mountain to get help, leaving Dovie back in the plane to look after Cokey. Shortly after Richard and Preston started down the mountainside, the earth began to rumble.

"It's a shame they didn't stay back at the plane," said U.S. Forestry spokesman Erwin Jones. "Even a well-equipped professional climber wouldn't stand a chance in hell making it down that mountain in these conditions, even if they *had* escaped the avalanches." On February 18 Dovie and Cokey were rescued by a group of *six volunteers* from Austin. Richard and Preston weren't so lucky. Their bodies were never found.

So the Rockin' Dog was cheated out of his comeback by a plane crash that occurred exactly 25 years after a similar tragedy ended the career of his biggest idol, Buddy Holly. Six weeks after the crash, more than five hundred fans attended memorial services in Austin, the biggest crowd the Dog had seen for way too many years. Richard and Preston were both 29.

After being given first aid at St. Ascot, Dovie and Cokey were flown back to Austin. The identities of the mysterious rescue team were not released. A spokesman for the group said that they "prefer remaining anonymous."

But anonymous is one thing that Dovie de Carlo hasn't been in the years since the crash. She has refused to talk about the tragedy, even though it's brought her the fame and success that the Rockin' Dog was unable to reclaim, and her albums of his songs—*These Walls, Broke Down in Paradise,* and *Cry, Cry, & Cry Again*—have all gone solid gold.

Everybody loves a survivor.

I skipped through the rest of the chapter. Opposite the title page was a shot of Richard James posing between giant display bottles of Seagram's 7 and 7-Up. The caption said: "The Rockin' Dog in Heaven? James poses here with the makings of his favorite drink, Seven 'n' Seven, a cocktail he claimed made his tail wag and his guitar howl."

The text on the next few pages was interspersed with several photos of James onstage with various band configurations, and one of Dovie that was taken at Richard's memorial services. There were two photos of the crash site, with FAA inspectors combing the wreckage. But there was no photo like the one I'd taken from Moreland's den.

I skimmed over the biographical account. Little Ricky James Gilmore had been the only child of an army major and, like Dovie's family, had moved dozens of times before settling in San Antonio, Texas, in the late sixties. And, like Dovie's mother, Richard's mom had also had been a Bible-toter. Mrs. Gilmore had reportedly bought her son his first guitar so he could learn spiritual songs to perform on church-sponsored camping trips. But Richard broke a finger playing baseball and quit taking lessons, much to his mom's disappointment.

When he was sixteen, Richard discovered Buddy Holly, traded the acoustic in for a Stratocaster, and set about teaching himself all of the West Texas rocker's songs. After graduating from high school, Richard's parents enrolled him in TLC (Texas

Lutheran College), but he spent most of his first semester hitch-hiking to the East Side of Austin, where he sought the tutelage of black blues musicians and big-chested women, who offered the good-looking boy TLC of a different sort. He learned a lot that semester, none of it from books or lectures.

Neither Richard nor his parents saw any reason to try for a second semester, so he packed his bags and drifted for several years, touching down in Memphis, New Orleans, Lafayette, Macon, Cincinnati, and a half dozen other places, working menial-labor jobs during the day, roaming the clubs at night. He came back to San Antonio in 1976 for his father's funeral and looked up some of the musicians he'd hung with in Austin during his abbreviated college days. When Richard popped into a late-night jam session at the One Knight, he showed his ex-mentors what he'd learned while he was gone: he sang every Jerry Lee Lewis, Al Green, Little Richard, and O. V. Wright song the guys could think of. Richard could also sing just like his favorite, Buddy Holly, though his natural singing voice, and the style he was to become known for, sounded like a unique blend of Jerry Lee Lewis and Howlin' Wolf. Richard bought his own microphone and a pair of snakeskin boots the next day, and a band was born.

Just a few weeks later, the band moved to Houston, rented an apartment, and started playing clubs. They cut a demo at a studio, and a couple of months later the small-appliance-store owner who owned the studio signed them to a contract and put out their debut album on his own label, named after his daughter, Loisann.

The record got quite a bit of airplay on southern radio. The band sharpened its chops playing the rowdy, often dangerous circuit of clubs that stretched between east Texas on through Louisiana, Mississippi, Alabama, Georgia, Florida, the Caro-linas, Virginia, Ohio, and Missouri, changing its name a half dozen times before settling on The Hellhounds. Along with the name changes, personnel came and went, too, and a year after the band had moved to Houston, Richard was the only original member. After leaving the band, the original guitar player, L-Tone Rogers, had a regional solo hit with an instrumental called "Sugar Bear" (and a dark fable about a swamp zombie called "Razor Blade Man" on the flip side) on the Loisann label. L-Tone also continued to work with Richard off and on over the years.

By the time the punk invasion had hit in full force in the late seventies, the kids with spiked hair and ripped T-shirts were coming back from the record store with a new album by Richard "the Rockin' Dog" James & the Hellhounds in the same bag with the Sex Pistols, The Damned, and Nick Lowe. Richard James wasn't punk any more than Nick Lowe was, but in the decade of Led Zeppelin, the Eagles, Yes, and *Saturday Night Fever,* he was a breath of fresh air. A rip-snorting, hog callin' blast of it.

It was just the blues, but it was the blues of a hot-wired white boy with the right combination of grit and charm to make those classic three chords sound fresh again for awhile. In '78 and '79, Richard had several songs that put sparks in the charts— "Six Foot Snake in Tight Blue Jeans," "Do the Dog," and "Train to Nowhere." He bought a '59 Eldorado and spent seven grand restoring it to showroom condition. He also bought a house for his mother in Lubbock, a town that, being the hometown of his idol, Buddy Holly, was a sort of rock 'n' roll mecca for him.

In the early eighties, disco faded and so did most of the seventies dinosaur rock groups. New wave became new music or just music, and MTV came on line, perverting more young minds in a couple of hours than Alan Freed had in a lifetime. Rock 'n' roll hadn't just sold out to the Establishment, it *was* the Establishment. At least once a year, a prominent critic would pop up and claim that rock was dead; hardly anyone seemed to think the claim was worth debating anymore.

As the decade turned, Richard found himself without a record deal. Following the success of his early independent records, he'd signed with one of the major labels, but sales were disappointing, and he was unceremoniously dropped. He hung around Austin and Lubbock a lot, but most people seemed to think his act hadn't aged very well.

Around 1982, he put out another album. Financed and produced by James (with semidiscreet financial backing from the Kilton gang), it was a bomb. He kept playing, but the venues kept getting smaller and smaller. February 3, 1984, Richard James's career ended when his plane went down on a mountainside near St. Ascot, Colorado, twenty-five years to the day that Buddy Holly's plane crashed in a corn field near Mason City, Iowa.

Some people had said he was on his way back.

I flipped through the rest of the chapter, which essayed the Dog's influence on subsequent generations of blues rockers, which was thought to be considerable. Typical rock journalism stuff—it didn't interest me. I wanted to know more about the mysterious rescue party.

The last bit of information on the rescue was at the end of the chapter. As I already knew, L-Tone Rogers had been slated to perform with Richard in Denver the night after the plane crash. After hearing that the Dog's plane was lost, L-Tone drove up to St. Ascot to hang out with the various search parties, and it just so happened that he was the only person on the field when the search party's helicopter landed, with Dovie and Cokey inside. The last paragraph ended with a quote from the guitar player:

I got to give old Cokey and Dovie a hug, then one of the boys give me the news about the Dog and the others. Next thing I know, they up in that plane and they outta here. I just stood there crying. Musta cried for a week straight.

I looked at the photo from Moreland's den. There were only five men in the photo accompanying Dovie and Cokey, but the book said there were *six volunteers*. Dovie had told me herself that there were six men in the search party. Maybe the sixth guy was the one who took the photo. Maybe they'd gotten L-Tone to take the photo, maybe the author of the book had made a mistake. Maybe Dovie made a mistake.

Maybe the sixth man was Otis Taylor.

I had a hankering to talk to L-Tone again. I called the barbecue joint he'd been playing at. They said he wasn't playing there anymore. No one knew where he was staying, either. The phone directory had no listing for L-Tone Rogers, and I wasn't surprised.

I went out and picked up the newspaper. I pulled out the club listings, but didn't find L-Tone's name anywhere.

I thought about calling some club owners and booking agents, but one of the ads in the paper distracted me completely. It was the Continental Club ad. Just as Ladonna had reported, it said:

SATURDAY NIGHT

WELCOME HOME

AUSTIN'S OWN

DOVIE DE CARLO

Wayne, who managed the Continental Club and had been involved with the Austin music scene almost as long as I had, might know where I could find L-Tone. Clifford Antone was a good possibility, too, but I needed to call Wayne anyway to yell at him about breaching our agreement about advertising the gig. But first I had to talk to Dovie. If we weren't doing the gig anyway, I'd have to apologize to Wayne instead of chewing him out about the ad screwup. But Dovie wasn't answering her phone.

I called Billy and got his answering machine. I called Leo, no answer. I started to dial Ray's number but hung up when someone started knocking on the door.

It was Ray.

"I was just calling you," I said.

Ray sauntered in and glanced around the apartment. Apparently he saw nothing that interested him. "Well, there's no need for that now since I'm here," he said. "How's your head?"

"Fine, I guess. You heard about last night?"

He nodded. "And the van situation, also."

"The van, yeah. You didn't lose anything, did you?"

He shook his head. "But I was just wondering if anyone had bothered to talk to George at the pool hall."

"I don't know. Why?"

"Because"—his pencil-thin mustache rose, snakelike, above the corners of his mouth—"as you may know, George often lets down-on-their-luck types sleep in the back. No more than one at a time, mind you, but he takes them in for a week or so, allowing them to mop up for room and board. Maybe there was someone there night before last and he saw or heard something."

I nodded. "The police might have thought of that."

"Doesn't matter," he said smugly. "George wouldn't tell the police because he doesn't want them to know he has transients sleeping in his pool hall. But he'll tell me. I'm about to drive past there now, so I thought I'd stop and ask."

"That's swell of you, Ray."

"Think nothing of it. You suspect the hillbillies?"

I nodded.

"You know how I feel about them. Why were you going to call me?"

I told him to hang on a minute while I went back to get the search-party photo. I handed it to him and asked if he recognized any of the Kilton gang from the gigs he'd played with Richard.

"It's been a long time, Martin," he said. "But I think I can safely say that four of these people were, at one time or another, with the hillbillies."

"Who are you leaving out besides Dovie and Cokey?"

"This one," he said. "The fellow with the nice jacket and the toothpaste commercial grin. Looks like a real poseur."

"He's a doctor, Chester White."

Ray ran a finger under his chin and said, "Chester White?"

"You know him?"

He shook his head. "No, but isn't that the name for a breed of pig?"

I thought about it. "You might be right, Ray."

"Of course I'm right. Look it up in the dictionary. Listen, I need to be going. I've a lot to do, and Kate is waiting in the car."

"One more thing," I said as he turned to leave. "You never said if there was a white-haired guy, real bony, real pale, hanging around with the hillbillies back then, did you?"

"No I didn't. I do think I'd remember someone like that. Sounds even more like a ghost than your average speed freak."

He opened the door and gave a little finger waggle as he went out. After he was gone, I got out my Webster's Ninth and looked for Chester White.

Ray was right. Chester White was a breed of pig.

I put the rest of my clothes on and made a pot of espresso. I drank the espresso and ate a bowl of oatmeal with the cat on my lap while I called Dovie again. No answer. I tried Billy and Leo again, still no luck. Lasko wasn't in.

I looked at B.B. Berry's bio on the back flap of *That Texas Thang*. It said that he lived in Santa Monica, California, and wrote for the *L.A. Weekly*. I called directory assistance and got his phone number. I called it, but it was disconnected. I called the *Weekly,* but no one there could help me. I left a message.

I could do a quick credit check on Berry down at the collection agency, but if I went down there, I'd have to put up with Jack Green, and I wasn't in the mood. But I did call the agency and leave a message with one of the collectors, saying that something had come up and I wouldn't be in for awhile. As if that would be a surprise.

I let the phone cool down while I finished the espresso. The cat stayed on my lap, rubbing against my hands whenever they came within range. When I petted him on his head or back, he purred, when I scratched the area just above his tail, he meowed.

When the phone rang, he jumped off my lap, and when I recognized the voice on the other end, my heart nearly jumped out of my chest.

"This' Dolph Moreland calling," said the heavy, gritty drawl. "I's wonderin' if you and me might have a little talk?"

16

"Looks like somebody tried to hammer you into the ground headfirst, son," said Moreland as he poured me a glass of ice tea from a pitcher and got comfortable in his lawn chair.

I didn't answer. We were in his backyard. I was sitting in the tractor seat chair again, and somewhere, a long way off, the dog was barking. An occasional breeze brought with it the scent of fire.

"What I want you to know, old Neville wouldn't kill that boy," he said.

"How about mistaking my head for a tent stake? I guess I just hallucinated that from all the glue I've been sniffing."

Moreland grinned. "Nope, I reckon it's a fact he did at that."

"If he didn't kill Otis, what's he hiding out for?"

"I 'magine he's got his reasons."

"Yeah, I'm sure he does. Like you've got reasons for forgetting the name of Sherm Caswell, a guy who used to be your pilot."

Moreland frowned and scraped his jaw with his thumb. "They say you can't say something nice, don't say nothin'. Fella runs off like that, I got no reason to say anything 'bout him at all. One day he's just gone, you know, just up and gone."

"Yeah, around the time that writer had the hunting accident."

He puckered his mouth as if he'd just bitten a piece of gristle. "You know, you and me ain't gonna have much of a talk here if you're gonna accuse me of lyin' ever' time I open my mouth."

"Did you know Sherm left a message on the writer's answering machine the day before the kid was killed?"

"Don't recall hearing 'bout that," he said.

"All right," I said, "let's try this: How many guys were in that search party?"

"Five, I reckon. I wasn't here when they left, and I's out in the pasture when they first got back. Ain't five how many's in that photo you swiped from me?"

"Who flew the helicopter?"

"I 'magine Sherm did. He had a license for that, too. Learned how in the army."

I didn't say anything. The dog kept barking in the distance, and the fire smell lingered, even though the breeze had died out.

Moreland said, "Son, I just can't do right by you, can I?"

"Maybe it's not you, it's the people who work for you, and you keep taking up for them. But then that just brings it back to you again, doesn't it?"

"Son, lemme tell you something. I'm kinda simple an' I got my own way of lookin' at things. I grew up around people who did everything for themselves. Grow your own food, shit in the woods when you feel like it. When they asked me, I give my country ten years. Killed a lot of the enemy, did whatever else they asked. Then I come home to this ranch to grow crops and raise cows, like my daddy did after he come home from the war he fought. Way I see it, what I do out here is my own damn business. Same with the boys who work for me."

"But the cops in the county next door don't seem to appreciate your damn business."

"Hell with them. Look here, I'm not sayin' those boys ever did make speed up there in that thicket, but if they did, so the hell what? My C.O. used to hand it out to us like peanuts. Wasn't any talk about it being a bad thing back then. My boys—say they did make the stuff—sure as hell didn't force it on anybody. What people do with their own life is their business, in my book. And if some fellas make a livin' off it, well, that's the American way, ain't it?"

"Yeah, they're just a bunch of red, white, and blue teddy bears."

"Look here, son, I ain't gonna beat around the bush with you. I know those old boys got a little outta hand with you, an' I'd like to make it up to ya. You seem like a pretty decent fella, an' I 'magine you'd agree with me that poor gal's been through enough. That plane crash would be enough to knock anybody outta kilter for life, but then that fella she was seein' out in California that old Taylor was worked up about gets himself shot. Now old Taylor went an' got his own head blowed off. You claim he used to play rough with her. Well, now that's over. Seems like you'd be kinda glad."

"I'm not shedding any tears. But somebody somewhere might be."

"I heard he didn't have no folks," Moreland said.

"Maybe your boys'll miss him. Maybe they'll just keep hanging around Dovie, and I wouldn't like that."

Moreland nodded. "Uh huh, well I don't think that's gonna happen. If I gave you my word that they're gonna have plenty of work 'round here to keep 'em outta trouble, an' I'd be much obliged to ya if you didn't keep doggin' 'round this thang, how'd that be, son?"

"How much obliged?"

"How's 'bout I bought you a new van? I don't know much 'bout guitars an' what all you boys use, but I could throw in a little extra, enough so's you'd be better off than you started."

"Are you serious?"

"Hell yeah, son. Hell, I could write you a damn check right now, if you's agreeable."

I thought about that for a bit, then said, "Agreeable to what?

Why do I get the feeling you're leaving something out of this deal?"

"You tell me, son. There something you'd like to throw on the table?"

I was hoping he'd say he wanted the tape back, but he didn't. "So you just want me to mind my own business from now on. Forget about all this, and you'll buy me a new van?"

He nodded.

I stood up. "No deal, Mr. Moreland. Your price is too low and too high at the same time. And maybe you haven't lied to me, but there are things you're not telling me. I'm gonna keep looking into this thing." I took a step back as the dog came loping up and added, "I don't think it'd be wise for you to try to stop me, either."

Moreland took the dog's head in his hands and kneaded it roughly. The dog rolled his eyes and panted, bathing the rancher's hands with saliva. Moreland said, "Goddammit son, I just can't do right by you, can I?"

"I think you've been shitting in your own woods too long, Mr. Moreland."

His expression soured. "You don't need to be lookin' over your shoulder for me, son. I had to try, is all. I just hate to see that poor gal put through any more trouble. Just bear that in mind, an' someday mebbe you'll see how I was right. Now go on an' git outta here, them cows wanna be fed an' daylight's wastin'."

I went out through the gate and got in the Ghia and drove away. When I got to the rise of the hill on the county road, I looked back in the mirror. The rancher was in his pickup, driving in the direction of the old landing strip. Rising up from the woods beyond it was a plume of dark smoke. It looked like the smoke might be coming from the lime pit.

17

The nurse came back out on Oak Tree's back terrace and gave
me a cheery wink as she wiped Cokey's face with a damp cloth.
The terrace overlooked several acres of green grass, shrubbery,
fountains, and trees. Birds frolicked in the spray of the fountains, pecking at the pecans on the ground, squawking. The
former drummer for Richard James had a smile on his face as
his glassy eyes appeared to drink it all in. But he'd been smiling
when the nurse had wheeled him out to the terrace, and his
expression hadn't changed in the interim.

"Sometimes he points to the birds," she said. "We bought
him a bird book once and he learned to recognize some of them
by name. But I guess he got tired of that. You're Martin Fender,
the bass player, aren't you?"

I nodded. Cokey just sat there, his mouth curled up at the
edges. But it was a bland expression, like the face of a person
sleeping with eyes open, like a video image frozen in the pause
mode. His clothes hung slack and shapeless.

"Did you and Cokey used to play together?"

"No. Does he ever communicate?"

She patted the drummer's shoulder and shook her head. "Not
really. Not, uhm . . . no, just not really."

I'd tried talking to him when she'd first brought him out, but had no luck. I got down on one knee and tried again. "Cokey, I'm a friend of Dovie's," I said. "Remember Dovie?"

A grackle swooped down and landed just below the terrace. The big black bird strutted over to a pecan on the ground, pecked at it, and strutted around it cockily, like a crack dealer commanding his street corner. Cokey raised a finger and said, "Bird."

I tried again. "Dovie, Cokey. Remember Dovie?"

"Bird."

The nurse patted my shoulder this time. When I looked up, she just smiled and shook her head. "I don't want you to upset him."

"What usually upsets him?"

"All sorts of things. Doors slamming, certain episodes of *Gilligan's Island,* jets flying overhead, eating."

"Eating upsets him?"

She laughed. "I wish I had that problem. I've got it the other way around, I guess."

"You look remarkably well balanced to me."

"Why, thank you. And I might say that you yourself look very nutritious—" Her face went pink as she caught herself. "No, I mean—"

"Don't say a word," I said. "And thanks." I took the former drummer's cool, soft hand and squeezed it. "Good-bye, Cokey."

For a moment there seemed to be a glint of recognition in his eyes. His smile widened.

"Cokey?" I said.

"Bird."

18

Though it was late October, the early evening sun seemed to pour on a little extra something for the nine-to-fivers' commute home. I didn't like it any more than they did and had no particular reason to put up with it, so I picked up an order of flour tacos at Tamale House and went home. After feeding the cat, I checked the answering machine. There was a message from Billy saying something about seeing me tonight, which was odd. I guessed that he meant he thought we were rehearsing, which seemed like a remote possibility, but then, the music business is fueled by remote possibilities, so I called Dovie. Once again, there was no answer. There was a message from Lasko, saying to give him a call. I did, but he was out. The next message was from Jack at the collection agency, saying something about getting together so we could come up with a work schedule. I fast-forwarded to the last message, which was from Carson Block. He was in town, at the Crest, formerly the Sheraton Crest, on Town Lake.

Now *there* was someone I wanted to talk to, I thought to myself as I shut the machine off. A guy who talks me into a gig, casually mentioning something about annoying creeps who hang around Dovie in Austin . . . But he wasn't in his room.

Immediately after I hung up the phone, it rang.

"Hey, fucker—" said the familiar raspy voice. "You think you're smarter than me, huh?"

"You really want me to answer that, Nate?"

"Think again, Martin. You people think you can keep going on taking things out of my head and claiming they're your own, you're gonna be sorry, pal."

"I assume you mean the tape?"

"Quit trying to be cute, man. I'm serious. I'm sick of being ripped off, hearing my songs on the radio but someone else gets the credit and the money for them. It's like after people get famous all these naked pictures of them come out in *Playboy,* taken back when they were nobodies, when they were willing to sell their soul for a nickel and throw in their body for free to get a break. But I got ripped off, Martin, 'cause I didn't sell my soul, I just got ripped off for it and never got a damn break. But you can't get away with that forever, you know."

"I would imagine there's a law against it, Nate. Why don't you hire a lawyer? Or better yet, go see a doctor. You need help, man."

He laughed. The laugh degenerated into a cough, and the cough into a torrent of words. "Man, don't try humoring me, OK? You can't steal somebody's soul 'cause that pisses off the man upstairs, you dig? It's against the laws of the universe, and it's a serious fucking crime. A capital crime, pal. So you better wise up, 'cause I'm righteous, I'm bad, I'm God's detective, armed and dangerous and on a mission for justice. You can't keep ripping me off, man. I'm everywhere, watching you, all over your ass. I'm in your telephone right now, man, slipping through the wires, and if you don't gimme back what's mine, I'm gonna drill a hole right into your head."

"Speaking of heads, Nate," I said, "How about cooking me up an order of onion rings in that deep vat fryer you're wearing for a hat?"

"You'll be sorry, Martin. I warned you, man. I warned you and—"

"Come and get me, asshole," I said, and slammed the phone down on God's detective's ear.

I called Wayne at home, but his answering machine said he was at the club. I called the club, but someone was testing the p.a. system and whenever I asked to speak to *Wayne,* the person on the other end apparently thought I'd asked who was *playing* tonight, because she just kept saying, "Dot and the Leopard Men, Dot and the Leopard Men. Come see 'em."

I was sure I had better things to do. I plopped down on the couch with my tacos and started throwing them in my face. They were as spicy and greasy as ever. I was well into the second one when I noticed that I'd left the cassette player on this morning, with the tape of "The Whole Damn Truth" still in the compartment. I laughed semi-deliriously at the situation: God's detective was so far ahead of me that he knew better than to break into my apartment again and look for that tape in the most obvious place.

And I'd fallen asleep while listening to it. Either it was a real lame song, especially for one that had caused so much trouble, or I wasn't getting enough rest.

I put the tape back on play again, then went back to the couch and stretched out. The same spooky chords jangled out, the same spooky voice drawled away like the voice of a lonely man in a cold marble cavern. Right away I started feeling very light, very rubbery.

Maybe I was just bored with the song. Why did it have to mean anything? My brain was tired. And who were Dot and the Leopard Men, and why should I care?

I wasn't really in this one, not physically. I was more of an observer, but the people in the dream knew I was there. Somehow.

The giant woman was still naked, still beautiful, but I was sort of hovering over her, above the scene. She sat on the ground with her legs crossed, and her skin, though as smooth and flawless as polished marble, was covered with leopard spots. The spots made her even more alluring, more mysterious. Tiny men swarmed over her, trying to steal the spots, and she wasn't doing anything about it.

I watched helplessly as one of the tiny men climbed up her face, pried open her mouth, and crawled inside.

At her feet was the familiar chunky outline topped off with a greasy pompadour, wearing the same mechanic's coveralls as when I'd met him shortly before his demise. His back was turned to me, and he was bent over, struggling with something. I changed perspectives—something that seemed quite normal at the time, sort of like going to another camera shot on a movie set—and viewed him from the opposite angle. From this viewpoint, I was able to see that he was struggling to pull a Stratocaster from the pool of concrete that he, too, was enmired in up to his knees.

"You don't know what it's like, do ya," he drawled, "to be boiled in concrete."

I gave no answer. I was only an observer.

Finally the guitar came loose, clumps of greenish gray muck still stuck to it, like gore clinging to a limb that's been wrenched from its socket. The big man in the mechanic's coveralls made a Pete Townsend windmill circuit with his arm, slashing out an E chord so loud that stars dropped from the sky, mountains fell, and oceans sloshed out of their bowls.

"I could tell you a thing or two about her that'd curl your hair," he snarled. Then he slashed out another thunderous E chord, threw his head back, and let out a bloodcurdling primeval howl that shattered all the crystal ware in Neiman-Marcus, exploded all the silicone breast implants in Beverly Hills, and set fire to all the motorcycle jackets on Hollywood Boulevard.

Suddenly I was no longer an observer. I was clammy flesh cold blood prickly skin. The man with the guitar wasn't Cyclone Davis.

He was Richard James.

19

It was dark outside when I opened my eyes. The bag the tacos had been in was on the floor, and little balls of chewed-up flour tortilla and taco stuffing were scattered in a radius of several feet around the striped mound lying passed out on his back next to the bag. Michael was sitting on the floor nearby, thumping on my bass guitar, and Ladonna was standing in the middle of the room, taking in the scene. She was wearing a short, tight-fitting cocktail dress, a strand of pearls, and the usual hoop earrings.

"What time is it?" I said.

"A little after ten," she said.

"You're dressed to go out."

"Uh huh. Don't you think you should be, too?"

I straightened up and thought about standing. I was still groggy, half expecting a giant naked woman with leopard spots to tell me what was going on. "I guess so," I said. "Where are we going?"

"To see Dot and the Leopard Men," said Michael. He looked very serious, holding my bass guitar, which was almost as big as he was.

"They any good?" I said.

Michael just smiled and thumped on the bass strings. Ladonna said, "I don't know, but I heard the bass player's pretty good."

"I'm sorry, man," said Billy. "But I thought Leo talked to you and Leo thought I talked to you."

We were in the dressing room at the Continental Club. Leo was back in the corner adjusting the tuning on a '59 Stratocaster with a custom finish of leopard spots. Billy was changing the head on a snare drum. Wayne was out in the club, watching the opening act, Ray was on his way, and Carson was bringing Dovie.

There was no need to chastise Wayne about the advertising for tomorrow night's gig. While I was out at Moreland's ranch, Dovie and the guys had gotten together. She explained to them that the thing with the van wasn't her fault, but she'd square it with us. Carson wanted to see the band, Dovie wanted to play to take her mind off things, and Billy and Leo were in a similar frame of mind, so all parties had decided that the best thing to do was to move the gig up a day and perform under the name of Dot and the Leopard Men.

"It's OK," I said. "Lucky for me Ladonna ran into Nadine at the supermarket and found out in time to come over and wake me up. But it's hard to believe Dovie would want to play tonight."

Billy shrugged. "It was her idea, and I've got no particular objection, especially if this is the end of all that bullshit with Otis and his pals. You're not too weirded out to play, are you?"

"No. Makes as much sense as anything else does around here."

"Well, whatever, and at least we're making money. Lasko's on the guest list, and I think there's a couple of undercover cops out there, too, but I don't think they're with him."

Billy was probably right. Lasko would be here for the music, and the others would be here because Watson sent them. "What about the gear?"

"We're using some of the opening band's stuff," he said.

"They got an Ampeg SVT bass rig, and I brought my kit over from the studio and Leo brought one of his amps from home. OK?"

I nodded and sipped some of my drink. It was bar scotch, but it would do. "No roadies?"

Leo looked up from his guitar and said, "Nick and Steve are out of town with Lou Ann Barton tonight, so a couple of guys from the club will set the stage for us and pitch in if somebody breaks a string or something. The house guy's running the board. He's pretty good, he's done Lou Ann, the T-Birds, Johnny Reno, and a lot of other bands like us, so I trust him."

"What about the set list?" I said.

"Dovie said to play a few songs on our own, then she'll get up and do the six we worked up with her," said Leo. "After that, I guess we'll just see what happens."

"Oh yeah," said Billy as he gave the snare a good whack, then tightened a lug. "I put Darlene Barnes on the guest list for you."

"Darlene Barnes?"

"Yeah, she said Lasko said it would be all right."

"What, is she a cop?"

"No, flight attendant. For Continental."

I thought about that for a moment. Billy whacked on his snare some more. Leo gave the Strat a final adjustment and said, "You wanna use this tuner, Martin?"

I strapped on my Danelectro bass and changed places with him. I'd brought the P-bass along, too, but I'd decided to use the Danelectro for the gig. Just as I sat down and got hooked up to the tuner, a big-eyed blonde in acid wash jeans appeared in the doorway.

"Martin Fender?" she said. I held up my hand. She smiled shyly and cautiously made her way back to my corner. "I'm Darlene Barnes. Sgt. Lasko said you might want to talk to me."

"Nice to meet you," I said. "Would you by any chance have been working on a flight from Austin to L.A. last Friday morning?"

She nodded. "Sgt. Lasko said you were curious about a white-haired guy who was a passenger."

"You remember him?"

"Sure. I mean, not many people look like that." She laughed. "It's a good thing, too, I guess."

"Did you notice anything else about him? Did he seem nervous, or act suspiciously in any way?"

She shook her head. "Well, he drank a few drinks, looked out the window, things like that. I offered him a magazine and he took it. *Premiere,* I think it was." Her forehead wrinkled as she glanced around the dressing room. "But you know what? I don't think he could hardly read."

"Why do you say that?"

"He just flipped through it, you know, like he was looking at the pictures. I had to show him to his seat, too, and when he paid for his drinks, he held the bills up real close to his face, like he could barely make out what denominations they were."

I thought about that. Billy and Leo got up and left the room. "Did he have a piece of tape on his ear?"

She shrugged. "I couldn't say. I think his hair pretty well covered his ears."

"Could he have been wearing a wig?"

"God, I don't know. I guess, but why would anybody wear a wig like *that?*"

"I've got a little theory about that," I said, "but I won't inflict it on you right now. Can I buy you a drink?"

She shook her head and blushed. "No, thanks. I don't drink, and getting me in free was real nice of you. I'm a real big fan of Dovie de Carlo. If what I told you helps her out any, well, that'd be kind of an honor, you know."

I shook her hand and thanked her and she left.

I checked the strings on the bass, but they were already in perfect pitch. Maybe Leo had tuned it for me when I was out talking to Wayne. It was nice of him to help out, but what are friends for if not to pitch in when their buddy's on the spot?

Like Otis's friends. Red Fred was about the same build as

Otis, and with sunglasses, bleached wig, and cowboy hat mashed down on top, he could use Otis's plane ticket so that, to all appearances, Otis Taylor arrived in L.A. the morning *after* Cyclone Davis was killed. But Red Fred, according to Dovie, was terribly nearsighted, and Otis, a guy with a gun in nearly every room of his house and a deer head trophy on nearly every wall, was not. How else could he have driven out to L.A. to shoot Cyclone Davis with a .30-06 on a canyon trail at night?

I was convinced that Otis *had* done just that. Now I just needed to know why.

The opening act finished their set and the stagehands started rearranging the gear for us. Ray arrived and told me that George over at the pool hall said no one had been sleeping in the bar the night our warehouse had been broken into. We smoked cigarettes, nursed cocktails. A half hour later Dovie still hadn't arrived, and the crowd was getting restless. Wayne came back to the dressing room and suggested we start without her. We were just about to take the stage when Carson Block brought her in the back way, looking paler than ever and shaky, too, but not much worse than the last time I'd seen her.

"Sorry we're late," said Carson as he pumped my hand.

"I've gotta talk to you," I told him as I strapped on my bass.

"And I've need to talk to you," he said. "Some weird shit has been going on back in L.A."

I gave him a nod and followed Dovie back to the corner of the dressing room, where she had dropped into a chair and hunched over to light a cigarette.

"Are you OK?" I said.

She nodded. Her eyes looked a little foggy and unfocused.

"Sure you wanna do this?"

She nodded again. "Quit worrying about everything, Martin," she said in a voice that sounded a little distant, but not too shaky, not too hoarse. "Everything will work out."

"We need to talk."

Out of the corner of my eye I could see Wayne and the rest

of the band standing in the doorway, waiting for me. And the crowd sounded like it was on the verge of getting ugly. Dovie took a deep breath, then reached out, grabbed my face in both hands, and kissed me on the mouth.

"Not now, Martin," she said. "If you want to talk, I'll need a drink. And you know I don't like to drink when I sing. Why do you think I wanted to play so soon? So I won't have to think. I just wanna forget. Is that OK?"

I told her it was. For now.

We started off with Link Wray's "Rumble." Leo stood at the edge of the stage, cigarette screwed into the corner of his mouth, his guitar cranked up to feedback levels. Billy's drums were nice and loud onstage, too, especially the heavy floor tom beats that punched up the menacing, martial rhythm of the instrumental tune. My bass felt a little cold and sticky, but that would pass. It sounded OK. Ray got up during the second song, Bill Black's "Smokie, Part II," and it was 1959 all over again. We were cooking by the time Leo stepped up to the mike for "Back for a Taste of Your Love," Syl Johnson's 1973 Hi records classic. Leo sang it in a passing imitation of Al Green, which made it a passing imitation of Syl Johnson, too.

The dance floor was packed and writhing like a bucket of snakes by the time we cranked things up on Howlin' Wolf's "Killing Floor," and it stayed that way until we took a pause, several songs later, to towel off and replenish our fluids. Leo lit up a cigarette, and I took the mike to say, "Now we'd like to bring up a friend of ours. Some of you may know her as Dot . . ."

There was a hush in the room, pierced by a few whistles and several shouts of "*Hey, Dovie . . . Sweetheart!!*" as Dovie strode to center stage, sunglasses in place, and her complexion looking whiter than seemed possible under the lights.

She steadied herself by gripping the mike stand, then looked at us and said, "Let's start with 'Sabertooth,' OK?" Billy clicked off a four-count, and the band fell in together like a well-oiled

but noisy machine. "Sabertooth Tiger (in a Little Kitten Suit)"
was one of Richard James's early singles, a twelve-bar rocker
that the band had been playing for years. It had a sexy, churning
beat, powered by a rude guitar figure not unlike the riff to
Rufus Thomas's "Walk the Dog." For the first few bars, the
crowd on the dance floor seemed too mesmerized to do anything
but watch openmouthed. Dovie sang:

> She tore down your drapes
> the night you brought her home
> She ripped up your couch
> 'cause it was shaped like a doggiebone
> And she drives you crazy all night
> with her sandpaper tongue
> Got a slick striped coat, white gloves and boots
> She's a sabertooth tiger
> in a little kitten suit . . .

But by the time the chorus came around, the crowd began to
dance again. Dovie's voice was a little flat, but it dripped enough
sassy twang into the wall of sound that it sounded just right.

After "Sabertooth," we played a couple more Richard James
songs, plus several of the originals we'd worked up with her,
the last of which was "Mystery of Love," the song I'd helped
her with the afternoon we'd met back in L.A. The crowd
seemed to like the new song every bit as much as they liked
the Richard James songs. A great number of folks, especially
in the back, were standing on their chairs; hardly anyone was
sitting in them, including rockabilly boys and low riders, long-
hairs and punks, office workers, drug dealers, and lots of musicians. More than a few of them were already decked out in
Halloween costumes. There were several commandos in desert
camouflage fatigues, more than a couple of Draculas, one Frankenstein, a Freddy Krueger, and the usual Vegas-vintage
Elvises.

Lasko stood against the wall to one side of the dance floor, about as far as he could get from the two short-haired men at the back of the club in dark suits and open collars, which was probably Watson's idea of plainclothes. Darlene Barnes was dancing with a guy, her eyes locked on Dovie. Ladonna and Michael shared a table with Nadine and Kate. It was hard to tell from my viewpoint, but it looked like the girls were giving Dovie the up-and-down, while Michael was more fascinated by the crowd than by Dovie.

After "Mystery of Love," Dovie mumbled thank-yous. When the applause had died down she said, "I wonder if someone would be so kind as to bring me a glass of wine?"

We killed a little time as Leo switched guitars and Billy tightened the lugs on his snare and gave it a few whacks to test the tuning. Ray sipped his martini and looked to me for a clue as to what we were going to do next. I just shrugged and kept an eye on Dovie. She wiped her face with a towel and took the glass of red wine that Carson Block handed her, took a few gulps, and went back to the mike.

"I'd like to do a song now," she said, faltering a bit. She took another gulp of wine and started over again. "I wanna do a song now, and this one goes out to a very special guy, Martin Fender, on bass guitar—"

There was a smattering of applause, mostly for her, though, and some shouts of "*Hey, Dovie . . .*"

"—and someone else who was real close to me. He was kind of a crazy guy, but I liked him a lot. One day he went out to Lubbock, though, and that changed everything. I don't know what it is about that town . . ."

"*Whoa! Hey, Dovie . . . Sweetheart . . .*"

"So I'd like to do this song, an old Buddy Holly song." She turned around and said, "That'll Be the Day," and we played it.

The crowd responded with renewed enthusiasm after Dovie's rambling, emotional dedication, and the other guys in the band rose to the occasion, diving into the pop chestnut with the earnest abandon of a teenage garage band. I gave it my best effort, but I couldn't help straying off the beat once in awhile as my mind wandered. One could naturally have assumed that the "crazy guy" she'd referred to was her dead lover Richard James, the legendary R&B figure and Buddy Holly fan killed after his plane crashed exactly twenty-five years after Buddy Holly's. Richard James was gone but she was a survivor, and like they say, everyone loves a survivor.

There was an awful lot of angst in that room, because now tragedy had struck again, with the murder of the man who owned the publishing rights to that legacy, a man who'd also been close to her, closer than I'd wanted him to be. Maybe some of the people in the audience had known Preston Drake and Cokey Kossmeyer, too. And everybody was a Buddy Holly fan, after all.

But I couldn't help wondering if she'd been thinking of another crazy guy who'd made a sojourn to Lubbock—Cyclone Davis. I had a cassette of a song taped to the inside of the wiring compartment cover on the back of the Danelectro that made me wonder, too. Leo was convinced that the tape had been made by Richard James. Cyclone Davis had seemed convinced that it proved that Richard James was still alive. I wasn't even sure it was a good song.

It was a dangerous song, though. It gave me strange dreams. At least one man, and possibly two, had fallen down dead over it. It had caused me to pack along my gun in my guitar case, just in case I ran into a guy who thought he was God's detective, a burn-out case whose only interest in Richard James being alive was so he could kill him for putting a wiretap in his skull and ripping off his songs.

But who was the Holly song really dedicated to? Was it Richard James, or Cyclone Davis? Otis Taylor was supposedly from Lubbock, too, but I would have unplugged my bass and walked off stage in a minute rather than play on a song dedicated to that freak.

I yearned for answers. The dreams weren't giving me any. The giant woman wouldn't talk to me, and Cyclone Davis had turned into Richard James.

Soon the song was over and Dovie took a bow, mumbled *"thank you, thank-you-very-much,"* and left the stage. It was only one o'clock, so the band would have to play for another hour without her, and I'd have to wait at least that long for my answers.

Much of the buzz of excitement caused by the enigmatic star's presence crackled through the room long after she'd left the stage, though people were no longer standing on their chairs and the cluster around the stage thinned out considerably. We had a job to do, and we did it well, I thought. It was, after all, the only job I was being paid to do. We kept the dance floor packed with Lightnin' Hopkins's "Jake Head Boogie," John Lee Hooker's "Drugstore Woman," Howlin' Wolf's "Down in the Bottom" and "I Asked for Water (and She Gave Me Gasoline)," and Roscoe Gordon's "Just in from Texas." Midway through the set I looked off to stage right and spotted Nehru Ellis, a keyboard player from Cincinnati who had played with the band off and on over the years. I gave him a wink and he jumped onstage and commandeered the opening act's Hammond B-3 for the rest of the night on a slew of Stax-Volt, Hi, and Goldwax classics. At one point, someone shouted out that we sounded almost as good as Booker T and the M.G.s.

A fine compliment to be sure, but all in all, it was still the longest, slowest set of blues I'd ever played.

When I stepped off the stage and went back to the dressing room, Dovie and Carson were gone. Wayne came back and said Dovie had collapsed in the dressing room immediately after leaving the stage, and Carson had taken her out to the house. Wayne also said that I had an urgent phone call. I followed him to the office and took the call. It was Sgt. Roman, calling from L.A.

20

Lasko and I were sitting in his pickup behind the Continental Club. The club had been closed for half an hour and the streets were quiet.

All Lasko would say about the Otis Taylor case was that the prime suspect, Neville Graves, was still at large. The slugs in Otis's skull and the wall behind his desk had been fired from a .38 revolver. The slugs were a perfect match with the slugs from the San Antonio murder that Graves had never been charged with.

"So does Watson still insist it was a drug deal disagreement," I said, "or did Graves just blow up when he and Otis got in a disagreement over how well done they were going to char those T-bones?"

Lasko picked at his front teeth with a wooden match and shook his head slowly. "Sorry, but that's all I can share with you right now, Martin," he said. "What'd Roman want?"

"He wants me to fly to L.A. tomorrow, on his nickel. Some cops, a deputy D.A., and some official types from the city want to ask me a few questions about Cyclone Davis."

"You gonna go?"

"Well, at first it sounded like it was a request, like I'd be doing him a favor, but while I was trying to decide if I had a choice in the matter, Roman kind of sneaked the term *material witness* in there."

"I get it. You'll be doing yourself a favor if you do him one."

I nodded. "They've got a flight booked for me and everything. You know anything about it?"

Lasko shrugged and scratched the back of his neck. "I heard there was some kinda mix-up out there. Speaking of the left coast, Carson Block seems pretty fidgety about some things been going on since you left."

"Like what? And what kinda mix-up?"

He scratched the back of his neck again and said, "Best you ask Carson about his fidgets, and Roman about the mix-up."

"Dammit, you can't talk about Otis, you can't tell me what Carson wants, you won't tell me about Cyclone Davis. What the hell is going on?"

"Look Martin, I told you before, you ain't a cop. But you're in this thing, and if somebody like me or Sgt. Roman is asking you to cooperate, I'd think you'd wanna do it, you know? You're the one all wrapped up in this Richard James thing, aren't you?"

"I'm not the only one," I said, watching as Lasko shifted in his seat.

"Oh hell, I guess you're right. You do love to be right, don't you?"

"Yeah. Tell me more so I can bask in the glory, why don't you?"

"Well . . . ," he groaned, stretching the word out as if it were a tired, sore muscle. "It's just, this Otis Taylor case is rubbing me raw. Nothing about his character is adding up right, except that I can feel deep down in my gut he wasn't a right guy. And tonight when I was in there watching that girl sing, it just tore me up to think about the things you said. That he beat up on her, that he was running her into the ground somehow. After turning up Darlene Barnes today, I did a little interview with Nubby Maxwell and Red Fred, looking for ways to prop up your theory that Red Fred flew out to L.A. as a decoy for Otis Taylor. The way Red Fred tells it, him and Graves drove out there in Otis's car so they could stop in Phoenix to visit a friend. Claimed they don't care much for flying, and Otis wanted to drive his own car in L.A. since he was a tightwad and didn't like to rent cars when he didn't have to."

"You swallow that?"

"I'd as likely swallow a fresh cow paddy as that crock of shit. But the friend in Phoenix backs up their story, and so do a couple other witnesses."

"What about the flight attendant?"

He shook his head. "I showed her Otis Taylor's driver's license photo and she said, yeah, I guess that's him." Lasko made a face. "I mean, you know, a guy looking like a redneck version of Andy Warhol, who's gonna look that close?"

"But she said he was nearsighted."

"So what? She give him an eye exam? Martin, cops need proof, not a bunch of wild-eyed maybes."

"All right, how about this: Dovie told me she saw Nubby Maxwell waiting to pick someone up at the airport the day we flew in. He must have been there to pick up Red Fred, because the two of them were there at our first rehearsal the next day. And Otis didn't show up here until Wednesday, four days later."

"So what does that prove?"

"That Otis *drove* back from L.A. with Graves. And that jibes with the fact that Otis didn't like to fly, that he drove to L.A. letting Red Fred fly out there as a decoy. Dovie knows he doesn't like to fly, but she apparently fell for the decoy bit. The only thing I don't get is that she apparently knew Otis was driving *back* to Austin, because she told me not to worry about Otis when we got back here, that he wouldn't be around for awhile. Maybe that was because he told her so, and she believed him. She is pretty gullible sometimes."

Lasko wrinkled his nose at me. "Martin, this is like trying to eat chili with a fork. I gotta have more than this."

"All right. I'll keep working on that part of it. What about the L.A. cops?"

"They still don't have much to go on, but they did find a .30-06 with a night scope ditched down a ravine not more than fifty feet from the place your pal was shot. Ballistic check showed that the rifle's the weapon that killed Cyclone Davis, but it and the night scope are cold. Both disappeared in a nighttime heist of an El Paso gun shop five years back."

Another dead end. The ensuing silence was awkward.

Lasko finally spoke up. "You know, Martin, I just feel like a big old wrong has been perpetuated here. Like I was saying about how a musician can't seem to die anymore without people robbing his grave. And when I saw the look on your face when she introduced that Buddy Holly song, that's when I decided it's a good thing you gotta fly out to L.A. and find out just who Cyclone Davis really was."

"What do you mean?"

"They fucked up out at the L.A. county morgue."

"What do you mean?"

"Cyclone Davis wasn't who they thought he was. I wasn't gonna tell you, but here it is: There was some kind of mix-up out there, and it turns out that Kyle Anthony Lynch was black. The situation is kind of hushed up right now. They've had nothing but a mess on their hands ever since Noguchi, the coroner to the stars, so I gotta warn you against thinking you can blast in there and make a big stink about it. So listen, I'm just warning you now, but . . ."

Lasko was wasting his breath. I kept watching his mouth move but I'd long since stopped hearing the words coming out of it. I'd stopped way back when he said that the LAPD had misidentified Cyclone Davis. I felt a sharp prickling sensation begin to erupt on the back of my neck, and it spread like wildfire as I considered the possibilities: If Cyclone Davis wasn't Kyle Anthony Lynch, who was he?

I wanted to see the body, to check it for old signs of frostbite, to see if the index finger on his fretting hand had been broken when he was a kid. Lasko's mouth finally stopped moving when I opened the door and climbed out of the pickup.

I stopped in front of the house and looked back down the drive. The woods weren't exactly quiet. Hidden back in the thick growth, night birds and insects made their night music, tree limbs and fingers creaked and rattled, bowed by a gentle intermittent breeze.

There were two other cars in front of the house besides Dovie's Lincoln and the Ghia. One was a Mercedes, the other a Chrysler LeBaron with a rental agency's name on the license plate holder. Carson met me at the door and let me in.

Dovie was wrapped up in a blanket, sitting on the futon by the window in the living room, staring blankly at the view. Her eyes looked dulled and unfocused. Chester White sat on the edge of the futon, talking to her in a low voice as he filled her wineglass.

"I guess it hit her all at once," said Carson. "You know the doctor?"

I nodded and walked across the room.

Carson called after me. "Martin, I don't think now is—"

"I'd like to talk to Dovie," I said. "Alone."

Chester White turned his head, narrowing his eyes at me. "Martin, this isn't a good time. Why don't you—"

"It's all right, Chet. Martin's a good guy," said Dovie in a low voice, her words slurred and soft around the edges. "Even though he likes things to be simple." She turned from the window and waved at the other two with a limp-wristed motion.

They hung back for a moment, then went outside. I sat on the edge of the futon and took one of Dovie's hands.

"You OK, darlin'?"

She nodded. "It worked for a little bit, Martin. I didn't have to think for a while."

"What didn't you have to think about?"

"You know, the whole thing." She was having trouble holding her head up. A lot of trouble.

"Does the whole thing include Cyclone Davis?"

She squeezed my hand, then rested her chin on her knees, her head tilted forward so that her hair hid her face completely.

"Otis killed him, didn't he?" She didn't answer. "Tell me why, Dovie. Tell me what that song had to do with it."

She still didn't respond, but she didn't let go of my hand, either.

"All right then, tell me how many men were in the search party."

"Why?"

"Just tell me. Can you remember?"

" 'Course I can." With her chin resting on her knees, the words barely escaped from her teeth. "Why you think my life is so fucked up? I remember everything. There were five, Martin, five scruffy little angels. Why?"

"You told me before there were six, and a book I just read said there were six."

"So? People make mistakes. Especially people who weren't there."

"What about L-Tone Rogers? What'll he tell me?"

She parted her knees so that her head sank into the blanket.

"Dovie, look at me."

I cupped her face in my hand and turned it toward mine. Her eyes glared for a second, then went dim. As they started to close, something like a snarl came out of her mouth. Even so, I had the feeling she was about to pass out.

"You said Richard's face was all messed up in the crash, that people would never pay to see him play again. Did he really die in that avalanche, or was he the sixth man?"

She just shook her head.

"Was Cyclone Davis really Richard James?"

A sputter came from her lips. "Of course he wasn't."

"L-Tone said Cyclone called him pretending to be Richard."

"So what? Cyclone was crazy. Are you?"

"Maybe I am, Dovie. Maybe I'm crazy and the rest of the world is sane." For a couple of seconds I actually considered the possibility, then gave it up—too depressing.

"Why you keep buggin' me, Martin?" She sounded like a seven-year-old going under anesthesia.

"You asked me to help you, remember?"

The flesh at the edges of her mouth and around her eyes crinkled. "Not as simple as helpin' me write a song, is it?"

"No, it's not. You loved Otis more than you thought, didn't you? Is that why you're upset now?"

She made a derisive sound with her lips. The effort seemed to exhaust her; her chin dropped onto her knees again, her head wobbled from side to side. "Love isn't enough . . . to put up with *that*."

"What did he have on you, Dovie? What are these Kilton creeps holding over your head?"

"Go 'way, Martin."

"Why?"

"Don't wanna talk n'more. Wanna sleep, an' don't wanna lie to you. You keep after me I'll either tell you something I don't wanna tell you . . . or I'll lie, an' I can't do either one too good. Momma didn't wanna raise no liar."

Her head rolled off to one side, causing her body to collapse into my arms. I didn't think she was faking it, the thing was too pathetic to arouse either pity or sexual attraction. Her eyes were starting to roll back under the lids, but she was mumbling something about being sorry.

"What's Chester White doing here?" I said.

"He brought me some pills. They help, a little."

"Help you what?"

Her mouth dropped down unvoluntarily, and she struggled to close it enough to speak. "They help me . . . stop."

I put her down on the bedding and pulled my arms out from under her. From outside, I heard a car engine start. It sounded like the Mercedes. Dovie was already snoring. I pulled the covers around her, adjusted the pillow under her head, and went outside.

Carson looked tired and worn-out sitting on the steps as the woods around the winding drive swallowed the taillights of Chester White's Mercedes. I sat down and lit a cigarette.

"I don't like that guy," he said. "But I guess he's just trying to help."

"I don't like him either," I said. "And I don't think I appreciate his kind of help."

"What's she supposed to do, Martin? Christ, have you seen the disaster area back in that bedroom? It's like something out of a horror movie. Tomorrow I'll get somebody out here to clean it out for her, so she doesn't have to drag that futon out to the living room every night. And it's spooky out here."

"No more than Laurel Canyon this time of night, Carson."

He folded his arms and shivered. "I don't know, man. It seems different to me. Like, why's that tree moving like that?"

He pointed to a spot where the drive looped back into the woods. A fat cedar tree by the side of the road seemed to be dancing back and forth.

"Just the wind trying to slip down to the lake for a moonlight skinny dip, Carson. What's shaking in L.A.?"

His forehead wrinkled. "You sure you wanna know?"

I said I did. He leaned forward and locked his arms around his knees and told me all about it while I smoked my cigarette.

Carson was stressed out. He'd been that way ever since Dovie de Carlo had been under contract to IMF Records. Disgruntled ex-roadies came to his office, demanding back wages. Drug dealers approached him at his home or in restaurant parking lots, claiming that either he pay the money Dovie owed them or there would be problems—*You know,* they said, *problems you don't want.* Six months ago, a rehearsal studio had presented him with a bill for several thousand dollars worth of rehearsal time, and he was almost certain Dovie hadn't spent more than an hour inside a rehearsal studio for over six months.

Anyone who'd been to one of her recording sessions could figure that one out, he said.

Dovie was no help. She'd just shrug and say she was sorry.

Trouble just seemed to follow Dovie around, he said, but he believed in her and wanted to keep her on the label. He also wanted to keep his job, so he worked hard to deal with these problems, as irregular or bogus as they seemed, and rarely told his superiors about them. Most were things that a manager would normally take care of, but Dovie hadn't had a regular full-time manager for more than a couple of months since Carson had been working with her. Some of the situations, when ignored, would go away. He took care of some of the others out of his own pocket, and still others through creative billing, which was something record companies knew a thing or two about.

But Carson didn't feel up to dealing with some of the situations, and some were out of his league. These he took up with Otis Taylor. All he had to do was to make a phone call, he said, mention the situation to Otis, and the problem would go away. Maybe Otis paid the people off himself, maybe he sent some of his backwoods torpedoes over to talk to the people. Carson didn't want to know, and he didn't like calling the man when he could avoid it, anyway.

But now there was another problem, one that he didn't want to deal with himself, one that he couldn't bring up with Otis, because Otis was dead.

"This time it's a studio engineer demanding to be paid for a session," said Carson. "I don't believe Dovie did a session with the guy, but I think she knows him. His name is Pep Soto. He did some work with Richard James back when Dovie was with him, on *Ninety Minute Man*. He has a little studio up in Laurel Canyon."

"Did he mention Cyclone Davis?"

Carson nodded. "That's why I thought maybe you'd wanna talk to the guy. And that homicide detective, Lasko, said you might have to go out to L.A. anyway."

I wrung a last puff out of the cigarette, then flicked it out onto the driveway, watching the sparks jump away from the butt as it tumbled under the Chrysler.

He chewed the side of his lip and drew his knees up closer to his chest. "Look, Martin, I know you don't think a lot of me."

"Let's just skip that part. You're here with Dovie. That counts for something."

He nodded, then went on. "I'm sorry I wasn't completely honest with you about Dovie's troubles before. But the fact is, they were so, uh, vague. You know? I don't know why in hell she's haunted by all these weirdos. They just keep coming out of the woodwork. But I'm starting to think that this Cyclone Davis guy was more to her than a wild romp in the sack and a dose of white trash raunch, you know?"

"Me, too."

He shrugged. "I mean, it's hard to tell with her. She's been through so much. You hate to bring it up because you feel like you're going to make her run through a lot of bad memories and maybe it's just not worth it. On the other hand, she seems kind of relieved that Otis is gone."

"There are reasons for that," I said.

"Yeah, well, and I hate to say it, but I guess I just wish she was a little *more* relieved, you know? I mean, I wish I felt like this was the end of it. But I just don't know, and I wish that damn tree would stop bopping around like that."

The wind had kicked up again, and with it, the fat evergreen had resumed its side-to-side sway. But things were swaying all over out there, and staring at things in the dark stirs the imagination. It seemed to me that we already had more than enough to keep our imaginations in a state of agitation.

We talked for a little while longer. One of the things we talked about was trying to do something about Nate Waco. Part of the problem was finding the guy, and we never came up with a solution for that. Maybe that situation would resolve itself; it seemed likely that sooner or later he'd show up to reclaim the guitar and amp that were stranded in the house when Dovie had the locks changed.

In the end I agreed to check things out for him in L.A. I told him that it would cost him money. LAPD was paying my airfare, but nothing else as far as I knew, so I took all the cash he had on him—a little over a thousand dollars—and got his promise to pay whatever other expenses I ran up. It was easy. Getting Ladonna up in the middle of the night and explaining the thing to her would be the hard part.

When I bumped down the drive, I slowed a bit when I came up next to the cedar tree that had been making Carson Block so nervous. The tree stood in a bank of cedars that hemmed in the road like a solid green wall. It was short and quite a bit fatter than the rest. Maybe none of the other trees would dance with it. Right then I couldn't say; the wind had died down and I was tired.

21

The phone rang at nine the next morning. I was still in bed. The answering machine picked up the call, and after the beep, I heard a low-pitched voice saying, "I'm trying to get in touch with a Martin Fender. You don't know me, but my name is Bill Jaworski. Sgt. Lasko gave me this number. He said you were asking about my son, Bob, the writer who was killed while he was working on a Richard James story. I'm in town and I was wondering if we could meet . . ."

We met at Jim's coffee shop just off the freeway on the south end of town. Bill Jaworski was a little overweight, a broad-shouldered man with big, powerful hands. The hands were clasped together around a steaming cup of coffee, not entirely steady.

"You don't know what this did to my wife, Martin," said Jaworski. "It's bad enough when you lose a son, but when he's murdered and nothing's done about it, well . . ."

I nodded but didn't say anything.

"You see," he said, "we come from Pittsburgh. I lost a brother back there in a Jimmy Hoffa–type deal. He was president of a union there, the one I belonged to, and the government came after him about something the union was doing. My brother took the fall for the big boys and ended up doing a couple of years in the pen. When he came out he was still real popular with the membership, and he wanted to run for president again. But the big boys had somebody else in there then, somebody they were happy with, and they told my brother not to run. He ran anyway. He would've won the election, too, but one day after his shift at the plant he stopped off at a bar, and we never saw or heard from him again. The police say they think he might've skipped town. It really upset my wife, so I lied to her. I told her I thought maybe they were right."

He sighed and tugged at the loose skin under his chin. "So that's why we moved down here. We heard things were different, you see. I had some savings and I set up a machine shop. Bob finished high school and was in college, working on a journalism degree, writing free-lance for several music magazines. It wasn't much, but it was a start, and Bob gave it his all, like he did with anything he did, and we were sure our son had a bright future ahead of him. But we were wrong.

"Bob was murdered by Dolph Moreland. The law over there said it was a hunting accident, but I wasn't able to fool my wife this time. Like I guess you heard, Bob was a vegetarian, and there's no way he would've gone deer hunting. Hell, we grew up in the city, none of us would know the difference between a white-tail deer and a cow, or which end of a hunting rifle is which, for that matter."

"What do you know about the story he was working on at the time, Mr. Jaworski?"

"It was some kind of big piece about Richard James. Bob wanted to play up the mystery angle, how they never found the bodies and all that. He was trying to talk to people who'd played with him, and he wasn't getting a whole lot of cooperation. But the way Bob was, that just made him more determined, you know. He was a determined boy, a good kid. He did talk to Richard James's mother in Lubbock, but that didn't satisfy him."

"Did he tell you much about what he did find out?"

He shook his head. "We didn't talk that much about it. I mean, I'm from a different generation. I mean, at that time, I couldn't have told the difference between a Richard James song and one by the Beatles. I think he understood. We knew he was supposed to meet with the pilot, because there was a message on his answering machine from the guy. You know about the photo?"

"You mean the photo of the search party?"

He nodded. "All we had to go on was that photo and the message on the answering machine. Bob kept all his notes on cassette, and he had his cassette recorder with him when he was killed. But we didn't find anything much on the cassettes in his room and the sheriff's deputies over there said he didn't have any tapes with him."

I didn't have to ask if he believed them. "Anything else?"

"All I know is, he was real excited about talking to Moreland's pilot. Before he called agreeing to talk, Bob was thinking he was going to have to go up to Kilton, but that would've taken him out of school for too many days, so he wasn't anxious to do that. He was serious about school and hated to miss a day."

"Why was he going to go to Kilton?"

"To try to find Preston Drake's parents."

"Preston Drake was from Kilton?"

He nodded. "Apparently so. But we checked into it after Bob was killed and found out that they used to live there, but they moved out several years back. Nobody could tell us where." His forehead creased with deep lines as he leaned forward and said, "You look like you think that might mean something."

"I don't know," I said. "It could explain how Richard fell in with the Kilton crowd, if Preston Drake was from there. I don't know if it means much more than that. What about the photo, Mr. Jaworski? Do you know how your son got ahold of it?"

"Well, we just always assumed the photo came from the pilot.

Sgt. Lasko seemed to think so, too. But the way I see it, the pilot wasn't so anxious to talk to Bob until that night he left the message, so why would he give him the photo beforehand? And what's the big deal with the photo, anyway? I know it must have been important to Bob, because he had it hidden inside a book, locked in a drawer in his desk. My wife and I started thinking he might have gotten it from that guitar player, L-Tone Rogers. I know Bob talked to him about a week before he was murdered. I tracked him down and talked to him myself, but he said he didn't know anything about it."

"Did you believe him?"

Jaworski just shook his head.

A waitress came over and refilled our mugs. When she was gone I said, "Mr. Jaworski, I don't know what to tell you. I'm glad Lasko told you I was involved in this thing, but I don't know what good is going to come out of it. I'm supposed to go to L.A. today. Maybe I'll find some answers there. If I do, how do I get in touch with you?"

Jaworski's face became set in a sort of pained expression. "You don't," he said. "My wife and I don't need answers, except to the question of how a boy can be murdered and nothing done about it. You know they tell all these stories about how in Central America people get taken for rides and never come back. Everybody knows, nothing is done. I don't want answers, questions, excuses . . . I want justice."

"I don't blame you. I don't like it either. Believe me, I'd like to do something—"

"So would I," he interrupted. "I'd kill Moreland myself, but I'm just not built that way."

He stared down at his hands. They were shaking.

"But I wish to God I was," he said.

After talking with Mr. Jaworski I was more determined than ever to find L-Tone Rogers again and ask him more questions about the search party. I called Clifford Antone, and he said he thought L-Tone was out of town, but he didn't know where. Wayne told me more or less the same thing. It looked like it would have to wait till I got back from L.A.

I took Ladonna and Michael to lunch. I promised to bring Michael back a souvenir, and Ladonna, too. We went over to my apartment, picked up the cat, and took him over to her place. I didn't want Ladonna coming over to feed him and risk running into God's detective.

I made some phone calls, and after Michael got involved in watching the *Dick Tracy* video, Ladonna and I went into her bedroom and closed the door. A little while later I drove to the airport and got on a plane.

1

Sgt. Roman met me at the front desk at the Valley Bureau
LAPD headquarters in Van Nuys and walked me back to a
conference room. Four people were already seated around the
table when we came in. Introductions were made, but we got
down to business so quickly that the names immediately faded
from my mind. There was a round-shouldered guy with black
curly hair, beard, and glasses in a rumpled suit. He seemed
slightly embarrassed about something, and was by far the least
belligerent one of the lot. At the opposite end of the hostility
spectrum was the bearish one with the booming voice and a
tendency to turn red in the face—Lieutenant Something-or-
other. I could tell he hated me, with every blunt, accusatory
question and every flick of his boyish eyes. But it was the bureaucrat with thick glasses and thin frame who rarely looked
me or any of the others in the eye who worried me the most.
The slender redhead in the expensive but conservative suit and
Chanel earrings I figured for a lawyer, probably from the D.A.'s
office. The thin bureaucrat had to be from the mayor's office,
and the bear with boyish eyes probably represented the LAPD
brass. The kindly bearded one had me stumped, coming across
as being too inwardly directed to be either a lawyer, bureaucrat,

or cop. His hands looked soft, and from what I could see of his legal pad, his handwriting was terrible. Then there was Sgt. Roman. I knew what he was, and he knew what I was. The others didn't share that advantage, so they asked a lot of silly questions about who I was, what I did for a living, and what I had been doing in L.A. before they got down to what really interested them, which was: (1) Who was John Doe #515, a.k.a. Cyclone Davis, and (2) what did I know about the involvement of John Doe #515, a.k.a. Cyclone Davis, in illegal narcotics trafficking?

The inquiry always came back to those two basic questions. By observing the range of emotions, attitudes, and senses of purpose—ranging from the malevolent stare from the big cop to the oblique probing from the mayor's boy—I gathered that there was more than a little embarrassment being passed around because of what Sgt. Roman had called "a little mix-up at the county morgue." They were looking for a whipping boy who wasn't one of their own, and for ninety minutes they took turns trying to size me up for the job or to get me to steer them to someone else:

DEPUTY D.A.: Mr. Fender, is it still your contention that you accompanied John Doe number five-one-five in his automobile on the night of October nineteen with absolutely no knowledge of any intention on his part to engage in an illegal narcotics transaction?

MF: I was supposed play bass guitar for him on a recording session. He gave me a ride home. He never came back to pick me up for the session. There was no mention of drugs.

THE LIEUTENANT: Did the victim mention to you where he was headed after he dropped you off?

MF: No.

THE LIEUTENANT: Have you ever been up to this canyon trail before, the one the victim was murdered on, either during the day or at night?

MF: No.

THE BEARD: Mr. Fender, did you say that you had absolutely no knowledge of this individual's actual identity?

MF: That's right.

THE BEARD: Did you notice a tattoo, a birthmark, or any other distinguishing characteristics?

MF: No.

THE LIEUTENANT: You say you threw away the envelope he gave you the hundred dollars in? How about the money?

MF: All gone.

THE BUREAUCRAT: Have you had any other occasions to speak with, or associate with, persons who may have been employed as law enforcement personnel in Los Angeles County?

The more unsatisfying my answers became, the faster the questions were hurled at me. The lieutenant wanted to know what Otis Taylor had to do with Cyclone Davis, and how long I'd known Graves, Red Fred, and Nubby Maxwell. The bureaucrat and the deputy D.A. kept asking questions about L.A. cops and the drug angle, and the kindly bearded one kept fidgeting in his chair, puzzling over what I knew of Cyclone's true identity.

They were a worried bunch. They kept pouncing on me and bouncing off, even though I told the truth about everything except for omitting the fact that I had the cassette tape of the song called "The Whole Damn Truth." The taste of irony provided by that omission helped me maintain my cool during the experience. They hated me, but as the questioning wore on and took them nowhere, their hatred dissipated and floated around the room, like a deadly gas or possessive spirit seeking a new target. People within the various ranks they represented were going to share the heat for something that the murder and consequent "mix-up" of John Doe #515, a.k.a. Cyclone Davis, had stirred up—and they knew it.

Curiously, they casually sidestepped any issues that tended to directly involve Dovie. The only conclusion I could draw was that, being a more public figure, her involvement with the dead man had already been probed to their satisfaction. Either that, or she was being protected.

Sgt. Roman asked only a couple of questions. I didn't get to ask any. Abruptly at 5:30 P.M. the bureaucrat from the mayor's office nailed Roman with a stare and said, "That'll be all for today."

The bureaucrat stood up, and the rest of the group trained nervous eyes on him as he snapped his briefcase shut, adjusted his glasses, spun on his heel, and walked out of the room. When he was gone, the other members of the group sighed nervously and avoided looking at one another.

Roman showed me the way out. When we got to the door leading out to the parking lot, he handed me one of his cards. Scrawled on the back was an address in North Hollywood.

He headed for his car and I headed for mine.

The address turned out to be an impound lot. Jammed behind the hurricane fence was a herd of Porsches, Mercedes, Jaguars, minitrucks, Jeep Cherokees, old Buicks, and new Japanese cars. Lots of new Japanese cars. Car thieves love them. Hondas hemmed in Cyclone's Cadillac on three sides. On the fourth side was a pearl white Bugatti replica. Sgt. Roman was admiring it as I walked up.

"Welcome back," he said dryly.

"When can I look at the body?"

Something in his face twitched as he stroked the side of the Bugatti. "That'd be a problem. That meeting was mostly because of the snafu at the morgue, you know."

"I gathered that much. The guy with the beard?"

He nodded. "He's from the county morgue, but not for long. The big cop, Lieutenant Rhodes, is head of a drug enforcement task force that's breathing down my neck on this thing. But the mayor's breathing down *their* neck. The skinny guy with glasses is the mayor's new appointee to the LAPD review board. They say the mayor bought him a brand new hatchet, and he wants to see some blood on it. The redhead, the deputy D.A., is a ball-busting career woman, and she doesn't care how many bodies she has to stomp over in her high-heeled climb to the top. You're tiptoing around a hornet's nest here, Martin."

"When do I get to see the body?"

"You don't."

"Why not?"

"Listen, Martin, what you have to understand is, since there was no ID on the body, your friend was processed as John Doe #515 when they brought him in. The county morgue processes over five hundred John Does a year. He was the two hundredth homicide we sent them this month. Plus they had a bumper crop of car wreck victims, drownings, and other miscellaneous causes of death, all of which call for autopsies. It's a lot to cope with under the best of conditions, and out here, the best of conditions is still a pretty grim situation. There's been a lot of trouble with the management—controversy, scandals, investigations, lawsuits, and you name it, so that's why I'm gonna have to ask you to keep what I say confidential."

"What are you trying to say, Sergeant?"

"There was a fuck-up. A disgruntled ex-employee at the morgue switched some toe tags. Your friend's tag got switched with another stiff's, that of Kyle Anthony Lynch. Another employee tried to put things right, but she didn't tell anyone. To make matters worse, she didn't exactly put them back the way they were supposed to be, either. One thing led to another, and your friend's body got mixed up with a bunch of stiffs who had gone unclaimed so long that they were set to be cremated. And that's what happened. John Doe #515 is nothing but a bucket of unclaimed ashes. Even the prints that the medical examiner took off him at the crime scene were lost in the shuffle. Right now we don't know any more about who he was than the night they brought him in. It's regrettable."

"It's regrettable?"

"Yeah, that's what I said. You want me to say I'm sorry? I can't do that, sir, because that's just the way it is. Welcome to L.A. Now I'd like to ask you a few questions. Besides all this bureaucratic rumpus, I've still got a homicide investigation to try and wrap up."

And so he asked his questions. He asked me about my theory about Otis Taylor driving out to L.A. to kill Cyclone Davis, why I thought he would do that, and if I knew of any other proof besides the LAX parking receipt, the flight attendant's comments, and the high mileage on Otis's LTD. I told him I had no other proof than what he'd mentioned and no idea for a motive other than jealousy. The tape was still my little secret.

"Well," he sighed, "I'd sure like to mark this case closed, but it's pretty hard to justify that with what we got. Jealousy's always a good motive, especially among friends. And this Taylor character did give this car to your friend. The way it turns out, your friend lived a pretty spare existence. The name Cyclone Davis doesn't appear in any of the usual nooks and crannies. The arson investigation on his apartment has gone nowhere. I'd like to know more about these characters from Kilton, to see how they might have fit into the murder and possibly the arson, too, to cover their tracks, but other people are working on that angle."

"Anyone I know and love?"

The cynical grin on his face gave him away. "I believe your

friend Sgt. Lasko refers to him as a born-again hardass from Amarillo?"

"Abilene," I corrected. Now a lot of my questions were answered. No wonder the LAPD had been so anxious to peg Cyclone's murder as a drug-related homicide; Otis Taylor and the Kilton drug gang had been suspected ever since Roman had contacted Austin PD after seeing that Cyclone's Cadillac was registered to Otis Taylor. Watson had jumped into this case with both feet.

Roman gave the Bugatti one last lingering glance before he moved over to the Cadillac, opened the driver's door, and motioned for me to get in on the other side. After we were both seated inside, he said, "So this car is one of the few things we've had to go on. There was a bottle of Seagram's under the seat, wiped clean, and a notepad in the glove box, also wiped clean and the used pages torn off. The killer or killers were pretty thorough, but not thorough enough. The top page of the note pad had the imprint of the last thing written on it, which turned out to be the address of a recording studio in Laurel Canyon. Talked to the guy, claims he never met your friend, just arranged the studio time over the phone. Is that normal, would you say?"

"It happens. What else?"

"Matchbooks from truck stops and other road stops, running out east through New Mexico and Texas. Seems he stopped in Lubbock last month for a few days, at a place called the Astro Motel. Talked to the manager there, said your friend stayed out pretty late at night and slept late in the morning. Called Ms. de Carlo's hotel twice, spoke for quite some time, and reversed the charges. Made one other call, to an Austin number. Phone company tells me that the number belongs to Ms. de Carlo's lake residence, and she tells me her estranged husband, Nathan Waco, was staying out at the place around that time. Watson's people in Austin are looking for him for us.

"The Astro manager also says Davis asked for directions to the cemetery where Buddy Holly is buried, then checked out at noon on the third day. We talked to the law enforcement people there, but they didn't have anything on a Cyclone Davis, or anyone of his description. That's it. No prints on the stolen .30-06 we found. The only other thing is the mileage here on the odometer."

I leaned over to get a look at it. The odometer read 65,363 miles. "This car's barely over two years old," I said.

He nodded. "I heard Taylor's car in Austin had pretty high mileage, too. Thirty-odd thousand, was it? Maybe he's the one who put so much mileage on this one, too. Looking at it that way, I guess him driving out here to shoot your friend isn't that preposterous. Still seems like there'd be a better way, or a better explanation for why he'd do it that way."

"I hear his friends can't shoot straight," I said.

Roman nodded. "Yeah, I hear that, too, but apparently one of them has been doing some practicing. Let's hope they find him before he gets real good."

"I'm with you there, Sergeant."

"I understand you bumped up against this Graves character once before in a restaurant parking lot. Any idea why he would want to shoot his buddy's face off or how that would tie in with your friend's murder?"

"You getting burnt out on the drug angle?"

Roman just grunted at my question. "Martin, so far you've gotten off pretty light in all this. I know you're gonna do some checking around while you're here, but just remember, this isn't Austin. You screw up, you'll find yourself in jail so fast it'll make your head spin. I suppose you've heard some bad things about L.A. cops."

I nodded.

"Well, bear that in mind. Don't push your luck, and remember what I said about keeping the mix-up at the morgue under your hat. If we need you for any more meetings, it won't be until Monday. I'll let you know soon as I hear. You need money for a motel? The city's obligated to pay for it, you know. Where you staying?"

I told him I didn't know. He recommended the Beverly Sunset, the cheapest decent place on the strip, he said, also conveniently close to Tower Records, in case I wanted to do any record shopping while I was in town. There was a good Thai restaurant nearby, too. He recommended the shrimp curry.

2

From the street, it looked like just another one of the stucco
monstrosities that are either crawling up the side of one of
Laurel Canyon's rocky hillsides or sliding down it, depending
on your point of view. A lime green '60 Coupe de Ville was
parked in front, and something shaped like a convertible Hudson sat waiting under a rain cover in the garage. The entrance
was on the second floor, above the garage. I climbed the steps
and used the antique knocker on a heavy wooden door braced
with steel. Bolts slid back, the door opened, and I stepped
inside.

Pep Soto was as trim and fit-looking as the matador in the
brightly colored oil painting in the foyer. He was about thirty
or thirty-five, with a fine, light complexion and coal black hair
parted on the side, just brushing his shoulders. Matadors not
being in great demand in L.A., he could have been a model.
The grip of a .45 automatic jutted out of the waistband of his
tight jeans.

"I just want you to know, friend," he said in a cool, carefully
modulated voice, "I'm not afraid of you."

"Big deal," I said. "Someday you'll forget yourself, reach
down to scratch an itch and accidentally blow your balls off. I
hope you realize that when you tell people you're not afraid of

them in a voice an octave higher, it won't carry the same weight. Friend."

His nostrils flared slightly as he glared at me, but otherwise, he retained his cool. "What do you want?"

"Not much. Just ask you some questions, maybe get you to listen to a tape."

"Is Carson going to pay me for that session you and Cyclone Davis stood me up on?"

"Maybe. Depends on the price."

"All I want is two hundred bucks. It was a late-night booking and I can't say for sure if I turned down any other business for you guys. But I kept a drummer waiting all night, and he's got to be paid something for his time whether he plays a lick or not. I'm sorry your friend got killed, but you see my position. What's two hundred dollars to IMF Records or Dovie de Carlo?"

"It all depends on how you ask for it, friend. But I've got the money. You don't even have to shoot me for it."

His attitude softened considerably, and a sly grin began to form on his thin lips. "Just answer some questions and listen to a tape?"

"Yeah."

"OK. Come on back."

I followed him through a small den and dining room. Though the rooms were crammed full of all sorts of handcrafted furniture, Indian rugs, and wild, Meso-American paintings done in primitive, wildly colorful styles, the house didn't look lived-in. The chairs and sofas had too many pillows and Navaho blankets for sitting, the tables were too cluttered with knick-knacks for eating.

The studio was in the back, in the part of the house facing the hillside. Behind a foot-thick, soundproofed door was a room with a formidable-looking 24-track mixing console and racks of accessory gear. The walls were covered with acoustic foam. There was a small refrigerator in the corner, with a microwave oven on top, and a trashcan overflowing with soft drink cans and take-out food litter. The room was barely big enough for the two of us to stand in, but, seated in the two high-back leather chairs behind the console, it was comfortable and almost cozy, especially after Soto took the pistol out of his pants and laid it down on a power amp. On the other side of the console was a soundproof window connecting the room to a small sound-stage equipped with a drum kit, guitar amps, microphones, portable partitions, and various stringed instruments.

"We seem to be the victims of wrong impressions," I said. "You expected me to come over here and play hardball with you, and Carson Block seemed to think you were pulling some kind of scam on him. Care to enlighten me?"

"Look, Martin," he said, "I don't like to get ripped off. Cyclone Davis called me and booked the session. I'd never met the guy, and normally I'd need a deposit, but he used Dovie's name. I did the sessions for Richard James's last album, so I knew the kind of people who hung around with him, and I heard they still hang around with Dovie. I guess I was defensive and maybe a little abrasive when I asked to be paid. I didn't mean to offend anybody, but after I heard that Cyclone Davis was murdered that night, I called Dovie and said if she'd cover me on the drummer then I'd forget about the rest of it. Some-body has to pay the guy. The next thing I know, my place is broken into. They didn't steal anything, but it pissed me off. That's why I called Carson, and came on strong with him. I was pissed off."

"Did you ever have any dealings with her publisher?"

"Otis Taylor? No, I've heard of him, but never met him. And the only time I've been around Dovie is when I did the last Richard James album."

"Tell me about it."

He leaned back into his chair and smiled, his eyelids droop-ing, as if recalling a medley of private thoughts and impressions. "Look, man, I suppose you've been in the business long enough to know what I'm saying here. Engineers working with a band see things in a pretty unique light. In some ways, we get treated like furniture, in other ways, like the closest friend you can have, but not always like a friend you respect totally. Sometimes it's almost like you're a dog or something. When you have a bunch of guys in a small room like this, doing their thing all night long for a bunch of nights in a row, not sleeping, a lot of things come out about them. Sometimes they do things or say things they wouldn't do or say around anyone else. It's like the outside world is completely shut out, and the rules out there don't apply in here. I don't know if that's really what they think, but that's how they act."

"I get the picture," I said. "Now tell me something good."

"OK, for one thing, Richard went through this big charade about how he was paying for the record himself, but several times during the recording, these cowboy lowlifes would show up and stink up the studio for no apparent reason, and I've been in the business long enough to know when drug money is being fronted for a record. But that's all I'm going to say about that. The money was green, and I earned it, and the bank didn't ask me where it had been when I put it in my account."

"Was one of the cowboys big and rangy-looking, kind of like the Marlboro Man?"

"Yeah, I remember him. Graves was his name. Snakeskin belt and boots. He didn't like coming here, the ceiling was too low for him. I don't remember the other two guys' names, but one was black, and the other had red hair. The black one had a finger missing, too. I think they called him Stubby, or something."

"Nubby," I corrected. "Nobody else, no one with long white hair?"

He shook his head. "Just those three. And Dovie's husband, Nate. I don't think he was with the drug guys. They flew him out, supposedly to play lead guitar on some of the cuts, but they ended up not using him."

"Why? Too strung out?"

The engineer shrugged. "A little shaky, that's all. But he played a lot in the short time he was here. You know he used to play with those guys, in a Top Forty band before Richard James took them over?"

I nodded. "The Number Sevens. Nate left them to play with Richard James, so the Sevens found another guitarist and went on without Nate. Then Richard dropped Nate when he appropriated the new incarnation of the Sevens."

"OK, but Richard had dropped that guitarist, too, by the time he did the last album. It was just Cokey, the drummer, Dovie, and Preston, the bass player. Richard played most of the guitar parts, and Preston played the rest. Preston was pretty good, but Nate was better. I thought they should have used Nate, but Preston didn't get along with him, and of course, things were kind of strange, with Richard being with his wife."

"How did Nate handle that?"

"Better than I would have. Nate's main interest was in playing. He had all these songs he wanted to show them, but they just cut him down and tried to discourage him. And Preston would take him off and get him so jacked up on speed he couldn't keep both feet on the ground, much less both hands on his guitar."

"I thought you said Preston didn't get along with him."

"I guess they had one of those love-hate things going. You know how that goes, with musicians."

I nodded. "What was Richard like?"

He fiddled with one of the faders on the console and said, "He was really cool, actually. You know, they tell a lot of stories about the guy, and I can't say I liked his friends, but he was real sweet. Once in awhile he'd act up, you know, drinking all that whiskey and 7-Up, but I think it was because he felt he had a reputation to live up to.

"I'll tell you one thing, he was crazy about Dovie. They were inseparable. In fact, if there's one thing bad I'd have to say about the guy, it's that he spent too much time playing with her titties and not enough playing his guitar, singing and writing songs. He seemed kind of spent, creatively, at that point. For awhile I wondered if they were gonna come up with enough songs for a record."

"That seems strange," I said. "Since he left such a backlog of unrecorded material for Dovie to record."

Soto gave me a look. His eyes were like two dark stones. "Yeah, strange, huh? What do you make of it?"

"I've got some theories. Wanna hear a tape?"

He nodded. I gave him the cassette and he put it in his deck, which was hooked into the mixing console and the huge studio monitors that looked big enough to shake the house from its hillside foundations. He made some adjustments on the console, then let the tape roll. We sat back and listened to the entire song without speaking.

Soto was the first to speak afterward. "'The Whole Damn Truth,' huh? Interesting. It sounds like Richard James, all right. What's your theory?"

"Cyclone Davis was pretty excited about doing the session here," I said, "but first, he said he wanted to 'meet a man about a song.' He said the song was going to change his life, that it would prove that Richard James was still alive. This was the song, and I think the man he was going to meet was Otis Taylor. I think Otis killed him and stole the tape back. That's probably why he and his goons busted in here, to see if you had a copy."

"How'd Cyclone Davis get it? From Dovie?"

"That's what she said. But I've got another theory about that."

"Which is?"

"I think we'd better listen to the song again before I say. Can you clean it up a little? I'm looking for some kind of proof it was recorded after 1984."

"I can tell you that right now, friend."

I was startled. "How?"

"Just listen," he said as he bent over the console, made some adjustments on a graphic equalizer, tweaked the pre-amp, and then pressed play again.

The song blasted out over the speakers with new clarity. You could hear the singer's intake of breath before each phrase, and you could hear the movement of his fretting fingers on the guitar strings as he changed chords. The enhanced fidelity also brought the drum track to new prominence in the mix, revealing it to be a drum machine instead of a live drummer. Soto stated offhandedly that it was an inexpensive low-end Yamaha, probably an RX11 model. Almost every word of the verses was now decipherable, even in the second, off-the-cuff verse, except for the grouping of words at the end of the second line, the phrase that rhymed with "hand of fate."

"See?" said Soto as the song faded. "You hear it that time?"

"What in particular?"

He smiled smugly. "The shadow of the reverb, that little clicking sound, with a distorted shimmer afterward. That's the signature of a Delta Deluxe VII model digital reverb unit. Delta came out with the Deluxe series to try to recapture that warm, spring reverb sound they used in a lot of rockabilly records back in the fifties. With the advent of digital technology, the emphasis on studio effects was all, you know, how clean and sterile you can get it. Then the pendulum swung back the other way, because people wanted some of the old sounds again.

"The Deluxe V and Deluxe VI models were almost perfect. They had that warm, cheesy sound of the old spring models, but very little distortion. Real nice for vocals and drums. But they were expensive, so they came out with an economy model, the Deluxe VII. That way, guitar players and home studio folks could afford them, too, not just professional studios. But they have that little click-shimmer-buzz to them, which you wouldn't care about on a home demo and you wouldn't notice in a noisy club. The Deluxe VII model didn't go into production until 1987, 1988."

"And you're certain that's what was used on this recording?"

His expression was that of a very confident man. "Absolutamente. Just like a wine taster knows his wine, friend."

"You own one of these gizmos?"

He shook his head cockily. "No, man, when I want a funky sound, I get the real thing. I've got Space Echo, an old Fender spring reverb, plates, you name it. But other people have used them here, and I've worked with just about everything they make. What's the rest of your theory?"

"I'll tell you in a minute. Can you clean up the vocal some more? I'm still trying to figure out the second line of the second verse."

"See what I can do. This was definitely done in some sort of demo studio setup, not anything up to what I've got here. Sounds like no more than eight track."

He yanked some cords out of the patch bay and plugged them into different places, adjusted some knobs on a compressor unit, changed the position of a couple of faders, then sat down again and replayed the tape. As it rolled, he made more minor adjustments, and I listened, taking sections of the lyrics apart and throwing the fragments against a swelling wall of suspicion. Most of them stuck.

Well I just can't shake the hand of fate
Spinning 'round a world of pain . . .

Sparse chords jangled, with the bass guitar sticking in the minor thirds, as the lyrics started out echoing a million other blues songs, but hinting at a deeper despair and self-pity than most.

You don't know what it's like
To be struck by lightning, and fall from the sky . . .

These lines could be either totally figurative, or very literal: Dovie had said the plane was struck by lightning before it crashed. I was voting for literal.

They say rest in peace but you didn't die
Hearing those angels singing
A sweet, sweet song, but not for you . . .

Literal, not figurative, except for the part about the angels, and that stuck to the wall, too. What if Richard James hadn't been killed in that avalanche? What if he was the sixth man in the search party? Dovie said Richard's face was mangled from his injuries, so much that she knew no one would ever pay to see him again. Maybe he knew it, too, and didn't want to come down from that mountain to face that kind of existence.

Cold as a coffin nail.

What was colder than a coffin nail? Frostbitten fingers? A TV picture tube showing a memorial service that you can't attend because you're the guy it's being held for?

Boiled in concrete.

Dovie said it was one of Cyclone's sayings. But she got mixed up while telling me about it, and said that Richard used to say it. Maybe she was right both times.

Buried alive in the blues.

Literal, figurative. Self-pitying to the point of cliché.

and you'll never know, boy you'll never know . . .
The whole damn truth.

Maybe, maybe not. But I was getting warm.

Soto reached over, pushed Stop on the tape machine, and said, "Well, did you get it that time, what he rhymes with *fate?*"

"Yeah. He was searching for a rhyme, found one, and mumbled it."

"I can see why. It's a pretty poor line."

I agreed. It was a revelation, too, but I'd already come to my conclusion before I figured out the exact words.

"Shit," said Soto. " 'This affair's all tangled, like *Contra*-gate . . .' "

I nodded. That was how I understood it, too.

"That's really poor, but I guess he was just vamping."

"Yeah. I've heard worse."

"Me, too, I suppose." He clapped his hands together. "OK, it's theory time. It *sounds* like Richard James, but it obviously isn't, because that model reverb didn't exist till late '87, '88, *Contra*-gate even later, and because Richard James died after his plane crashed on the twenty-fifth anniversary of Buddy Holly's death, back in 1984. So what's your theory?"

I took awhile to answer. Finally I said, "It's a fake." The word fell out of my mouth and died in the muted room, like the lie that it was.

"It's a *fake?*" he said, laughing. "Is that all there is to your theory? Is that what you came up here to find out, friend?"

My mind was spinning, not fast, but slow, like a tire wobbling out of alignment. At least two men had been killed over this tape. No, that wasn't right. They'd been killed for what it apparently implied.

The Whole Damn Truth.

The truth doesn't set you free: it kills you, like it had killed the curious rock critic and the disappeared pilot. But did I have the whole story? Dovie was still scared, still under some sort of spell. Maybe there were more secrets, ones that were darker than the possibility that Richard James had come down from that mountain and lived under the moniker of Cyclone Davis.

I didn't feel the rush of excitement that I thought I'd feel. I felt sad, fragmented. I was disappointed, more so than when I'd first heard the song. And Soto was disappointed in me. I didn't care.

"No," I said finally, pulling out my wallet. "I came up here to pay you your two hundred dollars. Sorry Cyclone couldn't make it."

"Put your money away, friend. And put your indignation back in check, too. I told you, I just don't like to get ripped off. I thought if I called Dovie and let her know that Cyclone had booked the studio and I'd lost money, well, maybe she'd want to make it up to me in some other way. You know, cut a demo here, or something. A small independent businessman like me has to look for every break he can get. You know how it is. But those guys broke in on me, and like I said, that pissed me off."

"At least they didn't burn down your studio. One other thing—did a writer by the name of Bob Jaworski ever get in touch with you?"

He thought for a moment, then shook his head. "Name sounds familiar, but I don't know. Why?"

"He was working on a story about James a couple of years ago."

Soto shook his head. "I know I didn't meet the guy. Maybe he called or something, but I don't remember. If he called and left a message and it wasn't about booking the studio, I probably didn't call him back, you know?"

"Forget it. Sure you don't want the two hundred?"

"Nah, keep it. Put some flowers on the guy's grave or something."

"I wish he had one," I said.

We shook hands and I left, holding on to that last thought as I drove back through the canyon. Cyclone Davis had no grave. Richard James had no grave. Even the bass player, Preston Drake, had no grave.

So many deaths, so few bodies to go with them.

3

It was just after nine o'clock, and the trendy eateries were buzzing and the glam rockers were already tottering down Sunset in their boots and spandex, their leathers, chains, and big hair. Expensive cars were humming past billboards advertising movies and concerts, the hotel valets were jumping, and the houses squatting on the slopes of the hill behind the cheap motel were escalating in value by the second. In the glittering basin on the other side of the Strip, the madness that was L.A. appeared to go on forever.

None of it had anything to do with me. In my cheap room with the mismatched furniture, there was nothing but the blues. I was drinking scotch and listening to voices from the past on my Walkman, wondering about their secrets.

Robert Johnson, the king of the Delta blues singers, murdered by a dose of poisoned whiskey at the age of twenty-seven, was every bit as compelling and disturbing over fifty years later. He played guitar like a man with three hands, and he sang like a man with hellhounds on his trail.

And there was something especially haunting about Memphis soul singer James Carr's bittersweet sixties-era soul ballads, too. Carr's awesome voice had been silenced after a brief but brilliant career, not by death, but a mysterious, unknown malady, something akin to a paralysis of spirit. Maybe after giving the world "Dark End of the Street" and "You've Got My Mind Messed Up," he'd felt he'd given all he had to give. Then suddenly, in 1991—after an absence of almost twenty years—he'd come back to record a new album. His singing was still chillingly good, and his story was still a scary one.

Another great Memphis singer, O.V. Wright, had died of cancer the year after a triumphant comeback tour of Japan in 1977. His "Nickel and a Nail," "Eight Men, Four Women," and "Drowning on Dry Land" were some of my all-time favorite songs, and I found some similarities between his career calamities and the case of Richard James and the Kilton gang, who'd financed his last album.

O.V. started singing professionally at the age of six and had already made a number of records with the gospel group, the Sunset Travelers, before meeting Goldwax Records' Roosevelt Jamison. Roosevelt felt certain that, with the right song, O.V. could have a crossover hit for his fledgling soul label. The two hit it off and began working together, O.V. dividing his time between performing in two different gospel groups on weekends, working as a garbage collector, and rehearsing with his bands in the blood bank that Roosevelt worked at during the week. Roosevelt eventually decided that "That's How Strong My Love Is"—a song he had written while dating a nurse—was the perfect vehicle for his new discovery. O.V. cut the song in 1964, and it was a hit.

Then O.V.'s past came back to haunt him.

A Houston nightclub owner/reputed numbers boss/record-label owner popped up with a contract O.V. had signed sometime previously as a member of the Sunset Travelers. O.V. hadn't told Goldwax about the contract because he thought it only obligated him as a member of the Travelers, not as a solo artist. But the Houston nightclub owner, who was reputed to conduct some of his contract negotiations with a .45 laying on his desk, wasn't the sort to take no for an answer, and Goldwax was forced to give up O.V.

It wasn't an unusual story. The same scenario had been played thousands of times before. But how many times had it happened to a performer who was supposed to be dead?

Apparently, after paying for Richard's failed comeback album, the Kilton search-party gang felt that they still had Richard James under contract, even as they let the rest of the world go on thinking he was dead. The undead Richard James kept writing songs. The songs were recorded by Dovie, and the royalties were collected by Otis, who fronted the gang and kept Dovie in line.

But there had to be more. This grift was screwy. Where was the glue that held it together?

A doctor, Chester White, was in on it. He could have fixed Richard's face during the same period of time he was working on Dovie's recovery at Oak Tree. She would have been vulnerable then, a physical and mental wreck from starvation, rape, frostbite, drug abuse, and what have you. It seemed to be a well-established fact that Otis had come into the picture during that period of time. Between the doc and the man called Otis, they'd talked her into the scam. Maybe even during the early months after her recovery, she hadn't even known it was a scam.

But still I had trouble seeing her keeping up the sham over the years. There had to be more. Where was the glue?

I thought about "The Whole Damn Truth" some more but gave up on it and thought about the guy who'd first told me about it instead, the wild man in the Cadillac, drinking whiskey and hollering about dead musicians. What was it he'd said about Dovie?

I know a thing or two about her that'd curl your hair.

Was he talking about himself, or about her? Dovie had said that the plane crash experience would always haunt her. Now the statement had new significance, but was she referring to the cover-up of Richard's non-demise, or the plane crash itself?

She'd said that love was not enough to keep her and Otis to-gether. Evidently blackmail and intimidation more than made up for it. What happened on that mountain? Was I going to have to fly to Colorado to find out? I hoped not; climbing and hiking weren't really in my line.

There had to be a way to find the glue. I thought about Cyclone some more. He was every inch a white trash blues monster: fat, with a greasy pompadour, sunglasses, mechanic's coveralls, and a Cadillac, swigging Richard James's favorite alcoholic refreshment, probably taking speed. He'd been to Lubbock recently.

Lubbock kept coming up in this thing. Buddy Holly was from Lubbock, and so were some other great musicians—Joe Ely, Butch Hancock, Jimmie Dale Gilmore, just to name a few.

Richard James had a thing about Lubbock. He bought his mother a house there. In Lubbock the Dog had stolen Nate Waco's old band away from him, and his wife, too. If Cyclone Davis was really Richard James, he'd have to go back to Lub-bock, to visit his mother, to hear the wind whistling over the plains, to hang around Buddy Holly's old haunts. But wait a minute, *Sgt. Roman said Cyclone had asked the motel clerk how to get to Buddy Holly's grave.*

That bothered me.

It also bothered me that there was no record of phone calls to a Mrs. Gilmore, Richard's mother. Maybe he'd just gone over without calling, but it still seemed odd. Dovie told me that Cyclone had called her from Lubbock, upset. Roman said there had actually been *two* such phone calls, both lengthy ones. According to Dovie, this was ostensibly after he'd stolen the tape from her.

Otis was supposedly from Lubbock, too. The high Texas plains were a long, long way from the backwoods of Kilton in East Texas. I wondered how he and the gang had gotten to-gether. Maybe Otis had met Richard in Lubbock, long ago. Maybe he had known Richard's mother before he made the publishing agreement with her.

Maybe Cyclone found out something about Otis in Lubbock, or maybe something in his brain pan went pop while he was there, causing him to make the distraught phone calls to Dovie, then decide to brace Otis, taking me along to back him up on the midnight meeting and in the studio.

Cyclone had said that the song was going to change his life. He was right about that. It ended it.

But was it his first brush with death, or his second?

I made another drink, then went over to the window to scowl at L.A. for awhile. A city that produces so many violent deaths that a man's body can get swallowed up, lost, and incinerated before it gets a chance to tell you who it belonged to was too big for me. A city where the cops threaten to squash you flat for squawking about that body getting lost was too evil for me.

The phone rang. It was Sgt. Roman. He said I wouldn't be needed for any more meetings. I was free to go back to Austin. All I had to do was book a flight and the city would pay for it. That was it.

I wanted to get out of there. I'd followed up my leads, answered a lot of dumb questions from the city's bureaucrats, asked a few of my own of Pep Soto. There was nothing else there for me, and prolonging my stay would only prolong my bitterness. But I was mad at Austin, too. It seemed too small and ingrown, too much like Sweet Bay City, where the cops call you "son" and warn you to go back where you came from. Dovie was there, and she'd lied to me. Our van was there, full of concrete. Graves and his pals were there, Nate Waco was there—though not all there—and Watson was there.

I owed Carson Block a call, but I didn't feel up to it. I did call Ladonna, and breathed a sigh of relief when I caught her answering machine. I left a brief, sincere message, then called my own number to check my messages. There were two.

LASKO—Hey, Martin, I just got off the phone with Sgt. Roman, and I just wanted you to know I didn't know about that cremation thing. I sure am sorry. Hope your trip didn't turn out to be just a pain in the ass for nothing. Gimme a call, let me know what's happening. Later.

WAYNE—Hi, Martin, it's Wayne. It's about eight o'clock on Saturday night and I'm here at the Continental Club. Listen, seeing as how last night went pretty well, I wanted to know if you and Dovie would like to try it again a couple of weeks from now, like maybe the weekend after Halloween. Sorry about the mix-up last time, Martin. Oh, and one other thing. You were looking for L-Tone Rogers. Well, this afternoon I was talking to my buddy up at the Blue Parrot and he said L-Tone's playing there, tonight through next week, maybe the week after, too. They seem to like him a lot there. Well, gimme a call when you get the chance. Oh, and that's the Blue Parrot in Lubbock, not Casablanca. Ha ha.

Lubbock.
Richard James's mother. Tornados. Cyclone Davis's distressed phone calls. Otis Taylor. L-Tone Rogers, the only man on the airstrip when the search party's helicopter landed, with either five or six men, besides Dovie and Cokey. Buddy Holly's grave.
Lubbock.
I would go there.

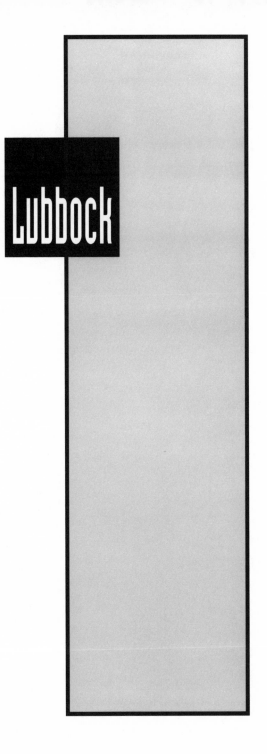

Lubbock

In Lubbock the air was cleaner and cooler. There were no palm trees at the airport. The people looked sturdier, hardly any looked like they belonged to a gym, and not many walked around toting Evian bottles and cellular phones. There were fewer Mercedes and BMWs, and hardly any vanity plates.

I rented a car at the airport and headed for the Astro Motel. I'd stayed there before, so finding it was no problem. The manager wasn't in and wasn't expected back. After all, it was Sunday, the clerk reminded me. I used the phone book in the lobby to look up Mrs. Varian Gilmore, then dropped some change in the pay phone and called her. A surprisingly lively voice answered, and when I told her I was a writer for *Rolling Stone* magazine, she responded by saying, "How nice. Did you wanna talk about Richard?" I said I did. She said that would be fine, but she'd just come home from church and could I wait until about four o'clock? I said that would be fine. She gave me directions out to her house, and I hung up the phone.

It was a little after twelve o'clock, too early to go by the Blue Parrot and ask about L-Tone's whereabouts, but not too early to go by Buddy Holly's grave. I was just about to ask the clerk to recommend a decent place to get some breakfast when I saw the metallic blue late '40s Mercury coupe parked in front of a room at the end of the wing. Fuzzy dice, Mardi Gras beads, and a gold L on a chain dangled from the rearview mirror. The door to the room was half open, and someone was sitting on the bed, playing his guitar.

L-Tone sat on the edge of the bed in his undershirt, baggy trousers, and house slippers, a gold-crowned tooth flashing in his grin and his fretting fingers flying over the neck of his guitar like a big black spider. His stage clothes were hanging in the closet, a purple lamé jacket with zebra-stripe lapels, matching pants, black-and-white Stacy Adams wingtips. His road-scarred twin Pro Reverb was at the foot of the bed.

"Yessir, Martin," he said as he riffed on the old semi-hollowbody Epiphone. "Doin' a week at the Blue Parrot. They dig my sound out here, man, dig that L-Tone sound."

"You're the man who has it, L-Tone," I said.

"That's right, sonny boy. Know how come I play so mean?"

I shook my head.

"When I's just startin' to play, no more'n a string bean of a fella playin' for nickels on the street, I met a girl. She was so cute, so fine, she made me hard all over. I got up the courage to talk to her, and she said why didn't I take her to the picture show? Pictures weren't no more'n fifty cents back then, you know, but fifty cents was all I had, so I said how 'bout a little walk downtown? So she said OK and we went for a walk. We walk by this restaurant, and she asked me could I buy her a piece of pie? So I did, even though it took my last penny, and afterwards I walk her home and she said her momma was out with a friend and why didn't I come on in? Well, I did, and she let old L-Tone into her love box and turned him inside out. Yes, sir. Man, I was walkin' on clouds all the next day. I look for her but couldn't find her nowheres. Later on that night, I walks by her house and peeks in the window, and there she is in her room, doing some other gentleman the way she done me."

L-Tone bent the treble strings up so high they kissed the low

E. "I hollered, Martin. I just couldn't hep myself. I just stood there'n hollered. Threw rocks at her house till she come out. The other gentleman lit out the back door. She comes out on the porch 'n says, 'L-Tone, whus wrong wit' you?' I says, 'I thought me 'n you had something.' She put her hands on her hips 'n says, 'Yeah, we did, L-Tone. Thanks fo' the pie. You bought me a piece'n I give you one.' "

He gave me a mock-serious scowl, then burst out laughing. "Man, I was so mad, I just wanted to slap her silly. But my poppa always told me, Boy, you don't hit no woman, no matter how riled she gets you. So I thought about that, and I just took it out on my guitar instead. And that's why I plays so mean."

I laughed and nodded in appreciation as he plucked out an exotic melodic riff that sounded like a cat meowing. "Was Richard ever rough with Dovie?"

"Hell, no," he said, bent over the guitar, strumming and riffing. "The Dog was just a big, overfed white boy fulla R&B 'n' white powder. Couldn't play guitar worth a shit or sing none too good, but he was a good fella, and no sir, he'd never hit no woman or treat her rough. Not when I's around, anyway."

"What about the guys who rescued Dovie and Cokey?"

He stopped playing for a moment. "What about 'em?"

"You said you didn't know them, right?"

"Naw, I told you I never run with that crowd. Not my type of folks."

"Do you remember a kid, a writer named Bob Jaworski?"

His lips folded into a rubbery frown. "Yeah, I 'member that boy. I don't talk much to reporters, Martin, you know that. They make up they own stuff, anyway, way I see it, so why I wanna waste my time tellin' em my own lies?"

"He was real curious about what happened to Richard. He was killed under mysterious circumstances, too."

L-Tone shook his head slowly, still frowning. "What I tell you? Make no sense gettin' mixed up in them Kiltonians. You die when you fuck with those boys, I don't see no mystery."

"But he did talk to you, right?"

"Well, he come to see me, but I run him off."

"Did you give him a photograph?"

"Nope. He already had one. Bought it off a fella worked at a film lab."

"I've got a copy," I said. "Wanna look at it?"

"Nope, no sir. Too painful."

"Who took it? Do you know?"

"Course I know. I's the one took it. One of them fellas had a camera, one of the Kilton boys. Don't recall which one. But I do recollect once I started to snap it off, a couple the other fellas got mad. Didn't want no picture, they say."

"How many were in the rescue party?"

"Six, I recollect."

"Six? Are you sure? There's only five in the photo."

"Hell yeah, I'm sure. Why you so curious?"

"Because there's only five in the photo, for one thing. Where was the other guy?"

"He was already in the plane, I reckon." L-Tone scratched the back of his neck and said, "See, that eggbeater they rented wasn't 'spose to carry more'n four people at a time. Gentleman at the airstrip who rented it to 'em kept on raisin' hell about it, 'cause he's afraid they were piling more in there when they went up over the mountains. So they took turns goin' up—two, three, or four at a time.

"Finally that last day they come back and dropped off couple of fellas back at the plane. I went over there and they run me off, said to mind my own business. Then they up 'n took off again. About an hour later, the beater come back, and that's when I saw they had Dovie 'n' Cokey with 'em. 'Bout that time couple fellas come on out of the plane, one of 'em was the doctor who was with 'em. That's when I snapped that picture. But I could tell they was somebody still up in that plane, way they acted. I figured it was one of the boys, and he got hurt on the mountain, or something. Coulda been frostbit, I reckon. Next thing I know, they up in that plane and outta there. Didn't stop to talk to the gentleman rented them that beater or nothing. That boy was pissed off. Civil Air Patrol boys were plenty mad, too."

He went back to playing, his right thumb gently massaging the strings, coaxing a tone out of the guitar that was much sweeter than the expression on his face. "You giggin' out here, Martin? Didn't see no van pull up."

"I didn't come here to play, L-Tone. Dovie's been having some troubles, and I've been trying to find out exactly why."

"What kinda troubles?"

"The Kilton gang has been dogging her. Otis Taylor was bossing her around, beating on her once in awhile, before he was murdered the other night. She was hanging around Cyclone in L.A. before he was murdered on his way to meet Otis about that song I told you about. I've been wondering if Cyclone was the guy who was hidden back in that plane."

"Hell you say, Martin," he said. "You saying this Monsoon Charlie was really the Dog, like he said when he called me? You trying to say you really think the Dog didn't die up there? I know you said that before, but it still don't set right with me."

"I'm not saying I like the idea, L-Tone."

He shook his head and played a jagged blues riff. "Now why would he go and do that?"

"Dovie said his face was pretty badly mangled in the crash. Maybe it affected his mind, too. It looks like Cyclone had some special business here not long before he was murdered, something that got him all worked up. When I was with him, I just thought he was a nut, but you know what he told me? He said, 'Sometimes crazy people don't act that way 'cause they're crazy, they act that way 'cause there's no other way to act.' "

L-Tone kept shaking his head. "Well that's a goofy-ass thing to say, but I can't hardly find no argument for it. One thing I do know, you sayin' that this other fella was beatin' on Dovie, but if the Dog was around, he wouldn't allow that kinda goin' on." He bent over the guitar again and picked at it. "Now a fella like old Preston, he was rough with his women once in awhile. Boy was a right prick of a fella, that Preston. Didn't much care for him.''

Preston, the one who raped Dovie up on the mountain. It figured. "Did you know him very well? I heard he was from Kilton, too.''

L-Tone looked up for a second, nodded, then went back to playing. "Yeah, I believe he was. I met him down in New Orleans before he hooked up with the Dog. Didn't much care for old Preston, but he was a good player. Had a damn good ear and played right behind the beat, real good. Like you play, Martin. I hate to say it, but he was funny, too. Always talkin' 'bout his dick. Never seen a white boy talk 'bout his dick so much.''

Suddenly his hands dropped to his sides.

"Shit, Martin," he said. "You really think the Dog would wanna go off and play dead? Never even give old L-Tone a phone call. What kinda predicament make a fella, even an old mangy fella like the Dog, do something like that?''

"I imagine it would be a pretty hard thing to do," I said. "It would make a guy pretty blue.''

"Blue, shit," he said. "Leavin' folks all thinkin' you dead. Like bein' buried alive, almost.''

"Yeah," I said, "and boiled in concrete.''

"Huh? Haven't heard that one in a coon's age.''

"Dovie said either Richard or Cyclone used to say it, about being in a tough situation or something. It's also in that song I told you about.''

L-Tone scratched his chin thoughtfully. "Well, I don't doubt that. Like I say, the Dog'd steal anything, your gal, your song, whatever. Guess an old bastard like him do it even after he's dead.''

"What do you mean, 'steal'? Richard wasn't the one who used to say it?''

"Not back when I's around. That was one of Preston's sayings, boiled in concrete. Cold as a coffin nail 'n boiled in concrete."

"That's real interesting, L-Tone."

"Yeah, if you say so. Like I say, the Dog'd steal your last nickel, too. Boiled in concrete, shit. I tell you something else, too, he wasn't talkin' 'bout no situation there. That's just Preston talkin' 'bout his dick. Boy was always talkin' 'bout his dick."

I stood up and shook hands with the guitar player. "Thanks a lot, L-Tone," I said. "You've been a big help."

"Shit," he said, the gold crown flashing in his smile. "I got nothin' to say. I do my eatin' with my teeth, my talkin' with my fingers, my walkin' with my feet, and you know what that thing hangin' down between the knees is for. And it ain't for talkin' 'bout, not to my way of thinkin'."

2

I got in the car and went for a drive through the flat wind-chafed town. Rolling down parts of the main drag, it looked as if the '50s had never left. I stopped at a little joint with curb service, ordered a Frito pie from a carhop girl with turquoise eye shadow and a bra that turned her breasts into missile cones. At a truck stop I picked up a regional map and a Joe Ely cassette, and then I just drove for awhile. There was a defect in one of the windows that caused the wind to leak in, producing a constant whistle. I cranked the volume on the tape deck but the natural accompaniment was still audible, like the whine of an unearthly steel guitar. Between Tokyo and Detroit, what did they know about the wind on the Texas plains?

The Panhandle-Plains region, where Lubbock is situated, is a long way from Austin, geographically and otherwise. Lubbock is closer to the capitals of New Mexico, Colorado, and Oklahoma than to the capital of Texas. Closer to Plainview, Plains, Plano, Muleshoe, Sundown, and Levelland than any sort of cosmopolitan metropolis. It gets cold out there, and you can see twenty miles in any direction.

In the rearview mirror, I could see the downtown buildings, but they didn't do much to compete with the giant blue sky as the main feature of the landscape. Something about its quaintness—the surplus of wind and sky and Baptist repression, the billboards advertising Prairie Dog Town—and its remoteness and flatness favored the impression that it belonged to one of several other times. It belonged to the Old West, its ghosts stirred up by the wind and songs like Joe Ely's "Me and Billy the Kid." It belonged to the Mexicans and the Indians, who still made up a good part of the population. It belonged to the time when oil was king in Texas, and Elvis was the king of rock 'n' roll.

Things still seemed a lot simpler here, even the complicated, ugly things I'd brought along with me. I kept thinking about L-Tone, grousing about how Richard would steal anything, even a deceased bandmate's macho boast, but still missing him, and still, in his roundabout way, praising him. And I kept seeing his mournful face, asking how was it that the Dog could treat an old friend like that, to pretend to be dead and not even give him a phone call.

Maybe his mother could tell me.

The white frame house with a picket fence was at the end of a mile of meandering dirt road. Sheep grazed on the grayish brown grass around a windmill, and chickens pecked at the gravel beside a brown Suburban station wagon in the drive. A trim gray-haired woman in a long blue dress was standing behind the screen door when I walked up the steps.

"Mrs. Gilmore?" I said.

"You must be the fellow from *Rolling Stone,*" she said as she opened the door. I nodded. "Come on in. Can I get you something to drink?"

I declined, so she started in with a tour of the house. "Richard bought this place for me, you know. After my husband died I just didn't care for San Antonio anymore, and one of my sisters lived out here. And Richard always liked it here, for some reason. Don't know why, there isn't all that much to like. Or dislike, for that matter."

Over the fireplace hung a huge oil painting of Richard James decked out in black leather and pomade. His curled-lip sneer was softened, though, by a pastel pink gloss on his lips, and there was a definite halo aura in the blurry neon glow behind his head. The mantel below the portrait was taken up by photos of Richard as a child and several of his father, in his army uniform.

I followed her down a hall decorated with more photos and several gold records, into a den with more photos, an acoustic guitar, a music stand, and some sitting chairs.

"You sure you wouldn't like something to drink?" she said. "It's no trouble, young man."

I shook my head and gazed respectfully around the room. I'd started feeling guilty about the purpose for my visit about half a second after crossing her threshold. Mrs. Gilmore was spry and almost bubbly, not at all the picture of a woman whose son who might have actually died as recently as the week before. Maybe she was a good actor, or maybe she wasn't aware of the scam any more than L-Tone was. Either way, I was starting to feel like I was on a bum errand.

"You must be very proud of your son," I said.

She gave me a funny look. A heart-shaped pendant on a gold chain hung around her neck, and as she fingered it, the light threw a glint on the stone of her wedding band. "Well of course I am. Richard had a God-given talent, and he used it to the best of his abilities. I wasn't always happy with his songs, but I'm too old to approve and just old enough to realize that I'm not supposed to. I mean, that's why they call it rock 'n' roll, isn't it?"

"You hit the nail on the head, Mrs. Gilmore."

"What did you want to ask me, young man?"

I put on my best journalistic mug. "What about some of the people Richard hung around with, Mrs. Gilmore? Surely that caused you some concern at times."

She frowned a bit and plucked at the fabric of her dress. "Well, you're right there. Richard was sort of a rebellious child. We tried to bend him to our will and, as children will do, he just naturally did his best to bend the other way. That's why he chose the life he chose. Richard, bless his heart, was a poor judge of character. He hung around the wrong crowd sometimes, and ofttimes when he got around good people, he brought them down with him. That's why I kind of felt bad for that girl, Dovie, when she started going with him. But they turned out to be a pretty good couple, and they were good for each other. That's what I told her poor mother."

"You know Dovie's mother?"

She nodded. "Uh huh. She called me after they went on the road together the first time. Apparently Dovie and her parents had a big falling out when she started with the music thing, and they never spoke after that. But that girl's mother loves her, and it's a shame they can't get together. I still talk to her once in awhile."

"How about Otis Taylor, Mrs. Gilmore? Could you tell me a bit about him?"

Her face grew quiet. "Well, isn't that just awful what happened to him?"

"Yes, it is. How did you two get together?"

Her gaze drifted over to the music stand as she fingered her pendant. "I'll tell you one thing, he sure thought highly of Richard's music. He offered me quite a bit of money for the rights to all Richard's unpublished songs. Well, I told him that I honestly didn't think he'd left all that much. There were a couple of boxes of tapes he'd left here, but I thought most of that was from when he was first starting out. But Mr. Taylor said he thought he could round up some more from studios Richard had worked in down in Austin, and I sure don't know a thing about the business myself, so I said, why not? It sure beats social security and an army pension."

"So he picked up all the tapes you had when you signed the contract?"

"Well, he didn't actually do it himself. Actually, I never met the man, not in person. We talked over the phone, and the men who flew out with the other fellow who had the contract picked up the tapes. I don't recall his name, but he was handling the legal part because his father, who was a lawyer, had drawn up the contract, and Mr. Taylor didn't like to fly."

"You said you don't remember the name of the guy with the contract?"

She thought for a moment. Her eyes brightened and she said, "I do recall that he was a doctor."

"Chester White?"

She shook her head. "I'm sorry, that could be it, but I really can't say. I guess I'm getting old and forgetful."

"Do you still have the contract? Maybe his name, or his father's name is on it."

She thought for a moment while she fingered the pendant. "Well, yes," she said, "I guess it would be. But I keep all that sort of paperwork down at my lawyer's office. Do you really need it for your story?"

The guilt came back. I swallowed. "No, I guess not." I scratched my head, trying to think of more questions that would go along with my journalist ruse, and couldn't think of any, so I just blurted out one of the others. "Mrs. Gilmore, did you know Cyclone Davis?"

She looked startled, not by the question, but its blunt delivery. "Well, no. I guess I'm not up on the music scene. He *is* a singer, isn't he? I mean, it sounds like a singer's name."

"Yes, he was a singer. He came out here to see Buddy Holly's grave and a couple of other things. I thought he might've contacted you."

She smiled. "Well, a lot of people do. That's what happens when you're a celebrity's mother. I'm on the tour right along with Buddy Holly's grave. People come out and look at me, look at Richard's stuff, and I tell them whatever they want to know, as long as it's not personal or dirty. They all have that look on their faces, too, like they're trying to figure it out, where it all came from. But I can't tell them. I was just his mother. Whatever is inside a person comes from God. It's up to the individual to make of it what they can, good or bad. You've got it, too, young man."

"What's that?"

"That look. I hope I've been able to help you some."

"You have."

"I'm glad. You sure you wouldn't like something to drink? I could make some coffee or tea."

I shook my head once again, thanked her for her time, and left.

As I drove back down the dirt road, huge dust devils roiled in my wake. Seeing them made me thirsty, but I was glad I hadn't accepted her offer of libations. She probably even had a bottle of Seagram's in the cupboard, but Richard James hadn't been by to drink any in a long, long time.

3

Richard James's mother said she'd never seen Mr. Taylor.

Mr. Taylor didn't like to fly.

When I pulled up at the cemetery and glanced at the odometer on the rental car, I thought about the high mileage on Mr. Taylor's LTD and the Cadillac he'd given Cyclone Davis.

I kept thinking about it as I walked through the cemetery, pausing to read names, dates, and words of affection carved into cold, hard stones. The words seemed so final and absolute. Why was it that marble and granite provoked people to reverence and thoughtfulness? Words of wisdom in Latin or lofty paeans to God were always being chiseled into them, never anything casual or intentionally flip. Was it because they were symbols of permanence, or was it because they were cold and hard, like the truth?

The whole damn truth.

Buddy Holly, died February 3, 1959.

You could almost hear his six-syllable "We-eh-eh-eh-ella" at the beginning of "Rave On" hiccuping in the wind. "Peggy Sue." The Crickets. Alan Freed. The Ed Sullivan Show. The Fifties—Cadillacs, nerd glasses, Stratocasters. Payola, rip-off-artist managers, plane crashes. The first song that the Beatles (even their *name* was a tribute) had recorded was a 78 RPM of Holly's "That'll Be the Day."

When I die.

I walked around some more in the soft ground and stopped at another grave. I looked back over my shoulder toward Buddy Holly's grave again. Standing there, you'd just be able to make out the name on the tombstone I was standing beside.

The inscription said:

OTIS WENDELL TAYLOR
Born Jan. 7, 1954
Died April 5, 1954
From His Mother's Bosom
to God's

If it hadn't been a Sunday, I could have gone down to the health department and, for a small fee, obtained a copy of Otis Wendell Taylor's birth certificate, and used that to obtain all sorts of false identification under that name. But I didn't need to do that. Someone else had done it a few years ago, and I had a theory as to who that someone else was.

So did Cyclone Davis when he flew to Lubbock and saw that tombstone.

I walked back to the car, got in, and drove back to the airport, looking forward to the flight back to Austin and further confrontations with the whole damn truth.

But I was also anxious to get it over with, because the theory was depressing. If true, it meant that Mr. Taylor didn't like to fly for the same reason that Dovie de Carlo didn't like to fly. That meant Mrs. Gilmore was wrong, she *had* met Mr. Taylor.

Mr. Taylor was her son.

Austin The Whole Damn Truth

Maybe I'd never know the true identity of the body of the man who'd called himself Cyclone Davis, but chances were that sooner or later, the body of the man who'd called himself Otis Taylor would tell its caretakers who it had really belonged to. It seemed likely that Graves would turn up soon, too, and he could answer whatever questions Otis Taylor's corpse couldn't. But I still wanted to know how they'd gotten Dovie to go along with the scam all these years.

"The Whole Damn Truth" had to be the key. Not just that song, either, but all the other songs that Dovie had been recording over the years. Where had they actually come from? According to several sources, Richard hadn't been all that prolific. Not while he was alive, anyway. If he'd been pretending to be dead all this time, he'd probably had a lot of free time on his hands. But where does a dead man go to record a hit song?

After my cemetery visit, I'd talked briefly with Carson. Carson told me then that he'd been bothered by the fact that there were no master tapes of *any* kind at Otis's house. Even if Richard James really *had* left behind three albums worth of unreleased material, master tapes had to be stashed somewhere.

Carson told me he had called around to all the studios in town, but none owned up to having any Richard James masters.

It was possible he had a studio in Lubbock, and maybe Cyclone had found it, in addition to the tombstone. I made a few calls before leaving Lubbock but failed to turn anything up, and it seemed more likely that Richard would want to stick close to the gang in Austin anyway.

Why would Richard James pretend to be dead in the first place, and how did he get Dovie to go along with him? I made Carson promise not to tell her what I'd found out on my trip. I wanted to ask her these questions in person.

I wasn't able to get a flight back to Austin until Monday evening. When I got in, I headed straight for Dovie's house. When I arrived, she was in the shower, and Carson was struggling with the futon, trying to cart it from the living room back to the bedroom. I gave him a hand. The mattress was dense and unmanageable, and carrying the thing was like trying to dress an unconscious fat man, but we finally got most of it off the floor and started walking it back to the bedroom. Between gasps for breath, Carson told me that he'd broken his promise.

"I couldn't help it, Martin," he said. "I asked her if Otis was really Richard and she denied it. But afterward she called Chester White and started drinking and taking pills again."

We made it into the bedroom. All the debris had been cleared out and the surfaces scrubbed down. The gap in the floor was still there, where the microcassette-corder had been. We dragged the futon over to the spot where the bed had been and let it drop, then went outside and sat down on the steps. Carson had picked up his jacket on the way out, and he held it in his lap, stroking it distractedly as he spoke.

"Listen, Martin," he said, still gasping from his exertion, "about the spying thing. She thinks it's Nate, and maybe she's right. She's not just paranoid. I hate it out here, man. You notice that dancing tree when you came up the drive?"

"No. I had other things on my mind."

"Well, I looked at it yesterday, and it's all dried up, man. Why would a dead tree dance?"

"You got me, Carson."

He frowned. "Another problem: The record company wants me to see if I can cut a deal with Otis Taylor's estate for Richard James's publishing. Well, guess who inherits the song catalog now that he's dead?"

"Three guys from Kilton, Texas?"

"Right, and guess who does their legal work?"

"Chester White's father?"

"Yeah," he said. "Like you suspected. So it looks like you may be right about Chester being involved in this thing up to his stethoscope. His dad is conveniently out of the country, and I don't get paid enough to talk business with Red Fred and Nubby Maxwell. And tonight I thought it might be a good idea for Dovie to get out and do something to take her mind off all this stuff, so I took her down to the Willie Nelson concert at Palmer auditorium. But no sooner do I pick up our comp tickets at the box office than we run into those two scumbags. So we turned around and came back here."

"I'm glad you did. I'm pretty anxious to talk to her."

He bit his lip and said, "And Christ, Martin, you should've seen the way those guys looked at Dovie, like she's some kind of freak or something. I mean, I know she's got problems, but, you know, it just gave me the chills. I know it upset her, too." He frowned, biting his lip again. "It figures those hillbilly hoodlums would be big Willie fans."

"Now, don't go putting Willie down," I said. "And you gotta respect this gang. Look how dedicated they are to their musical idols, Willie and the Dog. After all that's been going on, they still have the energy to go root for Willie. And that's nothing, they've been supporting Richard James for over ten years, first just giving him speed and carting him around in a private plane while he was alive, then keeping him underground, writing songs for you and Dovie after he was supposed to be dead."

He was slumped forward, one of his hands deep in the pocket

of the jacket, playing with something inside it. "For chrissakes, Martin," he said, "You really think he really *didn't* die on that mountain?"

"It sure looks like it," I said.

"Wow," he said, sighing wearily. "This is incredible, Martin. Major felonies and rock history, all tangled up with our little singer. No wonder she's a wreck. I don't see how she's been able to take it."

My muscles were still throbbing from wrestling with the futon. Dovie had been handling that thing by herself every night since she'd moved out here. I wondered what else she was more capable of handling than we gave her credit for.

"You know," I said, "I can't figure out why Graves would kill Richard. Why kill the goose that pens the golden eggs?"

"I don't care," said Carson, his hand still fidgeting inside the pocket of his jacket. "The guy was a sick puppy. You know what he did to Dovie that afternoon before he was killed? He tied her up, naked, and left her. Left her trussed her up like a Thanksgiving turkey, man. I think she was scared to tell you about it."

I thought about that while Carson kept fiddling with his jacket. Suddenly the sound of an electric guitar erupted from the pocket.

Carson blinked and jerked his hand out of the pocket. "Oops."

"What've you got there?"

He pulled the object out of his pocket and held it up for me to see. It was the microcassette-corder I'd found in the hole in the bedroom floor. When he pushed the play button, the electric guitar came to life again. The guitar meandered around a melodic figure for a few bars, exploring different notes and phrasings, then settled into a groove. After some minor variations on the rhythmic feel, the guitar riffed in a different key, meandered, then stopped abruptly. Someone coughed. A loud noise, like that of something falling or being thrown on the floor.

Another cough. More guitar, some of it just riffing, some of it exploring a song idea.

"Is that the tape that was in it?" I asked.

He nodded. "I bought some batteries for it this afternoon," he said. "I guess Nate used it to record his song ideas. Dovie says he's paranoid about people stealing his songs."

"That's putting it mildly."

Carson fast-forwarded the tape and let it play again. More riffing. Abrupt switch to coughing, the sound of a window opening. More riffing, tuning, lead figures.

"Lots of extraneous noise and doodling on it," he said. "There doesn't seem to be a dead spot on the whole tape."

"It's voice-activated," I said, reaching over to take the recorder from him.

"I know that, Martin. I used to have one for taking notes."

I fast-forwarded the tape and played another section. The fidelity was poor and, as Carson had pointed out, there was an awful lot of useless doodling on the tape in addition to the nonmusical sounds. I gave the device back to him and he put it back in his jacket.

"I didn't even think he'd still be able to play," I said. "You find any other tapes like this around the house?"

"No, but the guy's a nut, right?"

I started to embellish the comment, but didn't. Dovie was standing in the doorway of the house. Carson gave me a worried look.

"Give us a few minutes," I said.

"It's not true, Martin," she said. She was wearing a terry-cloth bathrobe and deck shoes. A full glass of wine was in one hand, a cigarette in the other. I noticed that Nate's guitar and amp were stuck in a corner of the living room. Occasionally she glanced over there.

We sat down on the couch. She drew the robe up around her, sipped the wine, sucked on the cigarette. "Otis was just a guy," she said. "They said he came from Lubbock but maybe he was from Kilton like the rest of them. I don't know. But Otis was *not* Richard."

"All right," I said. "But these songs you've been doing weren't recorded before the plane crash. At least 'The Whole Damn Truth' wasn't."

She didn't say anything.

"Where did Otis make the recordings?"

"I don't know. He just sent me tapes, that's all."

"What do Moreland and the doc have to do with this?"

"Chet takes care of me," she said. "And Otis used to spend a lot of time out at the ranch."

"Did he spend much time with the doc?"

She just shrugged.

"You know, I'd think you'd want to help me out on this."

She looked away and mumbled. "I can't."

"Why? Because you don't want to lie to me?"

She shook her head. "Because something happened to me a long time ago and I can't change it. I guess my mother was right. I sold my soul to the devil and I gotta take what comes, but because of it I've had a career I never would've had otherwise. Richard's dead. Cyclone's dead. Otis's dead. My husband is skulking around in the woods, spying on me for God knows what reason."

"You really think Nate is out here?"

"Yeah. I'm gonna take that amp and guitar and leave them out on the porch. Maybe he'll come get them and leave me alone."

"Is that all you're going to do?"

"What do you want me to do?"

"Tell the devil to fuck off," I said. "Tell me what kind of contract you signed with him."

She sighed and drew her robe closer again. "I don't want anyone else to get hurt. Just go home and forget about it."

"I can't do that. You asked me to help you, remember? When we first met, you were so sure Otis killed Cyclone that you wanted me to kill him. Remember? Now you want me to forget about it, to do nothing. Why?"

She just shook her head.

I started over, from another direction. "When we got confirmation that Otis flew into LAX the morning after Cyclone was killed, you believed it. But when we left L.A. a couple of days later, you said not to worry about Otis, that he wouldn't be in Austin for awhile. You saw Nubby at the Austin airport, and you knew he wasn't there to pick up Otis because Otis was driving back from L.A."

"So?"

"So if you knew that Otis didn't like to fly, why didn't it occur to you that he'd driven to L.A. and sent Red Fred in a white wig so he'd have an alibi when he killed Cyclone? Especially when you knew that he left L.A. by car?"

Her expression looked completely childlike. "I don't know. I guess I'm stupid, OK? He told me he was driving back to Austin. I didn't know it was supposed to mean anything, and when I saw the plane ticket for that Friday morning, I took that on face value, too. I'm sorry I'm stupid, Martin. Sorry to disappoint you."

"Knock it off."

She drew her knees up against her chest and held the wine-glass in both hands. "There's no use, Martin. I've done a bad thing that can't be undone. Sometimes the world's just stacked up against you and there's no use fighting it."

"Richard's dead. He can't hurt you anymore, can't make you feel guilty or obligated to him."

"You don't understand, Martin. Go away."

"Even if I go away, this thing won't. You know that."

The skin around her eyes quivered, but no tears came out.

"Did Preston really die in the avalanche, or did Richard and the gang kill him because he raped you?"

Her jaw dropped open. "No, Martin. Good God, no. I told you Richard died up there. Quit doing this to me."

"Did Otis really tie you up the day he was killed?"

She pressed her face against her knees and nodded, causing the wine to slosh out of her glass. I took the glass from her and tried to put my arms around her, but she fought me off.

I stood up. "Was Nate out here that day, too?"

She wouldn't look at me. "Just go, Martin."

"What have they got on you, Dovie?"

She put her legs down and got up, glared at me for a second, walked back to the bedroom, and shut the door.

I heard the lock click. I wanted to kick something.

Carson looked up anxiously as I came out on the steps. I could tell he was anxious to go back in. "What'd she say?" he said.

"To forget about it," I said.

He put his jacket on, looked out at the woods, shuddered. "Well?"

"That's the one thing I can't do," I said. I checked my watch. It was a little after ten. "What was the schedule on Willie's show?"

He gave me a funny look. "It started at eight. There were three opening acts. Willie wasn't supposed to go on till midnight."

"Good. Did you happen to see Chester White at the concert?"

He shook his head. "He could've been there, I don't know. Why?"

"Because I'm gonna make a house call. It'd be easier on both of us if he wasn't home."

"You aren't thinking of breaking into his house, are you?"

"Damn right I am. There has to be a studio somewhere. The doc's in on the scam. There's something missing here, something that's held this thing together all this time."

"And you think the doc might have the studio in his house? You think that'll be the answer to everything?"

"I don't know. But it sure could clear up a lot of things. All I know is I can't leave him alone until I find out."

Carson bit his lip again. "You can't do it, man."

"Why not? It wouldn't be my first burglary."

"It doesn't matter, the cops are watching the place."

"Are you sure?"

He nodded enthusiastically. "Oh yeah, I drove by there my-self yesterday. The neighborhood's crawling with plain-wrap cars. You wouldn't stand a chance in hell."

I looked away from him so I could think. Maybe Watson had Chester White tied into the Kilton gang, after all. Carson was right, there was no use trying to pay the doc a visit. Watson's men would probably pull me over before I got halfway down his block.

What the hell. I still had a hankering to break into somebody's house and find a recording studio. Dovie had been mum about Otis's involvement with the doc, but she did say that he'd spent a lot of time out at the ranch.

I nudged Carson's shoulder and said, "Gimme your keys."

He looked puzzled, but instinctively reached inside his pocket and took them out anyway.

"You don't wanna know," I said.

I took his keys, got in his car, steered it west.

2

I drove past Moreland's gate and turned in at the small dirt road leading into the thicket. I pulled the car off the road and parked in a cedar break just off the first rise and walked the rest of the way. I had a flashlight, the Beretta, and the large screwdriver that had put me on the other side of a number of locked doors and windows in the past.

The road was rough going even on foot, with so many curves that several times I had to stop and convince myself that it hadn't looped back over itself and sent me back the way I'd come. Finally it dumped out into a small clearing with a cabin and a round building made of stone on the right side of it.

The cabin was a ramshackle, unpainted wooden structure a little larger than a double-wide mobile home. No lights were on. The round building next to it was about twenty feet high and ten feet in diameter. Attached to the side was a plastic BEWARE OF DOG sign. A windmill stood a few yards from the round building, and the clearing around the place extended no more than twenty yards in any direction. There were no vehicles except for an old John Deere tractor, and, despite the warning sign, no hound of hell came charging up to rip out my windpipe.

The air had a smoky smell to it. I thought back to the plume of smoke I'd seen on my last visit to the ranch. I judged that the lime pit would be somewhere off in the woods to the right. Maybe I'd have to check that out, too.

The front porch was rickety, but the front door looked solid, secured by two dead bolts, and the windows had burglar bars. Twigs snapped as I crept around to the side and shined the flashlight in the first window, illuminating a kitchen. I bounced the beam of light over a combination wall phone and answering machine by the door, a microwave oven and lots of liquor bottles on the counter by the sink. Through the next window I saw a bed, a gun cabinet with lots of guns in it, and walls papered with pictures of naked women. I skipped the next window and crept around back.

In the clearing behind the place, several straw-back chairs were arranged in a semicircle around a tree stump. I walked over there. Mixed in with the leaves on the ground were hundreds of spent brass cartridges and empty liquor bottles. I trained the flashlight beam on the edge of the clearing. The trees had been shot up.

I turned my attention back to the cabin. The back door had two dead bolts, just like the front, but the unpainted wooden frame had started to rot. I picked up a rock and used it to hammer the screwdriver into the weakest looking area. The wood splintered easily. In a few minutes, the door came tumbling down. I climbed in over it.

There was a lot of life-style crammed in the back room: more guns, a modern television monitor, a VCR, a Nintendo game setup, a washer and dryer, two beanbag chairs, an army cot, and the rank ether smell that followed the Kilton gang around.

Flesh and steel winked at me from all sides—porno magazines and videocassettes scattered amongst an armory that ranged from Uzis to hunting rifles, from snub-nose revolvers to pump shotguns. A boar's head grinned at me over the door to the kitchen, and a six-foot rattlesnake skin was stretched out on one wall.

I stepped into the kitchen. It was an unenlightening mess. I checked the microcassette in the answering machine. No messages, not from Richard James, Elvis, or crooked DEA agents.

Two bedrooms were located on the left side of the house off the kitchen. I went into each one and found nothing that surprised me, or anything to justify the midnight mission.

The bathroom and one more room were on the other side of the cabin. The filthy bathroom held no surprises: no drugs in the medicine chest behind the mirror, plenty of browsing material on the toilet tank.

One room to go. The door was shut and padlocked. I jammed the screwdriver into the lock hasp, kicked the door, and the screws ripped out and the door swung open.

The room was empty, stripped and bare. The floor was carpeted, and the padding underneath the rug felt substantial. There were dents in it, where heavy things had rested for a long period of time. The inside of the door and the walls were dotted with upholstery tacks, with bits of foam material clinging here and there where the material had been ripped down. There were extra electrical outlets in the walls, and the ceiling had been sprayed with a layer of insulation that looked to be six to eight inches thick.

This was it. Not the studio, but the place where it had been until very recently. The room's raw emptiness screamed volumes. I went back through the house to make sure I hadn't missed anything, but I found no file cabinets full of dirty secrets, no recording gear, no musical instruments, and no tapes that weren't prerecorded commercial cassettes, although they did have an extensive CD collection. Heavy on the Willie Nelson and Richard James. Nothing but that empty room.

I chuckled to myself as I thought of Detective Watson. Maybe he was finally barking up the right tree by watching the doc. This hovel was no speed lab and I wondered if it ever had been. At least there *had been* a studio there.

I went out the back way and checked out the round building. There was a plank door on the right side but no windows. I tried the door. It swung open, creaking like a witch's cackle. I stepped over the threshold and flicked on the flash, illuminating a rusting water pump in the center of the room. I moved the flashlight beam down to the concrete floor and froze in my tracks.

Rattlesnakes.

At least a dozen, probably more. They hissed and shook their rattles as the light washed over their spade-shaped heads and their diamond-patterned backs, lying there in deadly knots, uncoiling in a liquid grace, their tongues flicking out, tasting the air.

I backed out slowly and shut the door with care, feeling that if I closed my jaws suddenly, I'd take a bite out of my heart. My gaze stuck on the BEWARE OF DOG sign. Some joke. So this was the "mean old hound" Moreland had warned me about.

It was time to get the hell out of there. I took two steps toward the road before I stopped. The smoky smell from the woods stinging at my nostrils pulled me back. I trained the flashlight around the clearing, wondering how far it was to the lime pit, stopping when the beam lit up a set of tire tracks in the dirt leading out through the woods to the right, heading in the direction I'd guessed the lime pit would be.

What the hell? It was no darker and stranger out there than the thicket I was going to have to walk back through, and I was still empty-handed. I checked my watch. I still had time.

There had been fire in the lime pit. I broke a four-foot branch off a dead tree and poked around in the ashes. The smell clawed at my nostrils and the stirred-up ash almost choked me, but I kept at it until the branch struck buried treasure.

A blackened power amplifier. An 8-track console. Cables, tape reels, microphones. Weird lumps of molten plastic, guitar strings, circuit board. A rectangular unit about the size of a boot box with wires dangling out the back.

I tugged this last item out of the pit, turned it upright, spit on the front panel, wiped it with a dead leaf. The engraved lettering was still legible:

DELTA DELUXE VIII DIGITAL REVERB

Pep Soto had been close enough. He'd said the reverb used on "The Whole Damn Truth" had to be a Delta Deluxe VII, proving that the recording had been made no earlier than three or four years *after* Richard James's supposed demise. The Deluxe VIII would be an even later model.

I'd found the studio and I'd found the equipment that Richard James's songs had been recorded on after his death. I was halfway home. I just needed to get out of the woods.

I banged the thing on the ground to knock the loose ashes off and picked it up. I wasn't going back to Austin empty-handed after all. As I stepped back from the pit, something rattled by my foot. I put the light on it. It was a microcassette.

I ran all the way back to the cabin.

I replaced the microcassette in the answering machine with the one I'd found at the lime pit and hit the play button. A cough, a loud sniffle, a fragment of a song . . . guitar noodlings, a lead figure, chords . . . a cough, a window opening, feedback, more riffing. A hoarse hum, a cough, a sniffle, more riffing, a fragment of a song. I hit the fast-forward button. More song fragments.

My heart did a flip-flop. The tape was just like the one in the microcassette-corder hidden at the lake house. I wondered how many more had been cremated in the lime pit. I wondered how long that cassette recorder had been hidden under Nate's bed.

Maybe Nate wasn't as crazy as I'd thought. Someone had been stealing his songs after all. I thought about what Cyclone Davis had said: "Sometimes crazy people don't act that way 'cause they're crazy, they act that way 'cause there's no other way to act."

Poor Nate.

Poor Cyclone.

Poor heart, gonna jump out of my chest.

I headed back down the road as fast as I could manage with the reverb unit, and only lost my footing and fell on the rocks twice. I made good time, I thought, getting back to the car. I figured Nubby Maxwell and Red Fred would still be bopping to "Whiskey River" or some other twangy anthem they'd heard a million times before. I figured wrong.

Graves, Nubby, and Red Fred were waiting behind an old tree when I got back to the Chrysler. I dropped the reverb unit just as Graves hit me in the stomach so hard my hands hit the ground before my knees, and Red Fred stepped on my fingers when I tried to catch the Beretta as it tumbled out of my pocket.

"God-dang nosy bastard," said Graves, kicking the reverb unit so hard it bounced several feet. "I told you not to fuck with me."

Red Fred laughed, his chest heaving with excitement under a tattered *Star Trek: The Next Generation* T-shirt. The large automatic was a gray blur in his shaky grip.

"I can't believe you guys walked out on Willie," I said.

"Me and Nub had a little business proposition goin' there," said Red Fred.

"You guys have a part of Willie's bandana concession or were you just renting out your jumper cables?"

Nubby cackled as his hand danced anxiously from his knife holster to the grip of the handgun jutting out from his jeans. Now I could see the Monte Carlo hidden behind some cedar trees on the other side of the road.

That and Graves's fist were the last things I saw before everything went black.

I came to in the empty room in the cabin. Graves had just hit me in the stomach. By the assortment of hurts in my body, he'd long since grown bored with my face. He towered over me, his snakeskin boots inches from my face. Red Fred and Nubby grinned from opposite corners, ready to pounce on me in case Graves let me bounce their way. Chester White stood in the doorway.

"Hit him again," said the doc.

3

When I came to again I was propped upright against the wall,
my right eye nearly swollen shut and something sticky running
down the side of my face. Red Fred leaned against the opposite
wall, hands in his pockets, hat tilted back on his head. Graves
stood beside him, rubbing his knuckles. Nubby hung back in
the corner, fingering his knife, sucking his lower lip under his
upper, the kind of nervous tic that is a dead giveaway for stim-
ulant abuse. Chester White leaned in the doorway, tight-lipped
and pale in a casual khaki blazer and red V-neck sweater.

None of them had a gun. My hands weren't tied.

"I say we chop 'im up," said Nubby.

The doc gave him a reproachful cluck.

"Looks like I busted into the right place," I said.

Chester White finally showed his teeth. "You know, Martin,
I now remember where it was I saw you play. Your band opened
for Albert King at a benefit at Antone's about five years ago.
I remember you played a candy-apple red Precision and wore
a black vintage suit, like the one you're wearing now."

"Same suit," I said, "and here I am, working for free again.
Things don't change much, do they?"

"I guess not," he said. "Just what did you think you found
here, Martin?"

"Well, it's not exactly Graceland," I said, "but what the hell, it's secluded. No neighbors to complain about loud music being played by a guy who's supposed to be dead. This was the studio, wasn't it?"

Chester White nodded. "But believe it or not, this is the first time I've been out here. I'm not fond of guns, Martin." He looked around at the hatted hoodlums. "You'll notice that there are none in this room," he said. Then he added, "At the moment."

"That's swell," I said. "How'd you guys get together, anyway, at a peace rally?"

The doc shrugged. "My father put us in touch when they heard about the plane disappearing. After the rescue, it was explained to me that these guys were anxious to recover their investment from the last Richard James album, on which they lost a considerable amount of money. It just so happened that I had some contacts who were able to procure recording equipment in such a way that its purchase can't be traced. So actually, things came together quite by accident."

"Love will always find a way," I said.

The doc clucked at me. "Believe me, Martin, I went along with these guys to try to rescue Richard James because I was a fan, plain and simple. Sure, I knew who these guys were and what they used to do, but the main bond we had was our desire to find our rock 'n' roll hero alive. It was a tough, grisly experience. The situation we found the survivors in was not a pretty one. In so many ways, dying in the crash would have been much easier for them. Over the years since that rescue, my sole efforts on their behalf were to help them deal with that crisis in the way that best suited their interests. So while I'm not denying that we've all benefited from our little enterprise, I'll remind you again that, first and foremost, I am and always have been, a fan. Believe it or not, Martin, that was always the bottom line."

"But it's all over now, Doc," I said. "Your fan club's about to go out of business, permanently."

His eyebrows went up a half inch. "Oh? How's that, Martin?"

"We found the microcassette-corder at the lake house," I said. "Dovie and Carson Block are trying to smoke Nate out of the woods, and when they do—"

Chester White jerked an accusatory finger at his companions and snapped, "Graves, I told you to tell Otis to get that thing out of there."

Graves responded to the doc's momentary loss of composure with a cold stare. The muscles in Chester White's neck twitched and he looked away. "I'll deal with that," he said quietly.

"What about him?" said Red Fred.

"Chop 'im up, I say," said Nubby, making a carving motion with his knife as he sucked in his upper lip. "Cut him up in little pieces an' leave 'em for the buzzards. That's what I say."

"That won't work," I said.

"I know," said the doc, tight-lipped and cool again. He reached in his pocket for his car keys and nodded at Graves.

Graves nodded back, icily matter-of-fact. "We'll take care of his car."

"What about the gear?" said the doc. "That was sloppy, burning it up in the lime pit. You'll have to get that stuff out of here tonight. And this room needs work. Very sloppy."

"Damn right, Doc," I said. "That was almost as bad as the deal with the van."

Chester White nodded, frown lines making his face appear decades older. "Sorry about that, Martin, but they got a little carried away after you insulted them. You shouldn't have done that. It turned out bad for everyone." He shrugged, looking around at his co-conspirators. "You come with me, Nub. This can't be messy."

"Oh great," I said. "You're gonna have Graves shoot me? He'll have all the cops in the county out here by the time he hits me."

The doc jangled his keys again and shook his head. "Right again, Martin. We can't have any shooting out here. Like I said, I don't approve of guns in the first place. On the other hand, Martin, when you go playing with snakes, don't complain when you get bit.''

For the first time, I saw a smile crease Graves's tanned face. Nubby shoved his knife back in its holder and stepped over me on his way out. The doc stepped aside to let him through and said, "Try not to hit him anymore, Neville."

He turned and left without saying good-bye. I heard their footsteps on the porch. Car doors were opened, then shut. The engine turned over, the tires crunched on gravel, and then the night was quiet again, except for the phlegmatic breathing of my two remaining captors.

Graves nodded at me to get up, and Red Fred stepped toward me, grinning anxiously.

I raised up on one knee, then slid down again.

"Get up," said Graves, "or I'll mash you up and tote your god-dang carcass outta here in a bucket. Them snakes is waiting for ya.''

"I can't," I said. "I think my leg is broken."

Graves nodded suspiciously at Red Fred. "Give him a hand, Red."

Red Fred pushed back his hat, squinting, and said, "Beam me up, Scotty. Eh?"

Graves said, "Come on, Red. Let's do it."

Red Fred held up his hand. "You watch the old *Star Trek,* Martin?"

"Not lately," I said. My heart was roaring in my ears.

"Know how on every episode they got a new guy in the landin' party when they beam down on a strange planet? He's a guest star, y'know, not one of the main guys on the crew? An' ya jist know this sombitch's gonna git it. He ain't gonna be back on the show, he ain't gonna go on any more missions, 'cause that fucker is gonna git his ass wasted by some weirdass alien. Ya know't I'm sayin'?"

I didn't respond. I feigned passive resignation.

Red Fred grinned, leaned in, reached for me. "Yer like that

new guy, Martin, an' it's too bad old Scotty cain't beam yer ass up."

Red Fred leaned over me and grabbed my lapels. When his head was close enough, I grabbed him by the ears and slammed his face into the wall above my head. I saw Graves coming over to kick at me as I made Red Fred eat sheetrock and upholstery tacks again, hearing the bones in his face crack, feeling blood spray down on my hands and face as his hat flew off his head.

I gripped Red Fred's throat and flung him into Graves's legs. Graves cursed and stumbled out of the way, giving me enough time to get up. I lunged for the doorway, pausing to kick the giant cowboy in the balls. It slowed him down for about one second, putting me one step ahead of him. His boots clomped behind me as he thrashed through the cabin, his size giving him a slight disadvantage.

The front door had been left open a crack. I reached the edge of it and swung it at Graves as he came within reach. He ducked aside and I plowed out onto the porch and lit out for the woods in a dead run. I made it a short distance, ducking low branches and jumping over rocks before colliding with a large tree. I managed to use the momentum to swing me around to the other side of the trunk. Graves came at me, I danced to the other side of the tree. He lunged around the other way, I took counter steps. He was panting heavily, cursing and grunting, and I was trying not to think of us as two kids playing tag when the *crack-crack-crack* of a machine gun got my attention with its heart-seizing song and a rain of kindling on my head.

I started to run. The gun erupted again, stitching a pattern of raw wood across the trees that blocked my path, and I pitched forward and ate dirt. Soon I felt hot steel on the back of my neck.

They dragged me over to the well house. Graves pressed me face first against the building as Red Fred opened the door. I could hear the rattlers break into deadly applause as Graves jerked on my collar and pushed me into the doorway. I grabbed the sides of the doorway and pushed back, trying not to look at the knotted moonlit forms on the well house floor. Red Fred bashed my right hand with the gun, Graves punched me in the left kidney. I held on and they hit me again. This time I felt myself double up into a ball, thinking that now they could just roll me in. But as my fingers touched the ground and my chin hit one of my knees, it didn't happen.

I heard a twig snap somewhere behind us, then the click of a hammer being drawn back.

"Dolph," said Graves.

I turned around as best I could without falling backward into the embrace of the legless creatures. Moreland stood about ten feet away, a double-barreled sawed-off balanced on his hip, leveled at Graves and Red Fred.

"Dolph," said Graves again.

"Drop that iron, Red," said Moreland.

The Uzi hit the ground with a clatter.

Not a muscle moved in the old man's face. It looked like a thing that had been carved out of something in the woods.

"Get off my property, son," said Moreland, not taking his eyes off his two ranch hands.

I was surprised to find that my knees held when I raised up. I backed away a few feet, out of Graves's and Red Fred's reach, then headed down the road on shaky legs.

"Hurry on up, son," said Moreland. "Head straight for your car and don't stop driving till you git to Austin."

It was a long walk back to the Chrysler.

Over the rise of a hill just before Sweet Bay City was a gas station and convenience store. I pulled over at the pay phone and called Dovie's house. Carson answered on the first ring.

"Call the police," I said. "Chester White may be on his way out. If he calls, don't let on that you've talked to me. In fact, you should take Dovie and get the hell out of there right now."

"But the doc *is* on his way out," he said excitedly. "He called on his car phone. He called while Nate was here."

"What?"

"Yeah, Nate was here," he said. "Putting his guitar and amp out on the porch did the trick. He came walking up out of the woods a few minutes later. Man is he spaced out. I think he's really been living out there, man."

"But he's gone now?"

"Yeah. He left a few minutes ago. Dovie talked to him for awhile, then he lugged his stuff back out in the woods. I gave him the cassette recorder, too."

"Oh Christ," I snapped. "That was probably the *worst* thing you could've done. Listen to me, Carson, take Dovie and get out of there. But call the police first."

"Why? What do I tell them?"

"Anything. I don't care. Take Dovie to your hotel and wait for me."

"OK . . . Hey, wait a minute . . ."

I waited for several excruciatingly long seconds. Finally he came back on the phone and said, "Martin, a car just came down the road, then another one came out on the drive, right where that dead tree was and—"

He dropped the phone. I heard gunshots.

I yelled into the receiver. A dial tone yelled back at me. I called back.

The line was busy.

Maybe I was too late. I wasn't sure if Chester and Nubby could've made it out there already or not; my watch had been broken during one of the beatings. I jumped in the car and floored the accelerator. Time stood still.

Everything else blurred.

4

Police cars blocked Dovie's driveway at the junction with the main road. I was treated to a faceful of flashlight even before I'd eased the Ghia over on the shoulder. The beam came closer, close enough for me to ask the uniform behind it to contact Sgt. Lasko. In less than a minute, I was escorted down the drive, to the spot where Dovie's black Mustang had charged out of the woods and collided with the Mercedes. Two cops were standing at the roadside, in the gap between the trees where the Mustang had gone through. There was a hole in the ground, where a dead cedar tree had been propped up, disguising the makeshift driveway. Tire tracks led out into the woods.

Now I knew why a dead tree would dance.

The Mercedes windshield was a silvery web with several bullet holes in it. Through the open door on the driver's side, I could see Chester White and Nubby sprawled dead across the seats, their faces masks of blood and gore.

Lasko came trotting out of the woods on the other side of the road, grim faced and breathless. "Dovie and Carson are OK," he said, "but—"

"But what?" I demanded.

"Come on," he growled, catching his breath. "Maybe you can get him outta that tree."

I followed him a short distance through the woods until we came to a group of about a dozen police officers, all facing the opposite direction, looking up—a battery of flashlights, hand-guns, and shotguns. Lasko nudged a break in the ranks so I could see better.

The cops were standing on an embankment about fifteen feet above a small creek that trickled peacefully over a rocky bed. On the opposite bank of the creek stood a huge oak tree. The guns and flashlights were aimed about twenty feet up the tree trunk, at the juncture of a large limb. Nate was up there, grip-ping a small branch with one hand, a revolver with the other. The microcassette-corder dangled around his neck, the revolver was pointed at his head.

Lasko nudged me with his elbow. "He won't let anybody in the creek. Say something, maybe he'll listen to you."

"Nate," I said. "It's OK. You can come down now. You were right."

"FUCK OFF, MARTIN!" yelled Nate. His voice was hoarse, his eyes wild, his hair a matted mop of burrs and leaves.

"Come on down," I said. "Nobody here wants to see you get hurt. You were right all along."

"Damn right I was right, man!" he screamed, jabbing the barrel of the gun into the side of his head. "They deserved to die, those fuckers."

"I know, Nate," I said. I pointed to the cassette recorder. "You've got the proof right there."

He let out a torrent of nervous laughter. "I told you, man, but you didn't believe me. That bastard was stealing my songs and beating up on my wife. I saw him tie her up and humiliate her, man. It made me sick. That's when I finally knew who he was and what I had to do. I went over to his place and waited for him in the bushes. When he got there, the redneck was with him. I waited till the redneck came out to light the barbecue, then snuck up and bopped him with a tire iron. THIS IS HIS GUN, MAN—I TOOK IT OFF HIM!"

"And then you—"

"Hell yeah, I shot that motherfucking song-stealing woman-beating sonuvabitch's face off, man. I told you before, man, can't keep running from God's detective."

The remark went over like nails on a blackboard—all around me, I sensed the twitching of itchy trigger fingers. "What about the doc?" I said. "Why'd you kill him?"

Nate snorted and tightened his grip on the branch, keeping the gun barrel jammed into the sad dark crown of hair. "Fuck him, man. He had keys to the place, used to come over all the time to make sure I didn't steal the plumbing fixtures and stuff." Nate glanced down at the recorder. "That goddamn yuppie probably put this thing under my bed, man. I don't know if that other motherfucker was helping him or not, but they came together so they went out together, too."

"Why don't you come down, Nate? I'll give you that song you wanted. Whaddya say?"

He shook his head. "What would I want that for now, man? I'm a killer now, not a songwriter."

"Come on, Nate. Nobody wants you to get hurt."

He laughed as he looked down at all the guns pointed at him. "Hey, man, I'm not stupid, you know."

I looked over at Lasko. His neck muscles stood out like new rope as he clenched his teeth, but he hadn't even pulled his gun. The eyes of the men next to him glistened in the moonlight. I didn't like what I saw in them. When I looked up at Nate again, he was smiling.

"HEY, ALL YOU MOTHERFUCKERS DOWN THERE! YOU THINK I'M STUPID, MAN?"

A crack, a muzzle flare from the .38—Nate's head whiplashed against the tree trunk, careening off again like a ball. I looked away, hearing leaves rustling as the spray hit them. I heard crashing branches and more rustling, then a clatter on rocks and a small splash. When I looked up again, Nate's body was sprawled out facedown on a lower limb, his arms flung out in such a way that he looked as if he might be flying. The revolver was in the creek. The cops gradually lowered their guns and climbed down the banks and waded out into the stream beneath the tree, trying to figure out how to get him down.

"What the hell happened to you?" said Lasko, eyeing the damage to my face and clothes. "Look like you took a dive in a garbage disposal and met up with a Roto Rooter."

"I've been out at the Kilton gang's place."

He scowled at me, shaking his head. "Looking for Richard James the hard way, huh? I mighta saved you the trouble, if you wanted."

"What do you mean?"

"I just sent off for his prints this morning. Should get everything tomorrow. You know Otis only had seven toes?"

"Seven toes?"

I watched him nod his head as I thought about the padded material I'd seen next to Otis's boots . . . *Frostbite*. I reminded Lasko that Richard James had broken his left index finger as a child. Maybe the X rays would show it.

Lasko's scowl turned into a pained expression. "Goddammit, this is gonna be a long fucking night. For both of us, you understand."

I understood.

5

Late Tuesday afternoon, Lasko and I were sitting on my balcony as a man in a gorilla suit drove a jeep up to one of the apartments along the creek. The gorilla honked his horn and a shapely woman in black tights with a skeleton painted on the front came out of the apartment, leading two Mutant Ninja Turtles. A few minutes earlier, a gang of youths in zombie attire had screamed through the parking lot on skateboards.

It was Halloween, and Lasko had the results of the fingerprint search. He knew Otis Taylor's true identity, and Nate's confession had been supported by a ballistics check of the gun he'd used on himself as well as the man who'd called himself Otis Taylor. Lasko had just spent the previous two hours talking to Dovie.

And we'd just listened to "The Whole Damn Truth."

Lasko pulled out a big black cigar, bit off the end, and lit it. I watched him lean back in his chair as a big cloud of smoke left his mouth and drifted over the balcony.

"I ran into Leo at Seis Salsas," he said, "and he said there's a big shindig Thursday night on Auditorium Shores, after the *Día de Los Muertos* parade down Sixth Street. I was thinking of going anyway to check out all the low riders. Leo said the thing is supposed to wrap up with a big jam session featuring you guys and some of the Antone's house band."

"So I heard," I said. "I haven't talked to anybody besides Leo about it. Billy's been shopping for a new van, Ray's been gigging, and I've had other things on my mind."

"I guess you have. You going out to see Dovie?"

I nodded. "How is she?"

"Not too bad, considering." He propped one of his boots on the balcony railing and blew out another stream of smoke. "At least that sonuvabitch Watson's happy as a fly on a turd."

"I heard something on the radio about a big warehouse bust that went down last night. Was that his crew?"

"Uh-huh, the holy roller made his big case," he said. "Chester White had a deal going with some heist artists who specialized in high-end gear—computers, photocopiers, fax machines, scanners, and recording studio equipment. The Kilton gang were in on it, too. The doc was fronting the warehouse outfit certain pharmaceutical drugs they had a market for and acting as a go-between with some of his friends who liked bargains. Watson had a warrant for the doc and apparently had a tip that he was supposed to be at the warehouse. They went on and rushed the bust before they knew whether he was in there or not because a truckload of hot merch was fixing to pull out, and he didn't want the evidence to slip through his hands.

"At worst, Watson didn't find a speed lab or cache of that stuff anywhere, but all the things that happened last night and this morning just add more proof on his side: drugs are evil and the people who sell them are, too. The sonuvabitch thinks AIDS is part of God almighty's plan for chrissakes, you know what I mean?"

"What do you mean, 'what happened this morning'?"

"You know, the big fire out at Moreland's place."

"Oh yeah. They seem to have a lot of fires out there."

"Uh huh. What time you say you were out there?"

"I lost track. Around midnight, I guess."

He shrugged and stood up. "Well, like I say, it ain't my

jurisdiction, anyhow. Watson sure hauled ass out there, though."

"He find any more of God almighty's plan out there?"

Lasko turned up a palm. "Two dead bodies. Lotsa guns. No speed lab, but I imagine the gear they found in the lime pit is gonna match up with the hot list."

Lasko tugged the cuff of his jeans down over his boot top and made a face. "Watson knew all along the gang did your van caper, you know. He just didn't want to mess up his warehouse bust."

"It figures. Does that mean the LAPD had the gang figured for Cyclone's murder all along, too?"

"Yeah, more or less, I reckon. You know that tape?"

"You wanna hear it again?"

He shook his head. "Maybe some other time. You realize I listened to it that night we brought you in?"

"You did? Why didn't you say anything? Why'd you let me keep it?"

Lasko laughed. "Hey, since when is having a tape of a dead musician a crime? If it is, we're all going to jail. I figured you mighta swiped it, but then maybe I kinda didn't wanna know. How was I supposed to know it meant anything?"

"What did you think when you listened to it?"

He took a deep breath and let it out slowly. "To be honest, I was disappointed. I guess I still am."

"Yeah," I said. "I guess I am, too."

6

Dovie and I sat at a patio table in back of the house. A wide black headband held her hair back from her face, but errant locks still fell forward into her eyes. She was wearing a large gray sweater that came down to her knees and faded jeans stained with fresh paint.

Carson had flown back to L.A. but would return for the weekend. A large American sedan was parked in front of the house, between Dovie's Mustang and the Lincoln. It looked like the kind of car someone's parents would drive.

"I didn't want to lie to you, Martin," she said. "I hate lying. It's the way I was brought up, and I've never been very good at it anyway. I kept things from you, but I didn't actually tell you that many things that weren't true."

"And then you had good reasons, I suppose," I said.

She nodded.

"Tell me about the plane crash. Did Preston really rape you?"

She nodded again. "As if things weren't bad enough. He'd always been jealous of Richard, not just because of me, but for everything. He . . . you know, he wanted to be Richard, he wanted to be in control. And after the crash he got his chance. Sort of."

"Did they really try climbing down the mountain to go for help?"

She shook her head, her chin down, her eyes lowered. "No. That part was a lie. But we had to say something. You see, it was a lot worse than I said. We were in shock, all of us, not just Cokey. Preston was the only one who had any will left in him, and his will was bad."

"What about Richard?"

Wind blew, kicking up dead leaves, making a sound like faraway applause. She looked down at her damaged fingers, then hid them in the loose material of her sweater.

Finally she said, "He died in the crash. We put his body out in the snow. And I lied when I said we had food on the plane. We didn't have any, not anything at all, just booze and speed. We were so weak, I knew we were gonna die soon. I didn't want to do it, Martin. I . . . it was so horrible, just considering it. Finally, I think it was on the tenth day, I was hallucinating. I was so weak I couldn't stand up, I could barely crawl. Preston made me do it. Oh God, Martin, don't make me say it now."

I put up my hand to stop her, but she blurted it out.

"We ate him, Martin. We cut little pieces off Richard and . . ."

Her lip was quivering like a leaf in a storm, even though she was biting it, and tears started streaming down her face. "That was the secret, Martin. That's what they had on me."

The wind whistled through the trees, and more leaves danced across the patio. I didn't know what to say.

"When the rescue party got there," she said, "the looks on their faces—oh God—when they saw what we'd done. But they didn't say anything about it. They never did. Not to me, anyway. They got rid of what was left of Richard's body somehow. I don't know how, I don't want to know. I cracked up. Everybody knew that, but they sure didn't know why. Everybody thought it was shock and drug abuse. But twenty-four hours a day I was still going down in that plane, you know, hurtling through the sky, crashing, eating the body of the guy I loved. I left my humanity up on that mountain, Martin. I was a monster, and I didn't think I'd ever be able to be around people again. After awhile in the hospital, I don't know how long, maybe a month, Chester brought someone to see me. Chester had fixed his face—as well as he could, anyway—but I knew who he was.

She brushed away her tears with her sleeve and said, "You'd think I would've run screaming, but I didn't. I know it sounds like a bad horror movie, but as mean as he'd been to me, I couldn't keep him away. I mean, he was my only link to reality, *my* reality. The rest of the world was just a stupid dream, and I couldn't relate to it. Preston was the only one besides Cokey who'd been through what we'd been through, and I don't think Cokey really knows it, because he was able to escape the whole thing in his mind. Sometimes I wished I was like that too, and other times I wished I was dead like Richard.

"But you know, I've never been that kind of person. Things happen to me and I'm just along for the ride. After I got out of the hospital, Preston kept coming up with songs and I sang them. I didn't know he was stealing Nate's ideas. The guys from Kilton did whatever they did to back us up, and Chester did what he did. As long as I had something to do, singing, that is, I could keep putting one foot in front of the other, keep getting on the bus and leaving the last town behind, almost like when I was little and everything was new when we'd move to a new town.

"Then I met Cyclone. He made me laugh, and he was so fanatical about the music thing, it kind of gave me a new perspective on life. I mean, I wasn't just singing so I wouldn't have to think anymore. Cyclone was so fucked up in a human kind of a way, it reminded me of what a monster Preston was. And Cyclone made me feel like I was really somebody important, not just a victim and a faker. Preston saw that and it drove him crazy. He liked controlling me by reminding me of the horrible thing we'd done, reminding me of how people would react if they ever found out. And when that didn't work, there was always the rough stuff, and I was too weak to fight back.

"Poor Cyclone," she said, stifling a sob. "He felt so broken-hearted and betrayed, thinking that 'The Whole Damn Truth' meant that Richard James was not only alive but that he had turned into a cruel asshole who went by the name of Otis Taylor. God, I hope Cyclone never realized what really happened up there."

"I doubt it," I said. "And you can't keep torturing yourself over it. It isn't a sin. In a situation like that, you have to do things to survive. The old rules don't apply. You survived, now you just have to learn to live."

Her eyes blinked, but no more tears came. "I didn't know they killed people, Martin," she said. "That writer, I thought that was an accident, like they said. And the pilot, well, they were such a rough crowd, I just thought—"

I just nodded my head slowly, breathed deeply, and twisted one finger around another deep inside the pockets of my jacket.

She twisted her mouth into a bitter expression. "I don't know why you should believe me."

"Let's not argue about it. Tell me about the song scam. You say you didn't know Preston was stealing songs from Nate, but how'd the whole thing get started, anyway?"

"It was Chester's idea," she said. "I ran up a helluva bill at Oak Tree, and I didn't have any money of my own. No insurance or anything. The gang had been supporting Richard for a long time, and Preston owed them a lot of money, too, from some botched drug deal of his. So Chester came up with the idea of doing the first single, planning to split the profits with the gang as a reward for rescuing us and for keeping quiet about what we'd done to Richard. He really dug being involved with the music thing and the gang, too.

"Preston already had some vague plan about staying underground, because the Kilton guys weren't the only people he owed a lot of money to, and with his appearance, well, he didn't ever want to set foot on stage again. The other guys pretty much blamed Preston for what happened to Richard, and for me being all messed up about it, but Preston had grown up with them, and they wanted to protect him, too. So the tribute single was supposed to be a one-shot deal, not just with IMF but with the Kilton gang, too."

"The single becoming a hit sort of pulled the whole scam together, then?" I said.

She nodded. "It took off right away, and Preston was smart and devious enough to think of buying the rights from Richard's mom."

"That forced IMF to do business with Preston as Otis," I said, "and the gang couldn't afford to get rid of him or let him tell your secret, either."

She nodded. "Besides, Preston wrote all the songs on Richard's last album, anyway."

"Or Nate did."

A look of shame fell across her eyes. "Yeah, I guess," she said. "You don't seem that surprised that Otis was Preston. It's almost like you'd been thinking it for awhile."

"Maybe it just took some time to realize it," I said. "I couldn't figure out why you'd stick with him if he was so cruel to you. I knew there had to be a reason, a bad one. And when I was thinking that Otis was Richard, I just couldn't get used to the idea that he would be so abusive to you, especially after talking to L-Tone. Then there was the song. It pretty much gave away what happened, but not to whom, except for the line about being struck by lightning. You said Preston had been hit by lightning, not Richard."

"I told you Otis wasn't Richard." She blotted her eyes with her sleeve again, but she wasn't crying. "What about the police? What will they do with me?"

"Apparently Preston had never been fingerprinted, and Richard James's prints didn't match those of Otis Taylor's. That's good enough for Lasko, and he's the only cop who knows who that white-haired corpse in the morgue really used to be. He'd just as soon leave Preston Drake up on that Colorado mountain with Richard."

She sighed as the wind blew more leaves across the yard.

"What about Cyclone? Will we ever find out who he was?"

"I don't know. Sometimes I wonder if we just dreamed him up."

She smiled, reached out to take my hands. "I do, too, Martin. You know, I told my mom about him. He was everything she used to fear as a mother, but when I told her about him, she just hugged me and said she wished she could've met him."

I didn't say anything. The air was getting chilly. Dovie let go of my hands and stuck hers in the folds of her sweater.

"I called her, you know," she said, "and they came right over. She understands. I was so worried about how she would take it, you know, but she was so . . . I don't know. So strange, so cool about it. It's like she's a—"

"A mother," I said. "They can be like that."

"Yeah," she said, smiling. "Thanks."

7

Wednesday morning Ladonna called in sick and rode out to Moreland's ranch with me. It was a nice day for a drive, with clear blue skies and the air just warm enough to leave the top down. I made sure I stayed under the speed limit while passing through Sweet Bay City.

Coming downhill on the county road, I felt a tightening in my gut as we caught a glimpse of acres of blackened thicket where the cabin had been. Closer to the entrance to the ranch, the road leveled out again, putting the thicket out of view. As we drove through the gate, Moreland's dog raced after the Ghia, barking.

Mrs. Moreland came out on the porch and shushed the dog when I pulled up in front of the house. "He's out back of the barn with the turkeys," she said. "He's working on the shed in the pen. Be sure and shut the gate so none get out."

I looked at Ladonna.

"I'll just wait here," she said.

The Cessna was still sitting on flat tires on the weed-dotted landing strip. The turkey pen seemed dangerously close to the landing strip, but then again the turkeys' wings were clipped, making them as incapable of flight as the dilapidated airplane.

Hundreds of the stocky white fowl were confined inside the pen, scratching in the raw dirt, pecking at pebbles as well as feed pellets, doing the things that turkeys do. There was a small shed in the far end opposite the gate, which was a four-foot section of fence hooked to a corner post. I released the two hooks that held the gate in place, then jumped back as the thing sprang out of my hands. A couple of turkeys that had been near the gate panicked and shot through the opening. I wished them good luck, stepped inside, and refastened the gate. Several of the escapees' feathered contemporaries stared up at me with button eyes, but the escapees didn't look back.

Moreland came out of the shed, nodded his head in greeting, then waded through the sea of white birds. "Let's get out of this pen, son," he said.

I followed him through the gate, letting him refasten it. The two escaped fowls were now strutting around in the shade of the barn. If Moreland noticed, he didn't say anything. We walked over to a cattle feeder and sat on two tree stumps.

He pushed his hat back on his head, wiped the sweat from his face with a bandana, then pulled the brim back down again. "Reckon she'll make it?" he said.

"She's come this far," I said. "I don't know if it's all over or not, but she's back with her family now. Whatever else happens, hopefully they can help her deal with it in a better way than you and your boys did."

"We just wanted what was best for her," he said. "I didn't want no more trouble for her, but you come along an' just wouldn't leave it alone. Well, maybe it all turned out for the best. Might as well look at it that way, we sure as hell can't change anything now."

He squinted at the sun and said, "You ever hear 'bout my boy?"

I nodded. "One of your neighbors ran over him."

"My only son. Just a teenager, but a big, strappin' boy fulla life and a harder worker than any three grown men. The doctor said he didn't die from being hit by the car the first time. What did it was the second time, when that drunk sonuvabitch backed up out of the ditch an' run over him again. The sonuvabitch went home an' went to bed with my boy's blood still on his bumper. Next morning he washed his truck an' drove into Fredericksburg for an auction.

"Well, I killed a lot of men in the war because we were right an' they were wrong. That's how I looked at it with that sonuvabitch. I took him out in the thicket an' shot him dead. Didn't bury him or try to cover up for what I done, just shot him an' leave him lay."

"What happened?" I said.

"Not a damn thing, far as you'd be able to tell. Neville Graves had come to work for me a few months before that. We never talked 'bout it, but I know he was the one got rid of the body. I didn't act obligin' to him, an' he didn't act like he had one over on me. Maybe that's why I let him bring his friends in from Kilton with their dope business an' let him use my plane an' have run of the place. But I think it's mainly 'cause I just didn't give a goddamn anymore. I just didn't give a damn."

"And that's how things were when they came back with Dovie?"

He nodded. "I just met her that once, when they brought her in an' told me what it was happened up there. She reminded me of a week-old pup been whupped an' drowned an' left to die. You couldn't get no more 'n six feet from her an' she'd try to crawl under her collar, bawling an' shaking."

"They already had the idea to keep the truth from everybody when they got back?"

He nodded. "I was the one got Chester to go up there with 'em, since I knew his dad. But his dad never knew about the big hush up. Old man White, bein' a criminal lawyer, is pretty open, but he ain't quite *that* open. Well, I felt damn sorry for that girl. An' I have to say it was the first time I felt much of anything at all since my boy been killed. I didn't hardly have anything to do with the rest of the deal, but I told Neville an' the boys if they were gonna do this thang, they'd have to get rid of the dope, an' I always thought they pretty much did do that. They quit makin' it out here, anyway."

"And they got rid of your pilot and the writer when they threatened to disclose the truth?"

"I won't lie to you, son, but fact of the matter is I didn't hardly have anything to do with it. The writer did borrow a rifle from me, saying he wanted to do some hunting, an' old Sherm did just disappear on me 'round that time, though I'm pretty sure nobody else seen him since then neither. I figure it was Preston did it that time. Neville an' the boys would've helped tidy up, but Preston was the one with the good eye. If I'd let him hunt out here more often, I wouldn't have no deer at all left. Boy was damn good with a rifle."

"You don't feel bad about it?"

He took off his hat and curled its brim in his hands. "What for, son? Wouldn't change the facts. And they were gonna try and take advantage of that poor gal's misery. I guess I'd have shot 'em myself if it'd come down to it."

"What about Graves and Red Fred?"

"Well, things pretty much got outta hand, didn't they? I think everybody pretty much had their own kind of good intentions, but Preston was gettin' crazier an' crazier, an' maybe the thing had just gone on too long, like when you got a sore an' the skin heals over but it festers inside, an' keeps getting worse 'n worse until you gotta get it cut out. Maybe it's 'cause I never had to answer for killing the sonuvabitch who ran over my boy, I don't know. But it wasn't doin' her any good anymore, an' I had to do something."

He looked me in the eye and said, "I locked those boys in with the snakes. When they quit screamin' I drug 'em out an' put 'em in the cabin, nailed the doors shut, set it on fire 'n watched it burn."

He put his hat back on his head and got slowly to his feet. "I let the snakes go first, though," he added.

"I won't tell anybody," I said.

"I don't give a damn if you do or not," he said. "If they

figure it out, they can come get me. They know where I am."

"It'd be hard to prove, anyway."

He took a deep breath, his chest swelling up impressively as he stared off at the hills. "I wouldn't deny it, son. I just don't give a damn."

"I guess I'll be going," I said.

"Your gun's in the mailbox. Be sure you git it on your way out. I 'preciate you coming out. Be careful you don't step on no snakes on your way back."

"I will," I said. "Your wife warned me, but I accidentally let a couple of your turkeys out when I opened the gate."

He winked at me. "That's a'right. That speeding ticket of yours?"

"Yes?"

"I never fixed that, neither. An' if I's you, I'd mail 'em the money instead of stopping by."

If I'd been wearing a hat, I'd have tipped it at him before I left.

I told Ladonna about the conversation on the drive back down the country road. We paused at the top of the hill just long enough for one last look at the blackened thicket.

"I keep thinking," she said, "about how of all the people involved in this thing who were supposedly just acting in Dovie's best interests, Moreland is the one who says he doesn't give a damn. It sounds to me like he gives a damn a lot."

"I think he meant he just doesn't care if he gets caught," I said. "But I don't know about that, either."

"You think he'd go quietly?"

"I wouldn't take bets on it, and I sure wouldn't want to get caught in the crossfire if he decided not to."

When we were back on the highway, Ladonna scooted over to lean against me. "Are you going to play that Day of the Dead gig tomorrow?" she asked.

"I don't know," I said.

"Sounds like a good gig," she said. "But maybe you're not

in the mood for costumes and Mexican food, tequila, and low riders. Could that be it?"

"No."

"I didn't think so," she said. "Could it be that you're sick of dead people? Sick of dead people hanging around after they're supposed to be dead, pretending sort of to be someone they never were? Death, murder, blood, guts, fire? Could you possibly be tired of all that?"

"Yes," I said. "Some tequila and Mexican food I could handle, but no men in skeleton costumes popping out of coffins, no parades of ghouls down Sixth Street, no laughing at death. Maybe it's a healthy attitude and a colorful tradition, but I'm not in the mood for it. Maybe I'll change my mind, though."

"You said you could handle some tequila and Mexican food?"

"Yes," I said. "Why? Have you got something in mind?"

She nodded. "See, the reason I was asking about the gig was, if you *aren't* playing tomorrow, we could start packing for a trip down to Port Isabel. We could leave Friday afternoon after Michael gets out of school."

"But it's November first," I said. "Isn't it a little off season?"

"So what? So the crowds won't be there but the ocean will. You don't have to get in it. It'll be romantic, and we haven't had enough romance lately to suit me."

"Baby," I said, "I'm yours. If you want me to dive in your ocean, make love under it, or walk on top of it, just say the word."

She smiled and kissed me quickly. "Martin, don't you realize that anybody can walk on water?"

"No, I didn't."

"Sure. Just depends on the temperature. If it's frozen, anybody can walk on it. But as for those other water sports—"

"You got it, Ladonna. You're the girl of my dreams."

"Honest?"

"Honest."

"What about the giant woman?" she asked. "What about her?"

"What giant woman?"

She smiled. "You were talking about her in your sleep that night Michael and I came over. I'd like to hear about her sometime."

I shook my head and downshifted as we approached a hill. "Giant women can take care of themselves."

"Oh yeah?"

"Yeah," I said. "And the regular-size ones do pretty well for themselves, too."

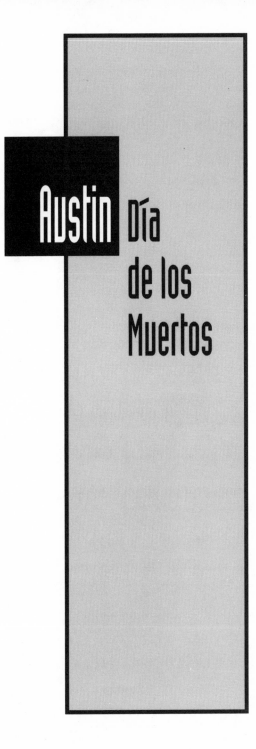

Austin Día de los Muertos

In the Meso-American culture, death is regarded as the happy denouement of life. *Día de los Muertos,* a holiday dedicated to honoring the spirits of the departed, has its roots in pre-Columbian pagan traditions that involved ritualistic bloodletting and cannibalism, among other things. The conquering Spaniards were able to wean the natives of some of those habits, but you can't keep a good party down.

So today, south of the border, *Día de los Muertos* lives on in a curious entwinement of pagan traditions and Roman Catholic mysticism. Nighttime vigils are held in cemeteries. Barefoot girls in communion dresses sweep off the graves of loved ones and turn the soil in the belief it will help the dead breathe. Thousands of candles are burned. Marigold petals are strewn about or hung in garlands on the graves or at elaborately decorated shrines. Schools let out and shops close for fiestas, ceremonies, and parades in which people made up to look like corpses rise up from coffin floats and wave their arms at the revelers. Much tequila is consumed, special foods are prepared. Bread is broken, special songs are sung. Death is ridiculed as "the stinker," "the bald one," or "the one with the teeth showing."

North of the border, *Día de los Muertos* art objects are probably the best-known aspect of the holiday. Skeletons and skulls made of papier-mâché, ceramic, wood, crystallized sugar, and tin are sold in shops, along with macabre, colorful paintings, ceramic devil figures, and tree of life candelabras. To some people, it's the party after Halloween. But Austin, a town that likes a good party, likes to celebrate Day of the Dead in style.

The parade was held on 6th Street that afternoon. A massive crowd of celebrants, a great many in costume, lined the sidewalks and cheered the low riders, coffin floats, and mariachi bands. The air rained marigolds, streamers, peppers, candy, tequila. Vendors sold Day of the Dead crafts and tacos and fajitas served with a commemorative *salsa muy picante* guaranteed to raise the dead.

That evening, the party moved to Auditorium Shores on the southern banks of Town Lake. Ladonna and Michael and I got there just as the sun was turning an appropriate pumpkin orange in a bed of purple somewhere west of town, maybe just over Dovie's lake house.

I had decided to do the gig, but I was as surprised as anyone when we pulled into the backstage parking area and saw the grotesque thing that had been towed to the side of the stage. The thing was our van, caked with Town Lake mud all along the lower part of the body and wheels, and a concrete filling inside, the tops of our amplifiers jutting out from the surface like prehistoric animals enmired in a primeval tar pit. Pumpkins, squash, corn, and marigolds had been strewn atop a bed of straw on the roof, and black and gold streamers hung down the sides where dancing skeletons had been painted.

The stage had also been festooned with skulls, pumpkins, and lifesize Day of the Dead figures. Crepe paper and weblike netting had been strung from the lighting trees, and amplifiers had been draped in black.

I checked in with Wayne, who was the stage manager, then went back to the guitar-tuning area behind the stage. Leo was back there, playing an old riff on an old amplifier that he'd just purchased, another tweed Pro-Reverb. It sounded damn good, and Leo looked as happy as a kid with a new bike.

"Hey, man," he said, beaming, riffing, "how you like it?"

"Sounds good," I said. "Nice warm tone with a lot of bite."

"Yeah, cool, huh?" he drawled lustily. "Just got it today. It's not quite as sweet as my other one, but close. You see the van?"

I nodded. "Hard to miss."

"It was somebody's idea, I forget who." He snapped his fingers, as if that would conjure up a name. "The guy who runs that shop, you know? That record store with the Robert Johnson poster on the wall. You know?"

"On the Drag?"

"Yeah, on the Drag. You know."

"The store on the Drag with the Robert Johnson poster."

"Yeah, that one. The guy who runs it, I think the van was his idea. You know the guy."

I just nodded.

"Everybody seems to get a kick out of it. Dovie coming?"

"No. I think she's with her parents."

"That's good, I guess. Probably needs to take a break and a couple of chill pills, you know?"

"Me, too."

"Heard you and Ladonna and Mikey going to Port Isabel tomorrow."

"You heard right, bro."

"Cool." He cranked the volume on the guitar, then slashed out a riff that sounded like a sex-crazed dinosaur attacking a pile of rocks.

"Nice amp, Leo. Almost as good as the old one."

"Yeah, cool."

I found Ladonna and Michael a good place to sit backstage, then I went looking for Billy and Ray. I ran into a lot of musicians I knew, found a cold beer, and warmed up my fingers. One of the local R&B outfits was churning it up onstage, and though the sound was familiar, I couldn't place them.

The air was crisp and the sky was clear. It was nice to be alive, nice to be home. I felt bad about Nate bouncing around out there in the ether zone, thinking a dead man had been sucking ideas out of his brain. I was glad that Dovie had made it down from that mountain, relieved to know what had really happened to Richard James.

Maybe someday I'd be able to tell Mr. and Mrs. Jaworski that the men who'd murdered their son were dead. It probably wouldn't lessen their grief, but it might ease some of their disappointment that nothing had been done.

Disappointment. I thought about the song that Cyclone Davis had been so excited about. He'd not only been wrong about what it signified, but he'd been wrong about its author.

"The Whole Damn Truth" was a lie.

But Cyclone had been right about the wrongness that it signified, and his fanatical enthusiasm had led to something being done about it.

I saw a black man wearing a purple lamé jacket with zebra-stripe lapels strutting toward me carrying a tweed guitar case. I was glad I didn't have to tell him why the Dog had been playing dead all this time and hadn't even given him a phone call. L-Tone was smiling a smile that said that people from all over were ready to rediscover that extra-special L-Tone sound.

L-Tone winced coyly as the sound of Leo's guitar rattled the night air like the wings of a low-flying angel skidding against a tin rooftop. I realized with a start that the sound had come from the stage. Ray's saxophone answered Leo's guitar with a primal howl, followed by a drum roll—too languid to have been executed by anyone but Billy—and a Hammond B-3 swirling through a Leslie speaker—the signature growl of Nehru Ellis, the Cincinnatian with the real Memphis sound. Somewhere a woman laughed lustily. L-Tone slapped me on the back and gave me a conspiratorial wink, nudging me toward the steps to the platform. I let him go ahead and hung back for a minute, taking one last look at the view behind the stage.

The postmodern buildings on the opposite shore of the lake

looked cold and staid as soldiers, reflected in the river stretched out on her back, a shimmering giant silver woman, her breath sweet and green, her secrets intact.

The stage was full of eerie silhouettes of musicians and their machinery basking in layered folds of light and dark. As I studied the picture, my eyes focused on a strange shape lurking behind a speaker cabinet as big as a casket. Its shadow bled out across the deck for a few seconds before being obliterated by a roving spotlight. The shape moved slowly away from the speaker until it was directly in the path of the spotlight, becoming an eclipse. The fiery silhouette revealed a burly outline of mechanic's coveralls, sunglasses, and a rockabilly pompadour as stiff and tall as a shark's fin. He was probably just a roadie, but he reminded me a lot of a certain wild man in a Cadillac.

I strapped on my bass and climbed onstage. I still owed him a gig.